CW00541081

COVER THE LIES

Carla Vermaat

ARMICHAEL
RIME

Also by Carla Vermaat

Tregunna

What every body is saying

COVER THE LIES

Carla Vermaat

CARMICHAEL
CRIME

Published in Great Britain in 2017 by
Carmichael Publishers, St Austell, Cornwall
Copyright © Carla Vermaat 2017

The moral right of the author has been asserted.

*This book is a work of fiction. Names, characters, businesses,
organizations, places and events, other than those clearly in the public
domain, are either the product of the author's imagination or used
fictitiously. Any resemblance to real persons, living or dead, events or
locales is purely coincidental.*

A CIP catalogue record for this book
is available from the British Library

ISBN 978-0-9933339-5-8

Typeset in Meridien by CeeVee-Design
Cover Image © Carla Vermaat – Cover design by Varwig Design

Printed and bound in Great Britain by TJ International, Cornwall

CARMICHAEL
CRIME

For Mike

PROLOGUE

There it is again: a knock on the door. Urgent. Loud. Determined.

A sudden draught hits her bare ankles, and sends a shiver up her spine. She is standing in the hall, the outline of her body silhouetted against the dim light that filters down the staircase. Too scared to switch on the light, she's trying hard to remember where she put her mobile phone. She wouldn't feel so vulnerable if she could hold it in her hands, knowing she'd only have a few buttons to press for help. Did she leave it on the charger in the kitchen or is it still in the pocket of her jeans on the chair beside her bed?

Another knock. This time, it is definitely more urgent. Maybe also more desperate. Is it her neighbour, worried that her 17-year-old daughter hasn't come home from a night out with friends? Or the man from across the street, looking for his cat? Worth a small fortune, the little spoiled-to-death animal escapes whenever the opportunity arises, especially when it's getting dark. No, if it were someone she knew, they would have called her name by now, having seen that the light in her bedroom is still on. They'd know she'd be scared at this time of night to open the door.

Unless it's … him. He wouldn't call her name while knocking on her door; he'd be only too aware that she would definitely not open the door if she knew it was him. Not after everything he'd done to her.

Another knock, softer. Hesitant. Again, only this time it is accompanied by a voice. Soft. Muffled. Is someone saying, begging, 'Please?'

She hesitates, her hand clutching the hem of the long T-shirt she's been using to sleep in since he left. She gazes over her shoulder into the darkened room where she can just make out the black metal hands against the pale enamel face of the clock. It was past midnight when she went to bed. Now it is ten to one. She's been reading a few pages of her book and she was just about to turn off the light when she heard it.

Again. A knock. A flat hand banging hard this time, which, she feels, adds to the sense of despair of her visitor.

Curiosity makes her move forward. She leans against the door, pressing her ear against the cool painted wood, trying to detect if she can hear something familiar in the voice. There it is again: 'Please?'

There is a growing tension in the plea now which distresses her. She stretches her arm, and her trembling fingers reach for the security chain on the door, one of the aftermaths of HIM.

'Please. Open the door. Please.'

The voice is muffled. She can't even work out whether it's male or female.

'Wait. Just wait one sec.' She has made up her mind. Someone needs help. Her help.

She turns and, taking the steps two at a time, runs up the stairs, to her bedroom and quickly pulls on her jeans, tapping the pockets: no mobile phone. She will make sure she has it in her hand before she opens the door, her fingers ready to make an emergency call. Just as a precaution. She dismisses putting on her bra. Instead she takes a loose, thick cardigan off the hanger and slips her arms in it.

Hesitating for a moment, standing still on the stairs, she can hear repeated knocking, not so loud as to alert the neighbours, but firm. Determined and desperate. And the voice again, now on the edge of crying. She goes down the stairs, her movements almost in slow motion. She's bare-footed, but otherwise she's dressed as though it's a cold winter's night. Her hair falls around her face as she fumbles with the key in the lock. She is certain now that her visitor is crying. Dispirited. Devoid of any hope.

Someone who needs her help.

It's not kindness that makes her forget any precautions but curiosity that makes her undo the security chain rather than have it in place to peer through the gap first to make sure it is safe. Instead, she pulls open the door, and is instantly swept aside, her back hitting the wall, as someone crashes in as though catapulted towards her. Her breathing stops and her eyes widen in shock and instantly she is overwhelmed by regret.

'Please. The cards. I need the cards.'

His face is a pale blur, but his dark eyes are glistening like ice. His solid frame steadies in front of her as he gazes at her with a steely stare. Then, with a shake of his head, he wipes his forehead with a hand that even trembles more than hers. She inhales, deeply, keeping the air in her lungs for a few seconds,

2

and then she exhales, releasing the tension as she recognises the familiarity in those eyes, albeit red and brimming with tears.

A pulse throbs in her neck and she can hear her blood rushing in her ears.

'The cards,' he whispers.

'Of course,' she says, her voice higher in tone than normal. 'Would you like to come through?'

She stifles a nervous laugh behind her hand and points to the unlit room beside her, reaching out for the light switch. When she turns to check if he is following her, the light falls across his face. His hands and forehead are streaked with something that can only be dried blood.

The woman's eyes are the most extraordinary colour. Colours. One is blue, the other is brown. Her eye make-up, waterproof, matches them: from the top of her nose her eyelids are blue, gradually mixing with brown towards the sides. Thick black eyeliner and bright red lipstick are smudged across her face. White, bare shoulders. Under her chin, a small silver heart on a necklace is stuck in a strand of wet blonde hair.

She doesn't blink when I enter the white plastic Scene of Crime tent and step on the small wooden jetty on the bank of the fishing lake. Having pulled on the obligatory white paper suit and blue shoe covers and dutifully signed the clipboard, I stand still in the opening for a moment, carefully taking in the situation. Behind me, a radio crackles. It belongs to the officer standing guard outside the tent, keeping a record of everyone entering and leaving the area that has been cordoned off with police tape. On the coast road, drivers slow down, hoping to catch a glimpse of what is going on. A police officer wearing a yellow fluorescent sleeveless jacket over his uniform is gesturing everyone to keep moving.

'Hi Andy.'

A familiar figure turns as a gust of wet wind disturbs the quietness. David Jamieson nods, frowns and points. Obediently, I help myself to a pair of blue latex gloves.

'You're late.'

He closes his case and scratches his ear under the rim of his hat. Apparently, the pathologist is just about to leave, making room for the three figures in white, who are crowding into the limited area. One is kneeling on an aluminium tile and covering the wooden edge of the jetty with fingerprint powder and sticky tape, concentrating too much to notice me. The planks are grey and weathered, wet from overnight drizzle. His body language suggests he is not hopeful of finding anything useful. His colleague is taking still photos and then videos of the crime scene and everything else that might be worth to record. By the look of the red clothes shining beneath the thin white of her suit, I recognise the third person, Andrea Burke. She's hunched down between her forensic bag and the corpse, briefly looking up and nodding at me by way of a greeting. She holds up a clear plastic bag, peers at its contents through her red-rimmed glasses, and scribbles something on a clipboard. The photographer swings his cameras around his neck and grins somewhat sheepishly, trying to remember my name. I can tell that he fails by the way he nods.

'You're the SIO, Andy?' Jamieson stamps his feet on the ground, trying to stay warm.

'For now.' I look away, hoping that he won't enquire after my health.

'Running errands again?' He grins to take the edge off his sarcasm.

I shrug. 'Maloney's on his way.'

'Sir?' Burke interrupts, passing her clipboard to Jamieson for him to read her notes. After he scribbles something on it, he looks up at me again, this time avoiding my eyes. I know what he is thinking but with the presence of Andrea Burke in mind, I decide that it's probably best to keep quiet. For now.

'Couldn't he get out of his warm bed?' Andrea Burke looks up, grinning.

'He was off yesterday.'

It was only a couple of months ago that DI Maloney gloated about having dinner at Rick Stein's famous restaurant in Padstow to celebrate the wedding anniversary of his parents-in-law. Now the couple are in a bitter and rather nasty fight over their divorce, arguing endlessly about who is to blame, who will stay in the house, how to split their money, and, more importantly it seems, what to tell their relatives, friends and neighbours. After thirty-odd-years of marriage, they should know better. As Maloney's wife is upset about it, and clearly desperate to seek reconciliation, he has driven her to Weymouth, where he was staying the night when the call came about the body in the lake. Which is why he forwarded the message, and the task, to me. I guessed he didn't want DCI Guthrie to know about the intimate details of his family life and I promised I would fill him in as soon as he got back. In truth, I'm happy to pick up the crumbs of whatever Maloney drops.

My rank as detective inspector is only effective on paper. I have a reduced salary and an official status as part-time police officer on a so-called zero-hour contract. The money isn't a huge problem; I still earn enough to keep me going but it is the underlying, much bigger issue that is concerning me. On a positive day, when I manage to see the brighter side of life, I tell myself that it is a good thing that I don't have to fill in forms and spend hours in meetings about strategy and budgets. Because I don't have any duties to fulfil in an official capacity, I am free to do the more routine police work which, I must admit, does make me wonder if a step down on the career ladder would make me feel my job was more worthwhile. I haven't been a DI long enough to get comfortable in the role, but I do know that working with people suits me well.

'Not much forensic evidence, I'm afraid,' says Jamieson, locking his case with a dry click. 'She's been in the lake for a good few hours.'

I step aside and peer down past Burke who is half obscuring the body, and my eye catches a small mole on the left shoulder of the dead woman. 'Isn't she dressed?'

'No. No clothes found either.' Burke shakes her head, adding sarcastically, 'I don't think she was going for a swim.'

She has a sense of humour that I don't always understand and I suspect it works both ways.

'Do we know who she is?' I ask, skipping the questions with obvious answers and bend over to look at the victim's face. She is staring at me with vacant eyes. Not blinking. I stare back and let the questions in her eyes settle inside me. I feel almost guilty that I can't answer them yet.

Andrea Burke lifts the sheet covering the rest of the body, pointing, and I see a clean thin cut where a sharp knife slit the neck. Or perhaps I should say a sharp object, as it is an unofficial, preliminary observation. Rules are strict nowadays. Even the slightest slip of the tongue can send a good lawyer into action and have the case dismissed by the court before you know it.

'No identification, unfortunately.' Andrea Burk eventually replies. She's not looking at me, but there is a tiny little smile lingering at the corners of her mouth.

'Where are her clothes?'

'We haven't found them yet.' She pauses briefly. 'But we have a handbag.'

'Don't hold your breath though, Andy.' Jamieson cuts off any ideas I might have that this will be an easy case.

'Exactly.' Burke shakes her head with vigour. A strand of ruby red hair pops out of her protective suit. 'There is only money in the handbag, I'm afraid. Fifty pounds in bank notes and some loose change.' She lets her words hang in the air with a sense of expectation.

'What? No ID? Bank cards? What about keys?'

'Nothing.'

'Anything else?' I ask, trying not to show my disappointment.

'Time of death ... about 24 and 30 hours ago.' Smiling sheepishly, the pathologist casts me a sideways glance. 'If that helps? Cause of death ... well, I can't disclose anything before I've done the official post-mortem, but at first glance ... the cut in her neck.'

'She didn't drown?'

'I will have to check that, but I don't think so.'

'What else have you found? Are there any signs of other physical injuries?'

'Sorry Andy, it's too early for that. I'm afraid I can only answer that question later.'

I turn towards the exit of the tent. A gust of cold damp air hits me in the face as the officer outside opens it politely. I smile but his face remains stoic. To make a point, perhaps, he slaps his arms against the cold, looking like a young bird that hasn't yet got the confidence to fly away.

His radio crackles and I watch him listening to someone called Billy who is reporting that no one in the only building that has a view over the lake has seen or heard anything suspicious. Helpfully, he points in the direction of a group of farm buildings nestled on the slope of the southern facing hill, where the sun is briefly reflected in a small bay window on the first floor. A ring of smoke comes out of one of the chimneys and a murder of crows sits on the rooftop, watching a buzzard circling over an area of gorse and hawthorn, scrutinising every centimetre with its sharp eyes.

Thanking the officer, I walk back to my car and, as I pull out, I make a mental note to check the statements of the residents as soon as they're brought in. I look around. The area is a black hole in the CCTV systems. A perfect location for criminal activities.

2

Josh Warren was unfortunate enough to have found the body. Clearly, he now regrets having called the police, wishing that he'd walked away, pretending not to have seen or heard anything. I know how he feels, but I'll have to treat him as a suspect. It won't be the first time that a murderer is so confident and arrogant that he calls the police himself.

'Mr Warren?'

I look at him through the half-opened window on the passenger side of a patrol car. He is lurking on the back seat, clutching a plastic bag as if it holds the crown jewels. He is in his early thirties with a round face and fine blond hair that is already thinning on the top of his head.

'Yes. Can you tell me how long this is going to take? I called my boss but I thought I would be at work within an hour.' His voice is tinny, his eyes wide, the memory of the dead woman still etched on his retina.

In the driver's seat, a uniformed officer is sitting behind the wheel with a mobile phone in his hand. His colleague is outside, walking across the parking area with his hands folded on his back as though he's looking for a lost coin. The area is cordoned off with blue and white police tape hooked around metal poles that have been hammered into the ground by the officers who were the first to arrive at the crime scene.

'They're sending more men.' The driver stifles a yawn and shoves his mobile phone in the breast pocket of his fluorescent jacket.

'Do you know the nearest place to get a coffee?'

The officer shrugs, automatically patting his chest, as, for a single moment, he believes he has somehow lost his phone. 'Up that hill. There's a pub at the top. Not sure if it will be open, though.'

I gesture towards Warren. He hasn't moved. Hope has flares up in his eyes, replacing an unfounded fear that he might end up in a police cell. Sadly, some people are like that in response to the power of the law, feeling guilty of anything, while they're completely innocent.

'The Swan Inn is further up the road.' He breaks off to take deep breaths. 'I know them. They'll open up for me if Ray is there. He's the manager.'

'Let's go there then, shall we?' I motion with my head and open the door. He nods with a shiver at a sudden gust of cold wind. The temperature must be somewhere around five degrees, but the wind makes it feel like it is below zero. The tips of my ears are almost freezing.

'Sir, we are supposed to take Mr Warren to the station for his statement.' The officer behind the wheel frowns, talking to me through the smallest possible opening of his window. 'We're waiting for our colleagues and then we'll go.'

'I will take Mr Warren to the station.'

'Okay.' He nods as if he's seen and heard it all before and lost interest a long time ago.

Beside me, Warren stamps his feet to stay warm. He scrutinises my ID card as if he thinks I am a fake policeman looking for a scapegoat. He slumps beside me in my car, putting the plastic bag in his pocket and fiddling with a woollen hat, contemplating whether to put it on. His padded jacket is thick and he wears a woollen jumper underneath it, his collar turned up, yet he is shivering.

'Where do you work, Mr Warren?' I ask, starting the engine and turning the heater on full blast.

He replies with a considerable amount of pride in his voice: 'I work at the Lobster Hatchery in Padstow.'

This immediately stirs up a memory in my mind. A clear day, Lauren's birthday. We had browsed the shops in the picturesque fishing village, and then walked on the beach. Her 10-year-old twin sons ran in front of us like young horses, flapping their arms and shouting in the clear air. We were supposed to go to the Lobster Hatchery afterwards, but something had happened and the lovely day had ended under a dark shadow. The promise of a visit to the Lobster Hatchery has still not been fulfilled ...

'Are you one of their volunteers?' I ask Josh Warren.

'No, no, I'm part of the team.' He looks almost offended.

'So what's your job exactly?'

'I look after the little ones.' His voice makes it clear that he is not going to disclose any more details.

As I pull out of the car park and wait for a supermarket delivery van to cross the narrow bridge, he sighs involuntarily.

'Glad to be away from that,' he announces. 'I've never seen anything like that before. Just as well Eddie could ... '

'Just as well what? Eddie?' The engine hums in protest when we climb the steep hill and negotiate a sharp, narrow S bend next to an old church.

'I'd thought he'd better go. My mate. Eddie. He was with me.'

I cast him a quick glance. 'Are you saying that you weren't alone when you discovered the body?'

'No. Yes. I mean, that is what I am saying. I thought there was no point for him to wait until you lot showed up. I decided that I would go back and ... show you.'

I try to hide my annoyance. 'I will need Eddie's name and address, Mr Warren. I hope you have that?'

'Whatever for?' His amazement is genuine. 'Eddie will tell you exactly the same as me.'

'To confirm your statement.'

'I haven't given a statement yet. The officer said you would deal with that.'

'Okay.' Obviously he is now wishing that he hadn't come to the fishing pond in the first place. 'It's okay, Mr Warren. It's just a formality.'

'I ... we didn't touch her, or anything like that. I didn't touch anything. Or Eddie.'

I give him an encouraging smile. 'Okay. Good. I will need a statement about the circumstances when you found the body. Both yours and Eddie's.'

I round a steep bend, nearly scraping the side of my car on the wall as another delivery van comes down at a dangerously careless speed. I can see the driver grinning before he disappears.

'It's right here, past the bend with a car park to the right.' Warren points.

The Swan Inn is closed, but a cleaner opens the door and Warren walks in as if he has every right to be there. The place is dark and gloomy; the smell of stale beer mixed with cleaning detergent and food preparation. A variety of cooking smells assails us as we move into the pub: a hint of curry, garlic, tomato sauce, roast meat, pastry, freshly baked bread. I feel my stomach rumbling and realise I haven't eaten except for a slice of toast with my morning coffee.

Warren knocks on the kitchen door and I hear a muffled conversation with only a couple of recognisable words as the cleaner switches on a vacuum cleaner.

'They will bring us some coffee.'

We sit at one of the tables close to the window and I retrieve a small notepad from my pocket. I rarely use it, but the sight of it normally puts people at ease.

'Let's start with your details please, Mr Warren, and of course I will need those of your friend Eddie.'

He gestures with two hands. 'Your colleague has my details already.'

'I'd like to have them too.' I smile gently.

'How long will this take?' he asks, impatiently waiting as I write down the information. He lives in Rumford, next to his sister and her family; they share a car, a dark grey VW Polo, to minimise their costs.

'It takes as long as it takes, Mr Warren. I'm sure you'll understand that this is a serious matter. A woman was found dead and we are treating her death as suspicious.'

His lower jaw drops and he licks his lips nervously. 'I didn't kill that woman! I don't even know who she is! I have nothing to do with it.'

'Why were you there this morning, Mr Warren? Let's start at the beginning. You and Eddie arrived at the scene and … what happened?'

He hesitates, stares at my face and decides that the best and quickest option is to cooperate. 'I pick Eddie up for work in the morning. We both work in Padstow. As I said, I work at the Lobster Hatchery, and Eddie works in the harbour. Sand dredging.' He looks at me, half expecting me to ask for an explanation. I wait quietly and he continues. 'Normally, we don't take the coast road, but today … well, let me explain first that the Swan Lake is owned by an angling association and I'm a committee member.'

'Last Saturday, we had our first angling competition of the season. I wasn't there myself, because I had to work, but most of our members were there, and some guests too. Anyway, the system is that our members can use the lake for free but guests have to pay a fee. There's a moneybox in the little shed at the entrance to the car park and you leave the fee and a forms with your name and other details on it in the box. Sometimes people put the money in an envelope.'

For some reason, he is avoiding my eyes, playing with a cardboard beer coaster and studying the images on either side as if he's never seen them before. 'Erm ... because I drive by on my way to work, it's my job to collect the money every week. Sometimes our treasurer does it himself, but I do it normally on Monday after work. Obviously our members are mostly there on Saturdays and Sundays. I'll go extra times when we've had a competition, like this weekend.' He pauses and is silent for a moment or two. 'I was supposed to collect the money on Saturday evening after work, but I forgot. And yesterday ... well, I had been out on Saturday evening.' His face turns a shade of red and I can see him struggling with on the one hand being honest and on the other the fear of admitting that he'd probably driven home with too much alcohol in his blood stream.

I don't say anything and he shrugs. 'The moneybox is safely attached to the wall but, still, there would be a considerable amount of money in it because it was the first competition of the season, so I thought it would be best to collect it this morning before work and take it to the bank in Padstow in my lunch break.'

'So you went directly into the shed.'

'Yes.'

'But the woman was in the lake, which is at least twenty yards from the shed. Could you see her from there?'

'Erm ... no. But my male Eddie got out of the car ... to have a pee. Then he saw her.' He grins sheepishly. 'Eddie likes to pee in the pond.'

'Was that unusual for him?'

'No.' He shakes his head, embarrassment crossing his face. 'Well, uhm, I shouldn't say this, maybe, but Eddie is ... a bit ... you know.'

'I'm afraid I don't understand, Mr Warren.'

'Eddie is ... damaged, that's perhaps the right word. He was abused by his father when he was young and now ... he is kind of ... strange himself.

'So it was Eddie who discovered the body?'

'Yeah. First, I wasn't interested. I had collected the money and I wanted to go to work, but he kept yelling at me about floating boobs. Of course I thought that it was ridiculous, but his voice sounded like he was somewhat upset, so I thought I'd better calm him down a bit. If he gets in a state, he can be awkward all day and since, things haven't been all hunky-dory with his boss lately, I thought I'd better sort him out before he got himself sacked.' He shrugs with a sheepish grin. 'And then I saw that he was right. She was naked, you see, all white flesh in the water. She looked like a mermaid, with her hair floating like weeds.'

'What did you two do next?' I am slowly getting the picture of the events that shocked the two men.

'I told Eddie to go back to the car. He was crying, you see, saying how beautiful she was, and all that. Uhm, I don't think he understood that she was dead. He said something like we needed to rescue her, mouth-to-mouth, that sort of thing. But he did as he was told. I secured the rope around the gate, so that it would be a bit more difficult for anyone to get into the car park and we drove up the hill where I stopped to call the police.' He pauses briefly. 'I have no reception down at the lake with my mobile.

'You didn't touch the body? Either of you?'

'Definitely not. I watch those programmes on TV, inspector, I know everything about DNA and fingerprints.'

I suppress a smile. 'And what happened then?'

'As I said, I stopped to call the police. The person I spoke to said they would send a patrol car within half an hour and I thought … if it takes them half an hour, I'll have plenty of time to drive to Padstow and drop Eddie at his work.'

'How long had you been away from the scene?'

'Not more than fifteen minutes.' He shrugs, tugging at the collar of his shirt. 'I had secured the rope at the gate, using a special seaman's knot. It was exactly the same when I got back, so I knew nobody had been there. I parked exactly where I had parked before, in case police would be looking for tyre marks, and I stood at the gate, waiting for the police and making sure no one else came in there.'

'We appreciate your thoughtfulness, Mr Warren. Now, going back to the moment you and Eddie discovered the body, was there anyone else? Did you see anyone?'

'There was no one. Nothing.'

'Did you recognise the woman?'

'To be honest, I didn't look at her again once I realised that she was dead.'

'As you come here quite often, was there something out of the ordinary?'

'No, but ... uhm...' He grabs another beer coaster and flips it on the edge of the table. Catches it between his thumb and index finger. Flips it again. 'I wasn't sure whether someone had dropped them there on the day of the competition ... but that didn't make sense. I mean, you would miss them immediately, wouldn't you?'

'What are you saying, Mr Warren?'

He bends to pick up the beer coaster from the floor.

'I found these. I picked them up before I saw the body.'Putting the beer coaster down and placing his cup on it, he leans back and, as if the significance only occurs to him now, he produces a set of keys. There's a car key and two other keys on a key ring with a small children's doll made of light blue plastic. The doll has a capital A on its stomach.

3

The incident room is deserted. Several tables are set out in neat rows, reminding me of a classroom at school. The tops are wiped clean of greasy fingerprints and spilled coffee, and chairs are stacked against the wall on one side. The smell of disinfectant hangs in the air, giving the room a sense of expectation.

In the meantime, forensic investigators are still scrutinising the area around the lake, gathering samples that will hopefully turn out to be connected to the crime, while other officers are out looking for witnesses. In the mortuary, the pathologists are taking samples from the body for DNA testing and taking fingerprints and dental impressions in preparation for the official autopsy which is scheduled for early afternoon.

Putting my coffee on the table nearest to the whiteboard, I grab a handful of magnets from a plastic tray underneath it. It annoys me that the board is not properly clean but covered with the faded remains of the details of a previous case. Someone had also pinned up a newspaper cutting about an incident that happened a few weeks ago, its headline screaming 'Teenager in hit and run', and for some reason, it has been left behind. The article describes a nasty hit-and-run: a sixteen-year-old without a driver's licence but with seven times the limit of alcohol in his blood. On the pavement, a caring father was collecting his young teenage daughter from a friend's birthday party. Miraculously, the father was physically uninjured, but the 13-year-old girl was left with two broken legs, and head and back injuries. The young man was sent to prison, but the girl was paralysed from the waist down. Two families ruined for life.

I take down the newspaper cutting and find the wiper for the whiteboard in a drawer of one of the desks. Soon enough the board will be filled with details of a new case, a new investigation, this time about a woman found dead in a fishing lake. I pick up the photo and, for a moment, I stare at a mainly black-and-white image of the victim, her skin is unnaturally white and the dark sheet underneath her is wet from water dripping off her hair. Sadly, she doesn't have a name yet.

The shrill ringing of my phone interrupts the quietness of the empty room. I sigh, not even attempting to hide my annoyance when I reply curtly, 'Yes?'

'Is that Tregunna?'

It's the new desk officer. I can't recall her name. Something like Annie or Allie. She sounds as though she is being careful not to get into a long conversation with me. We haven't had a good start. I can't think why she's been so hostile towards me. Unless it's because I seemed to have totally ignored her on her first day. I remember vaguely that I was introduced to her, at which moment my phone rang and I turned my back to her to take the call.

'It is.'

'Sorry sir, Philip isn't here yet and I can't find anyone else in the team. But you are in the building, right?'

Philip, that must be Maloney. I am Tregunna. Not Andy, but just Tregunna.

'I am.' I sigh. 'Did you say that Philip hasn't arrived yet?'

'That's right, sir. We think he might be held up on the A30. There's been a collision near Launceston.'

I stare at the clock. It's approaching twelve, the time I scheduled the first briefing in the expectation that Maloney would be back by then. But as there is still no sign of him, I suspect I will have to take the lead. In a few minutes the room will be charged with excitement. The first hours of an investigation are crucial for its success and although I am glad for the opportunity, I also dread the responsibility. Perhaps I am not quite ready to do my job a hundred per cent after all.

'I've got someone here to see you, sir.' The desk officer sounds curt, formal and there's something else I can't fathom. I suspect that this isn't the right moment to find out what it is.

'Okay, I'll come down,' I say and she ends the call without a word.

The hall seems to be filled with more people than there actually are. Two uniformed officers, hands in blue latex gloves, are standing firmly behind a man who is leaning heavily on the desk with both arms. Further away as is another man, his back to the wall and his eyes raised towards the ceiling, breathing heavily through his mouth, as dried blood obstructs his nostrils. A third officer has placed himself deliberately between him and the trio at the desk.

With a sinking feeling, I hear the man leaning at the desk muttering obscenities and one of the officers telling him that he is only making his case worse with his offensive language. The man doesn't seem to be bothered. Nor is the desk officer. Although her face is slightly flushed, her stare is fixed and firm and she speaks with authority as she tries to calm the man.

She stops mid-sentence as she spots me opening the door. 'Tregunna.'

Following my gaze, she smiles faintly but there is a certain triumph in her eyes when she picks up a single sheet of paper and nods towards one of the interview rooms opposite her. Half expecting her to ask the two officers to escort the abusive man into the room, I can't hide my surprise when she points in the direction of another man sitting on one of the seats against the wall, his arms folded across his chest viewing the scene with a mixture of impatience and amusement.

'Can you have a word with that gentleman, Tregunna?'

She – her name badge still doesn't help me with her name as it only says A. M. Barron - hands me the sheet and I see a one name written in the corner in neat and tidy handwriting that corresponds with her air of competence. Kenneth Poole.

Our eyes meet for a split-second and I realise that she knows perfectly well that my initial thought was that she called me to deal with the abusive man.

'Erm … thanks,' I say, glancing at him and the man with the bloody nose who have clearly had some kind of fight and haven't calmed down yet. A word, a glance, a gesture, anything can ignite the situation again into a serious fight.

'Mr Poole?'

My voice attracts the attention of the three officers as they try to keep the two angry men apart. Even the man leaning on the desk turns his bald head to stare at me. He has a puffy, pink face with small blue eyes and ginger eye brows. I can see beads of sweat on his forehead. The silence continues and the beads join up, trickling down the side of his angry face. He scowls, casting me a threatening glance, then turns back towards the man with whom it appears he had the fight.

'Sir,' one of the officers begins, his eyes darting towards his colleagues for support. But they all seem frozen rigid, as if they are waiting for someone to make the first move.

More silence, broken only by the rustle of the sheet of paper in my hand and the drama starts again.

'You listen to me,' shouts the abusive man, as he leans further over the desk towards the desk officer who, I must admit, is holding the fort with admirable patience and stoicism.

'No,' she says firmly. 'You have said enough. You have sworn enough. Now you listen to me. I need to know your full name and address.'

'What for?' He peers down at the desk, trying to focus on a form she's holding up.

'You will be held in custody.'

I don't wait for the eruption, which, surprisingly, ebbs away as if there had never been a threat. As I turn towards the man on the seat in the waiting area, I hear the abusive man behind me blurt out of a stream of apologies explaining that it has all been a misunderstanding between him and his mate. It is his mate, yes, not his enemy or the future victim of his murderous rage.

Patiently, I wait until he stops for breath and in the moment of silence, I turn to the man in the waiting area.

4

Kenneth Poole squeezes his steel grey eyes and rises slowly, running a hand back through his thick, sandy-coloured hair. Clean shaven, he is tall and carries a bit too much weight around his waist.

'Mr Poole, how can I help you?' Showing him my ID card, I shake a firm, cool hand and gesture towards interview room number 1. 'Shall we find a quieter place?'

He glances at me as I open the door and I see a look in his eyes that suggests, for some reason, he wouldn't have minded continuing to watch the events between the two men.

'Yes, but I'm not sure …' He pauses, apparently reluctant to disclose the reason for his visit; almost as if his worst fears won't come true if he says nothing. 'My wife.' His voice is low and coarse and he seems slightly out of breath. 'I heard on the radio that you found the body of a woman.'

I stare at him, waiting for more. When he remains quiet, avoiding my eyes, I ask, 'And you think it may be your wife?'

'I hope not, of course but … it could be her.'

He looks straight at my face and I know he doesn't want to beat around the bush. For that reason, I avoid the obvious questions like why he seems to believe that his wife is dead.

'What does your wife look like, Mr Poole?'

He shakes his head, lost for words for a moment, then he says, clearly deep in thought, 'She is … beautiful. Just beautiful.'

I suppress a smile. 'Can you describe her … features? Hair? Length? Weight?'

'She is naturally blond and she must be … she is about five inches shorter than me. And her weight … I don't know. She's just … perfect.'

There is something about him that makes me feel he may be right. Without a word, I take the Polaroid photo from my pocket and lay it on the table, upside down, thinking of her eyes.

'And what is the colour of her eyes?' I ask casually, but my voice must have acquired an edge that gives something away because he gasps for breath and looks me straight in the eyes.

I already know his answer. I can read his mind and, unfortunately, he can read mine too. His head sinks and his shoulders drop and all of a sudden, he looks twenty years older.

'Her eyes are different, inspector. One is blue, the other is brown.'

'Of course that doesn't mean … I'm so sorry, Mr Poole.'

He swallows hard, fighting a lump in his throat, trying to remain composed and not bursting into tears.

'This is a photo of the woman we found this morning, Mr Poole. It isn't a pleasant photo, so I don't blame you if you don't want to see it.'

'You don't need identification?'

'We have several options to tackle that, Mr 'Poole, but maybe it is best if you let me ask you some questions first.'

He nods, relieved by the delay, maintaining a vague hope that at least for another few minutes he can believe this is all one huge mistake. Then he sits quietly for a while, staring at trembling fingers, perhaps half wishing he was a woman so it would be ok to show his pain and sorrow.

'For now, Mr Poole, just to make sure we're not making any mistake, can you tell me which of her eyes is blue?'

'The left,' he says promptly, not hesitating at all. 'Her left eye is blue.

I nod, putting the unseen photo back into my pocket. 'Eh … can I get you something? Tea, coffee, a glass of water?'

He doesn't move. 'Coffee would be … no, it'll make me sick.'

'Perhaps later,' I say gently. 'What is your wife's name?'

'Alicia. Alicia Poole.

I write the name under his on my notepad and wait patiently. Once more he is quiet, gathering his thoughts, trying to grasp the enormity of what is happening to him, the impact it will have on his personal life, and trying to fight the hope that this is a dream, a bad joke, not the cruel reality.

'Sorry.' He covers his eyes with his hands, his shoulders hanging low as if in defeat. He is locked in a cocoon of disbelief and denial. Raw grief will catch up with him later.

There are sounds from the hall, shouts and laughter. The normal day-to-day life of a working environment. Somehow, it seems to wake him up. His head jerks backward and for a moment he studies the ceiling, then he clears his throat and eyes me suspiciously.

'I'm sorry you had to find out … the way you did, Mr Poole.'

'Not your fault,' he replies brusquely. 'I suppose you'll have questions, but I have lots of them too.'

'Of course. I will tell you as much as I can but you must understand that the investigation has just started. We found … it is only a few hours ago that we found … her.' I clear my throat. It seems wrong to speak of his wife as 'the body', let alone 'the corpse'. 'When did you last see your wife, Mr Poole?'

'It was … on Saturday morning.' His eyes widen and it is obvious that he is surprised that it is less than two days ago that he saw his wife alive for the last time, and that his life has now changed in about the click of two fingers. 'At about nine. We'd had breakfast and I went upstairs to change. I was going off to play golf with some of my business partners.' He pauses, then shrugs. 'Nothing unusual.'

'And your wife stayed at home?'

'She did, well, she doesn't play golf. Didn't, I should say, I guess … uhm … she never learned to play and when I suggested that she have lessons, she laughed and said … did I really think playing golf was something she would like to do? I didn't expect she would want to learn but I thought … I'd just thought I'd suggest it, you know?'

'How long have you been married?'

'More than four years.'

'Children?'

'Yes, well, but not together, if that is what you mean. I have two sons, from my previous marriage. They're both married. Alicia … has … had a young daughter from her marriage.'

'How old is her daughter?'

'Briony is nine.'

'Does she live with you?'

'Yes, of course, she lived with her mother, obviously, but … I suppose everything will change now.'

'Does she see her biological father regularly?'

'Every other weekend. That was this weekend. Trevor just came to pick up Briony at the same time when I was leaving.'

'Trevor?'

'Trevor Bennett. Briony's father. Sorry. I must have his address somewhere but, at the moment, I can't think. I'm sorry. His number is on our phone at home.'

As I write the names down, I make a mental note to have this followed up as soon as I can. I will have to organise a family liaison officer who is confident enough to handle a child of that age. Nine years old, a difficult age, too young to deal with a horrible loss like that, yet old enough to understand. The poor girl needs to be informed sensitively and quickly.

'You were out playing golf and Briony was with her father, so Alicia was at home alone on Saturday?'

He shrugs. 'She was going to see her friend, Denise. They were going to do some shopping and then go to a cinema later maybe, and I assumed she would stay the night at Denise's.'

I don't like being fed snippets of information that I have to put together until I have the full picture. I much prefer to listen to everything in a more logical and chronological order.

'Okay, let me get this in the right time frame. Last Saturday morning, what time did you leave?'

'It must have been close to half past nine when I got in my car and saw Trevor stop on the road. I remember thinking that I hoped he wouldn't park in front of the drive, like he does sometimes. But he parked a bit further along and walked up the drive as I pulled out.' He pauses briefly, catching my eye. 'We aren't enemies, inspector, but we aren't friends either. Frankly, we have nothing in common, nothing to talk about other than the weather. So I didn't stop to have a chat with him.'

'Did you see him enter the house?'

'No, but I'm sure everything was all right. I'd forgotten to put my laptop on the charger and I phoned Alicia about forty minutes later. She said I was just in time, as she was just about to leave the house also. So I assumed that by that time, Trevor and Briony had already left.'

'So when you left that morning at half past nine, it was the last time you saw your wife?'

'Yes.' He is suddenly fiddly and fidgety. Nervous. Uncomfortable. I can't understand what has caused this unexpected change of attitude.

'You didn't go home that night?' I'll have to ask him about his alibi again when I've seen the post-mortem report and the time of her death.

'Uhm … no. Didn't I say? I thought Alicia was going to stay at Denise's. And the golf was, well … we had a good time on the golf course and we stayed and had a meal afterwards. I enjoyed myself and … I realised that I had drunk a bit too much. I knew Alicia and Briony weren't at home, so I decided to stay in a hotel near the golf course.' He offers a faint smile. 'I suppose you want the name of that hotel?'

'And the people in your company.'

'Company?' His face flushes and I don't need to ask him if he spent the night alone. Finding out the lady's name will have to wait until later and perhaps it won't be necessary to get her involved. There's no point in disclosing personal secrets without good reason.

'When did you get home, Mr Poole?'

'On Sunday evening. Around six, maybe it was five or ten past six. Trevor would normally bring Briony back after she's had her tea with them, so I didn't expect her back home before seven.' He shifts on his seat, thinking, calculating, and trying to make sense of what now seems to occur to him as unusual.

'I did think it was strange that Alicia wasn't home yet,' he says thoughtfully. 'She would always make sure she was at home when Briony came back. She thought that was important to Briony. She would never be late. Unless something had happened to her, of course, like when she'd been held up somewhere for some reason.' He sighs. 'I checked the answer machine and there were several messages from Trevor. Apparently, Briony was feeling unwell and he had tried to call Alicia to ask if it was possible to bring Briony home earlier, but he'd not got through to her. In his last message, he said he would keep their daughter with them and if she cared to call him back, they could discuss the matter. I suppose he was annoyed that Alicia wasn't there.'

'Go on.'

'There's nothing more to say, really. I tried to call Alicia, to find out what time she'd be home, but her battery must have gone flat. She didn't answer. There was nothing to eat in the house that appealed to me and I decided to go out for a meal.'

'Alone?'

'Well, yes. To be honest, I was also a bit annoyed with Ali. So … uhm … I met some friends and we had a few drinks.'

'In your local?'

'No,' he says, with a bit of a sneer. 'I rarely go to a pub. No offence, inspector, but it's not really my scene. No, when I go out like that, I go to the golf club where I'm a member.'

Deciding not to push the matter at this moment, I smile and ask, 'What time did you come home?'

'It was around midnight. Uhm … someone dropped me off at home and she picked me up this morning to take me to my car.'

'She?'

'My secretary.'

The classic mistress. It is not my intention to involve the secretary at this stage, but he seems to fear it is. He launches unto a lengthy explanation about his evening to play down any involvement with his secretary. I listen, only half convinced.

'How do you make your living, Mr Poole?'

If he is surprised by the sudden change of the subject, he doesn't show it. 'We have an estate agency. We have several offices in the region. I am more or less based in Wadebridge.'

'We?'

'Uhm … Julia and me.'

'Is Julia your secretary?'

The thought seems to amuse him. 'Good heavens no! Julia is my first wife. We set up the business together, just after we got married. But then we had our children and she worked less. But … she was still involved and has remained involved as a full partner, as one of the conditions of our divorce.'

'I see.' His first wife must have had a grudge to insist on that condition. 'Sorry I interrupted you. Go on, please, Mr Poole.'

He clears his throat, a look of concern in his eyes. Something tells me he is going to ring his ex-wife as soon as he walks out of the station.

'As I said, my secretary dropped me off at home around midnight. I had a bit too much to drink and, as much as Alicia likes her wine, she hates it when I've had too much. The house was dark and I reckoned she was already asleep. I thought her car was in the garage. It never occurred to me to check that. I decided not to wake her and I slept in the guest bedroom. When I woke up this morning, I thought she was having a lie-in. I knew that Briony was still with Trevor, and I thought I'd let Alicia sleep and enjoy a lazy morning. Besides, I had to prepare for a meeting which was scheduled for ten o'clock and I had to get my car from the golf club before that. My secretary collected me at eight and I drove straight to work from the golf club.'

I cast a quick glance at my watch. Hopefully DI Maloney has arrived by now. The woman's identity is crucial to progress with the investigation. We also need to speak to Alicia's friend Denise, with whom she spent most of the Saturday. But it'll have to wait. Something tells me that Mr Poole has more important information.

'When did you discover that Alicia wasn't at home at all?'

'This morning. As soon as I arrived in my office, I realised I'd forgotten my laptop. I thought about asking my secretary to pick it up, but Alicia didn't answer the phone and I didn't want Jenna to enter the house with my keys and frighten Alicia to death.' He gasps in horror as he realises what he's just said. 'Sorry, that wasn't what I meant.'

'You seem to make a habit of forgetting your laptop.'

He smiles faintly. 'In this case, yes, it sounds a bit odd, doesn't it? I normally don't take my work home. Home is home, work is work. I used to work more than was good for me, which was the reason for my divorce from Julia. Understandably perhaps, but, after that, I worked even harder until I got a serious warning. Chest pains.' He smiles faintly, almost embarrassed. 'The pain turned out to be gall-stones, but I thought it was a heart attack and I was so scared that I swore that I would change my lifestyle and I did.' He stops abruptly, realising that his thoughts have wandered off. 'The reason why I took the laptop home this weekend was because of the meeting this morning. It was an important meeting and I wanted to go through the details again to make sure I was on top of everything.'

'But you didn't.'

'As I said, I went out last night and came home around mid-night. I thought, sod it. I knew all the ins-and-outs of the contract and I didn't really need to check it all over again.'

'How did the meeting go?'

'What?' He stares at me, surprised.

'You said you had a business meeting this morning at ten o'clock?'

'Oh yes, of course. It went alright. No problem at all. We signed the new contract, much to my satisfaction, to be honest.'

'But how ...?'

'How did I discover that Alicia wasn't at home and that she hadn't been at home at all? Well, Trevor called me. He told me that Briony had developed a fever and that she was really ill and he was adamant that she should stay with them. Of course, he was also annoyed that he couldn't get hold of Alicia. It got me thinking that it was unusual for Alicia not to answer her phone.

Like most people nowadays who have mobile phones glued to their hands, Alicia was no exception. It occurred to me that she could be ill as well. Flu or something, just like Briony. So I went home to check. That was when I discovered that her car was gone, her bed hadn't been slept in and, by the looks of it, she hadn't been home at all.'

'And that wasn't like her.'

'No, definitely not. I mean, she liked to go out with Denise, you know, girly nights and all that. That didn't bother me. I could understand that, because Denise lives alone and ... they've been best friends for years.'

He stares at his hands again, his fingers trembling, eyes filling with tears as the grim reality hits him right in the face.

'When I heard on the radio that they found a woman's body ... I don't know how, inspector, but I just knew it was her.'

5

People who practice the art of Feng Shui would instantly feel their whole body itching when they enter DCI Guthrie's office. The furniture and colours are a disturbing mismatch that makes me feel uneasy and uncomfortable. If someone told him about the invisible forces that bind the universe, earth and humanity together, and explained the philosophy of harmonizing as with the surrounding environment, Guthrie would instantly dismiss the person as a nutcase.

His desk is placed against the wall so that, when he turns in his black leather chair, he can look out of the window and enjoy the stunning view across the bay. On the opposite wall is a painting of a golden sunset casting sparkles of light on the waves entering a Cornish cove. The remains of an old tin mine are silhouetted on the cliffs to the right, and on the left, a lone figure balances on the edge. I can't explain why the painting has always appealed to me. Or perhaps it's just that I can't understand that a man like Guthrie can feel the emotion in it, the desolation of the lone figure in particular.

'Tregunna. Have a seat, please.' Briefly looking up from the newspaper in front of him, he waves a hand towards two chairs on the other side of his desk. They are notoriously uncomfortable, purchased, they say, for exactly that reason.

In his fifties, Guthrie's face is unnaturally smooth and mostly devoid of wrinkles. According to PC Jennette Penrose, who, admittedly, holds a grudge against him, his looks are a result of numerous Botox injections, and possibly some small surgical procedures. His dyed brown hair is just half an inch longer than is in fashion, some of the curly ends escaping to brush against his collar and his cheekbones. His complexion has the unnatural sheen of a fake tan out of a bottle from a beauty salon. From an old photo, I know his teeth used to be stained and slightly crooked, now they have been transformed into two even, dazzlingly white rows.

'How's the investigation going?' He leans back and his eyes stare over a pair of half-rimmed reading glasses.

'It's early days, sir.'

'But you were at the crime scene, were you not? So what can you tell me?'

I stare at him, seriously considering asking him why he didn't bother to drive to the fishing lake, or attend the briefing which had been postponed till after my conversation with Kenneth Poole.

'This morning, at about quarter to nine, two men discovered the body of a woman in a fishing lake between St Merryn and Padstow. Blond, white, naked. A knife wound in her neck. No clothing, no possessions except for a handbag, no car. Initially, we didn't have an ID either, but someone came forward about a missing wife. Of course, the identity needs to be confirmed officially later, but we are reasonably certain that the victim is Alicia Poole. Wife of Kenneth Poole who is the owner of an estate agency with several offices around the county.'

'Ken Poole? I believe I have met him at the golf club.' He shakes his head. 'Well, Maloney is back now and he'll take over from you.'

He rises from behind his desk and makes a show of pulling down the blinds. He doesn't seem to notice that the sun has already disappeared behind darkening grey clouds. Raindrops of the latest shower are still stuck on the glass and it looks like there's more to come.

'Yes sir.'

He turns on his heels, frowns, and changes the subject abruptly. 'You claim that you can read someone's mind from their body language.'

It isn't a question that needs a response. Whatever the reason for this bold statement, it doesn't sound good. When he asked for me after the briefing, I half expected him to let me know that, on second thought, he'd decided to keep me in charge of the new investigation.

'I don't claim anything,' I say, adding 'sir' for good measure.

'Oh well, it's what they say about you.' Clearly, it isn't an opinion he shares.

He sits down again, drumming his fingers on the armrests of his chair. His eyes are fixed on my face as if, he too, is trying to read my mind. For the sake of our working relationship, I hope he fails.

'Now, where were we?' He frowns and I am seriously starting to wonder why I have been summoned into his office. Clearly, we don't have the kind of relationship that allows for a cosy chit-chat.

'How are you, Tregunna?'

The question, opening a completely different line of conversation, needs some time to sink in before I can formulate an answer in my head, let alone form the words on my lips. 'Very well, thank you, sir.'

He leans back, drumming on the edge of his desk with two fingers, and stares at a newspaper in front of him as if he's hoping that it will give him some inspiration to go on.

'I have a dilemma, to be honest, Tregunna. I am short staffed, our sick-leave rate is too high, and I need an officer with the right expertise and the right skills.' He pauses to scrutinise the expression on my face. 'And I have a problem with you.'

I swallow. So this conversation isn't going to be as straight-forward as I thought. 'I'm sorry, sir.'

'Yeah, well, I'll be completely honest with you now, Tregunna. I have read your latest medical report and, based on that, I was happy to welcome you back on the team. Full-time.'

I hear the words, but I also hear that they will shortly be followed by a 'but' and I get that sinking feeling that things are not going to proceed the way I was hoping. I clear my throat to say something, but think better of it when I see the dismissive glance he casts in my direction. Perhaps it is wise to let him speak first.

'Physically, you seem alright to get back to work.'

That is a surprise to me. During my last visit to the police surgery, I was told that the operation and the aftermath of it had been disastrous for my overall fitness. Exercise, a healthy lifestyle and nutritious food, were what he'd recommended, adding, with more optimism than I could fathom, that it would take time but I would get back to being a hundred percent fit again soon.

'That is the problem,' Guthrie nods. I imagine that I see a hint of sympathy in his eyes.

'Your case has been discussed with the team from the HR department. Within the team, there seems to be a disagreement about whether you are truly fit for work or not. And, of course, this matters not only to you but to your colleagues and members of the public.'

'I don't understand.' I lie. I do understand. He is carefully trying to tell me that the powers above, perhaps with his agreement, are planning to sack me. I could get up and leave the matter unspoken, keep it to myself and hand in my letter of resignation, but in a perverse way I want to hear him spell it out to me.

He moves the newspaper to one side and opens a folder from the top of a small pile, retrieving his reading glasses from the left-hand drawer of his desk.

'You've been through a lot, Tregunna. First, you found out that you had cancer, then you had a major operation and now you're dealing with that ... colostomy. It can't be easy for you.'

'No sir, it wasn't, but it's now nearly a year ago since I was diagnosed and the oncologist is optimistic.'

'That was precisely what I've told the HR team, but I'm afraid they have a different opinion. Understandably, from their point of view. And I must say, I'm not disputing any of that.'

He pauses, staring at me expectantly, but I can't find the right words. When he asked me to come to his office, I'd thought it would just be a formality to let me know that I could get back to work full-time rather than working more or less on the side lines, running errands for my colleagues. Not that I wasn't grateful for these crumbs that kept me occupied and focused in the period after my operation during which I was drowning in misery and self pity, but I wanted more. And since my latest visit to Treliske Hospital, when my scans were clean and I seemed to have got rid of the tumour, I was hopeful to return to proper police work officially.

'The problem is, Tregunna, that there are too many officers signed off for stress, depression, anxiety, or post-traumatic stress disorder, you name it. And sadly, that number has increased since the previous year. Now, you can argue that a lot of stress comes from the constant workload, which also relates to the reduction in the number of officers by government cuts. A vicious circle, more or less. We all know the problem but, unfortunately, we have to work within our financial budgets. Obviously, this is a national problem, not just in our region, and several commissions have been researching the precise causes and potential solutions.'

He pauses for breath. His eyes are searching for something on the desk.

'One of the issues that has become clear is that we must re-act quickly to help our officers and staff through tough times. We know from a range of surveys and research that the levels of uncertainty and change within the service are increasingly stressful. The current government is doing all it can to make it easier for the police to do their job. We have cut red tape and unnecessary targets to free up police time, we have given officers discretion to use their professional judgement and we are working across the government to stop the police having to pick up the pieces when other public services are not available. The message is that we should never be complacent. That is why money has been allocated to help support emergency services personnel and volunteers, and to focus on mental health, physical recuperation and bereavement support. We have to make sure that we are there for the public and, for that reason, we can't be in a position that we fail because we haven't looked after our own.'

He stops for breath again and I take the opportunity to interject.

'How does all this relate to me?'

He shakes his head. 'Now, I must say first, that I disagree with the opinion of the HR team, but I'm afraid this is not my decision. I can't afford to go against their recommendations.'

'In case they turn out to be right.'

He smiles vaguely, without humour. 'I'm pleased you get the picture, Tregunna.'

'Hm. I presume then that I won't be officially returning to work full-time yet?'

'Not yet. Believe you me, Tregunna, I have fought your case. I really have. The outcome is that you remain on my team. You will be working part time officially, but it is entirely up to you how many hours that will be. The downside, from your perspective, is that you will not have direct responsibility.'

'So no change,' I say, trying to keep the bitterness out of my voice.

He picks up the newspaper again as if he's hoping an answer is somewhere to be found between the lines Kim Naylor wrote about the Lady in the lake.

'There is a small change, though, Tregunna. There is a condition. You will have sessions with a psychiatrist who will then decide if and when you can be declared 100% healthy.'

'Why? What are they thinking? That I will pick up a gun and start a shooting spree?'

'That hasn't been mentioned as such, but yes, Ia presume they want to make sure that your mental health issues, if any, will not cause problems that might put other people in danger.'

'This is madness.'

He nods, 'I totally agree with you, Tregunna, but I'm afraid there is nothing I can do about it. Decisions have been made and, to be honest, I think you are lucky that you are still wanted by the police force.'

'I'm very grateful, sir.'

'Indeed. Well ...' He searches in the file and finds a business card. It is dark grey on one side and bright yellow on the other. The name of a psychiatrist and his address details are printed in black on the yellow side, with a few statements from famous philosophers in yellow on the dark grey side. I have no intention to take it and I leave it on the edge of his desk.

Guthrie closes the file. 'Call him, make an appointment and let me know when you have. Keep me posted about your progress so I can give positive feedback to HR. And don't pull a face like that, Tregunna. I'm not a fan of things like this either, but we all have to work within our limits.'

It sounds like the conversation is over and I put my hands on the armrests to get up. But he isn't finished. He shakes his head, placing his elbows on the edge of the desk, and lacing his fingers. He rests his chin on them as though he is deep in thought.

'Coming back to the beginning of our conversation, Tregunna, as I said, people say that you can read body language. Now, I'm not saying I agree with that, nor with the idea that it might be a useful skill to have within the force. But it made me think about what we can do with you and how you can be an asset for the force. For obvious reasons, I can't send you out on the streets. HR seems to believe that there is a possibility that you may become a liability and I'm sure you'll agree that we have to do our utmost to avoid casualties. HR had some suggestions, but I know that we're both convinced that those options are not workable.'

He pauses, looking me straight in the eyes. Perhaps he is trying to be kind, understanding, but I don't want that. Not while he is making decisions about my current life and my future without consulting me first. I can't believe that he is seriously thinking that I could put the lives of other people, let alone colleagues, in danger. However, at this moment, I would ever come that far, I would happily pull him across his desk and strangle him with my bare hands. But I would never harm or hurt someone without a reason.

He looks thoughtfully. 'Have you ever had thoughts about attacking someone?'

Maybe he is a better policeman after all. 'Yes sir.'

His eyebrows rise. He hasn't expected an answer like that. 'Honestly?'

'Yes sir. At this very moment.'

For a few moments, our eyes meet. Then he shakes his head and turns his attention back to his papers.

'I have told HR that I have another task for you and that, despite your illness, you have done an excellent job preparing the court case against that woman, Trewoon.'

He stops. He is waiting for some kind of reaction from me.

'Thank you, sir.'

'The prosecution is hopeful that the case is solid enough to have the judge send that despicable woman to jail indefinitely. She's mad, if you ask me, and it would be a disaster if she was released in a few years' time. We all owe that to you. Your role in that hasn't been unnoticed.'

He stops. He is waiting for my response.

'Thank you sir.' Having heard those words from his mouth, made me feel embarrassed rather than pleased. But he still had that edge in his voice that suggests he might have been taking the Mickey after all.

'Now.' He picks up a pen and draws a curly line on the top margin of the newspaper. 'Our next problem is that we have yet another murder on our hands. The case with the body parts found around the coast didn't make us popular with the tourist industry in Cornwall and we can't afford to be in the spotlight again with this new murder. Clearly, it doesn't help that the victim is the wife of one of our most prominent businessmen.'

He taps on his desk with the end of his pen. 'We need a specialist in our team. An intelligence officer who can deal with this case and I believe you will be perfect for the job. Your role will be to gather information and evidence. Of course, we have HOLMES 2 but, however sophisticated the system is, it is still a computerised one. We use it of course, but I think we can do with an analyst alongside it. Eyes and ears. Common sense. Logic. The ability to see the trees through the wood. And instincts, of course.'

'I thought we already have …'

'Yes. Of course. Bill Yates is doing an excellent job, but he has been transferred to another area. His own choice, apparently. His wife's father is terminally ill and she wants to be close to him. Look after him. They are moving as we speak.'

I feel embarrassed that, despite seeing the man almost daily, I had no idea what went on in Bill Yates's life.

'You will be our new Bill Yates, Tregunna. You have the experience to see what is important and what is not, you have the knowledge of what prosecutors want. You will be a spider in the web, the one who keeps an eye on all the threads, who makes sure that everything stays linked together where necessary, who can find the flies caught in it as soon as possible.' He smiles briefly, pleased about his range of metaphors. 'You won't work on the front lines. Leading an investigation isn't your mission any longer, but the information you collect will be of great value to each of us. Don't forget that we are a team and we have to work together. You will be organising and arranging extra briefings when necessary, you will provide everyone with the right information, after you have sifted sense from the nonsense.'

The end of his lecture comes as abruptly as it started. He nods, smiles, and, with a sense of relief, dismissively waves towards the door behind me when the phone rings on his desk. Obediently, I rise, deliberately leaving the business card of the psychiatrist on his desk, but although Guthrie is listening to someone on the phone, he is aware of my intentions. He points and I pick the card up, knowing very well that I can't ignore it.

6

The passage of time often results in suspects and witnesses forgetting the most crucial details of an incident. As a consequence, statements must be obtained at the earliest opportunity, especially from key witnesses. The accuracy of fresh memory ensures the evidential integrity and content of the statement. However, we always have to take in consideration the individual circumstances of the witness, their vulnerability, their emotional state and the impact that particular incident has on them. Although, in theory, consideration also needs to be given to whether the evidence should be recorded on video, it is rarely the case. Which presents me with a problem.

As Guthrie had mentioned, but what he didn't really understand is that I find that what I observe during an interview is as crucial as what is being said. Some of my colleagues say I can read body language. I am not so sure about that, but as I stare at the sheets of paper that are almost meaningless to me, I am getting frustrated with the feeling that I am missing the point. I am uncomfortably aware that the words don't mean enough to me to be able to determine what is important and what is not. I have no clear impression of the witnesses. As far as I can tell, they are all telling the truth or they are lying through their teeth. Either way, I have to admit that I am not good at this.

I know that this is not what Guthrie had in mind when he assigned me to the role, but I can't do much else than gather and sift through information for anything that has perhaps been missed by the investigating officers. It's not that I am looking for errors or misunderstandings that could easily jeopardise the investigation. I simply need to clarify the things I don't understand, any answers that are not clear, or questions that have not been asked. It's the only way I can make sense of all the paperwork. It's the only way I can find any discrepancies or uncover any lies.

Picking up a sheet from the pile, I stare at the name at the top. It is written in capital letters, bolder and larger than the rest of the statement.

Denise Shaw is 35 years old, divorced, and has one child, a 14-year-old son. She works as a management secretary of an international company that has its regional office at an industrial estate near Truro. She was the last known person who saw Alicia Poole alive.

I call her office, but a tinny voice explains that she has called in sick that morning. I scribble her address on a slip of paper and take my coat, hoping that Guthrie or Maloney won't notice me sneaking out.

A skinny teenager with red spots on a pale face opens the door. An unruly tuft of greasy dark blond hair falls across his forehead almost covering one eye. With sullen grey eyes, he stares at me in the hope that I will dissolve on the doorstep and he can continue with whatever he was doing. Playing on a tablet or mobile phone, probably. As I retrieve my ID card and hold it up for him, his face reddens, his spine stiffens and his eyes shoot from left to right and back, checking if the neighbours are paying attention. Or perhaps he half expects an army of uniformed policemen to appear, just waiting for my sign to storm the building.

'Is it possible to speak to Denise Shaw?'

'Mum's having a shower.' His voice comes out in randomly uncontrolled high and low notes.

'I can wait,' I say gently. Relief appears in his eyes as if he hopes I will wait in my car.

'Can I come in?' I suppress a smile. Subtlety seems lost on him.

'Uhm ... I dunno.'

A woman's voice calls from the dark interior of the house. 'Jake? Who is it?'

'Police.'

'Oh. Tell them to come back later, will you, darling? I can't ...'

Bare feet and the lower part of slim legs appear at the top of the staircase, the hem of a faded black bathrobe just covering her knees.

'Jake?' She sounds hesitant, less confident. Clearly, she can feel the draught from the open front door.

'He's here, mum.' The boy sounds as if he knows he's done something wrong.

'Mrs Shaw? Denise Shaw?'

She descends the stairs until she can see my face. Her dark hair is wet and hangs on her shoulders in curly wet strands. Eyes matching her son's in colour and expression, she stares at me, clearly wondering about the best policy to get rid of me. Her eyelids are swollen and her nose is red and wet.

'Is it about …?' She stops, sniffs. She can't speak her friend's name without bursting into tears.

'Yes, I'm afraid I have some more questions, Mrs Shaw. Since your memory is still fresh, it is important that we get as much detail from you as is possible under the circumstances.'

'Oh.' Tiny drops of water from her hair have gathered on her forehead. She wipes them with the side of one hand.

'Okay, give me a few minutes. Uhm … Jake can make you a coffee?'

The boy looks less pleased. His mother disappears upstairs and, with a sullen shrug, he steps back and I follow him to an open-plan living room.

The room is warm and colourful with one wall full of mostly abstract paintings in all kinds of shapes and sizes. Whoever painted them, Denise Shaw must have a preference for bright colours. There is a red leather sofa and two armchairs in a patchwork of red, blue, yellow and black pieces of leather, sewn together with big stitches, scattered with corduroy cushions. In the middle sits a coffee table of dark brown wood with sculpted legs, carved on its top surface and inlaid with ivory. A large, pale wool rug covers the polished wooden floor.

'Coffee?' Jake offers. 'We've just made some.' A lopsided grin on his face gives him a completely different personality. 'Filter coffee. Mum's got one of those new machines.'

Upstairs floorboards creak and footsteps can be heard moving about. I sit in one of the armchairs which is as comfortable as it looks and, muttering 'no milk, no sugar', I watch Jake into the kitchen area.

There is a pile of glossy magazines on the floor and a book lies open, upside down. The cover shows a young woman with a veil, leaving only a pair of black eyes that have no expression. The title and the author mean nothing to me.

Jake returns with two red mugs and a biscuit tin tucked under his arm. Placing my mug on a small table next to me, he puts his furthest away. He opens the tin and offers me a biscuit from a chocolate biscuits selection. I shake my head and he takes a handful of them, not minding which ones. It is obvious where the greasy spots on his face come from.

He piles them up behind his mug and picks a magazine from the pile. Outdoor Living. He doesn't open it and stares at the cover that has an abundance of pink flowers surrounding a set of garden furniture that is draped with cushions and blankets in matching colours. It is only then that I notice that there is no TV in the room. And Jake doesn't appear to be addicted to his mobile phone, as most young people are.

'Is this about Alicia?' He glares at me.

'Yes.'

'Mum's pretty upset about it.'

'I understand they were good friends.'

'Yes.' He opens the magazine randomly, clearly uncomfortable where to put his hands. 'Have you found the murderer?'

'Not yet. But we will.'

'Mum's a bit scared. She thinks he might come after her as well.'

'Why does she think that?' I ask casually.

'Dunno. She thinks she might have seen him when they were out.'

'Do you think she might know him?'

A small smile creeps over his face. 'She would have told the police, wouldn't she?'

'I hope so. Sometimes people withhold information. For no particular reason.'

'Like because she is scared?'

'For example, yes. But some witnesses are just scared because they don't want to be involved. Like they would rather not go to the police because they might have to give evidence in court.'

He nods, seriously. 'Mum's not like that. She wants Alicia's murderer locked up in prison.'

'And we will do our best to get him there.' I pause. 'Did you know Alicia well?'

He shrugs with the indifference of his age, not at all interested in the friends of his parents' generation. 'A bit. She is … was alright, I guess. I mean, she and mum were good friends.'

'But you didn't particularly like her?'

'She's mum's friend. Was. Not mine.'

A short silence. In the absence of the all too familiar sounds of a TV, we listen to the silence that is interrupted by his mother moving from one room to the other. Denise Shaw seems to need some time to get ready before she feels able to speak to me.

'Do you know Mrs Poole's daughter? Briony?'

'She's younger than me.' Another statement indicative of his age. A five-year gap is unbridgeable. To him, they are from different generations and it would be embarrassing for him to admit that he is friendly with a 9-year-old girl. 'She can be awkward,' he continues after a hesitation. 'But sometimes ... I kind of feel sorry for her.'

'Why is that?'

'Sometimes ... I thought that Alicia was ... unkind to her.'

I nod, waiting for him to go on.

'Like last summer, when we went on holiday to Portugal. Mum and me and Alicia and Briony. We were on the fourth floor in one of those modern apartments buildings, which wasn't too bad considering the lifts were never working. It could have been worse; the building was twelve storeys high.'

'You are young, you wouldn't have a problem with that,' I say, smiling sympathetically.

'Alicia was complaining about it all the time.'

'I can sympathise with that.'

He shrugs, uncertain.

'I guess you went out every day? Any places of interest you visited?'

He pulls a face. 'Mum and Alicia were only interested in sunbathing and going to the clubs at night. And all Briony wanted was to read her books. Alicia bought her an eReader.'

'So you didn't enjoy your holiday?'

'I could have, if they'd let me go out on my own.' He shrugs, anger on his face. 'I made some friends and it was alright in the daytime, but I could never join them in the evenings, when they met somewhere on the beach or at the swimming pool.'

'How old are you?'

'Nearly fifteen.' He examines the red coffee mug from every angle. There is something in the way his eyes are avoiding mine that alerts me.

'Most evenings I had to stay in the apartment because Alicia couldn't leave Briony there on her own. I didn't really see the point, because she was always reading or watching TV or playing on her mobile phone. I knew she didn't mind that I went out, but ...' He stops abruptly, his spots blazing on his pink face.

I hunch forward in my seat. 'What happened, Jake?'

'Well … I'd better not talk about that. She will never forgive me.'

'Your mother?'

'No. Alicia … oh … sorry.' His eyes drift to the door. Clearly, he is hoping that his mother will come down to his rescue and he'll be able to escape.

'Is it something the police should know, Jake? In relation to the investigation? Not in direct relation to her death perhaps, but to help us with a background picture?'

He picks up his mug and stares into it, regretting his earlier slip of the tongue.

'I don't know if I should tell you this.' He hesitates, torn between loyalty and excitement about getting involved somehow, getting noticed, which, at his age, would have made him feel important. I wait. I let him make up his mind. His thoughts are chasing across his face like clouds on a blustery day. He has already made the decision but doesn't know it himself.

'Well, I guess you'll discover it anyway.' He says eventually, lowering his voice as he continues. 'She was arrested by the Portuguese police when we were on holiday.'

'Arrested? Who?'

'Alicia. Well, she was nearly arrested, but even so,' He grins 'Mum was frantic about it.' His eyes sparkle, but suddenly his face turns pale, then red, and pale again. Stumbling to his feet, he almost forgets that he's still holding his mug. Coffee spills over his hand and drips on his shoes.

7

What was I frantic about, Jake?'
Her voice cold and sharp-edged, Denise Shaw sizes me up in the doorway, as if she's not sure whether I'm the person she was expecting to see. She's wearing black jeans and a yellow turtleneck jumper. Her bare feet slipped into green cotton espadrilles with soles made of straw. Her dark, shoulder-length hair has undergone what PC Ally Poldeen quirkily calls a 'blow-job': blown dry by a hairdryer switched onto the highest and hottest level making her hair look like a fuzzy halo. She has applied so much make-up that I can only just see that she's been crying.

'Mum! I didn't hear you coming down.' Jake rises from his seat, realising that what he has just said has really annoyed her. Tugging at the cuffs of his shirt, he seems anxious to get away. He twists around on his heels, trying to find an excuse to leave the room, then he heads for the coffee machine, while Denise turns to me.

'I've already spoken to the police. Or is there something else?'

It is a rather an odd question, almost as if she knows that she's been holding back some information but she's not sure what it might be.

'I hope I'm not interfering with your plans, Ms Shaw.'

'No.' She barely looks at my ID.

'If this is about … Alicia … then it is difficult for me,' she says defensively, touching her hair with her fingertips that are slightly trembling. Clearly, her cold exterior can't disguise her shattered inner emotions.

'I have read your statement about what happened last Saturday evening, Ms Shaw, but there are some points I would like you to explain to me. If you don't mind?'

She can't stop her eyes filling with tears. 'I find it very difficult to talk about it.'

'I appreciate that but we need your help. You were one of the last people who saw … your friend on Saturday night.'

She nods, accepting the situation, and steadies herself as she lowers herself slowly on the arm rest of the sofa, folding and unfolding her arms and absentmindedly turning a ring round her finger. 'But I thought …' Her voice drifts of as if she's forgotten what she wanted to say.

'I am sorry that you will have to go through all this again, Mrs Shaw. As I said, I have read your statement which is very helpful but now, with more witness statements, we're able to compare and check everything and …'

Her eyes flare up in anger. 'Are you saying I lied?'

'No, no, it's just that some of your answers have raised additional questions. And it's just that we'd rather check and double-check than make mistakes or miss something.'

'Okay.' She opens and closes her hands, unsure whether to leave them on her lap or put them in the pockets of her jeans. She smiles briefly when Jake emerges with a steaming yellow mug of coffee for his mother. He raises his eyebrows in a silent question and she responds by telling him to leave her alone with me. A flicker of doubt and concern crosses his face, but he shrugs and disappears with the biscuit tin tucked under his arm, closing the door behind him with a soft click.

'I'm sure you want us to catch the person who did this to your friend, Ms Shaw,' I say gently, glancing at my watch. I have a feeling that this visit will take longer than I anticipated and I foresee that I might not be back at the station in time for the next briefing. The report about Kenneth Poole is on Penrose's desk. If she isn't back in time, someone will find it there,

'Call me Denise, please, inspector.' She smiles faintly, but I can see her thoughts are far away. 'How can I help?'

She runs her tongue over her lips. A speck of red lipstick is stuck to her front tooth.

'I'd like you to tell me everything about last Saturday.'

'Oh.' She picks up her mug and blows the steam away before recounting what happened on Saturday in a monotone voice. At eight o'clock, she went to the local swimming pool where she swims every morning, then picked up her shopping which she'd ordered online the previous day. Then she came home and had breakfast with her son, and did some house work until Alicia Poole arrived.

I interrupt her. 'What time was that?'

'After twelve o'clock. Jake had just popped out to see some friends.'

'Did she arrive in her own car?'

'Yes of course she did.' For the briefest of moments, amusement lights up in her eyes. 'Alicia wasn't particularly sporty. She would never walk a step if she could avoid it.'

'And her car is a VW Beetle?'

'Yes. Light blue with a soft black top.'

I nod and she continues, creating images of a day in the lives of two friends who know each other well. They had a long chat and laugh in the afternoon, and later, when Jake came home they ordered an Italian takeaway and did each other's hair and make-up until they went out in the evening. By that time Jake had also gone out again to see another friend to watch horror films in a small cinema in the basement of his friend's father's house.

'Everything was normal? Alicia didn't seem distressed or anxious about anything?

'No. We just had a good time together.'

Thinking about it and realising that it was the last time she would ever see her best friend, makes her take a deep breath. Fighting tears that seem to have dried for a bit, she stares at me blankly, miles away in her thoughts.

'What time did you go out?'

'About half past nine, I suppose.'

'Did you go by car?'

'Of course, as I said, she would never walk a step if she could avoid it.'

The set of keys Josh Warren found at the lake's car park have been identified as Alicia's by her husband but, as far as I know, the car hasn't been found yet.

'Where did you park?'

'In the car park opposite the cinema. First we went to the Central Bar. We met a couple of friends there and we had a few drinks before going to some other bars.'

I can't recall that she mentioned in her statement that they had met friends in the Central Bar.

'I will need their names.' I say, almost sounding like an angry school teacher. 'That also applies to the bars you went to after you left the Central Bar. Was it normal that you went from one bar to another?'

She frowns as if something has occurred to her. 'We do, actually. I mean, we used to. Everyone else does that and it's good to mix with different friends rather than staying with the same ones all evening.'

'Was there something, that night, that you felt was different?'

'Not really, no.' She shakes her head thoughtfully. A strand of dark hair falls across one eye and she flicks it away hastily. She looks worried as is she's afraid she's missing something.

'We saw each other about once a month. Briony goes to her father every fortnight and we regularly meet and go out on a Saturday night.'

'And you are certain that everything was as it should be? Nothing happened?'

'No, but … well, now that you mention it, there was something, but it's more of a feeling.'

'Feelings can also be important.'

'At one point Ali was in conversation with a man. I had been to the Ladies and, when I came back, he was sitting at our table. But I bumped into an old school friend and it must have been about ten or fifteen minutes later when I came back to our table. She was alone then but … I knew something was different.'

'The man was gone?'

'Yes.'

'Did she say anything about him?'

'I asked who he was, but she said it wasn't a friend. She said it was just someone who had come and pestered but for some reason I thought she was lying. When I saw them together, I thought they were … they seemed to know each other. It wasn't like he was a good friend, but I could tell that he wasn't a complete stranger either. You know.'

'Did you get his name?'

'Wouldn't I have told the police that already?'

'Perhaps, but I'd prefer to ask rather than find out later that certain information is missing because I didn't ask.'

She nods as if she accepts my explanation. 'She said she didn't know who he was and that he was just a guy who fancied her.'

'Can you describe him?'

'I didn't really give him that much attention. I suppose he was ordinary, average. Between 30 and 40. No glasses. Short hair. Dark blond, I think.' She stops abruptly, her eyes wide. Astonished. 'Yes! I do remember something! He had an expensive looking watch, although I suppose it might have been a cheap copy.'

'Good. That's the sort of detail I'm looking for.'

She continues with new energy. 'After that, Alicia seemed a bit distracted. Not really worried or concerned, but there was something. She was different. Quieter than usual. She kept looking at the door as if she was expecting someone.' Denise stops talking and grows pensive, her teeth biting into her bottom lip. 'Perhaps she thought that he was coming back,' she adds.

'Did he?'

'No, she suggested going somewhere else and that's what we did.'

'You went to Barrie's Bar.'

'Yes.'

'This is at the other end of town. You said Alicia wouldn't walk if she could avoid it.'

'That's right, but we'd both been drinking. And besides, there was no point in getting her car and trying to find a place to park near Barrie's.'

'So you walked from the Central Bar to Barrie's.'

'We did. Oh no, we stopped at Angelo's.'

'Angelo's? You didn't mention that in your first statement.'

'I must have forgotten.' She looks embarrassed, almost on the brink of tears. 'I'm sorry.'

'Not to worry, Mrs Shaw, it's perfectly normal to forget some things. You have probably remembered more details since you spoke to my colleagues.'

'We didn't stay long at Angelo's,' she says by way of apology. 'There were a couple of rather noisy groups on a stag night. It was as if the two groups were competing to be noisily. As soon as we entered the bar, one of the groups saw Ali and they started shouting at us. Sent from heaven, they said. We turned and left the place without even having ordered a drink.'

'And then to Barrie's Bar? What time was that?''

'It was about half past ten. We met some friends there and we had a good time. Alicia … she enjoyed it. I'm glad that she had a good laugh on her … last evening.'

I nod, not giving her time to burst into tears. 'Was there any sign that someone showed more interest in her than normal?'

'Not that I noticed. She was relaxed again, after the incident with the man. When we went to the ladies together she told me she was relieved he hadn't followed us.'

'You didn't go anywhere else after Barrie's Bar?'

'No.' This is the part where she starts feeling overwhelmed by guilt. 'Well ...' Her face is pale. Ashen. 'It must have been well after eleven when I saw Alicia on the dance floor with a different man. Again, for some reason I thought they knew each other. Although, I had never seen this guy before, it was clear that Alicia knew him.'

'Hm. Did she introduce him to you?'

'I think she said his name was Chris. When he went to the bar to fetch us some more drinks, I asked her about him but she was a bit vague. I can't quite remember, I'm sorry. She said that she knew him from way back, from school even, maybe, and that she hadn't seen him for a while. Anyway, her tone was so casual that I didn't think anything of it. Then he came back with our drinks and he sat between Ali and me, so we couldn't really finish our conversation.'

'Can you describe him?'

'He was about our age. Slim built, about as tall as Alicia. Blond curly hair, a bit of a tan but not the same as surfers have. Grey eyes. His nose looked like it had been hit on one side. You know.'

'That is a pretty good description,' I say, thinking it shouldn't be difficult to find him on camera images and take a detailed shot of his face. 'Do you remember what he was wearing?'

'Faded blue jeans, a white long-sleeved shirt over a white T-shirt.'

'Was he alone, or with anyone else?'

'Not that I was aware of.'

'Would you recognise him again?'

She frowns, uncertain. 'I can try.'

'Okay. Now, back to that evening. He sat between you and Ali, and then what?'

'He ... he whispered something in her ear and she smiled and they both got up. I wasn't really paying attention because, at that moment, I received a message from Jake asking if it was alright if he came home half an hour later. I can't remember the reason but I said yes. I mean, I was having a good time, and I hoped he was too. I was texting him when Alicia and the guy got up. She said something to me, winking at me meaningfully, and I understood that they were going off somewhere.'

'Off somewhere?'

She seems surprised. 'Yes, have a bit of time together. Private. You know.' I don't know, but I can guess.

'Was that her normal behaviour?'

She shrugs. 'She had always been faithful to Trevor. Then they split up and she started being … a bit more reckless, I suppose. I mean, like, having one-night-stands. Then she met Ken and … well, she didn't seem to have changed. I mean, it didn't really seem to bother her so much any more that she was married again and that she ought to be faithful. She always claimed that Ken was rather open-minded. But only on our nights out, which happened only once a month. It was like she felt free for that night and she could do whatever she wanted.'

'Did Ken know?'

'I'm not sure. Ali knew that he had an affair with his secretary, who is also in a relationship of some sort, and she didn't care about that either.'

'So, on Saturday night, the two of you went out. Alicia had intended to stay the night with you and she would go back home the following day. But she left Barrie's Bar to go somewhere with that guy. Did you see her come back to the bar?'

'No.'

'And she didn't show up to sleep at your house?'

'No.'

'Did you try to call her?'

'Of course I did but she didn't answer. On the other hand, she'd done it before, you see, not coming back to my house, but instead she went straight back home. I thought she'd done the same on Saturday.'

'But you didn't check.'

'No, it was …' Her face turns pink and her eyes are swimming in tears. 'Jake had come home sick and I was a bit worried about him.'

'You mean he had been drinking?'

She shrugs, well aware that her son is underage to drink alcohol. 'He was feeling sick,' she says eventually.

'Okay,' I nod, deciding to let the issue go. 'Would you mind coming to the station to help us build up a picture of both of the men you saw with Alicia?'

8

Harradine Curtis, infuriating to most of the residents of our apartment building, is a very unlikely man to have as a friend. He is very opinionated and expresses his thoughts to anyone whether they want to listen or not. He works for Newquay town council dealing with people either living on the poverty line, or those trying to claim benefits when they have undeclared income from undisclosed sources. That's what he told me in a determined kind of tone when I came to live next door to him, as though he was warning me that he wouldn't tolerate it if I ever had the nerve to apply for benefits.

Aged fifty-three, he looks about twenty years older. His shoulders are hunched like a modern day Atlas carrying the weight of the world. The corners of his mouth are consistently pulled down and his watery grey eyes seem never to sparkle as if he can see a bright future ahead.

We had brief conversations in the beginning but, other than the fact that we were both living alone, we didn't have much in common. Then an issue over a parking space created a miniature cold war between us, which seemed to bother him more than me. It was a surprise to us both, let alone to other residents who wouldn't speak to him, when he helped me out once in a rather difficult situation. Since then, we are once again on speaking terms, both of us benefiting from it in some way.

He must have been looking out for me, because his front door opens as soon as I climb the stairs.

'Tregunna,' he says, as per usual, fervently ignoring my repeated requests to call me Andy. 'Just the man I wanted to have a word with.'

'That sounds serious, Mr Curtis.'

'Yeah well, it is.'

'How can I help you?'

He chuckles good-naturedly. 'It is not me who needs help, Tregunna, but you.'

'Do I?' Since we have reached a stage in our relationship that comes close to being friends, I have stopped wondering how his mind works. I have learned to take him as he is, at his pace, in his time. He can't be pushed, forced, let alone manipulated. He is more likely to do that to me.

'I am sure you do, Tregunna.' Placing one foot over the threshold of his flat, he grins expectantly. 'Coffee?'

I sigh. Mr Curtis has the habit of inviting himself into my home and never seems embarrassed by it. He doesn't seem to care if it is convenient for me. He doesn't even ask. He claims that he prefers the strong black coffee from my coffee machine, but then pours so much milk into it that I doubt if he can taste the coffee. He brings packs of cheap biscuits that contain the most preservatives and E-numbers imaginable, then munches his way through half of them and takes the rest home. If he ever notices that I never take one, he doesn't say anything about it.

'Coffee, Mr Curtis. Yes, why not?' My sarcasm is lost on him.

He wraps a woollen scarf around his neck, makes sure he locks the door behind him, and follows me into my flat. I have two heavy shopping bags, but he doesn't bother to offer to help. Making himself comfortable on my sofa, he pushes newspapers and magazines to one side and grabs the remote control to turn on my TV. Having the TV on in the background, albeit with the sound muted, is one of his other habits. At first, I turned the TV off again, but he declared he liked to have it on as it made him feel he had people around for company, in the background.

I have grown used to his funny habits by simply ignoring them, as there is no point in even trying to discuss them with him. In his job, I suspect he is a man who always wins an argument. Or, more likely, people just give up, worn down by his stubbornness.

Having said all this, he isn't an unpleasant person to deal with and I have got used to his visits, usually a rather colourful, but otherwise reliable source of information about the neighbourhood and what goes on in the council offices.

I make two coffees, one in the special mug he brought with him once - yellow with purple pansies painted on one side - and give him a plate for his biscuits. This time, he has brought dark chocolate digestives. The packaging says that it contains 30% more biscuits, which may be the reason that he didn't buy the cheaper plain biscuits. Along with his other rather peculiar habits, he is also careful with money.

'I'm here to assist you,' he announces rather pompously, as I sit down, trying to keep my eyes off the TV screen. I have discovered it is rather difficult not to look at it, even though I can't hear it.

'With what, Mr Curtis?'

'That young lady of yours.'

I feel myself stiffen. I know who he means: Lauren. He knows her and he persists in trying to put things right between us. In other words, he feels bound to act like a modern Cupid.

'Which young lady?' I ask, evasively.

He sniffs disapprovingly. 'I hope you're not telling me that there are more young ladies in your life?'

'I'm not telling you anything, Mr Curtis.'

He grins stubbornly. 'Indeed not. Anyway, I am talking about the redhead. The one with the two boys.' He pauses briefly, then he adds, mockingly, 'You remember?'

Reluctantly, I nod. 'Lauren.'

'I'm glad you remember her name,' he says sarcastically.

'Mr Curtis ...' I start, but he interrupts me without even acknowledging that I've spoken.

'I met her in town today,' he declares with a hint of pleasure, as if he is telling me a secret. 'As it happened, she was in front of me at the till in the bakery shop and I invited her for a coffee.'

I'm sure the fact that he was behind her at the till, was not a coincidence but orchestrated with the intention of inviting her to have coffee with him. I get the distinct feeling that I don't want to hear any more.

'I felt honoured that she accepted the invitation. She is a looker. As a man, it feels pretty good to be seen with her.'

He looks at me expectantly, but all I offer is, 'Hm.'

He grins again, satisfied with my reaction. 'We talked. Mostly about you.'

Suppressing a sigh, I say: 'You mean that you, Mr Curtis, talked about me all the time?'

'If you like to put it that way, then yes. I talked about you. A lot.'

There is no point in asking him what he told Lauren about me. In fact, I think I prefer not to know.

'And your point is?'

I pick up a chocolate digestive and take a bite, ignoring the look of surprise on his face. Consequently, he realises that he has achieved his first goal: my undivided attention.

'She is not happy about the way your relationship has developed.'

'Oh.'

'Or, rather, the way it has ended.'

'We haven't fallen out, Mr Curtis. And besides, it is ...'

'None of my business. I'm sure you were going to say that. And you are right. But I have a different opinion about the two of you.'

'I'm sure you have, Mr Curtis, but Lauren and I ...'

'You just walked out of her house. Without a word.'

'Uhm ...' I feel my cheeks reddening. 'Did she tell you that?'

'Not in so many words, but I can read between the lines.'

'It was weeks ago.'

'Exactly. She invited you for an evening meal. Then you played games with her sons, who seem to adore you. Then they went up to bed and ...'

'I know exactly what happened, Mr Curtis,' I interrupt breezily, wondering why I allow this man to interfere in my private life, and, worse, tell me what I should do.

He ignores me. 'She went upstairs to say goodnight to her sons and when she came back down the two of you had some more wine and ...'

'I know, Mr Curtis, probably better than you do.' For some reason, I almost doubt that.

'One of the boys called down that he wasn't feeling very well, so Lauren went upstairs again. And when she came down, you were gone.'

'It wasn't exactly like that,' I say lamely, knowing very well that only a truthful explanation would make him, and Lauren, understand what I am not prepared to explain. To anyone.

'I'm sure there is a lot more to it but, indeed, that is not my business. The only thing I would like to say is that, clearly, she is still upset about it, and I can see now that you are uncomfortable with the situation as well. Which tells me that there are feelings between you. And that is what matters to me. And the two of you.'

'There isn't the two of us.'

'And I beg to differ, Tregunna. The poor lass was almost in tears.'

I swallow. Although I can't imagine Lauren crying in the presence of Mr Curtis, or in a public environment, the thought of it doesn't make me feel better about it. On the contrary.

'She thinks it has something to do with your illness. She thinks you haven't told her everything about it.'

Once more I swallow. My throat is dry.

'She thinks that your illness is terminal and that's the reason why you don't want to commit to her. You don't want her to get hurt when you die.'

'I'm not dying, Mr Curtis.'

'That is the only reason she can come up with.'

'I am not dying,' I repeat. 'The tumour was removed and the doctors decided to keep a close eye on me, but any further treatment was, or is, not necessary. Lauren knows that, because she was there when I spoke to the oncologist just a couple of weeks before … that evening.'

'It is now nearly six weeks later, Tregunna. She believes that they have found more tumours in your body and that you can't be treated any more. She believes that you are giving up.'

'Do I look like a terminally ill person, Mr Curtis?'

'Sometimes you look very pale and very tired,' he replies, with alarming honesty.

'We all have those periods, but that doesn't mean we are going to die. I certainly have no intention to do so. And there is no reason for her to think that I would lie about that.'

'You haven't spoken to her since then. You didn't call her to apologise, to explain or anything. You did nothing.'

'I know. But there are other reasons …'

'Of course you have your reasons. Believe you me, Tregunna, I don't want you to tell me, but you should tell her. I think that you need to speak to that girl and see how you can patch up your relationship.'

'We have no relationship.'

'Maybe so, but you two do want a relationship.'

'Who says … ?'

'I do, Tregunna. I have seen the two of you looking at each other and it must have been special for her to invite you for dinner at her home. Alone. I mean, who else did she invite?'

'There was nobody else …'

He nods triumphantly. 'Exactly my point.'

'Mr Curtis, I don't …'

'All I ask is that you go and see her and explain to her why you left her that evening.'

I close my eyes and press my fingertips against my temples. My head is aching. Against my will, the evening is floating back in my mind. I can't deny that I was over the moon when Lauren invited me for a meal with her and her ten-year-old twins, Joe and Stuart. It had been a pleasant, rather quiet meal. The boys were suitably impressed with the presents I'd brought for them. They were also looking forward to the next day, which they were going to spend with their father and his new partner. Lauren had made an effort with the meal. Beautiful fillet steaks, and burgers for the boys. Home made apple crumble with Cornish cream and for her sons a choice of ice cream cones in different flavours.

There was coffee with strange shaped muffins afterwards which had been made by the boys under the supervision of their mother. Not a word of protest came when Lauren announced that it was time for them to go to bed. She'd opened another bottle of wine and we sat next to each other on the couch, watching a silly but enjoyable comedy on TV. It was all very cosy and relaxed, and so homely that I realised I had dreaded the moment I had to get up and go to my own home. Cold. Empty. No one to talk to. No one to hold in my arms and caress, nobody's lips to kiss and no red hair to bury my face in.

I couldn't remember who had made the first move, but suddenly her head had rested against my shoulder and she had wriggled into a more comfortable position, eventually with my arm over the backrest of the sofa in a protective way around her. Then there was an outburst of laughter on the TV, a giggle from her and she turned to look at me with a happy laugh in her eyes. I couldn't resist her. I pulled her closer, murmured her name and kissed her. It was like a promise, the start of something that could no longer be ignored. I had known all along that I was attracted to her, but I was too afraid to dare to hope that she felt the same way.

But then she pulled me closer. I could taste a sweet sensuality on her lips. I could feel her hard nipples under the soft fabric of her sleeveless top that had silver metallic threads along the edges. She made it quite clear how much she wanted me.

I'm certainly not proud of what I did. I just panicked. I can't rationalise it any better than that. I knew I couldn't give her what she wanted. I knew I wouldn't be able to make love to her, not properly, not in the right way, not the way she wanted me to, anyway. I felt her hand under my shirt, hesitating as it went in the direction of my stoma bag. Then she pulled back a little bit, probably sensing that I had held my breath. Her hand crept down my stomach, teasingly slow. I couldn't stop her. I didn't want to stop her. Against all the odds, I wished something miraculous would happen to my body. But it didn't. She mumbled something like I needn't worry about my stoma bag. She knew it was there. She didn't mind. But it wasn't that.

Then, without any warning, the moment passed. A cry from upstairs and her motherly instincts took over. She lifted her head, listening. 'Stuart,' she said, recognising instinctively the voice that sounded no different to me from the voice of his twin brother. 'I think he must be feeling sick. Too much ice cream. Uhm ... Andy, I am so sorry, but I'll have to go up and see to him.'

She kissed me on my lips, softly and full of tenderness, a look of innocent promise in her eyes that she wouldn't be long.

'Of course,' I said, not feeling sorry at all. Instead, I was relieved. Clearly, she hadn't realised what my real problem was. She'd thought it was embarrassment, discomfort, because of my stoma bag.

I couldn't help myself. I heard her talking to her son. I heard the running of taps and the toilet flushing several times. She had to change his bed sheets. I felt sorry for her, for Stuart, but I was relieved by the opportunity. I put on my shoes and sneaked out of the house with my coat under my arm. Ten minutes later, I sent her a text message: 'I am sorry.'

It was senseless and cruel. God knows what must have gone through her head when she found that I had gone. Deliberately, I pushed aside my guilt, my regrets, everything that had to do with feelings and emotions. When she called me the next day, her voice was soft and hesitant but, like a coward, I told her I had received a call from the station. She knew it was a lie. She said 'oh, I see' and after a long silence, disconnected.

'Well?' says Mr Curtis, pulling me back to the reality. 'Will you go and see her?'

'I ... I don't know.'

'That is nonsense! Why not? I know you feel for her. Your face changes completely when I say her name.'

'It isn't that simple, Mr Curtis!'

'Why not?' He smiles but grimly. 'I care for you, Tregunna. I've made some big mistakes in my life and I've regretted them right up to the present day. If I could turn back the clock, I would certainly swallow my pride and make different decisions. I was stupid, I was proud and arrogant, and it was too late by the time I realised it. By then, the woman I loved had married someone else and she was pregnant. I didn't want to disrupt her life. I knew she was happy, but I also knew that she never stopped loving me. And I never stopped loving her. I never got married, Tregunna. I didn't think I deserved to be happy with anyone else, and maybe there was a bit of hope that one day we would meet again.'

'But now …?'

'She died two years ago.' He shakes his head to indicate that he won't answer any more questions. 'I don't want you to become a miserable old sod like me. You and your Lauren are made for each other and I want to make sure that you don't make the same mistakes as me.'

I stare at him. He won't let this go before I make him a promise. I can't tell him the truth, as no doubt he will make sure he sees Lauren again. So I do the only thing I can do. I lie and say that I will do my best.

9

In his mid-thirties, with short black hair and thin lips, Trevor Bennett lives on the outskirts of Liskeard. He stands in the doorway, his arms hang down beside his body from rounded shoulders, nodding slowly, biting his bottom lip, and blinking away tears when I explain I have more questions to ask about the death of his ex-wife.

'It's so very sad. I can't imagine why anyone would want to … harm her.' He falls silent, looking over my shoulder as if something has caught his attention.

'We are treating her death as suspicious, Mr Bennett. We want to find out who is responsible for her death.'

His shoulders shiver as he forces a smile that isn't reflected in his eyes. 'Of course, of course,' he says, pulling his gaze away from whatever had caught his eye and focusing on me for the first time. 'I'm sorry, excuse my manners … do come in, please.'

The pale carpet is pristine and I am politely asked to take off my shoes. He waits for me to undo my laces, frowning disapprovingly as he notices that part of my big toe is poking out through a hole in my sock. I hear music and outbursts of laughter from a TV comedy behind one of the closed doors in the hallway. The door he opens leads through the kitchen to a side room that must once have been part of a garage. It smells damp, musty and feels very cold, as if the room isn't used very much. It makes me wonder why he has taken me into this rather unwelcoming place; it seems as though he's trying to make some sort of point.

The room is cluttered with an old desk, a computer and a printer, some old, battered, black files in a dirty white bookcase, and a drying rack with three towels and a single dark sock draped over it. In a corner is an exercise bike with a few men's shirts and children's white school blouses on coat hangers hanging on the handle bars and an ironing board with a pleated skirt waiting to be ironed. There is also a stack of clear plastic boxes containing all sorts of items, from Christmas decorations to children's shoes and boots. Out of a small rear window I can see the back garden sloping slightly upwards, with a square patch of worn grass covered by a circular trampoline with safety nets around it. Beneath the shrubs all along the border are yellow daffodils and primroses. Further back is a large greenhouse with broken panes of glass.

'Maureen's,' he says, as if to answer the question that, I assume, is reflected in my face as I catch sight of the glasshouse. 'She loves it. We are pretty much self-sufficient in vegetables here in the summer.'

'And you?' I ask casually.

'No green fingers here, inspector. I just mow the lawn when I'm asked to.' He gives a shy grin, moving the only chair from behind the desk in my direction. He clears the edge of the desk and perches on it, one foot resting on the rim of a metal waste bin.

'I'm sorry,' he says uncomfortably. 'If I'd known what time you were coming …' He stops, eyeing me suspiciously as if he's wondering whether it's wise to go on or not.

'No problem.'

'Erm … Maureen is out.'

'I came primarily to speak to you, Mr Bennett.'

He carefully laces his fingers together and rests his hands on one knee, looking miserable, as if the fact that his wife is out and she can't back him up makes him feel vulnerable. 'I suppose this is about what happened … this weekend?'

'I'm sorry that you have to go through it again, Mr Bennett. I know that we already have your statement, but there are a few more questions we would like to ask you.'

He nods, his eyes cast down. I can't tell whether he is nervous because he has something to hide or because he is stricken with more grief than he wants to show. His marriage with Alicia ended five years ago, but he might still have strong feelings for her.

'I'll make it as quick as possible, Mr Bennett.'

He doesn't appear to hear me. 'My stepdaughter, Gillian, it was her birthday last Saturday. We went out with the family. And Briony came as well, of course.' He pauses briefly, closing his eyes and pinching the bridge of his nose as if he wants to blow the memories away. 'Today, Gillian is having a party for her friends. A sleep-over party. They're off school tomorrow. Some catching-up-day for the teachers. Maureen and the girls have gone out and will be back shortly and I'm going to make them pancakes and … Anyway, Maureen and I … we didn't want to cancel that.' He takes a deep shuddering breath. 'We didn't think it was right … it isn't fair to Gillian. She … she's hardly ever met Alicia.'

'Of course.'

'I would have gone with them, but Maureen's asked one of the mothers to help instead. I … I don't feel like partying at all.'

'How old is Gillian?'

'Eleven. Nasty little bitches, that age.' This rather bitter comment is followed by a quick grin as if to say that he didn't mean it like that. 'Girls on the edge, says Maureen.'

'Is Gillian your wife's only child?'

'No, she's got a son too. Alfie. He's seven.'

'I understand you were out for the whole weekend. Would you like to tell me about it?'

'We went up to Devon. Maureen's sister has a few holiday bungalows and we stayed in one of those. Mind you, it was bitterly cold that night.'

His voice drifts off as it has occurred to him how cold it was when his ex-wife died.

'And Briony was with you?'

'Of course. She's my daughter; she's part of my family.' He pauses. 'I know now why Alicia didn't pick up the phone. She was dead and I … oh my God … I … I was so angry with her. I mean, Briony was sick and Gillian got the same bug a few hours later. Briony wanted to go home, to her mum, to her own bed.' He gestures vaguely towards the ceiling. 'Unfortunately, we have only three bedrooms. When Briony is staying here, she sleeps in with Gillian. Not an ideal situation, but the girls get on very well, so it hasn't been a problem yet. Only that day, when Briony was so ill … I'm sorry, you were saying?'

'Perhaps you can start from the beginning. Saturday morning, when you picked up Briony from your ex-wife's home.'

'Okay.' He sums up the times and events as if he'd rehearsed before I knocked on the door. I duly write down the details, but with every word, he more or less confirms what he said in his original statement and also what Kenneth Poole told me earlier.

He collected Briony on Saturday morning, waved to Kenneth who he saw driving off at about half past nine, had a brief word with Alicia about some domestic matters, mainly about the possibility of Briony and Gillian going out horse riding, and then went back to his home in Liskeard with Briony. By then Maureen had packed their bags and, about fifteen minutes later, they were on the road to his wife's sister in Devon. They had planned to return at the end of the Sunday, but because Briony got ill and the rest of the family wasn't feeling very well either, they drove back home around lunch-time instead. At Briony's request, he repeatedly called Alicia but he didn't get much further than leaving messages on her answer phone, to which she didn't respond.

'I called her names, inspector, I mean, I thought how irresponsible she was being, not being there for her daughter when she needed her most.'

'You couldn't have known.'

'No.' His eyes widen. 'Of course not! I hope you're not thinking that I ...'

'The investigation is at an early stage, Mr Bennett. We have no suspects yet.'

'But I suppose you're targeting family and friends first.'

I nod slowly. 'Statistically, most murder victims are related to domestic disputes.'

'Yeah, I've read that somewhere. But clearly, I have an alibi for most of the weekend.'

'Where exactly were you staying in Devon?'

His expression is grim and bitter. 'Are you trying to pin me down, in case I drove back to Cornwall, killed my ex-wife, and then drove back to Devon? Without Maureen missing me?'

'We'll have to look at every possibility, Mr Bennett. And we'll have to question your wife as well.'

'Exactly.' He grins cynically. 'I had no reason to want my ex-wife dead, inspector. Our divorce was ... not a mutual thing, but I accepted it. Besides, she had met Kenneth. He seemed a decent enough bloke. And what was most important to me was that he and Briony got on well and that it wasn't his intention that I would be estranged from her. He was her stepfather and he would never be more than that.'

'Do you have any idea who might have wanted to harm your ex-wife?'

'Uhm ... No.' He stares at his hands. One of his nails is broken and there is a clot of dried blood under his nail bed. 'I can't think of anyone. I mean, Alicia was just a normal woman. Beautiful, yes, and maybe someone was jealous about that, but ... she didn't have enemies. She wasn't like that. But still ... who could do that to my beautiful Alicia?'

There is a movement behind me and, as I turn my head, I see a small woman on the doorstep, her eyes on Trevor with an expression of disgust and despair. It is clear that Trevor hasn't stopped loving his first wife and that his current wife is only too well aware of it.

10

DI Maloney seems relaxed about the on-going dispute in his parents-in-law's divorce. Unprompted, he confides in me that he is relieved that his wife has stayed in Weymouth to support both her father and her mother. She seems hopeful that she can mediate between the two of them and achieve an amicable outcome for them. Maloney is doubtful.

'It transpires that my wife's mother has had a long-term relationship with another man, who was also married and had a family. It is even in doubt whether Brian, my brother-in-law, is actually my father-in-law's son.'

'That's terrible.'

'Yeah, of course, but as the affair is out in the open now and the man in question has died of a heart attack, why bother breaking up a marriage that was good, as far as we all know?'

'She lied to him.'

'Yes, but she has confessed now, hasn't she?'

I shake my head, wondering if he really believes his own words. After all, does a confession, albeit forced by the man's death, heal the wounds or cover the lies?

'Anyway, Tregunna.' He rubs his hands together as if they have gone cold. 'What's the latest on this murder case?'

'I have scheduled an extra briefing in about two hours.'

'So I've been told, Tregunna, but I would like to know now. I don't like to be confronted with surprises I have no forewarning of.'

I nod, irritated, but have to admit that I would feel exactly the same. 'No problem.'

'I may be late tomorrow morning again, if the missus calls me to collect her. I hope you can do the morning briefing tomorrow.'

'I have a hospital appointment later in the morning.'

Maloney nods gravely. 'How are you doing? I meant to ask you for ages, but … you know …'

'I'm doing well, thank you.'

'Good.' He nods, annoyed and relieved at the same time.

We enter the incident room where Jennette Penrose is hunched over her desk, watching blurred black and white images on her computer screen. Her expression tells me that, for some reason, her mood has sunk below freezing point and I can only hope that Maloney acts diplomatically enough not to trigger her anger. She is one of those people who is paranoid about privacy and fears that 'Big Brother' knows too much about all of us. So she hates watching CCTV footage as she thinks she is secretly spying on innocent people. She asked me once what to do if ever she saw someone she knew on one of the tapes and found out that he or she had committed a crime.

'If it has nothing to do with the particular case you are investigating, then I'd leave it to your own judgement, Jennette,' I replied, which I knew, didn't help her.

The memory stirs something else in my mind. If someone in Maloney's wife's family had known about the secret affair, what would that person have done? Tell everyone or keep quiet about it? Either way, there seems no right or wrong in matters like that.

Briefly, Penrose looks up, raising an enquiring eyebrow, but she just nods by way of greeting. Her shirt is creased and one of the buttons is open, revealing a white vest underneath.

'Hi,' Maloney says casually, but I suspect he's forgotten her name. She seems to think so too, as I see her stiffen. She begins to scratch vigorously at her head. Her mouth moves noiselessly and she mutters something under her breath as if she is talking herself into getting up and running away. Clearly, she is disappointed that Maloney isn't staying away for the rest of the week. The two have never really got on and she sees no point in hiding her feelings about him. But apparently oblivious to her hostility, Maloney ignores her in his usual way. Perhaps just as well.

At the end of the room, he stops and stares at the photo of the victim which is attached to the top of the board. 'Who found her?'

'The guy who collects the money in the shed, Josh Warren. There was a fishing competition going on this Saturday and he is a committee member of the fishing group, called The Swan. He lives in Rumford and works in Padstow. On his way to work on Monday morning at about quarter to nine, he went to the lake to collect the money and he found the body.'

I have spoken to Josh Warren's friend Eddie, and decided that it wouldn't be in anyone's best interest to have Eddie come to the station for a statement. He was so nervous about the whole business that he could barely talk about it. I may be wrong but I have no doubt whatsoever that Eddie had nothing to do with the death of Alicia Poole.

'I presume this Warren has been questioned?' Maloney asks.

'That's right. I don't believe he had anything to do with it. He didn't know the victim; he had no motive to kill her.'

'Alibi?'

'Warren was out in Padstow with friends on Saturday night. We have checked the pub where he was drinking and the people working at the bar remember seeing him. We have the names of his friends, but we haven't spoken to them yet,' I explain, meanwhile thinking that, in theory, and within the time frame as we know it at this point, Josh Warren could have driven to the lake and killed Alicia. The only thing is that I can't see him as being in Alicia's circle of friends and relatives. He wouldn't be so daft as to find the body himself and call the police.

Instinct, rather than hard evidence.

'Do we have any other suspects?' Maloney gestures at the board, looking at me as if I am about to present the name of the murderer on a silver platter.

I shrug and point at the photo on top of the board: Alicia Poole, blonde hair wet and bedraggled but happily laughing at the camera. It is a partial enlargement from a photo her husband gave us, taken on a beach during a holiday last summer. There was a tear in his eyes as he asked to have the original photo back.

'Nothing positive so far, I'm afraid. Victim is Alicia Poole, 34 years old, mother of 9-year-old Briony and wife of Kenneth Poole who runs several estate agencies in the county with his ex-wife Julia. His company seems to be very successful, no sign whatsoever that the death of his wife is related to his business.' I point at the question mark behind Kenneth Poole's name. 'We haven't been able to find a motive and his alibi for Saturday night is solid. He played golf all day on Saturday and he spent the night with his secretary in a hotel which is close to his golf club.'

'Alibi checked with the secretary?'

'We have. Her story is the same as his. The night receptionist of the hotel remembers them checking in. He said it was obvious that they weren't married and he could spot an illicit liaison a mile off.'

'Poole can't have left the hotel to kill his wife and come back before his secretary woke up?'

'There is only one exit in the hotel at night, and that is through the lounge. You'd have to pass the reception desk and the door is locked from the inside between 11pm and 6am. The night receptionist is certain that no one left the hotel that night. Or came in.'

'Did Poole's wife know that he was having an affair with his secretary?'

'We believe so, yes. But it didn't seem to cause friction between them. Up to a certain level, they seemed to have an 'open' marriage.'

'Perhaps things got out of hand,' Penrose jumps in gravely.

Maloney stares at her blankly. 'The secretary might have a motive. Had he promised her would divorce his wife and marry her instead?'

'According to her statement, she has no obvious motive. Jenna Saunders. She is bi-sexual. She lives with a woman. Every now and then she wants to have sex with a man and it seems that she and Poole have a mutual understanding about that. It is more or less a business arrangement. Her partner knows about it and doesn't seem to object, and, in her own words, she isn't a threat to Poole's marriage because she would never want to have a proper relationship with him.'

'Okay. Go on.'

'Trevor Bennett. He and Alicia divorced five years ago. He is now married to Maureen, who has two children from a previous marriage. Trevor and Alicia have only one child, 9-year-old Briony. The arrangement is such that the girl sees her father every other weekend. This doesn't seem to be causing any friction. He collects the girl on Saturday morning and he takes her back Sunday night.' I pause as he steps forward to scrutinise a 'selfie' from Briony, curly brown hair, smiling widely into the camera of her own phone, her teeth white and uneven, blue eyes sparkling with vitality.

'Then there is Maureen, Trevor's wife, who may be the only one so far who has a motive. She was interviewed by DS Reed and he said that she seemed anxious that Trevor and Alicia would get back together again.'

Maloney's eyebrows arch. Before he can jump to the wrong conclusions, I add quickly, 'Both Trevor and Maureen have an alibi. They drove with the three children to Devon on Saturday for a weekend at her sister's, who has some sort of a holiday site in Devon. Apparently, the trip was chosen by their 11-year-old daughter, Gillian, because it was her birthday. They spent the night in one of the sister's holiday bungalows. Their alibi is solid as a rock.'

'Hm. Who was the last person who saw Alicia Poole alive?'

'We're not sure yet. She'd gone out in Newquay with her friend Denise Shaw. From her statement, we know that Alicia left Barrie's Bar with someone she half introduced to Denise. Alicia told her that this chap, Chris was an old friend of hers, but Denise is certain she'd never heard of him before.'

'So we are focusing on him?'

'For the time being, yes. That's why we are investigating how Alicia ended up dead miles from the bar in Newquay where she was last seen.' I turn towards Penrose. 'Jennette? Can you tell us what you've discovered so far?'

'Sure.' Penrose shrugs and stretches her arms above her head, releasing the tension from her shoulders. Then, before getting up to join us at the board, she quickly sifts through a pile of prints. Her face has turned pink and I can see a gleam in her eyes, suggesting that she is pleased with what she's found out. I hope that Maloney will realise that she's spent many hours pouring over the computer screen.

She steps forward and starts to speak in a confident voice. 'Barrie's Bar is the last known place where Alicia went with her friend Denise Shaw. Fortunately for us, this bar has cameras everywhere. The manager told me that there were some incidents last summer, when a drug dealer decided that Barrie's Bar was as good as any place to sell his stuff. There were some fights between competing gangs. Then there was the stabbing of a young man, outside but on the doorstep. He only just survived. You may remember that, sir, it was last November. For Barrie, the owner of the bar, it was the straw that broke the camel's back. He's had cameras installed everywhere, with warning signs as well. Like 'you are being watched – if you're doing nothing illegal, you've got nothing to worry about'.' She pauses briefly. 'The cameras are even in the toilets.'

'Looking in?' Maloney asks incredulously.

She nods severely. 'Even in the cubicles. But they are attached to the ceiling, looking straight down, so you don't see …

uhm … much.' She blushes and shakes her head disapprovingly, like a prude old spinster. 'Anyway, I have images of Alicia and her friend for the whole time. Every movement. I can tell you how many drinks they had and who they spoke to and how many times they went to the cloakroom to powder their nose, so to speak. More importantly, I've seen them arrive … and leave.' She pauses, as if she's waiting for a pat on the back.

'I have pictures of everyone Alicia spoke to or exchanged a greeting with.' She points with her thumb to one side of the room where a printer has a small pile of black and white pictures in its tray. 'I even managed to see who she left with,' she says as an afterthought, but knowing very well how important it is.

I hold my breath. 'Good enough to be identifiable?'

She nods, glowing with pride. 'I got him from every angle. They left together, Alicia and this man. On the photos, her friend Denise Shaw didn't seem to be worried, so at that point, as far as Mrs Shaw was concerned, there wasn't any indication that something was amiss.'

'Good job, Jennette,' Maloney exclaims, almost rubbing his hands together in his enthusiasm. 'Looks like we'll make quick progress with this case.'

He stares at me as if what he believes is a big breakthrough is down to him coming onto the investigation.

'Let's hope we will find someone who recognises this man,' I say thoughtfully, knowing very well that it isn't always so straight-forward. Generally, images from surveillance cameras aren't as clear and useful as we like them to be. Faces can be blurred and distorted, in other words, unidentifiable.

'Of course we will!' Maloney isn't put off easily.

I exchange a glance with Penrose before she spreads out printed images of the man. They are all black and white, but, from what we know about Alicia, we can work out his height and weight. She danced with him, she stood with him at the bar, sharing a joke with the barman, they sat with Denise and, briefly, with a couple that had joined Denise for a while. Finally, they are seen exiting the bar, Alicia with her coat draped over her shoulders,

Unfortunately for us, Newquay council doesn't have as many cameras in the town centre as in Barrie's Bar, but Penrose and Ollie have found images that show them leaving Barrie's Bar and sitting on the low wall of the nearby Victoria Hotel, sharing a cigarette. Then they went in the direction of the old railway track, now a public footpath, and after a while, they appeared at the other end of the railway track, at the junction where the council office and the library are. They went past the library up to Manor Road car park and left in a car.

'Licence plate?'

She shakes her head. 'Not yet,' she says grimly, like a film director keeping up the suspense. 'We have been able to follow them as they drive out of Newquay, taking the coast road, but we kind of lost them there, as there aren't many cameras out of town.'

She points at the map on the wall, marked with red and yellow pins.

'Assuming that they followed the coast road along to the place where she was found, we have tried to get our hands on any CCTV footage along the road. Unfortunately, we didn't have much luck there. Most people have their cameras focused on their own exits and entrances. Where we do have a view on the road, the images are vague and distorted, I'm afraid.'

'What do we know about the bloke's car?'

'All I can see of the licence plate is that it start with a W – which isn't very helpful as it means the number is from the South West.'

'And the make?'

'Possibly a Toyota. Unfortunately, the CCTV images are in black and white, but we can assume that the car is probably white or silver grey.'

'Good work, Penrose.'

He lets out a deep howl like a wolf sniffing to locate a nearby prey. 'Next step is to find this car and the owner.' He sounds like he is already drawing up the official papers to charge the driver with murder.

11

Having been diagnosed with bowel cancer and having undergone a major operation to remove the malignant tumour doesn't necessarily mean that I am free of cancer cells that might decide to settle somewhere else in my body. I hate the regular check-ups. I hate the fact that I can't feel what the cancerous cells that might have been left inside my body are doing. I hate the fact that I am powerless, that I can't do anything about it and that I am totally reliant on doctors and nurses and laboratory technicians to find out what's happening to my body and make decisions before I've even been told about it.

Worse, I hate the fact that I have to sit in a waiting room full of people, all with the same problem. I hate the way we look at one another and guess who is going to make it to the next appointment.

I dread the moment when the doctor opens his mouth to tell me his findings. I even dread the relief when I get the all-clear, as the next appointment already clouds the horizon because I know I have to go though the same ordeal again soon.

The appointment is later in the afternoon and I wish now that I hadn't told anyone, let alone Maloney as he more or less forced me to go home early to 'get myself ready'. Clearly, he hasn't got a clue what this friendly gesture means for my nerves.

Earlier, Penrose ventured the suggestion that we could try and trace cars which had driven past the petrol station near the crime before the estimated time of the murder and shortly after it. Maloney looked dubious but, in fairness to him, he studied the map before he pointed at several other roads and lanes the murderer could have taken to get away from the crime scene unseen. Penrose flinched at the total dismissal of her suggestion, which I didn't find so unreasonable. Whether I'm supporting her idea or I'm desperate to find a distraction before I have to go to my hospital appointment, I'm not sure, but I have promised Penrose to the camera tapes from the petrol station.

It is situated on a junction on the coast road which runs between Newquay and Padstow, only about half a mile from the lake where Alicia Poole's body was found. The building looks as though it hasn't been painted for decades. The windows are splattered with dried dirt on the outside and condensation inside. The once white walls have become grey and grimly from vehicles driving in and out and the remains of rusty advertising boards and disused hooks for hanging baskets.

Opening the door, there is a strong smell of a mixture of petrol and freshly baked pasties. Along the walls, the shelves are stacked with all sorts of odd items that look as if they have been there for years and never sold. On the floor is a pile of plastic containers of engine oil and windscreen wash that seem to be the only items anyone buys.

A man is sitting behind a counter, one elbow on the top, holding his head as if it has become too heavy for his neck to carry. He is wearing a washed-out red sweater that is now faded pink. Behind him is an old bulky computer with a split screen displaying four different images from the cameras inside and outside. One camera must be somewhere above my head, covering the till and the door, the other three are outside, two covering the petrol pumps, the other covering the main area in front of the building. The one over the petrol pump nearest to the road gives a clear view of the junction opposite.

'Good morning.'

The man lets out a grunt as I approach him, seemingly annoyed that I am disturbing him. He's looking at a magazine spread out in front of him with a very short article and lots of photos of young women lying across car bonnets wearing little else than high-heeled boots and lacy thongs.

'Hi,' he says, not even bothering to close the magazine or cover the photos. He gazes at the screen on the till and his eyebrows rise as he realises that I haven't filled up with petrol. 'Yeah?'

'I hope you can help me,' I smile encouragingly.

'Depends with what,' he replies with an indifferent shrug, already making up his mind that he won't make any effort.

Once more I smile and produce my ID card at the same time, but he doesn't bother looking at it at all. 'I hope you can help me with some information from your security camera system.' I point at the computer screen behind his back.

'Yeah?'

'Are you the manager here?'

A shrug. 'Sort of.'

'I need to see the images from your security cameras.'

He looks doubtful. 'It's a very old system.'

'Do you still use video tapes?'

'I guess.' Another shrug. He looks over his shoulder and notices a young woman crossing the street. She is wearing a uniform from a nearby bakery shop, clutching a newspaper and a glossy magazine under her arm. He licks his lips and grabs his crotch.

'You'll have to ask my boss. All I know is that it is a very old system. Marge complains about it all the time but the boss says he doesn't want to pay for a new system while the old system is still working.'

'And where is your boss?'

Outside, the woman has disappeared out of his vision and, reluctantly, he turns his attention back to me, pulling a face to let me know that the answer is obvious. 'You'll have to ask Marge.'

'Thank you.'

He doesn't move.

'Where do I find Marge?' I ask, patiently.

'In the office.' His chin moves in the direction of a door that is covered with local advertisements, posters announcing local events and business cards, all pinned on with coloured plastic drawing pins.

'Alright.' I'm slowly losing my patience. 'What is your name?'

'I am W.P Torrington.' He produces a name badge from beside the till and holds it in front of his chest. 'Sales assistant '

'Alright, Mr Torrington, can you call Marge for me, or, your boss?'

'Of course I can, sir.'

He picks up a cordless phone and presses two buttons. 'Marge, I need to know where Mr Reeves is. There is someone here ... uhm, I dunno. What? Yes, hang on ...'

He gazes at me. 'Who did you say you are, sir? Marge wants to know ...'

'Andy Tregunna.' For some reason, I don't remind him that I'm a policeman. I doubt if he paid enough attention to my ID card that he can remember.

He repeats my name and I can hear the annoyance in a woman's voice without exactly hearing what she says.

'Yes, Marge. Hang on.'

'What is the nature of your enquiry, sir, Marge asks.'

'I would like to see the security tapes from last Saturday night.'

He frowns as he listens to Marge again. It is obvious that she is not pleased with his attitude. 'She'll be here in ten seconds,' he announces, putting down the phone.

'Thank you.'

He smiles, showing an expression of relief when a customer comes in. 'Hi. Pump 2?'

Intuitively, I follow his gaze through the dirty window. Only one car is parked next to the petrol pump. Only one pump is lit up on his till screen.

The sharp click-clacking of high heels on the tiled floor announces the appearance of Marge. She is in her late forties, dressed in a black skirt which covers her knees and a long-sleeved white blouse. Her glasses are an old-fashioned style, her lips as pink as the small scarf tied around her neck.

'Wilbur?' Her voice is sharp and unforgiving. 'What is your problem?' She makes it sound as if he is the problem, and that his days at the petrol station are numbered.

'Mr Tregenza would like…'

He pauses as she turns on one high heel. I am half expecting it to brake and to have to catch her in my arms as she falls.

'Actually, I am Andy Tregunna.'

'Uhm … Marge Flynn. I am the administrative assistant and book-keeper for Mr Reeves, who is currently on holiday.'

The till rings as Torrington opens it. The customer, a short man in his fifties, clearly well known to Torrington, patiently waits for his change and a for his loyalty card to be stamped.

I produce my ID card and Marge Flynn stares at it over the rim of her glasses. Her bottom lip drops as she studies the card, then there is a flicker of excitement in her eyes and her cheeks turn a shade of red.

'Is this about the murder?' she blurts out, making the departing customer pause halfway to the door. 'The woman they found in the fishing lake?'

I give her a brief nod. 'Yes Ms Flynn. I would like to have a look at the camera tapes from last Saturday night.' I am aware that the customer has stopped to follow the conversation. Marge Flynn looks round as if she expects a whole army of policemen to emerge. Meanwhile her brain is working overtime. Clearly, she doesn't want to consider the possibility of there being any connection between the petrol station and the murder.

'Ehm, yes,' she says hesitantly.

A husky gasp from behind the counter makes us turn to the sales assistant who is now slumped back on his seat and stares at me with a mixture of horror and panic.

12

I am still light-headed when I leave the hospital. I was planning to visit Becca after my regular check-up, but I am not in the mood. I can't bear the thought of sitting at her bedside, staring at her pale face, feeling the coolness of her skin, listening to her shallow breathing and wondering about the quality of her life.

Becca is a young woman but her existence is fragile, dependent on others for her life support and like a white lily floating on a pond, there are hidden daggers beneath the surface. Nine months ago she was shot by a bullet that was meant for me. A team of surgeons fought desperately to save her life, and although she didn't die, but they weren't able to do more than remove the bullet from her brain. She slipped into a coma and hasn't woken up since. At first, there was some hope, but gradually that has been replaced by disappointment and, eventually, acceptance of her condition.

I can't go and see her. Not now. My head is spinning. Having seen Roy Wood today has had much more impact on me than I ever expected. His skin ashen, eyes hollow, body slumped in a wheelchair, has shocked me to the core. The rapid deterioration of his body reminds me how fragile life really is.

Roy and I had the same operation on the same day less than a year ago. Unlike me, he had chemotherapy afterwards, followed by an additional course of radiotherapy. None of the treatments worked for him.

I know I will never see him again.

I almost feel nauseous when I walk back to my car. Shock, pity and frustration. All are normal, logical emotions but there is also something else. From the moment I saw Roy today, I felt a sharp spasm like a hot wire snaking up from the base of my spine, hitting every nerve.

Fear. Simple, raw fear.

I sit in my car, key already in the ignition. I clench my fists and rest my forehead on the steering wheel. I can't go home. I can't be alone. I know I'll sink back into the black swamp where I found myself months ago, after the operation. I don't want to go back to that awful time because this time, I know I won't be able to climb back out of it.

The busy traffic takes me out of Truro. I take the exit at Kingsley Village in Fraddon, staring at the front of a coffee shop. The smell of coffee appeals as much as the desire to be surrounded by happy, healthy people. Looking at them will undoubtedly make me feel even sorrier for myself but I'll go mad if I go straight home.

My phone vibrates. It makes me feel reconnected to the real world. Without looking at the number or the name, I press the red button. I don't want to talk to anyone. I won't be able to concentrate on a conversation. The desperate eyes of Roy Wood keep swirling in my head. I'm sure the caller will be able to hear a tremble in my voice. There is also a real possibility that I will start crying if it's my mother.

The caller seems determined to speak to me. Briefly, I contemplate switching the phone off altogether. It vibrates again. I look. It's Penrose and it means work. Distraction.

I press the green button and take the call.

She says she is sorry to interrupt whatever I'm doing, but I had insisted that she should call me with any updates. True to her word, she tells me about the latest developments in the investigation. New statements have come in, waiting for me to read and add to the computer system. She asks how soon I'm coming back to the station. I almost tell her about Roy Wood and the miserable state I'm in and that I won't be going back to the station today, but she doesn't give me the opportunity to interrupt her. Lowering her voice, she explains, almost apologetically, that she's had a call from a neighbour and she has to go home to her father.

As she finishes with a long sigh, I hear myself promising her that I will drive to the crime scene to talk to the owner of a nearby farm. She has studied the area on Google Earth and has discovered that one of the windows of the farmhouse is visible from the car park by the lake, hence it is possible that someone looking out of that window saw something at the car park. One of the detectives has already spoken to the farmer, Mr Carthew, but there is no mention in his statement that the question has been asked.

It is pushing three thirty when I pull through the gates of Carthew Farm, dodging potholes and splashing through puddles before parking in the cobblestone yard. .The farm is situated on the hillside, with clear views towards the coastline, across the valley and, most significantly, down over the fishing lake. Fields stretch out towards the bottom of the valley where a small stream flows into the sea at Harlyn Bay. The farm itself is a cluster of old and new buildings, with a wet and dirty yard where a tractor is parked alongside a battered Mercedes. A black-and-white dog is watching my movements closely when I park on the grass verge beside the road.

A baggy man in green corduroy trousers and battered old boots with mud stuck to the sides of the soles comes out of one of the buildings, stopping abruptly as I climb out of the car. He is probably in his seventies, with a thick mop of white hair and a wrinkled, weathered face in which his eyes are barely visible. Looking down at my shoes, he motions that there is no need to get them dirty

He leans over the metal gate between us. 'Are you looking for the holiday cottage?'

I'm certain a holiday cottage hasn't been mentioned in his statement either.

'Uhm, actually ...'

He shakes his head and continues in a disgruntled tone: 'I don't understand some of those fancy companies. They spend thousands of pounds on advertising, but they don't seem to see the need to put proper instructions on their websites. You won't believe how many people show up here in my yard to ask for directions.' He pauses for breath. 'You're here for the weekend, I presume?'

He looks over my shoulder as if he's expecting to see at least a quartet of tired and bored looking children on the back seat of my car, their mother reclining in the front seat with her eyes closed and a migraine coming on.

'I'd like to have a word with Mr Carthew.'

He cocks his head. 'Which one?'

More surprises. 'I wasn't aware there's more than one.'

'I'm Vincent Carthew,' he says helpfully. 'My son Derek's gone shopping. He'll be back at tea time.'

'Do you live in the farmhouse?' I ask, retrieving my ID card.

'Yes.' His easy manner has now completely gone, his eyes widen and the stern expression on his face seems set. 'Police? Is this about the dead woman?'

'It is.'

'I've told you lot everything I know.'

I nod. I have read his brief statement: he didn't see, hear or notice anything on Saturday night. He watched TV and went to bed early, as usual. He wasn't asked if, by any chance, he looked out of his window before closing the curtains. He didn't offer that information either.

'I would like to know what you can see from your house, Mr Carthew. You told my colleagues that you can't see the lake, but I have noticed that there is a room upstairs …'

The dog comes forward and sits down beside Carthew as if it senses that he needs moral support. Carthew's left hand digs automatically in his trouser pocket. He finds something that looks like a twig. The dog takes it, chews once and swallows, hoping for more.

'We don't use the rooms upstairs anymore. My wife can't climb the stairs and, with all those cuts in health care nowadays, we couldn't get one of those stair lifts installed. Besides, the children have all moved out and we're using the dining room as our bedroom.'

I try to recall but I can't remember that a Mrs Carthew was mentioned, or a son, for that matter.

There is something in the way he stretches his back and shoulders that makes me press on. 'Where does your son live?'

Putting his hands in his trouser pockets, he motions with his head. The dog briefly stirs in anticipation. 'They live up the road. It's half of Carthew Cottage. It's is a converted barn. One part is our holiday let; our son lives in the other half. They take care of the letting. Cleaning and stuff, but the bookings are all done online.' He shrugs almost apologetically. 'My wife and I weren't happy in the beginning. We weren't so keen on having strangers on our land, but I must admit that it helps us financially.'

'Is it possible to have a word with your wife, Mr Carthew?'

'I don't see why …'

'I believe we haven't spoken to her yet.'

For a moment he looks like he is going to refuse. 'That's right, but …'

'I have only a few questions, Mr Carthew. It won't take long.'

'She isn't … I doubt if she'll be able to help you.' he hesitates, not meeting my eyes. Then he shrugs as if he's aware that refusing won't help either. 'All right then. Just a few seconds, please. I'll have to sort out something with Will first.'

He doesn't bother with any more information, but walks over to one of the barns and disappears inside. It takes him less than half a minute to emerge with a young man, as thin as a piece of straw, with matching straw-coloured hair, and a red face spattered with freckles. Hands hidden away in low slung jeans, he doesn't appear to be keen on doing anything that involves any effort. He listens to Carthew's instructions as if he's heard it all before, then shrugs sulkily and climbs onto the tractor. Carthew opens the gate and closes it behind him as the vehicle wobbles away on the muddy track.

Carthew grins mockingly. 'Best use the road, inspector, we wouldn't want to spoil your shoes, huh?'

He guides me in the opposite direction towards a track of patched-up tarmac with grasses and weeds growing down the middle. It leads between two shoulder-high stone walls overgrown with brambles and hawthorn. At one point the branches are broken and it looks like they have been pushed aside. A rusty iron gate hangs crooked at the end. He opens it, making a gesture to me to follow him to the house. As we walk along a short flagstone path leading towards the front door, which is clearly rarely used, I turn and look back over the valley. The fishing lake shimmers like a bright mirror, reflecting the sun and a cold blue sky. I can see a few parked cars and a person in a yellow fluorescent jacket walking towards one of the fishing shelters that are scattered alongside the water's edge.

'You can see the lake from here,' Carthew explains defiantly, following my stare. 'But not from inside the house.'

Looking up at the only bay window on this side of the house, I make a mental note to check if he is right.

'What happened there?' Changing the subject, I turn and point at the damaged branches.

'What? Oh, I dunno. Happens all the time.' He shrugs indifferently. 'Badgers, probably. Or sheep.'

'Do you keep sheep, Mr Carthew?'

'There're in the field on the other side of the hill.' He gestures with his thumb over his shoulder.

'It will soon be lambing time, I presume?'

He shrugs, as though recognising my ignorance. 'That depends on the breed,' he replies patiently. 'Some are really early, even lambing in December or January. But ours are later.'

He unlocks the front door of the house and goes in, taking off his boots in the small porch, calling, 'It's only me, dear. I've brought you a visitor.'

There is no reply, but I can hear the soft tones of classical piano music and a voice humming along.

His wife is sitting in a comfortable reclining chair by the window that looks like a framed oil painting of the valley. Acres of green fields are dotted with sheep, and bright sunlight is shining on the distant sea. She turns her head towards us. A ray of sun falls across the deep purple fabric of her dress, over her fragile hands and on the pearls around her neck.

'This is a police inspector, dear,' Carthew explains curtly. 'He has some questions about the night before the woman was found in the lake. I have already explained that we sleep in our former dining room and that we can't really see the lake from downstairs.'

She nods vaguely, stretching out an arm to me as if she is a member of the royal family. Obediently, I shake a pale, weak hand with rings on three fingers.

'I'm sorry I can't get up, inspector. But please have a seat. Would you like a cup of tea?' Her voice trembles and she licks her lips as though she is almost dying of thirst herself. 'Vince, can you put the kettle on, please?'

Looking uncomfortable, he duly disappears, his feet in just his socks silent on the old slate tiles and rugs, and mutters under his breath about him being a farmer, not a housewife or a maid.

'What can I do for you, inspector?' Mrs Carthew nestles her spine into the backrest of the chair and smiles, folding her hands together as though she's preparing for a silent prayer. Her watery blue eyes are darting over me from top to toe. However, her expression is vacant and she doesn't seem to be taking anything in. I am already starting to wonder if this visit is going to be a waste of time.

'This is about Saturday night, Mrs Carthew. Were you at home as usual? All night?'

'Of course we were.' Her surprise seems genuine. 'Where else would we be?'

'You and your husband?'

'Yes, of course. Vince has to get up early, because of the ewes, you see. Some are about to have their lambs. He checks them every so often.'

'Aren't the sheep in the fields on the other side of the hill, Mrs Carthew?'

'Oh, are they? Oh yes, of course. Why do you ask? Is it important?'

'Yes, Mrs Carthew, it might be important. Were you and your husband together all the time on Saturday night?'

'Of course we were. Well, our son came round, of course, and they had a chat in the kitchen. I was here, watching TV, but I could hear them talking.'

I frown. Clearly, the officer who interviewed Vincent Carthew failed to speak to his wife or to his son. 'What time was that?'

'Oh, I know exactly, inspector, because it was nine o'clock. We were about to watch something on television and Vince was annoyed. He never likes it when he misses the beginning. But I said we were recording it anyway, because he always falls asleep.'

She chuckles as if she's told me a secret, but her eyes are vacant. I understand her husband's reluctance to let me see her.

'What is your son's name, Mrs Carthew?' I ask gently.

She giggles girlishly. 'Don't you know?'

'No.'

'Well ...' She smiles and spreads her fingers as if she has just painted her nails, studying them as though she suspects that she has forgotten to paint one of them. Avoiding the question. 'What was your question again? Was it about the ewes?'

I am becoming aware that the gaps in Mrs Carthew's memory won't be much of a help.

'Did your husband and son go out that night?'

'Why would they? It was pitch-dark. No, it wasn't. It was full moon.' She smiles and loses herself in thoughts that make her smile and frown. 'I love it when the sky is clear and you can see the moon and the stars, don't you?'

'Yes, I do, Mrs Carthew. Maybe your husband or your son had to check on the ewes?'

'Our Derek had just done that and he thought he didn't need to do it again until the morning.'

I nod, uncertain how to proceed. 'Were you watching television from the chair you are sitting in now, Mrs Carthew?'

'Of course, my darling. You know I do, because you always help me into it.'

'Did you look outside?' I ask, trying not to remind her that I am not her husband.

'Of course. I have to keep an eye on everything, don't I? If you don't watch everything, you won't notice what's going on behind your back.'

'That is very true, Mrs Carthew. Did you, by any chance, look outside on Saturday evening?'

'Saturday? Is it Saturday today?'

'No Mrs Carthew, it is ...' I stop, realising that there is no point in continuing. Even if there turns out to be something relevant in her statement, she won't be a very convincing witness in court.

Vince Carthew has appeared without making a sound. He places a tray on a small table next to his wife, nodding as if instructing her to do the honours.

'How do you take your tea, inspector?'

'No sugar, please, Mrs Carthew.'

'I'm not sure if she can help you with your enquiries,' Carthew says slowly.

'No,' I say gently. 'I understand.'

His wife claps her hands like a teacher demanding the attention of rebellious pupils. 'I was upstairs, Vince! I wanted to see where you and that young man were going, you see.' Her voice is high with a note of anger. 'You always sneak out with him. I know it! You won't even tell me ...'

'I was with Derek, love, our own son Derek,' he says calmly, without raising his voice, his face expressionless. He has clearly given up arguing with her.

'Who is Derek?' she asks, angry because she feels left out.

Her husband looks embarrassed. Despondent. Pained. His eyes move around the room, focusing on the clock on the opposite wall, the blank television screen, but his mind is elsewhere. He wants to be elsewhere.

'You understand now, inspector?' he says lamely, avoiding my eyes.

'I'm sorry,' I nod, taking my tea and wishing I hadn't accepted it.

'I saw them, you see. Down by the lake.' Mrs Carthew claps her hands in enthusiasm. 'They were beautiful.'

'Were you upstairs, Mrs Carthew?' I ask, really jus to break the silence.

'She can't go upstairs anymore, inspector,' Carthew interrupts.

His wife giggles again, clamping her hand over her mouth like a naughty schoolgirl. 'Of course I can go upstairs, you silly man! I'm not even thirty years old! You keep saying that I can't climb those stairs, but I can. And I do it, when you're not looking. I can see so much more from the window upstairs!' She chuckles, a faint blush over her cheeks. 'I saw them that night! They were so beautiful!'

'Inspector, please don't pay attention to what my wife says. She will tell you this today, but tomorrow it will be a totally different story.'

'I saw them, Vincent.' Her eyes have come to life. I can see fury and frustration in them and for some reason, I am inclined to believe her. 'You didn't see them, Vince, because you were asleep. I went to our bedroom upstairs, you know. I don't understand why we sleep in the other room. Is it because of your knee?'

'Yes love,' he says gently. 'It is because of my knee.' He smiles sadly, then looks at me and adds in a low voice: 'I had a knee replacement seven years ago.'

'You were snoring so loudly that you might have disturbed those lovely creatures at the lake.' Her eyes are shining and a happy smile trembles on her lips. 'They were so beautiful.'

'Who were beautiful, Mrs Carthew?'

'Oh! Why do you keep calling me Mrs Carthew? I'm Molly! You know that, don't you?'

'Yes of course, Molly. What was it that you saw, down by the lake that was so beautiful?'

'The swans of course. So bright and white in the light of the moon. I could even see their reflection in the water. And they moved ... sometimes gently ... as if ... as if ...' She frowns and stops, uncertain suddenly, clearly trying to work out whether what she saw was real or a long-forgotten memory. She looks at me thoughtfully. 'Don't they say that swans have only one male or female in their life? When one dies, the other never finds another mate? Well, I could see how much they loved each other!' Her eyes sparkling, she smiles, licking her lips.

'That is very helpful, Mrs Carthew. Thank you for the tea, but before I go, is it possible for me to have a look out of your window upstairs?'

'Of course, inspector. Everything is clean and tidy.'

'Thank you.'

'But I'm sure you don't have to go yet? I thought you were staying for lunch. I've cooked a lovely joint this morning. There is plenty for all of us.'

'We've already had lunch today, my dear, and I'm sure the inspector's had his as well,' Carthew says with an apologetic look at me. 'It's almost time for our tea.'

Rising to my feet, I smile at her. 'Thank you for the offer, Mrs Carthew, but as your husband said, I already had lunch.'

'No problem, my son.' She chuckles again, her cheeks pink and eyes gleaming. 'Those white swans were all making love, my dear, it was so lovely to see. So romantic.' She pauses and frowns, as though something is worrying her. 'Those swans ... in a way, they looked like ... people. Real people.'

13

Despite the age of the petrol station's surveillance system, the images are surprisingly clear and sharp. Penrose has spent hours going through the tapes, only persevering because of her usual stubbornness. Every now and then stopping to stretch her muscles, her demeanour telling me that she's nearly given up, but she doesn't. The fact that Guthrie told her that it would probably be a waste of expensive police time, has only increased her determination. Eventually, she drops three piles of print-outs on my desk, neatly stapled in the top corner. Her face is flushed, but I can't tell whether it is caused by tiredness or triumph. She pulls a chair up next to me and leans forward, resting her forearms on my desk as she waits, watches me flick through the papers. Two sets have three columns: Time, Licence plate number, Make of car. The third has one extra column, headed Returned.

'This is better than I expected, Jennette,' I say, hoping that she can't hear any doubt in my voice.

She scrutinises my face. 'Do you think so? So far, of all the cars passing the petrol station that night, there is only one car that can be identified.'

'Okay, but it's a start,' I say, suspecting that I am saying exactly what she is thinking.

She points at a printed image of a white van. It has a logo on the side with a picture of a fish and the company name underneath it; the address and phone number aren't clear, but Penrose has already found them on the internet. 'This van drove past the petrol station in the direction of the fishing lake at about quarter to twelve on Saturday night. However, we don't see the van going back.'

'We'd better not tell Guthrie or Maloney at this stage.' I know that I sound more like a boy scout than a mature police officer, but I think it is what she needs to hear.

I glance at my watch. 'Let's go, Jennette.'

'What? Now?'

'We both need some fresh air.'

'Right.' She sounds pleased, but doesn't show it.

'Do we have the address?'

'Of course.' She's typed it in her mobile. 'It's a company that supplies fishing gear. It's based in St Dennis. You know, where they've built the new incinerator.'

She drives with her usual impatience, bent forward towards the window screen as if she's trying to make the car go faster. A heavy-metal band on the radio is trying to burst my eardrums. She only turns the sound down when I ask if she has any further information.

Arthur Bristow is the owner of ABAS, short for Arthur Bristow's Angling Services, a company that supplies fishing equipment to shops throughout the county and to professional and casual fishermen. We find his warehouse on a small industrial estate on the outskirts of St Dennis, about 10 miles inland from Newquay. Several clay pits are scattered around the area, but none is visible from the road but if you park alongside the road and look down to the valleys, you can see the man-made lakes. The water has a bright turquoise colour that reminds me vaguely of a tropical beach.

A dirty white van is parked in front of unit 2B. The sliding door on one side is open and inside there are boxes stacked one on top of the other. A tall man is leaning against the back of the van, talking to the driver of a small refrigerated van that has prints of richly filled sandwiches and rolls on the sides. It makes me realise that I am hungry.

The tall man has a few thin strands of blond hair combed across his head. Otherwise, the bald shiny scalp is covered with scabs where he forgot to duck. His grin is wide and shows yellowing teeth and one with gold crown.

Their banter stops abruptly when we park opposite the door with a board with a picture of fish above it. It is definitely the same fish as the one printed on the side of the van caught on the petrol station camera. The sandwich van driver shouts something, winds up his window and drives to the corner of the car park, where a similar, smaller van is already parked. Two small conifer trees in purple pots on either side of the door are suffering from severe dehydration.

'I could do with something to eat,' Penrose announces, getting out of the car. 'I'm going to find out if I can get something from that sandwich company. Would you like anything?'

'A BLT if they have one.'

'I won't be long.'

She nods, already walking away. Above the garage door is a sign. 'Cornish Artisan Food'. I wonder what the actual meaning of the word 'artisan' is.

The tall man closes the van's sliding door and enters his premises, apparently oblivious to the fact that he has visitors. Two seconds later, he emerges with three boxes stacked under his chin.

'Mr Bristow?'

'Yes?' He places the boxes on the tarmac and scratches his head, finding a bunch of keys in the pocket of his jeans to unlock the rear double doors of his van.

'My name is Tregunna. Does this vehicle belong to you?'

His eyes flick up and down, sizing me up. 'Half is mine, the other half belongs to my wife.'

'The wife is better than the bank, I suppose,' I reply lightly.

His face darkens. 'I'm not so sure of that. It only works until you fall out.'

He opens the van and places the three boxes in an obscured area with more boxes. Locking the door with his keys.

'Mr Bristow, would you mind if we go into your office?'

Raising his eyebrows, he looks at me suspiciously. Thoughts cloud his face as he tries to figure out whether I am a tax man or a health inspector. 'Eh ... what are you after?

'My name is Detective Inspector Tregunna, Devon and Cornwall Police. I would like to ask you some questions.' I hold up my ID card. 'My colleague will join us in a minute.'

His head jerks towards the building opposite of his unit. 'Is it about those guys?'

'Which guys?'

'Oh. Clearly not. Never mind.'

'Which guys?'

'Sorry, my fault.' He scratches his head. Uneasy. 'I just assumed it was about the guys from number 4. A group of bike riders. You know ... or perhaps you don't know ... like in Easy Rider.'

'Easy Rider?'

'A film. Before your time perhaps.' He shrugs. 'Anyway, it was rather silly of me to think of them immediately. They're good guys. They don't do any harm. They just gather here to work on their bikes and have a beer. But ...' he gestures towards a place behind me, 'there are always people complaining, although they only see the exterior. Black leather, long beards and tattoos everywhere. You know.'

'This isn't about them.'

'Okay.' Once more he shrugs. His body language tells me that he isn't concerned about the reason for my visit. Evidently, someone with a clear conscience, unless he is a good actor.

'My office then.' He grins and I follow him inside, where the floor is covered with pieces of cardboard, piles of boxes in different shapes and sizes on top of them. It feels like a labyrinth without any escape routes.

'You're lucky,' he says over his shoulder. 'I was just going to Penzance and I wasn't planning on coming back today.'

'I have your address in ... St Blazey.'

'Not anymore.' He unlocks a door that has several dents in it. 'The wife has kicked me out.'

That explains his remark about who owns the van. For his sake, I hope his wife is not the revengeful type.

His office is a small room at the back, with no windows. Cobwebs cling to a light bulb that hangs down a plastered ceiling that has come loose at the corners. Someone has tried to prevent them falling down by hammering large nails in them randomly.

'It won't come down,' he predicts, following my gaze. 'Not today.'

He pulls a chair up from behind the desk and gestures that I should sit down. He pushes away piles of papers on his desk and perches on the edge, one leg dangling, the other secured firmly on the floor to keep his balance.

'Mr Bristow, I have reason to believe that you were at the fishing lake near St Merryn on Saturday evening.'

He almost chokes. 'Uhm ... How do you know? And why?'

I smile. 'So you were there last Saturday night?'

He looks thoughtfully before saying, 'Since you already seem to know, there is no point in denying it.'

'What time were you there?'

'Uhm ... late. About midnight.'

'And what were you doing there?'

He stares at his feet. 'Uhm ... this is rather embarrassing.'

'Please answer the question, Mr Bristow.'

He doesn't ask why. 'Well, I just told you that my wife has kicked me out. I ... I have nowhere to go. I pay the mortgage on the house. I pay for the children. There is nothing left for me to rent a place for myself. I … uhm, most nights I sleep in my van.'

'At that fishing lake?'

'Anywhere, really. Officially it's not allowed to stay in a car park overnight, so I try not to go back to the same place twice.'

'Were you there all night?'

'Uhm, well, actually, no, I wasn't.'

'What time did you arrive?'

He scratches his head. 'I can't remember. Eleven? Twelve?'

I pull the photo of Alicia Poole out of my pocket and hold it out for him to look at. 'Did you see this woman, Mr Bristow?'

He stares at it. 'No. I have never seen her before in my life.' His eyes avoid mine and he looks at the door as if he is planning to run out. 'I have seen that photo in the paper, though. She was … was she found in the lake?'

'She was. Were there any other cars in the car park when you were there, Mr Bristow?'

He opens his mouth to reply, but the door sweeps open and Penrose is on the doorstep, her face flustered. She's holding two brown sandwich packets against her chest.

'Can I have a word, sir,' she says, her expression serious.

'Not about the sandwiches, I presume? Do you need any money?'

'No sir.' Her eyes drift to Arthur Bristow's face. 'It's about the investigation, sir.'

'Okay, will you excuse us for a moment, Mr Bristow?'

'Of course,' he replies. 'How could I object?'

I follow Penrose outside and she walks to the side of the car park, to make sure Bristow can't overhear us.

'What's up, Jennette? Did you get a call from the station?'

'No sir. I think we have to be very careful with Mr Bristow, sir. It might be best to contact Maloney or Guthrie to get a warrant.'

'For?'

'Mr Bristow, sir.' She gestures over her shoulder with her thumb. 'There's a smudge on the side of the van, sir. I think this is blood.'

14

In films on television, a police officer in charge of a case might have an excuse to travel to some sunny part of the world to question someone loosely linked to the investigation. Sadly, this is not what happens in real life. Even if it were possible, I'm sure a trip to Portugal would be dismissed by Guthrie. I can understand why. In all honesty, the idea that what happened when Alicia and Denise were on holiday with their children in Portugal last summer might be important for this case is a bit far-fetched even to me. Yet, it keeps nagging at me and I know myself too well that I will only be able to let it rest once I've dealt with it.

I decide to use Maloney's office for my phone call to the Portuguese police. He has left the team with enough instructions to work through the night, while he collects his wife from Bodmin Parkway train station.

I fear I shall have to talk to someone who speaks only a few of words English with an accent that is as hard to understand as someone from a foreign call centre. I pull the door shut and perch on the corner of the desk.

Commissioner Ricardo Mateus Pimentao Pereira de Carvalho speaks fluent English, albeit slowly. I hear the rustle of paper when he goes quiet, wondering if he has found a file on Alicia's case, or is reading a newspaper as we speak.

Again, I needn't have worried. Before I was put through to him, I explained to one of his officers what I wanted so after we've exchanged some pleasantries and formalities, he gets straight to the point.

'I have here on my desk the file on Mrs Poole,' he says slowly and precisely. 'I can send it to you by email, but I'm afraid most of it is in Portuguese.'

'Did Mrs Poole understand the accusation?'

'I expect she did, yes. I wasn't there at the time. But she signed her statement so we have to presume that she knew what she was doing.'

'Okay. Can you tell me, in your own words, what happened?'

I hear him sigh. 'I will send the statement over to you anyway, so that your translators can tell you exactly, but for now … it was rather an unpleasant case, to be honest, Inspector Tregunna. An irresponsible act. But the charges have been dropped, so what can I do?'

'She wasn't charged?'

'No.'

'Why not?'

'I'll have to find that out for you, inspector. But for now, I can tell you this.' He clears his throat. 'Mrs Poole and her friend were staying in Hotel Aqua Sun, which is situated on the edge of Tofani, a town with a lot of tourist hotels.' He sounds like he disapproves of tourism altogether. 'This is a little bit ... outside the area where ... the tourists usually go out in the evening.' Another sigh. It makes me wonder how old he might be.

'That night, the 22nd of July, as usual, as is my understanding, Mrs Poole went out clubbing with her friend. First, they had their evening meal at the hotel with the children, and then they took the children to their rooms and then got themselves ready to go out.'

'You mean Briony, Mrs Poole's daughter, and Jake Shaw, the son of her friend?'

He rustles the papers. 'Exactly. It appeared that this happened most nights. The boy, who was fourteen at the time, was more or less baby-sitting the girl.'

I nod. Jake Shaw had told me the same story, but I still make a note to check this with his mother as well.

'That night was different, though, inspector. Apparently, the boy, or shall we say, the young man, was not so happy with the situation. And that particular night he refused to baby-sit the girl. His exact words, although translated now, were that he didn't like watching girlie films with her all the time, and listen to her giggling. In reality, I believe that he had his eye on a young waitress and I believe that he lied to her about his age and arranged to meet her that evening. So, what happened was that he left the girl in the room she shared with Mrs Poole and he went downstairs where he met the waitress in the garden. She realised soon enough that he was a little bit too young for her and she left him. He then went back to his own hotel room, without checking on the girl. As it happened, there was some problem with the hotel's electricity supply which caused a temporary disruption to the internet connection, which meant the girl wasn't able to watch any films. As she didn't speak Portuguese, she couldn't watch our local channels so she got bored and decided to try and find young

Jake, to persuade him to go with her to the garden where a local band and some dancers were entertaining the guests. Young Jake didn't open the door and, given his earlier, rather furtive behaviour, she assumed that he had already gone downstairs. She went after him. Unfortunately, she didn't have a key for her room, as her mother had taken it with her. She sneaked into the garden and watched the band and the dancers for a while, but then she got tired and went back up to her room to find the door was locked. She went to the reception desk, but there was only one girl working there and they couldn't understand one another.'

He stops for breath and I take the opportunity to ask what has been nagging me since he started. 'How come you know all these details? It wasn't like it was a major crime?'

'No, you are right. But this case was forwarded to me because we have a ... how do I say this ... an investigation going on about the tourists in this area and I received the files.' He pauses briefly, and then adds, 'I have a daughter of the same age as the girl and I found it unacceptable that a mother could leave a girl of that age on her own in a hotel room.' His voice rises with his frustration. 'Personally, I was of the opinion that Mrs Poole should have been charged and fined. To set an example, although these people can afford to pay the fine without it causing them any hardship.'

Sensing that this is a subject he likes to lecture on, I ask gently, 'What time did Mrs Poole come back?'

'Let me finish the story first, please, Mr Tregunna.'

'Of course. Sorry.'

'The girl went to the garden again to look for the boy, but he wasn't there. It was late. The band had gone and so had the dancers. Everyone had more or less gone to bed. By the time the girl found someone who understood that she wanted the key to their room, it was very, very late. The night receptionist was sensible enough to send a female colleague to the girl's room to check on her at regular times. Meanwhile, in Tofani, the tourists were still dancing and drinking. So were Mrs Poole and Ms Shaw. I'm not sure about this, as I have no proof, but I understand that Ms Shaw found ... someone to spend the night with. Someone from England, I believe. It was normal for the two women to order a taxi to go back to their hotel, but this time Ms Shaw was ... occupied elsewhere. Mrs Poole was alone and she couldn't find a taxi. Oh, her version of the events is a little bit different from what the taxi driver told us. She claims that he attacked her after it appeared that she didn't have enough money to pay for the ride and he suggested she paid him ... in a different way. Ahum. You know what I mean inspector? Only he claims that he didn't say that, but that, instead, he offered to take her as far as she could pay for and she could walk the rest of the way. It wasn't far. Uhm, to be quite honest, inspector, I think that he was of the opinion that Mrs Poole could do with some fresh air.'

I must have made a noise, because he interrupts himself with a hint of sarcasm in his voice. 'Yes, I agree that it wasn't very polite of him towards our ... foreign guests, but so be it. Anyway, he got another customer and he assumed Mrs Poole would try to find a more ... understanding taxi driver. But it was already getting late and even taxi drivers have to sleep, don't they? So Mrs Poole ... well, she ended up at the police station, after she was found drunk in the streets. She was then arrested.'

'What were the charges?'

'In my country, we don't like it when ... ladies ... behave like, shall we say whores, inspector. And believe me, she was so drunk she couldn't even remember the name of the hotel she was staying in.'

'You kept her in a cell?'

I glance at my watch. The conversation has already taken too much of my time and I don't think I will get very far with this. It's a dead end, unless the taxi driver followed her back to England and found her in a bar in Cornwall.

'One of the duty officers spoke to her at about five in the morning around the time, when Mrs Poole woke up. She seemed worried about her daughter, so the officer who got the impression that she was a very young girl, did the only thing she could do and phoned the girl's father, as we found his number in Mrs Poole's handbag.'

'How did you know he was the girl's father?' I ask, incredulously, making a mental note to check this with Kenneth Poole, and see his reaction.

'Well, we assumed he was and that they were on holiday as a family. We didn't know that the girl's father was still in England.' The Commissioner pauses and I can hear him rummaging through his papers again. 'Mr Bennett was not very happy with the situation.'

'Bennett? You spoke to Trevor Bennett about this?'

'Of course. He's the father.'

'But Mrs Poole was married to someone else.'

'We didn't realise that at the time, I'm afraid. We called the mobile number we found and we spoke to a Mr Bennett, not to Mr Poole.'

I scribble this down, wondering if this might be significant in the case. Probably not, unless this caused some friction between Bennett and Poole, which might have led to Alicia's death.

'What time was Mrs Poole released?'

'At about eight o'clock, according to this file. She had some coffee and she had sobered up, as you say. She made a few phone calls and was released without charges. Then she was taken back to her hotel to be reunited with the girl.'

His story has come to an end and I thank him. But he isn't finished. 'Why all these questions, inspector? This happened last summer and, as I've already told you, there were no charges, so Mrs Poole didn't have to appear in court and she was free to leave the country when she wanted.'

Prior to my talk with the Commissioner, I had already explained our case to his colleague, but he doesn't seem to have been told about it. 'Mrs Poole was murdered a couple of days ago,' I say, emphasizing every syllable. 'We are following all lines of enquiry.'

'She is dead? Oh, I'm so sorry to hear that, inspector, and, of course, I feel sorry for the poor girl. But to be honest, inspector, it doesn't surprise me. These things happen too often and besides, she acted irresponsibly with regards to her daughter, don't you think?'

15

By the time I leave Maloney's office, the sun is breaking through the clouds that have influenced my mood since I woke up. The buzz of excitement has disappeared. Everyone was hopeful and optimistic when it was confirmed that the smudges on one side of Arthur Bristow's van were blood. He was brought in earlier for questioning, or as was politely explained to him, to help us with our enquiries. Detectives are now checking his statement and making further enquiries, coming back with some answers and some more questions. Although Penrose keeps saying that finding Bristow was a combined effort of hers and mine that we found Bristow in the first place Maloney has given her all the credit. She deserved it, but all the same, it left me with an immature sense of frustration and jealousy especially as I've been given some boring errands to run for Guthrie.

The corridor smells as if a sweaty football team has just come in after a long training session. A half-empty bottle of diet coke has been left on one of the seats in the waiting area, an empty sandwich box is on the floor underneath it. A lettuce leaf drifts in the draught as the door opens in front of me.

.A woman in her late fifties comes in and leans against the desk. She has swollen feet in sandals with wide straps. The straps are tight and flesh comes up like padded fabric. One hand is clutching the lead of a small dog: a pale brown creature with long floppy hair and a wet nose sticking out from beneath it, eyes barely visible.

'I would like to speak to a superior officer.'

The desk officer frowns. 'Sorry, madam, there isn't anyone available at the moment.'

It's the same new recruit again, Annie or Ally. She's on a fast-track course and has too little experience for the job. The only problem is that she thinks she knows it all.

'But you're the police. You are supposed to be here day and night.'

The desk officer manages a sickly smile. 'We are here, madam. I'm talking to you, aren't I?'

'There's no need to be rude, young lady.'

'I'm not …'

'Yes you are.' The woman holds up her head with a touch of arrogance. Two pinks spots on her cheeks, she half-turns, inwardly debating whether to leave and go home. Then she turns back towards the desk. 'Who is your superior?'

In fairness, the desk officer responds calmly. 'That'll be SpongeRob. But he is not here at the moment. In fact, He's enjoying life on some exotic island with his wife.'

'I can see he's not here,' the woman sneers, not bothering to say something about the nickname Rob was rightfully given when someone, possibly referring to the animated TV-series Sponge-Bob, joked that he inhabited such a wealth of information that it seemed as if he absorbed everything like a sponge.

Irritation is rising on both sides of the desk. The dog is the only one unperturbed, wandering round the hall, sniffing at every square centimetre as if he's determined to examine everything.

'Can I help?' I step forward to face the woman, meeting a pair of eyes full of contempt. Annie, or Ally, isn't pleased by the intervention; perhaps she feels that I'm undermining her position.

My bad start with her began even before SpongeRob had introduced us and I recognised her voice. I had overheard her earlier that day in a conversation with a colleague who had been explaining to her who to contact and forward messages to for different eventualities. I happened to walk past when I heard my name montioned

'... and Andy Tregunna, you can forward cases like this to Andy.'

'Tregunna?' she chipped in. 'Oh! I've heard of him. Is he the one with the poo bag?'

When SpongeRob introduced us a few hours later, I could only acknowledge her with a cold nod. I didn't shake her hand or welcome her to her new job.

Now, she shrugs and offers another version of her sugar sweet smiles that aren't reflected in her eyes.

'Of course, be my guest,' she says with enough sarcasm to make me wonder which part of the conversation I missed. Before I can ask, a mobile phone on the desk bleeps. As I turn towards the woman, I catch the screen of the desk officer's mobile in the corner of my eyes. Colours of a game flash. Her limited playing time must be running out. It doesn't seem to matter anymore that she's supposed to be working. It isn't even allowed nowadays to say something about it. Not even jokingly.

'Are you a policeman?' The woman turns to me almost aggressively.

'I am. Detective Inspector Tregunna.'

With one hand brushing aside a brownish-grey curl from her face, she blinks slowly. 'You're not wearing a uniform.'

The words come out like an accusation. A former colleague always used to snigger when someone said that to him jokingly replying: 'I'm too important to wear a uniform' or 'that's because I'm currently working as an undercover agent.' The humour will be lost on Annie or Ally and on the woman.

'No, but how can I help you anyway.'

She stretches her back. 'I want to report someone.'

'That sounds serious,' I reply, suppressing a sigh and wondering why I let myself in for this.

I want to disappear quickly back to the incident room and hear about the latest developments in the case. Instead, now I'm stuck in the entrance hall, knowing that there are so many more important things to deal with than listen to a middle-aged woman who is probably holding a grudge against someone.

I force a smile. 'Shall we go to an interview room?'

A pair of sharp blue eyes shoots in my direction. Uncertain if I'm joking or not. A red flush falls across her face.

'I've already made some notes for you, sir.' Unexpectedly, Annie or Ally is being helpful, presumably because I'm gesturing toward the open door of interview room and relieving her of the woman and she can then turn back to her game.

As if on cue, her mobile phone bleeps again. She frowns at the screen and the light reflects back on her glasses. She turns it off and, with a hint of embarrassment, she shoves a piece of paper in my direction. Mrs Emma Davis. Number 63 Hockney Crescent.

'Mrs Davis, will you come with me, please?'

'Are we going into that room?' Mrs Davis follows me in the interview room. The desk officer's phone bleeps again. Otherwise, there is silence, like the world is holding its breath.

'Do you take criminals in here?' she asks with excitement in her voice.

'Sometimes.'

'Oh. Okay.' Duly impressed, she moves swiftly to one side of the table. The dog sniffs the air. His claws slide on the slippery lino floor as he runs to keep up with her.

'I want to report someone,' she says firmly.

'Oh.'

Leaning forward, she lowers her voice and adds, 'Someone who spies on naked people.'

The dog obediently sits next to her feet. Well trained. Well behaved. Closing the door, I shut out the noise of a deep chuckle from the desk officer which seems to come from deep in her throat.

'I guess it is difficult these days to find the right people for the job,' Mrs Davis observes, her tone so innocent that I'm not sure if she means people in general or the new desk officer.

'I think that applies to most jobs,' I say neutrally.

She leans back and her shoulders relax. 'I wouldn't normally come to the police with things like this, inspector. Live and let live, that's my motto. We all have our own funny ways and we all make silly mistakes. I wouldn't like to get someone into trouble if there is a slight possibility that there might be a totally innocent explanation.'

I put my elbows on the table between us, and stare at her, waiting, rather than asking what on earth she is talking about. The feeling that I have been lured into this by the new desk officer creeps up on me.

'I wouldn't have come here, inspector, but then I realised that it was on the same night. And at the same place.' She stops, uncertain about the lack of any response.

'The same night?'

'That's right,' she continues. Encouraged. 'It was that night when that poor woman was killed. I've read about it in the paper.'

'Yes.' I shift on my seat, my impatience gone along with the feeling that I have been lured into this by the new desk officer.

'Perhaps you can start from the beginning, Mrs Davies?'

16

There are several stories explaining how Bedruthan Steps got its name. One story refers to one of two cliff staircases used by miners to get to the mine workings. As evidence of mining has been found in the area, this seems the most likely explanation. However, romantics would rather believe that the name was taken from a mythological giant called 'Bedruthan' who used the granite rocks on the beach at high tide as stepping stones to go from one headland to the other.

The cold stings my face and my fingers as I get out of my car. The air is crisp, like a typical frosty winter's day. Smoke rises from the chimney of a single-storey building on the edge of the car park; it currently houses a gift shop and tearoom.

Looking inland, the sky has darkened and I can see a shower hitting the distinctive shapes of the clay hills in the distance. I feel a few spots of rain, but the clouds overhead are breaking, their shadows chasing each other across the barren fields above the cliffs and out to sea. Towards the horizon, the sky is almost completely clear, with rays of sunlight shimmering over the water and creating bright halos around the clouds that look like cotton wool balls.

A young couple discovered the body of a man lying on a bed of rocks below the cliffs. As it was initially thought that he was alive, a coastguard helicopter was called out. Apparently, the man had been there since the previous tide, but miraculously he wasn't washed into the sea because he was lying on a tiny stretch of rocky beach that remains dry when the tide is at its lowest point and there is no wind to whip up the waves. At least that is how the events are described to me by the car park attendant, after he has studied my ID card, suspecting that I'm trying to get free parking in the National Trust car park.

Tall and willowy, he seems to have the perfect shape for a job where he's constantly exposed to all types of weather. His hair is cut short and his ears are red from the cold. One ear has a small gold ring in the lobe, and a police radio is attached to his belt.

'Were you here when the body was found?' I ask.

'No. I hadn't arrived yet.' His face tells me he regrets having missed the excitement. 'I arrived just before the ambulance came.'

I look around. The National Trust gift shop has its door open, but the windows still have the blinds down. A woman dressed in dark green is hoisting the black-and-white Cornish flag in the pole beside the building. On this cold and breezy day, everything comes to life slowly. Except for the man whose life ended on a beach below the steep cliffs. For the sake of his family, I hope he didn't jump; it leaves too many unanswered questions and feelings of guilt too hard to deal with.

'Is the car park closed at night?'

The car park attendant looks thoughtful and then reaches into his little cabin and plants a hat on his head, not noticing it is inside out. A label with washing instructions flutters in the wind.

'No. There is an honesty box at the entrance of the cliff path,' the park warden explains.

There are five cars parked; his is on the verge behind his cabin. 'Have those cars just arrived?'

He scratches his head where the label flutters. 'The blue one belongs to the lady who runs the gift shop, the white belongs to the couple who found the man on the beach, the other three belong to the people who work in the tearoom.'

'Are you sure?'

He shrugs. 'I'm here every day. I keep an eye out.' His life, his job in a nutshell.

'Okay, thanks. Are you here all day?'

He shrugs stoically. 'Till five.'

'Where is the ambulance?'

He points. Beside the tearoom is a rusty gate that opens to give access to a track that has a low stone wall on one side. The field is barren, dark brown clay dug up by a tractor to make deep trenches planted with what look like cabbage plants. I remember the distinctive smell hanging in the air when the cabbages are picked, the annoyance of drivers when they get stuck behind the tractors pulling the heavily loaded trailers.

The field slopes down towards the cliff edge and at the bottom the top half of an ambulance is just visible above the wall. Trying to avoid the biggest chunks of clay, I walk alongside the wall and wish it was higher to give more shelter from the wind. Wishing I'd brought a woollen hat and some gloves, the cold northerly wind bites into my skin. I bury my hands in the pockets of my coat.

By the ambulance are two paramedics in green overalls and yellow fluorescent vests. The passenger door is open and one of them half leans inside. The other one has spotted me and comes forward, arms stretched in front of him as if he is diverting traffic and trying to stop me.

'Police. I'm Andy Tregunna.' It's too cold to take my hands out of my pockets and dig for my ID card.

'Oh. Hi. I'm Dan.' He smells vaguely antiseptic and dried blood. In his late twenties, he has a boyish smile to cover a natural shyness. 'On your own? No partner?'

'We're short-staffed.'

'Sounds familiar.' He grins sympathetically. 'I was just on my way to the tearoom. Can I get you some tea? Or coffee?'

'Coffee will be much appreciated.'

He nods and almost runs, looking forward to the warm shelter of the tearoom and the smell of freshly baked cakes.

His colleague doesn't appear to be affected by the cold. He is in his early thirties, with an open face, freckles on his sun-tanned skin and hair bleached blond by the sun and sea. His name is also Dan, but to avoid confusion, he says I can call him Matt. He is eating the remains of a sandwich, picking fallen lettuce and grated cheese off his chest. Straightening up, he pulls his ear and looks at me expectantly.

I hold up my ID. He reads my name.

'Ah, Tregunna! A true Cornishman!' he says, crumpling up the sandwich packet, chucking it on top of his closed paramedics case and wiping his hands on his thighs, meanwhile looking over my shoulder as if he's expecting to see a dozen of my colleagues pop up from behind the low wall that surrounds the field.

He jerks his head towards the stretcher trolley with the shape of a body in a grey zipper bag strapped to it. The corners of the white sheet beneath the body bag are flapping in the wind. Crows and seagulls circle and squawk above us, every now and then swooping down to peck at the bare soil.

'We're waiting until we're told we can take him away. Nothing we can do for the poor sod.' Matt shakes his head. 'Dead for a good few hours.'

'Where was he found?'

He shrugs. 'The heli lifted him up from the beach an hour ago. They left him with us because they were called out to an emergency in Polzeath. Some surfers got caught in a rip tide. Two of them are missing.'

I can't help shivering. I never really understand the desire to go surfing, especially in the cold and wind and when the temperature of the water is far too low for my comfort.

'Are you alone?' It almost sounds like an accusation. 'We were told to wait for forensics.'

'I'd like to see the body.'

'Of course.' Annoyance clouds his face.

'We didn't get much information,' I say by way of apology, not telling him that a red-faced Maloney had only shrugged with impatience when the call came in, and declared that he was too busy with the murder case to deal with a presumed suicide.

Matt leans against the side of the ambulance, finding shelter from the wind. He shakes his head and blows in his hands.

'I don't think it was suicide,' he says matter-of-factly.

'I assumed he jumped.'

So close to the edge of the cliffs, I can hear the constant rhythm of the waves crashing against the rocks nearly fifty feet below us. In the distance is the outline of a containership, just discernible on the horizon.

'Nope.' He reaches in the ambulance and retrieves a clear plastic bag from the passenger seat. Inside it is a blood drenched shirt. 'The guys from the heli took it off him because they tried to save him.'

'Save him? Was he still alive?'

He sighs. 'He was found on the beach by that young couple. They're in the tearoom, waiting for police to take their statement. As soon as they found him, the girl climbed up the steps from the beach and called 999. No signal down there. Some time later, the coastguard heli arrived.'

He shakes his head and adjusts his crotch again, looking thoughtfully. 'At that point, all they knew was that an injured man was found on the beach. He was bleeding, but he was breathing. They tried to stabilise him, but he'd lost too much blood. He was unconscious when they hoisted him up here. Meanwhile, they'd received a call about the emergency in Polzeath. The two missing surfers. By that time, we were in the area and we were sent here to take over. Unfortunately, he was dead when we arrived.'

'Did he say anything?'

'You'll have to ask the couple who found him. As I said, they're in the tearoom.'

'Have you found a suicide note?'

'I don't know anything about a note.'

'Car keys?

'I don't know. 'Listen, Tregunna, your questions are pointless, because I know as little as you do. All I can say to you that this isn't a case of suicide.'

'He didn't jump?' I ask, incredulously.

He shakes his head. 'Me and Dan have been here a while. We've had a look around and we've more or less worked out what happened to him.' He points over his shoulder. 'There's blood over there. I reckon he was stabbed there and was then pushed over the edge. Or he stumbled and fell, but I'd say the person who stabbed him, chose an easy way to finish him.'

'I can't understand how he survived a fall from that height.'

'You 'will see that something broke his fall. There is a bit of a plateau down there and he got stuck in some gorse or what have you. Then, by the look of the state of his hands and knees, I'd say he tried to cling on and perhaps he tried to scramble back up, but he slipped. From there, half of the rock is a bit like a slide, so from there he didn't actually fall. Only the last two or three meters, I think.'

'You obviously thought this through,' I say, not able to hide my sarcasm.

'As I said, me and Dan have had plenty of time to examine the place.' Continuing, he grins wryly. 'Forensics will have a job getting down there. Don't say I haven't warned you. That bit looks alright, but it is dangerous. I hope you won't need to call us again if one of your men is too reckless.'

I don't respond to his mockery. 'You didn't realise that you were destroying forensic evidence?'

'At that point he was already dead. It was only when Dan read the notes from the coastguard, that we realised it wasn't a case of a man jumping or falling from the cliffs.' He shrugs by way of apology. 'We only saw the stab wound at the side of his body when we searched for any ID.'

'Did you find any?'

'Nothing.'

'Anything in his pockets?'

'The couple who found him on the beach, also found a wallet lying beside him. They thought it must have fallen out of his pocket.' He retrieves a second plastic evidence bag from the passenger seat. 'Two ten pound notes, a till receipt from a superstore in Newquay, and one from another in Wadebridge. No bank or business cards.'

'Mobile phone?'

'I haven't found one.' He looks in the direction of the sea, clearly thinking that there isn't much chance that we'll find a mobile phone and, if we do, we won't get it working.'

'Car keys?'

'In his trouser pocket. But there was no car in the car park when the couple got here.'

'I'll check that with them later.'

'Of course.'

'Can I see him?'

'Be my guest.'

He opens the zipper of the body bag and I stare at a round puffy face. He is in his forties, shorter than the average man, and heavier also. His hair is dark and wet, stuck to his skull. His hands are dirty, with brown mud under his nails, dried blood in the corner of his mouth. There is something vaguely familiar about him, but I can't remember if and where I might have seen him.

'You know him?' Matt has noticed my hesitation.

'Not that I can remember.'

He looks over his shoulder and a wide grin appears on his face. 'Perfect, Dan,' he takes a white mug from his colleague. 'Brought one for the inspector?'

'Thanks,' I say, peering at the milky coffee as though I'm trying to make the milk disappear.

'Okay.' I retrieve my phone. 'I'll make the necessary phone calls.'

He shakes his head as if he's amazed by my ignorance. 'No reception here, I'm afraid. I've tried too. You'd better use the phone in the café. The shop isn't open yet, but there's a landline in the tearoom.'

People are arriving at the car park. I see the attendant collecting money from a couple with two children on the back seat. His hands are so cold that he has difficulty tearing a pink receipt from his ticket book. He slips it under the windscreen wiper and gives the driver a soldier's salute, disappearing into his cabin as they drive away to park closest to the building.

Some of the visitors are watching us from a distance trying to get a glimpse of what has happened. They're more interested in what they can tell their friends than the tragedy of a man's death. But it is too cold to hang about so they disappear into the tearoom. The odd brave couple walk the short distance the coastal path to take some photos from there. A few others don't even seem to notice that an ambulance is parked at the edge of a field with young cabbage plants.

'Where can I find the couple who found him?'

'In the tearoom.' Matt pulls his ear again. 'I've given the girl something to relax. She is shocked by the discovery.'

With the empty mugs in my hand, I walk over to the old, low building which houses the tearoom. There is a small garden looking out over the sea, sheltered by the building and an overgrown wall. The door is ajar. I hear soft music and laughter and the smell of home-made food reaches out as I enter the building.

'You're police,' the woman behind the counter declares as if she has to convince me. She has frizzy hair the colour of beetroot mixed with chestnut brown. A badge on her breast pocket says her name is Lyn.

'Hi, I'm Lyn,' she says cheerfully, then realises the reason why I'm here and her face turns sad. 'Sorry. It must be horrible to find someone like that.'

'Can I use your phone, Lyn?'

'Of course, this way.'

I use a small office behind the kitchen to call the forensic team and return to Lyn who has poured me another cup of milky coffee. She has such a warm and sympathetic smile that I can't ask her for black coffee.

'Where can I find ...?'

'In the back,' she waves a hand. 'The girl is in quite a state.'

As expected, there is little information to gather from the young couple who were unfortunate enough to go down the 149 steps to find the body on the beach. Dermot and Lizzy are in their early twenties, having their first holiday together. I hope the horrible experience won't cloud their relationship. Looking at the girl, seeing a nervous twitch to her left eye, I foresee that she will have a hard time dealing with this. Dermot seems a bit tougher, but I can already see in his eyes that he doesn't know how to comfort her. She sniffs and blows her nose repeatedly in a paper napkin. Lyn has supplied them with enough napkins for the next couple of days. I ask them if they noticed whether the man on the beach was still alive when they found him. They exchange looks. Lizzy starts sobbing and hides her face in a napkin, Dermot answers. 'He tried to say something, but we couldn't understand him.'

'Did he speak a foreign language?'

'No ... I don't know. It was just ... there was blood in his nose and his mouth and ... I thought at one point that he said 'blood', but that was all.'

Lizzy sobs louder and Dermot takes her in his arms and strokes her head. I take their details and those of all the people in the tearoom and the gift shop, as well as the car park attendant who has come in for a coffee and, more likely, to get any more information about the event that will no doubt occupy his thoughts for the next few days.

Back in the tearoom's office, I use the phone again, this time to call the police station. Maloney is far from pleased when I tell him about the stab wound, which means that we have a second murder on our hands.

'Do we know the deceased's name?'

'Nothing, so far.'

He mutters under his breath. 'Right, Guthrie isn't here yet. You act as SIO, Tregunna, until further notice.'

I stare out of a window that has four small panes of glass and looks out over the cliff tops and the sea. A blue and white fishing vessel dances up and down on the waves, followed by at least a dozen seagulls. I wonder if Guthrie will let me lead this case. Clearly, Maloney has enough on his plate with Alicia Poole's murder.

I swallow and let my thoughts rewind and play them again. All of a sudden, I know where I have seen the man who is now lying in a body bag in an ambulance waiting to take him to the morgue in Truro after the forensic team release him. It is Torrington, the sales assistant in the petrol station near the fishing lake.

bump into Guthrie in the corridor. He is holding a takeaway coffee in one hand, tucking a bundle of newspapers under his other arm. I'm probably doing him a disservice but it seems to me that he is more interested in what the papers have written about him and his role in finding the murderer of Alicia Poole than he is in hearing how the detectives are getting on with the case. He rarely comes to the briefings to hear about our progress, our successes and disappointments. But in a way it is also a relief not to see him there with his piercing eyes as he tries to find some-one to blame. He likes to be in the limelight and credited for the success stories in the media. His handsome face, his hair combed to perfection, his uniform meticulously clean, everything perfect in front of the cameras.

'We've scheduled a meeting with the press in less than an hour,' he tells me. 'Mr Poole is going to join us to make an appeal to the public. He's offering a reward, and I mean a significant reward, and hopefully someone will come forward with infor-mation that will lead us to the murderer of his wife.'

'What about the Torrington murder?'

He ignores the question, pretends he didn't hear me.

'Ken insists,' he says, using Kenneth Poole's first name cas-ually as if to make me believe that they are best friends.

I clear my throat. 'I think that the two cases are connected.'

He shakes his head. 'As I said, it'll have to wait. Talk to Maloney about it after the press conference.'

I step back as he pushes past me, heading for his office, no doubt to prepare for the conference - comb his hair, straighten his tie, brush the dandruff from his shoulders. I shrug and turn away from him, knowing full well that I could have pressed harder to make him listen to me. Stupid. I'll regret it later if I've bitten off my nose to spite my face, but I cherish the little triumph that I know something that he really ought to know too.

I walk past Maloney who is leaning against the wall. He looks bored, listening to someone on the phone. For some reason, his expression suggests that he is speaking to his wife. Perhaps she has returned to Weymouth in another attempt to clear the air between her parents. Judging by his expression, I doubt whether he will be interested in my news either. Nevertheless, he turns and faces me, pressing the phone to his breast.

'Have you got a minute, Tregunna?'

I nod and wait until he finishes his call, which appears to be with his daughter. Sixteen years old and very opinionated about the behaviour of her grandparents, her grandmother in particular. She's also of the opinion that her father at fault as well.

He pulls a face as he slides his mobile phone back in his pocket and gestures to me to follow him to the incident room. 'I gather you have a theory about Alicia Poole and the man they found at Bedruthan Steps,' he says over his shoulder.

'Guthrie thinks it's better to treat both cases separately.'

He puts his hands in his trouser pockets, clutching something with his left hand. 'But you think otherwise?'

'I believe that the cases are linked.'

He frowns doubtfully. 'Alicia Poole was the wife of a businessman. Torrington worked at a petrol station. She was 34, he was 45. What can they possibly have in common?'

I shrug. 'They were both stabbed. In a rural area. No CCTV, no useful witnesses. He must know the area pretty well.'

'Do you have any hard evidence?'

'No. Not yet. But it is too much of a coincidence to keep these as two separate cases.'

'What about the MO? Alicia Poole was found naked, clothes gone. Torrington was pushed over the edge of a cliff. He was fully dressed.'

'I am not talking about a serial killer who chooses the same kind of victims,' I say patiently, 'All I'm saying is that I think there must be a link between the two murders.'

'Okay.' He runs his hand through his hair, looking exhausted. 'Let's talk this through, then, shall we?'

In the incident room, DS Ollie Reed is adding information to the white board. He sticks a photo of Carthew Farm onto the board and steps back as though he's studying a work of art.

Maloney points at the photo of the farm building, clearly not understanding.

'So. Andy, convince me.' He sounds like he needs to be brought up to date again. Perhaps he does. His interest in the case may be affected by his current problems at home because, although the divorce of his parents-in-law doesn't involve him directly, it must put a strain on his marriage.

The white board is filled with photos and copies of statements. Photos of Alicia's closest relatives are lined up on the left-hand side. Kenneth Poole is beside her, Trevor Bennett is just above him with his wife Maureen next to him. There is a blurred photo of Briony, taken from her Facebook page. Denise Shaw stares at me from a coloured photo, on her red lips a smile as though she's about to wink at me. There are several enlarged photos of the man Alicia Poole left Barrie's Bar with on Saturday night. There's a blank piece of paper with a big black question mark which relates to the man Denise saw talking to her friend in the Central Bar. There's a photo of Carthew Farm with the names of the family, and photos of Arthur Bristow, Josh Warren and Eddie Rowse. Warren and Rowse already had their alibi substantiated by several of their friends and Bristow is no longer a suspect after his friend confirmed that he'd picked him up to have a drink at his home in St Columb, where Bristow stayed the night until his friend drove him back to his van on Sunday morning.

I pick up a blue marker pen and add Wilbur Torrington's name on an empty spot in the middle. 'Torrington worked in the petrol station a stone's throw from the Swan Lake.' I add arrows. '

'Is that all?'

'I have no proof yet.' I shake my head. 'His body was found on the beach, below the cliffs. We haven't seen the official post-mortem report or the forensic report, but I talked to the paramedics and I had a look at he scene myself. He had injuries from his fall, but there was some blood on top of the cliffs, which suggests that he was stabbed there. He didn't die instantly and my guess is that his killer pushed him over the edge to finish the job. However, at that particular point, he didn't fall down straight away. He more or less slid down the slope and only fell the last few meters, which was why he was still alive when he was found.' I pause and look at his face. 'Of course this has to be confirmed by the official reports.'

'The motive?'

'I haven't got that far yet.'

'Tregunna, I have to agree with DCI Guthrie that, at this moment ...'

I interrupt him. 'Torrington was more than shocked when I came to the petrol station to collect the CCTV tapes after Alicia's murder. Perhaps he knew Alicia Poole. Don't forget that she went out in Newquay every now and then. He lived in Newquay. He may have met her in one of the bars. Maybe he fancied her. After all, she was a beautiful woman.'

'I still can't see why ...'

I shake my head. 'Or perhaps he saw something that night. Don't forget that he was working in the area until eleven. If he had gone home to Newquay straight away he would have been going in the opposite direction to Alicia. And as the lake is beyond the petrol station on the way to Padstow, he can't have passed the fishing lake. But how much do we know about his whereabouts that night?'

I feel like I'm a key witness in a court case where I have to defend myself and I don't even know what the charges are.

Maloney turns to me, a flicker of doubt on his face. 'Does he appear on the camera tapes?'

'I'll ask Penrose to go through the camera tapes again to find out if he was in the same clubs as Alicia that night. Otherwise, we'll have to look at all the tapes again now that we know the colour and make of Torrington's car.'

He shakes his head. 'Tregunna, I still think...'

'It is also possible that he knew her killer.'

'Or Torrington killed Alicia Poole and someone else killed him?'

'Far-fetched, I'd say, but it is also a possibility.' I press my index finger under Torrington's name on the board. 'Philip, these two murders must be linked.'

He sighs as though he's dealing with an unwilling child. 'So what do you suggest?'

I hesitate. 'There is something else,' I say slowly, uncertain, as this is just a hunch. 'A woman came forward with a rather strange story but, somehow, I believe this is significant.'

'What is?' He is getting annoyed and impatient. He glances at his watch and is about to say that it is almost time for him to collect his papers and go to the press room.

I pick up a marker and write another name on the board.

'Emma Davies,' he reads, tutting his lips. 'Who is that?'

'She came forward with a story that didn't make sense to me at the time, but looking at things now ... it seems crazy but ... it might be something.'

'You've got two minutes.'

'Mrs Davies returned from a family visit with her husband. He drove. When they came down the hill from St Merryn, on the bend, there is a small patch of grass on the verge. Not large enough for a car to park, but nevertheless, a car was parked there. Mr Davies cursed, as the car had no lights on and he hadn't expected it to be there. In their headlights, they could see that there was someone in the car. At the wheel. Mrs Davies peered at the car, to try to indicate to the driver that he should find a less dangerous parking place. But he wasn't looking at her. He was looking through a pair of binoculars.'

'And the significance is?'

'Mrs Carthew, from the farm halfway up the hill beyond the lake, claims that she saw white swans. Making love, she said.'

'Is that the woman who took you for her son?'

'Uhm … yes.'

'So what makes you think that we should believe this woman? I mean, swans, making love, in the middle of the night? What medication is she on? Was she sleepwalking or hallucinating?'

'I think they weren't swans she saw, Philip,' I say slowly. 'I think she saw people. A man and a woman, perhaps a woman and two men, one of which might be our killer.'

'She mistook a man and a woman for mating swans?'

'There was a moon that night. Alicia might have been naked at that point. Her skin must have seemed white in the moonlight. Mrs Carthew got confused.'

'She's definitely confused, Tregunna.' Maloney shakes his head, thinking how stupid I am.

'And then who was the guy with the binoculars?'

'I have checked it, Philip. There are marks on the grass verge. From there, you can see the car park at the fishing lake.'

'Yes, but who is he?'

'That's not the point, Philip. What I'm trying to say is that he was there for a reason. He didn't stop for nothing. And his eyesight must have been better than Mrs Carthew's. She mistook people for swans, but the driver of that car knew better. He was playing Peeping Tom with his binoculars.'

'What is … ?'

'My point is, Philip, that, the couple who Mrs Carthew and the driver saw, I think at least the woman must have been naked.'

'Alicia Poole?'

'I think that is highly likely.'

'Naked? Do you know how cold it is at night?'

I shrug. I have no answer to that.

'Uhm … suppose your theory, however absurd, is true, then what has that got to do with Torrington? What does the husband of this woman say? Has he confirmed what she said?'

'He didn't look at the car.'

'Pity. Do we have details of the car?'

'No. It was all too fast for Mrs Davies. All she could tell me was that it was a smallish car, and a colour that didn't stand out, as she would remember otherwise. And she didn't see the licence plate either.'

'A perfect witness.' He grins cynically. 'Does this answer my question about Torrington?'

I shrug, well aware that my story is like a bad detective story. 'I think Torrington was that driver with the binoculars. He owns a silver grey Toyota. That fits with Mrs Davies' description. He might have seen the killer's face. Or he knew him already and recognised him. Maybe he tried to blackmail him, but he misjudged the situation and got himself killed.'

Maloney is quiet for a few moments. 'Alright. I don't really see why you think it may be worth investigating, but I know that, sometimes, you do have a good hunch. It wouldn't necessarily follow it up as a possible link, but I know you. You won't let this go until you get to the bottom of it.'

He looks at his watch again. 'Let's leave this for now, shall we? I've got that press conference in a few minutes.' A sardonic smile passes over his face. 'Can you imagine the reaction if I were to sit in front of the cameras and reporters and say what people will say that we have a witness who said she saw white swans making love, but who were, in fact, our victim and her killer?'

18

The press conference has overloaded us with phone calls and new information that needs to be followed up and checked. Most of it turns out to be useless but we can't dismiss any of it. The detectives are working overtime and, by the look on his face it is clear that Guthrie is worrying about his budgets. With two murder cases on our hands, there are few resources for anything else.

Consequently, with some degree of reluctance, Guthrie tells me that I am in charge of a small team investigating Wilbur Torrington's death, but emphasises that the death of Alicia Poole remains a priority.

'Why?' I ask him angrily. 'Torrington deserves as much attention as Mrs Kenneth Poole.'

He shakes his head. 'You've heard me, Tregunna.'

I press on stubbornly. 'I also believe that these two murders are linked.'

He smirks. 'Philip told me about the white swans making love in the moonlight.'

I open my mouth to explain but seeing his blank expression, I bite my tongue. Sometimes it's better to keep quiet. We stare at each other like two predators fixed on our prey. Whether he is aware of this battle of wills or not, he speaks first, shrugging. 'I suppose I can't stop you pursuing your theory.'

But this doesn't feel like a victory.

Half an hour later I drive to Wilbur Torrington's last known address. Trewinnick Crescent is one of several rows of one-storey detached bungalows, scattered in a parkland area like matchsticks fallen from the shaking hands of a chain-smoker. With weathered slate roofs, gutters sprouting green moss and brown window frames, they look as though they need an urgent make-over. Evidently, someone has made a start in modernising them, but as far as I can see, they have got no further than replacing the front doors with white, glazed PVC doors which stand out against the dirty pebbledash on the walls. The residents of the estate represent a cross-section of much of modern day society: there are single mothers with one or two small children, young couples saving for their first step onto the housing ladder, -

if the bonus-focused bank managers will ever give them the opportunity – elderly retired couples, and refugees from countries where normal life seems to have become impossible. Safety is normality for some, a luxury for others.

Jeremy Torrington lives at the end of a row facing a paved area with three benches arranged in a triangle and, at one corner, a bin displaying a picture of a dog pooing. A very large, tall man hovers on the pavement. His dog is the size of his hand. He sees me looking at him and walks away.

Most of the small front gardens have been transformed into private parking spaces. I park on the kerb and walk up to Torrington's front door. I press the doorbell but I can't hear it ringing. A frail old lady appears in the doorway of the house next door. She has thinning white hair and her bottom lip can't stop trembling. In her hands, misshapen by rheumatic arthritis, she clings onto a walking stick with one hand and a tea towel with the other.

'The bell is not working,' she says with a brittle, shaky voice. 'Are you here for Mr Torrington?' Not waiting for an answer, she continues, 'Joy asked me to keep an eye on things, in case you arrived early.' She narrows her eyes. 'Although I'm certain that she said that you were coming tomorrow.'

'Does Mr Torrington live here?'

'Yes he does.' She pauses. Her watery eyes switch from my face to my car and back. 'Are you not from the care home?'

'No. My name is Andy Tregunna, Mrs ...?' I hesitate, contemplating whether to show her my ID.

'Rendle. Betsie Rendle.'.

'I want to have a word with Jeremy Torrington. Do you know if he's at home?'

She nods slowly. 'Oh, he's at home alright, but he is asleep. Joy had to go somewhere, but she'll be back soon. She asked me to keep an eye on the house. The doors and windows are all locked, but you never know.'

'Mrs Rendle, I'm not sure ...'

'She's given him a sleeping pill, Joy.' Mrs Rendle continues. 'I expect she'll be back in about half an hour. Jeremy will be awake by that time.' She cocks her head, her eyes bright and intelligent 'Is it important?'

I nod.

'In that case, you might as well come in and wait here. Joy always lets me know when she's back.'

'And Joy is?'

'Jeremy's daughter, of course. She and Wilbur take it in turns to look after their father.' She shakes her head as if she's amazed by my ignorance. 'He has Alzheimer's. A rather desperate situation for the family. That's why I thought you were from the care home. They're supposed to come and see how … bad he is. But do come in. I'll make you a cup of tea while you wait.'

I follow into a sitting room and feel the gloom of old age descend on me like an invisible veil. The room is dark, furnished in the sixties. Nothing has changed since then. Barely used. The carpet, furniture and walls have different flowery patterns, making the room feel claustrophobic. The curtains have bleached vertical lines where the fabric has been exposed to the sun. They're half drawn to keep out the light. Or intrusive eyes.

Emerging from the kitchen, she pushes a blue trolley in front of her. Teaspoons rattle against the crockery as she negotiates the threshold. On top is a tray with china cups and saucers, a glass jug half filled with milk. In a basket beneath, beside a teapot covered in a flowery tea cosy, is an open biscuit tin with a flower print on the sides, loaded with muffins in pink paper cases. Enough to feed an army.

Slightly out of breath, she places the trolley between us. Her hands shake as she places the tray on a small side table. Her legs wobble as she slowly sits down and presses a button on the remote control of an electric reclining chair. It has a pocket on each side, in which is a flowery case for glasses and a folded newspaper. Today's. The chair hums until she is in a comfortable position with her feet dangling above the floor.

I clear my throat. It is twenty minutes after I rang the bell. 'Mrs Rendle …'

'The tea has to brew another few minutes, but please help yourself to a muffin. Apple and cinnamon. My husband's favourites. They're home made.'

'Thank you.'

'If you're not from the care home, and clearly you aren't, then why are you here, Mr Tregunna?'

'I'm a policeman, Mrs Rendle. I need to speak to Mr Torrington.'

'I see.' A lively sparkle brightens her dull eyes but she doesn't seem to be curious or nosy.

I lean towards the muffins; I might as well have one while I wait for Torrington's daughter.

'My husband died fifteen years ago,' Mrs Rendle says, out of the blue.

I sigh. The home baking comes with loss.

'He walked to our car which was parked in front of our house. He waved a kiss to me, like he always did in the morning, before he went to work. He climbed in the car, started the engine, but he never drove away. My neighbour called me ten minutes later. The car was still running and my husband was slumped behind the wheel. The doctor said it was so sudden that he didn't think my husband felt it coming.'

'I'm sorry.'

'As you can understand, inspector, it was a terrible shock. But my neighbours were brilliant. Jeremy and Rose were rocks for me. Somehow, I pulled through, but I couldn't have done it without them.' She pauses briefly. 'We never had children.'

A life in a nutshell.

'How long have you lived here, Mrs Rendle?'

'Over fifty years. We came here when these houses were built. Jeremy and Rose came much later when Wilbur and Joy were both already married.'

'Wilbur was married?' I interrupt.

'Well, yes, that's what Rose told us, but … it's funny that you should query that, inspector, because I remember thinking that it was odd that she was always showing me Joy's wedding photos, but I barely saw any of Wilbur's. Anyway, I don't think his marriage was a success because he came back to live with his parents again. That was on the same date, exactly two years before Rose died.' Her face contorts as she remembers. 'She went out shopping and never came back.'

'She disappeared?'

'O no! It was a horrible accident. A lorry driver reversed in one of those narrow streets in the centre of Truro. He didn't see her in his mirrors. She was … crushed between his truck and a wall.'

She stops for breath, shivering and fumbling with her hands.

'It was a horrible accident. Jeremy and Rose were very close and Wilbur was a great support to his father after his mother died. I suppose Wilbur found it convenient too because after that, he didn't bother looking for a place of his own and his father was happy with his company and it suited Wilbur too.'

'I guess they were both glad that you were next door, Mrs Rendle.'

'I hope so,' she says humbly. 'But ... why are you here, inspector? Has something happened? To Wilbur?'

'What makes you say that?' I ask.

'Because Joy was complaining about him. He's off work today. He'd usually look after his father all day. But he said he had something to do so he asked Joy to come in for an hour or so.' A deep frown has appeared between her eyebrows. 'He said it would only be for an hour, but he hasn't come back. Joy had to call in sick at work.'

'What time was that?'

'Some time after nine this morning.' She gazes at an old clock on the wall ticking the seconds away. 'He said he wouldn't be long.'

I clear my throat. As she seems to be quite close to the Torringtons, I may as well tell her something about what happened. She'll hear about Wilbur's death soon enough anyway and, by the sound of it, his sister Joy will need a bit of support as well.

'I'm afraid Wilbur Torrington has been involved in an accident.'

She swallows. Blinks, swallows again. 'You're not saying ... How bad?'

'Bad, I'm afraid.'

She looks at me and I see a hundred questions on her face. None of them is formed into words, though. She shakes her head in disbelief, sensing the worst, not wanting to accept it.

Her face has gone a few shades paler and her eyes look sad. 'I was concerned, I must admit. And when I saw you arrive ... I thought ... I don't know what I thought. I ... I spoke to Wilbur last night. I had a cup of tea with him and his father. That's why I baked the muffins. Wilbur loves them, but he only had one last night. Which was unusual for him. He seemed ... distracted. He was looking at his mobile phone all the time, and that was quite unusual for him too.'

'Do you happen to know the number of his mobile phone?'

'Of course. I have Joy's number as well. In case I need to contact them urgently when there is something wrong with Jeremy. Let me get it for you.'

She finds a tattered address book in a drawer. She opens it and starts searching with the letter A. She's nervous, shaking, deeply concerned. She turns the pages one by one. She's not concentrating. By the time she has reached the letter J, she realises what she's doing and stops.

'Joy Spicer,' Mrs Rendle mumbles. 'I have Joy's number here. Now Wilbur's.' She's obviously listed them under Christian names.

I type both numbers in my own phone and press the button to call Wilbur's phone. It goes directly to answer-phone. It doesn't surprise me, but I shall need his phone records.

'I did wonder why he didn't come back this morning. It wasn't like him at all, but … You hear about it sometimes … I mean, people walk out for a packet of cigarettes and never return. All of a sudden, they decide to jump of a cliff or in front of a train. Or they get in their car and drive away, not looking back. I never thought Wilbur would do a thing like that, but I could understand his frustration with Jeremy. Jeremy needs to be looked after all the time. And I mean, all the time, inspector. Even when he's gone to bed. They have to lock the windows and the doors, but he can be very determined.' She shakes her head. 'A couple of months ago, Jeremy cut open a cardboard box and wrote on it that he had locked himself in. He got the attention of a woman in the street. He told her that the key of the front door was under a flowerpot in the garden. He ran out as soon as she opened the door, knocking her over. She broke her wrist and it took Wilbur and Joy almost four hours to find him.'

'Was he hurt?'

'Not at all. He was tired. Exhausted. He'd walked all the way to the house where he used to live with his parents. He knocked on the door and explained who he was and they invited him in for a cup of tea. He told them stories about his childhood and they never realised that he could remember all that, but he couldn't remember his own name or were he lived.'

'It must be difficult to have to live with someone like that,' I say gently.

'Definitely. But when Wilbur … he wouldn't have left his father like that.'

'You say that he would never leave without warning; he wouldn't do that to his father. What about his sister? Could he have left her to cope with him on her own?'

'I am ... I was pretty sure he wouldn't, but, since last week ... I don't know, Wilbur seemed very different. Joy noticed as well, but she thought it had something to do with a woman. He might be in love, she said.'

Whether she notices that I am using the past tense in relation to Wilbur, she doesn't show.

'Did he have a girlfriend?'

'Not to my knowledge.' She chuckles. 'He was seeing a woman, I know that, but not in a romantic way. A fortune teller of sorts, she is. Wilbur believes in all that. He reads his horoscope every day. If there is something bad in it, and he has planned something, he cancels it.'

'He wouldn't walk under a ladder?'

'Certainly not!'

'How did he get on with his sister?'

'Joy? A busy-bee, that girl. I don't think they talk to one another that much. She rushes off to go home as soon as he arrives from work. She's always very happy to leave their father in his hands.' She nods thoughtfully. 'Of course, she had her hands full with Jeremy and her own family. And to be fair, she has the worst time with him. When Wilbur comes home, it is more or less time for a meal and then Jeremy goes to bed. As I said, they give him pills to relax and to sleep. He can get anxious sometimes. Aggressive. I know a man up the street whose wife has the same condition as Jeremy. She gets up in the night and wanders round the streets, apparently looking for the school she used to go to when she was little. But the building was demolished years ago and there is now a big supermarket on the site. It's easy to find her, though, sitting on a bench opposite the entrance, confused and crying.'

She shakes off her thoughts, realising they have nothing to do with Wilbur. 'I'm sorry. I'm drifting off, aren't I? I suppose Wilbur and Joy were afraid that Jeremy would do things like that. With the pills, he seems to sleep all night through so Joy has her hands full with him during the day. And so of course does Wilbur, when he's off work. And poor Jeremy .... Sometimes he is confused and he believes that Joy is his wife and ... he can be aggressive towards her, you know. That's why she locks him in every now and then and she comes to me for a cup of tea. To relax, she says, but I think it's also because she likes to have a bit of a moan. Well, to be fair, her life isn't so rosy anymore. This thing with Jeremy is ruining her life. That husband of hers doesn't make it easier for her either. He thinks Joy does too much for her father. He says that the government should look after Jeremy, not his children. Jeremy's worked all his life, paid his taxes and all that. He says that the government has a duty to look after Jeremy, not his children. But if he's looked after so well by his children, they won't help. Poor Joy, caught between a rock and a hard place. I never really liked her husband, nor did Rose or Jeremy for that matter.'

She stops. Her face is sad and her eyes moisten as she wipes the back of her hand across them, not wanting to give in to tears.

'No point in crying,' she says abruptly. 'I do feel sorry for Wilbur. He's never had much luck in life. Bullied at school, Rose told me.'

'What about enemies?'

She shakes her head vigorously. 'Enemies? Definitely not! Wilbur wouldn't hurt a fly, inspector. He is a big softie.' She shakes her head despairingly. 'Always been, if you ask me. Certainly with Sandie. He adored that girl and he was over the moon when they got married, but it didn't last very long before she cheated on him with one of his mates. His best man at their wedding, would you believe it?'

I push away the memories of my own short marriage. 'Does Wilbur have many friends?' I ask, interrupting this avalanche of information.

'Never seen one of late. But I'd guess he doesn't want them to know about his father. I mean, Jeremy has to wear incontinence pads and he often has … little accidents, if you know what I mean.'

I nod, hoping she hasn't noticed the bulge under my shirt.

'Wilbur takes his father out to the local pub every so often. They play pool or snooker and have a meal sometimes. Jeremy is always very excited about it. It wears him out though so when they get home after one or two pints, Wilbur puts him straight to bed. Joy always tells him off because she thinks it's wrong to let Jeremy drink, because of his medication, you know, but Wilbur doesn't agree. Jeremy seems to enjoy himself, so why not? And what does it matter for him now anyway?'

She stops and looks up at the clock, cocking her head as she listens. 'I think I hear Joy's car.' She chuckles girlishly. 'I might be a bit shaky nowadays, inspector, but there is nothing wrong with my hearing.'

I get up and stretch my back. There is a thoughtful expression on her face as she walks me out, repeating that I can come back any time if there is anything else she can help me with. As I step onto the path in her tiny front garden, I realise that I have learnt more about the Torrington family than I would have done if I'd been back at work in full capacity as a policeman, like Maloney. I would never have had the time to listen to all of Betsie Rendle's stories – or eat her home made muffins.

19

Betsie Rendle's front door closes behind me with a dry click. She says she'll join me later at the Torrington's house, but she would rather not be there when I told the family about Wilbur's death. 'They'll need some time for themselves, inspector.'

I wait for Joy Spicer to get out of a battered red car that looks like it's been hit on one side by another vehicle. She has small hips, broad shoulders and a big bosom. Her hair is dyed blonde and her eyes are swollen. She's been crying. I wonder if she already knows about her brother's death. She opens the boot and takes out a blue Ikea shopping bag with a pile of neatly folded and ironed bed clothes and towels balanced on top of it.

Then she tries to lift a second bag out of her car. I hear her speaking sharply and notice that she hasn't come on her own. In the passenger seat is a man speaking on a mobile phone.

Mrs Spicer passes me, carrying one of the laundry bags as if it weighs a ton. She looks at me warily, standing in Betsie Rendle's front garden.

'Mrs Joy Spicer?'

As I step forward, she looks up with an indifference that suggests a life full of dissatisfaction and disappointment. Joy. I can't think of a name more unsuited to her

'Mrs Spicer? Mr Jeremy Torrington's daughter?'

She stops halfway along the path, opening her bag to search for her keys. 'I am, yes, but I'm not sure ...' She pauses, frowning. 'Are you selling something?'

'No, but I would like to have a word with you and Mr Torrington, if that's possible.'

Finding a bunch of keys, she looks over her shoulder with a wry smile. 'As you say, if that is possible.' Her voice is full of sarcasm.

'I would like you to be present too, Mrs Spicer.'

'Oh?' Suspicion is now settling in. She senses that something is wrong, but she still thinks that I'm trying to sell her something – double glazing, a conservatory or solar panels.

'I'm Detective Inspector Tregunna. Andy Tregunna. Can I come in?'

'Oh.' She swallows heavily. An unsteady hand tugs at the collar of her coat. Finds her throat.

She looks over my shoulder as if she's hoping someone will appear to help her. 'Police? What is it about? My father?' Her mind is working overtime and all she can think of is what her father might have got himself into.

'Shall we go inside, Mrs Spicer?' I say gently.

She hesitates. Fearful. She knows intuitively that whatever I have to say, it will be bad news.

She can't find the right key. Preparing herself for the worst, she rubs her eyes and a single tear trickles down her face. She looks like someone who has too much on her plate and can't take any more.

'Let me help you.'

'I can manage.'

She unlocks the door and puts one foot on the threshold, cocking her head, listening. The house is quiet. Her father isn't awake yet. She turns.

'Sorry.' She's recovering, finding her composure. 'Do you have an identification card?'

'I have.' I hand her my ID and she scans my features, comparing them with the photo which was taken when I had longer hair and my face was fuller and my eyes brighter.

'Okay.' Giving it back to me, she shrugs off her coat and hangs it on an empty coat hook. 'My father is … not well.'

'I've just spoken to your neighbour, Mrs Rendle.'

'Oh. Come through, please.'

She locks the front door securely behind us, putting the key in the pocket of her fleece. Then she opens a door into a gloomy living room where the curtains are half drawn and the heater is on full blast. We are engulfed by heat. Automatically, I start unzipping my jacket.

'My father is always cold,' she says apologetically.

Two armchairs are by the window, one has an upturned open book and a pair of reading glasses on the seat. A matching sofa is pulled away from the wall and full-length curtains behind it divide the room into two narrow spaces.

'Shall I … make a brew?'

I could tell her that I have already had two cups of tea and two muffins with her neighbour but she needs to do something. She needs time before we sit down and I tell her the bad news.

'That would be lovely, Mrs Spicer. I suspect your father is still asleep?'

'I hope so. Let me check first.' She disappears between the curtains behind the sofa. 'Father? Are you awake?'

'Huh?'

'We have a visitor, father.' Her voice trembles. She's trying hard to sound cheerful in an attempt to let her father think that he's been expecting a friend or relative to call in to see him.

'A visitor?' The curtains slide open, revealing a small dark area just big enough for a hospital bed and a matching bedside cupboard. On the floor are packs of incontinence pads and paper towels.

'Yes. He is a policeman.'

I guess it's her way of warning him of any bad news. She hasn't asked me anything about her brother, but I'm sure it won't have crossed her mind that he is dead.

'Police!' Panic sounds in his voice and he gets up as if he wants to run to the door. Joy puts her arm round him quickly, casting me a worried look.

'We haven't done anything wrong, father,' she tells him re-assuringly and she gently steers him towards the chair by the window. 'He just wants to ask us a couple of questions.'

'Oh.' He looks round, trying to remember who he is. Or where he is. He is dressed in grey track suit trousers and a light blue shirt with a red bow tie. His grey hair is long and wispy, wafting around his head like a constantly moving halo. His eyes, a greenish brown clouded by cataracts, are wide and vacant. In a way, he reminds me of Mrs Carthew, but she was joyful and happy and this man is frightened, frustrated and aggressive.

'Greg is here too, father. He'll take you out later.' As if on cue, I hear a key unlocking the front door and heavy feet are wiped on the door mat. 'You hear that? That's Greg.'

'I'm going out with Will.' Torrington shakes his head, his hair falling over his eyes.

She doesn't argue with him. I've read somewhere that by arguing with people with dementia or, in Torrington's case, Alzheimer's, they tend to get upset and angry. They don't understand, they can't remember, yet they are aware of some-thing they can't fathom anymore. Joy Spicer has been dealing with her deteriorating father long enough to know what is the best way to handle him and respond to him.

'This is Andy Tregunna, father. He is a policeman, but he is very nice. You don't need to worry.'

'Police? Is this about George?' he asks.

At the same time, a man emerges in the doorway. He is tall and muscular, his head and face closely shaved, except for a bushy red moustache. Clearly, he has heard overheard his wife and he assesses the situation in one gaze.

He nods in my direction and sits down on the sofa. 'George? No, I don't think so,' he says sarcastically. 'George is dead, don't you remember, old man?'

'Have I not told you to go?' Torrington spits back at him.

'Father ...' Joy tries to smooth over the situation. Not successfully.

Her father half rises from his seat, hands on the armrests to steady himself.

'Who is this man?' he yells. 'Why did you let him in? I don't like him, Rose, I don't trust him at all. Where is my wallet? I have to check if my money is still there.'

Joy shakes her head, frowning at her husband, pleading him not to make the situation worse. 'Don't argue with him, please, Greg. Do as we've been told, otherwise he'll get upset.'

'I'm just fed up with it,' he replies harshly. 'We keep saying the same things to him all the time he never...'

'Inspector, this is Greg, my husband.' Joy Spicer interrupts him, forcing a tiny smile. 'He can't handle my father. It is hard when ...'

'O please, woman! Of course it is hard, because you're making it hard for yourself. I told you ...'

She shakes her head, wiping perspiration from her top lip. 'I'll make us a brew,' she announces, her voice steady and she disappears into the kitchen without waiting for his reaction. I suspects her earlier tears were from an argument with him before they arrived.

I sigh. I hate it when people fight just for the sake of it. Just to prove who is right and who is wrong. Pointless battles between people who once loved each other, who have now become bitter. Disappointed. Unforgiving.

I sit on the creaking sofa, conscious of the lumps of the metal springs protruding through the upholstery. As I move into a more comfortable position, my jacket falls open and the bulge beneath my shirt becomes clearly visible. I see Greg Spicer stare at it, and then he stifles a stupid, embarrassed grin behind a hand.

'Rose, is this about our George?' Torrington asks, hands restless in his lap.

Joy can't hear him but Greg responds spitefully.

'She's Joy, father, your daughter. Rose is dead.'

I feel like I have been dropped into a theatre where the actors are speaking lines from different pages in the script and no one seems to understand each other. I wish I had listened to Betsie Rendle when she told me about Jeremy Torrington's situation. I should have realised that there is no point in telling him about his son's death or asking him about his whereabouts from the last few days.

'Joy? Where is Rose?'

'Why are you here, inspector?' Greg asks, ignoring his father-in-law.

'I'm afraid I have something to tell you.'

'It's Wilbur,' Joy says softly from the doorway, an empty mug in her hand. 'Something has happened to Wilbur. I knew it.'

'Oh, don't be so melodramatic, woman!'

'I knew it. It's not like him not to come back.'

'If I were him, I'd be gone ages ago.' Greg Spicer seems to have lost all sense of sympathy.

'Yes Greg, I know that.' Tears are rolling down her cheeks.

'What's up with Will?' The old man is puzzled, looking around as if he thinks there are more people hiding in the corners and behind the sofa.

'I would like to ask you some questions about him, Mr Torrington.'

'You won't get much out of him, I'm afraid,' Greg Spicer says bluntly. 'He has totally lost it.'

'Is this about George?' the old man repeats. Shakily he rises from his seat and he unties the string around the waist of his track suit trousers and pulls them down. 'I don't like these trousers. They're too hot and they make me itchy.'

Joy hurries towards him to pull his trousers up over a bulky incontinence pad, quickly re-tying the string.

'George was his brother,' she explains, her face red. 'Died in car crash years ago.'

All of a sudden, the room is quiet. A sense of dread hangs in the air and three pairs of eyes are staring at me, waiting for the inevitable.

I clear my throat. 'Mrs Spicer, take a seat, please.'

'No.' She fumbles with her hands.

'Okay,' I say slowly. 'I'm afraid that I have to tell you that Wilbur has been involved in … an accident. He's dead.'

'That's impossible,' Greg says bluntly. 'I spoke to him this morning when he called Joy.'

'But he was here this morning,' Joy says incredulously, face ashen. 'We called his boss. When he didn't come back … we told his boss that he wasn't well. We had no idea he was … dead.'

'What happened?' Joy whispers, reaching out for her father's hand but he doesn't seem to notice. He is staring into oblivion, not aware of anything or anyone. He doesn't even listen when I inform them briefly about Wilbur's death, adding that we are treating his death as suspicious.

'I'm sorry, Mrs Spicer.'

'He works at the petrol station in St Merryn. He works mostly evenings and weekends, when the others don't want to work.' It sounds resentful, as if her brother wouldn't have died if he'd been able to work normal hours from nine till five.

'It's on the road to Padstow,' her husband adds.

'We know where it is.' I don't tell them that I had spoken to Wilbur earlier this week.

I lower my voice. Torrington seems to be dozing. 'I need to ask you some questions, if I may. Do you know a woman called Alicia Poole?'

'No,' Joy shakes her head, but I notice that her husband's expression changes.

'Isn't that the woman who was in the papers the other day? The woman they found dead somewhere in a lake?'

So far police haven't disclosed the exact place where Alicia Poole was found, but no doubt that will change after the press conference. Still I am not about to enlighten Spicer about this.

'Yes.'

'And you think … Wilbur knew her?'

'We have some information that may suggest that,' I say carefully, recognizing Greg Spicer as the kind of man who would happily sell the story of his brother-in-law's life to anyone who is interested in it. And pay for it.

'That woman? Who was killed? ' Joy's eyes are big as saucers. 'No. I'm sure he didn't know her. He would have told me about it.'

'Do you recognise the names of Denise Shaw? Or Trevor Bennett? Kenneth Poole? Arthur Bristow?' I ask, but their faces are blank.

Joy starts to cry and her husband seems annoyed with her attitude. I stare at Jeremy Torrington. His head has dropped to one side, resting on a pillow his daughter has gently pushed under his shoulders. His mouth is half open and some saliva drips on his chin. There is no point in asking him what time his son came home last Saturday night. Let alone if he knows who Wilbur was meeting today.

'I would like to have a look in Wilbur's bedroom. Does he have a computer?'

'Are you taking his laptop? When will we have it back?' Greg asks bluntly. 'It isn't like it's an oldie, you see. Our Nick will be very happy with it.'

'Greg! We haven't even … It's only happened a few hours ago!'

'I know, but there is no point is there? Your brother won't be using that laptop anymore. And I'm sure he'd be happy if we give it to Nick.'

'I'm afraid our forensic team will need some time to examine it to see if there is anything on it that can lead us to his murderer.'

The last word silences even Greg Spicer and he has the decency to look down at his fingers. I rise to my feet and Joy gazes at the empty mug she's still holding in her hand.

'Mrs Spicer, your father needs to be told.'

'Yes.' She sniffs and blows her nose. 'Perhaps it is for the best that he won't really understand or remember when we tell him.'

'But it is bloody annoying that we have to tell him the same thing time and time again,' her husband says harshly.

'It's not as if you have to deal with him much, Greg,' she retorts, wiping the side of her hand over her face. 'And now that Wilbur is gone, I will have to deal with him all by myself because I get no help or support from you whatsoever!'

20

Curtis, my neighbour, has been nagging me ever since he spoke to Lauren. He told me that I am a coward and a fool, and that I should know better than to let a woman like Lauren go. He calls her a jewel, a little gem, a 'one-in-a-lifetime-woman', someone who can make me happy. She loves me, he is certain of that. The bitterest pill to swallow is the fact that I know that he is right. Perhaps not that she loves me, but he is right about the rest.

I promised him I would contact her. I don't know how he knows, but he is certain that I haven't called her.

This morning, I took Mr Cole's prescription out of the drawer from my bedside table and put it in my wallet, securely folded. I have parked at Truro Crown Court and walk down to the city centre. My hand is in my pocket, holding the prescription as though a gust of wind might take it and blow it away like a dying leaf from an autumn tree.

I look over my shoulder, scanning the streets to my right and to my left. It is highly unlikely that I will be spotted by someone I know, but I can't bear the possibility. For that reason, I came to Truro to find a pharmacy where nobody knows me.

'Mr Tregunna!'

I freeze. I hear the voice as she enters my vision from a little alleyway between two shops in Pydar Street. I feel like a school-boy who has just worked out the best way to buy condoms and gets caught by the head master.

'Mr Tregunna! It is you!' She is slightly out of breath, as if she's been running to catch up with me.

I stop and force a smile, crunching the prescription in my hand. 'Miss Shaw.'

I turn away from the pharmacy door. She can't possibly know that I was about to get Viagra pills, but nonetheless I feel like I've been caught in some sort of criminal act.

'Do you always walk so fast?' she asks. Her hair is pulled back from her face. Silver blue eye shadow matches the collar of a blouse that pops out from her coat.

'It's going to rain.

She laughs, making me feel like a fool. 'I didn't think you are the kind of man who is afraid for a few raindrops.'

'I didn't see you.' It sounds even worse.

'You weren't trying to escape me?' she asks with a wink.

I shrug. The cry of a child gives me an excuse not to answer that question. I turn my head and I see a young woman pushing a pram with an unhappy toddler in it. She stops, obstructing the pavement to a man who is partially visible under an umbrella, and she wipes melting chocolate off the child's face. In her other hand, she has a plastic bag with chocolate Easter eggs, holding it up like a matador's red rag to attract the attention of a raging bull. Not surprisingly, the child cries for more, stretching its arms out towards the bag. 'Well, all right then, but this is really the last one, okay? I'll have your tea ready in a minute as soon as we're home.'

'Are you working?' Denise gestures vaguely over her shoulder in the direction of the city centre.

I'm about to tell her that I just spent an hour on a hospital ward, sitting next to a bed in which young Becca Trewoon is vegetating, but I swallow and shake my head. I suspect she might think it is a ridiculous and weird thing to do. She won't probably understand that I feel kind of guilty, or, more accurately, that I feel somehow connected to the young woman in the hospital bed. In a rather sad way, I have gotten used to thinking of Becca as a friend. I have told her about the previous case, when we were investigating the origin of several body parts scattered along the coast of Cornwall and the disappearance of two schoolgirls. I told her about my theories about that case and, listening to my own words, things started to make sense to me. With this new investigation, I've been doing more or less the same. I have told Becca everything I know about Alicia's and Wilbur's death and I have this weird feeling that, somehow, she will help me and guide me to the killer.

'Are you alright?' Denise Shaw pulls me away from my thoughts and I grin sheepishly at her. 'Sorry, I was miles away.'

'I was going to call you, but ... now that you're here ...' She stops with a vague gesture. 'How can I help you, Miss Shaw?'

'Denise, please, inspector.'

'Okay, Denise. I'm Andy.'

'Right.' A smile trembles on her lips. They are cherry red. I wonder briefly if they also will taste like cherries.

'Sorry, were you going to the pharmacy?'

I shrug. 'It can wait.'

'I'm going in too. I have to collect my prescription.' She steps beside me and pulls open the door. 'And then … can I invite you for a coffee?

A Costa Coffee just around the corner, opposite a Starbucks. Although her smile is genuinely friendly, she gives me no chance to refuse. 'Why not?'

Her smile becomes wider and for once I don't compare her to Lauren. There is no comparison anyway. Lauren is younger, soft and gentle; this woman is mature, more hardened by life.

'If you order a cappuccino for me, I will join you in a minute.'

Somehow, I feel trapped in a situation I know I can't handle. Nerves make me clumsy. I know I could tell her that I have just come out of the pharmacy, that I took in a prescription for … my neighbour … Mr Curtis ... that I'll have to go back later to collect the pills. It would be so easy. It would also be easy to tell her that I am too busy investigating the murder of her best friend to have a coffee with her. Instead, I can only nod passively.

'Uhm … do you want to go to the pharmacy first, Andy?'

'It is not important.'

She casts me a quick look, then nods. Women know some pharmacy purchases can be embarrassing. My ex-wife never asked me to buy sanitary towels or tampons for her. I can't help thinking that Denise Shaw presumes that I was after condoms. Coloured, flavoured, with or without extra add-ons. I wish …

'Okay. Costa? Alright, I won't be long.'

Before I can find an excuse to escape her, she has opened the door and enters the shop. I stare at her back, cursing inwardly because I can be so clumsy and inadequate with women sometimes.

I order two cappuccinos and choose a table at the back as if I'm not sure if I want to be seen. She comes in with a big plastic bag dangling from each hand. Grinning, she places them under the table and wipes a strand of hair from her nose. 'Weak bladder pads,' she explains, without worrying that the couple at the table next to ours can hear her.

'Not for yourself, I hope?' I try to joke, but fail.

'I probably wouldn't have told you if it was for me,' she admits, taking off her coat and draping it over the back of her chair. 'They're for my neighbour.'

And I was getting Viagra pills … for my neighbour I think to myself and I can't help a small smile, but at the same time I know that I can't explain it to her.

'Poor woman,' she says. 'I feel sorry for her. She doesn't feel comfortable or confident anymore and so she hardly ever goes out.'

'It can be very distressing,' I nod, wondering whether I should tell her about my stoma bag. Maybe not. Or perhaps she already knows. For some reason, I get the impression that very little escapes her sharp eyes.

'Hmm.' She picks up her tea spoon and scoops out some of the froth layered with cocoa powder. 'You are a remarkable man, Andy Tregunna.'

'Why is that?'

'Most men would be embarrassed by bags full of pee pads under their table.'

'I'm not most men.'

'That's why I say you're remarkable.' She smiles and leans forward and it feels like I'm about to be attacked.

'You said you were about to call me,' I remind her. 'About Alicia?'

'Yes.' She is taken aback, hiding her emotions behind a blank expression. 'Yes, of course.' She makes it sound as if she can't think of any other reason why she would want to talk to me. Perhaps I'm being vain in thinking that she might be interested in me as a man, not as a policeman.

'Have you remembered something, Mrs Shaw?'

'Denise,' she corrects me. She leans forward again, crosses her legs and puts one elbow on her knee, resting her chin in her hand. 'I hope so. Do you remember that I told you that Ali went off with someone that night? She told me his name was Chris. Did I tell you that? Yes, I'm sure I did. But I didn't think that she had mentioned his last name. That was wrong because I realise now that she did tell me. I'd simply forgotten it. I'm sorry, inspector, I don't know how I could have forgotten it. Anyway, I hope I'm right because I'm not sure if the name I remember is the same Chris, but …'

'Go on, please, Mrs … Denise.'

'It was a while ago that Ali told me that she had met up with someone who she used to know years ago. Long before she was married to Trevor. He was an old schoolmate of hers. And I remember this clearly, because she told me a little anecdote about the boy.'

She takes a sip from her cappuccino and carefully wipes the froth from her lips, leaving a smudge of cherry-red on the paper napkin.

'There was something about the pupils having to do a little talk in front of the class about a character of their choice from a book,' she continues slowly, as if she is reliving the scene. 'This boy Chris's last name was Eyre and he chose Jane Eyre as his subject. When his friends heard the romantic story, they rolled over with laughter. First of all, it wasn't really a subject that appealed to his friends, as they had all chosen footballers or Formula-1 drivers, but one of them knew things about Chris's family. 'What, he said, are you going to do your talk about your mother?' It appeared that this mother of Chris was called Jane Eyre. It wouldn't probably have been so much of an issue, but Chris's parents were just splitting up and he was rather emotional about the whole thing. He beat up the other boy after school and was banned for three days because he wouldn't apologise.'

'Chris Eyre.' I write the name on the back of a till receipt. 'So he must be the same age as Alicia?'

'I guess so.'

'I don't suppose you happen to know where he lives.'

She shakes her head, taking a few more sips of coffee, drawing my attention to her lips again. 'I'm sorry. I hoped this would be helpful to you and that you will catch Alicia's murderer.'

'Do you think it might be this old school friend?'

She shrugs. 'He seemed a nice guy, although he was a bit … he seemed to need to touch women, if you know what I mean. Some men do that. They flirt not only with their eyes, but also with their hands. Very subtle, so they can never be accused of sexual harassment, but all the same, it is there. Like touching your hips when they pass you in a crowd, or your arm or shoulder when they speak to you. You know what I mean.'

I don't, but I won't tell her that.

'I'm sure we'll be able to find this son of Jane Eyre,' I say flippantly, but her gaze remains serious. 'Sorry, this is a serious matter, of course.'

'I haven't been thinking of anything else, to be honest,' she says softly. 'I mean, I can't imagine that anyone would want to hurt Alicia, let alone kill her.'

'If this Chris Eyre is a suspect, what do you think his motive may be?'

'A motive? None, I'd say. I mean, he was a little bit possessive towards Alicia that night, but at the time I didn't think anything of it. She was beautiful and a lot of men looked at her. Chris seemed smitten by her too, but ... what can I say? If I don't know the man, how can you ask me what he is capable of?'

'Do you think there was more than just the previous friendship going on between them?'

'Oh yes, definitely. It was obvious that he fancied her and I could tell it was mutual.'

'She was married.'

'They had an open marriage. Alicia knew about Kenneth's affair with his secretary, and perhaps other girls occasionally, but she didn't mind. She had her ... flings, if you like, and they both seemed okay with that.'

'Kenneth Poole isn't the jealous type?' I ask her.

'Certainly not. Well, I haven't met him that much, but from what Alicia told me about him, he was okay with it.'

'That night, Alicia was supposed to sleep at your house. Were you not concerned when she didn't show up?'

'Not really. She is ... was a grown up woman. She knew what she was doing. She said Chris, Eyre, was a friend of hers and I thought perhaps she'd stayed the night with him. Although I did expect her to come back to my house some time the following day.'

'Did you try to contact her?'

'Of course I did.'

'What time was that?'

'Uhm, when I came home. After two o'clock.'

'At night?'

'The next day. Afternoon.'

I move awkwardly on my seat, but she stares at me with an open face. 'I spent the night with someone. Do you need his details?'

'To eliminate you from our list of possible suspects? Yes.'

'Am I a suspect?'

'In theory, anyone could have murdered Alicia Poole. Even you.'

'I have an alibi. I was with John. And I don't have a motive.'

'Perhaps you were jealous. She had a wealthy husband. She was a beautiful and attractive woman. She left you on your own in Barrie's Bar when she went off with Chris Eyre.'

She shakes her head, unimpressed, not even offended in the slightest. 'Alicia and I have been friends for ages,' she says quietly. 'There was no such thing as jealousy between us, simply because we fancied completely different men. I have never gotten on well with Trevor, for instance, and Kenneth is definitely not a man I fancy. Not even with all his money, his big house and his cars.' She pauses and smiles gently. 'I am more attracted to men who are more down to earth. Working men, you know.' Once more she pauses, then says, 'Men like you.'

She flutters her eyelashes and I can see the smile trembling on her lips. I am not sure if she is being truthful or just playing with me, flirting.

'It's late,' she says, looking at her watch, reaching for her shoulder bag. 'Time to go, I suppose.'

There are four empty coffee mugs on the table between us. Behind the counter, the staff are busy with new orders and they don't seem to have time to clear the tables and collect the dirty trays. Outside, people are rushing past, wet umbrella's shiny in the light of shop windows and street lamps.

'Do you still need to go to that pharmacy? You've got fifteen minutes before it closes.'

'It can wait.'

'But can your neighbour?'

'My neighbour?'

'You said you were picking up a prescription for your neighbour.'

'Oh yes. Yes, he isn't in a rush. He's got enough pills for this week, he said.' It is amazing how easily the lies seem to come out of my mouth when they don't seem to have come from my brain.

'But will you have to come back to Truro for them?'

'Uhm … yes.'

'Let's go now then.' She rises to her feet, slipping her arms in her coat without expecting me to help her, grabbing her plastic bags in each hand, reaching to put the strap of her shoulder bag over her shoulder, and waits for me. I am shocked at the speed she's set this in motion. I try to find an excuse, but there is none.

Then she says casually, 'If you're free tonight, I'd like to invite you for a meal.'

Somehow she has grabbed my arm and we duck under an umbrella she produces from her shoulder bag, close to each other to shelter. I can smell her shampoo and; I can feel the warmth of her body through her coat and mine.

I don't want to be here, with a woman I hardly know. She's the best friend of a murder victim whose death I am currently investigating. I think of Lauren, her light blue eyes, the freckles on her skin, the sound of her laugh, the love in her eyes when she looks at her twin sons. Perhaps I'm wrong but I sense that Denise Shaw never has a smile like that in her eyes when she looks at her son Jake. And perhaps she never will. Yet, there is something about her that tells me that I can trust her. That I can share my deepest worries with her, whereas I can't face talking to Lauren about them.

'You are right,' I say, as much to my own surprise as to hers. 'I'd better get that prescription before the pharmacy closes.'

21

The decision made, we hurry through the pouring rain. We stand next to each other at the counter, my heart pounding but not able to get out of this awkward situation. Next to me, Denise is studying a shelf containing a huge variety of vitamins and other health supplements.

The young man behind the counter calls my name as though there is another customer behind me waiting for his prescription. He puts a small box on the counter, his face expressionless and professional.

Denise turns towards me. I don't know if she can see the writing on the little white box.

'Thank you,' I say to the young pharmacist. My throat is dry.

'For your neighbour?' Denise laughs, as she opens her umbrella again once we are outside. 'Come on.' She hooks her arm into mine and cocks her head to one side, looking at me with something in her eyes that can't be mistaken for anything else than a flirtatious tease. 'Let's go to my home. Jake's out with friends tonight and I'm a good cook.'

I can't argue with that. Not with anything else. Her eyes have betrayed her intentions. I feel hot and cold at the same time. Like I'm a schoolboy approaching a girl for the first time, knowing what I want, not certain at all about what to do, scared by what might happen. The small box with the pills is burning a hole in my pocket, waiting to be used. I have already decided that I will not be able to use one of them with Lauren; I can't bear the thought of failure. But it's different with Denise Shaw. I hardly know her and I'm not emotionally involved with her.

I follow her as she drives home. Perhaps the drive will cool me down, but it doesn't. My heart is racing. I want to do this, but at the same time I don't. Do I want to know if the pills will work, or do I prefer to live in hope and uncertainty?

Too soon, I see her slow down and she turns into the street where she lives. Her house is in darkness and the faint hope that her son Jake will be at home after all, is fading fast. She climbs out of her car and I climb out of mine. Our eyes lock and I know that the promised meal will be delayed. She wants me. I hope I won't disappoint her.

'You alright?' she asks softly, as we step inside and she closes the door behind me, pressing her body against mine. I can taste mint on her lips and there is something else that reminds me of printer's ink.

'Andy.' My name is said in a sigh so soft that I'm not sure if I heard it. 'Relax. I'll get you some water.'

For the pill.

'Come.' I feel cool palms on each side of my face as she holds my head and brings her lips to mine. 'Relax, hon. Nothing to worry about.' Smiling softly, she stares into my face, lightly tracing her fingers across my chest.

'I'm ...' I wonder, if she's aware of my stoma bag. Should I tell her now, watch her face as disappointment or disgust settles on it before she releases me quickly? Or should I wait and let her find out herself, let her current feelings of lust dissolve in anticipation?

Without a word, she shakes her head and takes my hand. I follow her up the stairs, still unsure what to do, what to say, but it seems I have no say in the matter.

'I'll get you some water before I use the bathroom,' she says in a low voice. 'Let me get rid of that awful office smell first.' I know what she's doing. Whether from experience or just internet-knowledge, she's well aware that it'll be some time before the pill starts working. If ...

She pulls the curtains closed and, blowing me a kiss on her fingertips, she disappears in the bathroom. I take one of the pills from the strip and swallow it without reading the instructions and warnings. With my pants and T-shirt on, I slip into her bed and listen to water running in the bathroom, her voice humming a currently popular song. There is no going back now. I'm not even sure if I want to turn the clock back.

She's wearing lacy underwear. A push-up bra and a thong. Her hair is hanging over her shoulders and her eyes are dark with passion. I know that this is all wrong, but I don't seem to be able to move. I wanted this, but not for the right reason. And, fearing that the pill won't have any effect on my body, I know that I will be embarrassingly disappointing for her. I want to say something, but she is already leaning over me, her hair touching my face, her lips on mine.

The proximity of her body to my own causes a flutter in my stomach. I close my eyes and reach for her breasts. Waiting and hoping for a miracle. The scent of her perfume is overwhelming, the warmth of her soft, smooth skin even more so as she slides over me. Thigh on thigh as she moves between my legs, leaning her body on top of mine, hard nipples pressing into my chest. Her breath is in my face, her hands are on my body, caressing, starting from my neck and shoulders and going down very slowly. Desperately, I grab her arms and flip her over on to her back and I hear her gasp of surprise. My mouth finds hers again and my hunger for her body increases. I feel myself losing control, driven, possessed.

Then, all of a sudden, it's over. I feel her stiffen beneath me. I know what it means, but I don't want to admit it. With wide eyes, I stare up at the ceiling and follow the pattern of shadows. She lies beside me, her breath slowly coming back to normal.

Finally she says, catching her breath, 'I'm sorry.'

So am I, is what I want to say, but only an unidentifiable noise comes from the back of my throat. She hoists herself up to lean on one elbow and I know she is staring at the stoma bag under the white cotton of my T-shirt.

'Andy …'

I swallow. Tears are running down the sides of my face. I cry and I can't stop. I need to explain this to her but I can't find the right words. Nerves are taking over my body. I am shaking as though I have been in cold water and my body isn't warming up quickly enough. I'm in the semi-darkness of her bedroom and, if there was to be an opportunity to share my true feelings, then this is the moment. I cannot keep this in and still I am afraid to address what it is I can't say. I turn my head to see her half-frowning, half-smiling

'I'm so sorry,' she says again.

'No,' I say, my voice broken. 'It isn't you. It's me'

22

Chris Eyre lives close to the showground at Wadebridge, where the Royal Cornwall Show is held every year at the beginning of June. I have always had a liking for the old cottage. Recently, I have passed it several times and I remember that it had been derelict for a long time. Occasionally, it had 'For Sale' signs in the windows, but they have disappeared. It looks like someone has taken on the job of giving the cottage a new lease of life. The hedges around it have been cut and the walls have been freshly whitewashed. The double-glazed windows are brand new. With pleasure, I notice that the frames are made of solid wood, painted in a colour that can be described as blue, green or grey, depending on how one sees colours.

The man who opens the door is wearing blue jeans and a black jumper smudged with white paint. His brown hair is short and he has a lopsided grin and a dimple in one cheek. He barely looks at my warrant card. As I put it back in my pocket, I explain that his name has come up in an investigation we're currently working on. He doesn't seem bothered, not even interested. Nodding briefly, he steps back to invite me in, his attention more focused on the mobile phone in his hand, checking his emails or messages continually, probably without even being aware that he is doing so. It is almost second nature these days for people to be checking their mobile phones all the time. Chris Eyre is no exception.

We climb stairs made of solid beech wood. Sheets of newspaper stained with drops of dried paint are taped onto the treads.

'The living area is upstairs,' he explains matter-of-factly. 'It was Cilla's idea. She was right. It's brilliant.'

Whoever Cilla is, she has an eye for design. The first floor is open plan with windows on all sides, a combined kitchen-diner-lounge area. The kitchen is brand new with white, handle-free doors and a shiny top of black marble. Several copper coloured pans are hanging above a modern Aga. The floor is made of the same wood as the stairs; the walls are white and bare. He hasn't bothered yet about the furniture; a settee and two chairs are covered with dust sheets. Bits of old tree trunk serve as coffee tables.

'It's not finished, as you can see,' he days dryly. 'I'm doing what I can, but it all takes time. Everything comes down to my spare time and of course ... within the limits of our budget.'

'Did you do this all by yourself?' Having two left hands myself, I am duly impressed. 'It must have been a lot of work. '

'It still is.' He grins shyly. 'As I said, it takes a lot of time. More than I ... than we expected, to be honest. My wife has given up, sadly. She couldn't bear it anymore. She's moved back in with her parents.'

'I'm sorry to hear that.'

'She'll be back,' he says with more self-confidence than his sagging shoulders suggest. 'Take a seat, please, Mr Tregunna, but be careful where you sit,' he grins again. 'Sofa is a bit old.'

He takes the dust sheet off the sofa, revealing a base of burgundy fabric sofa, blankets and throws draped over it, probably to cover up holes in the upholstery. Saying that the sofa is a bit old is an understatement but I understand what he means when I feel myself sink into what seems like a swamp, thick mud slowly absorbing me.

'Told you!' he says jokingly. 'Coffee?'

'Thanks.'

He doesn't seem to be too interested in finding out why I'm here, which I find unusual. I'd like to see his reaction, the expression on his face, when I explain that this is about Alicia Poole's death. It'll have to wait until he sits down.

'Do you have children?' I ask casually.

He shakes his head. 'We've been trying for years, but then ...' A strange expression crosses his face. 'Is that why you are here?'

'What do you mean?'

He is quiet for a few moments. 'So this isn't ...' He stops and turns his back to me to deal with an expensive looking coffee machine, saying over his shoulder, 'So, tell me, Mr Tregunna, what can I help you with?'

The machine hisses and lets out steam and the smell of freshly ground coffee fills the atmosphere. People say you will sell your house twice as fast with the smell of baked bread, but coffee would do the trick for me. Although the place is barely finished, I suppress a mad idea of asking him if he would sell me his house.

Unaware of my thoughts, he picks up two white mugs and places them on one of the tree trunks. 'Milk? Sugar?'

'No thank you.'

He sits opposite me in one of the chairs, not bothering with the dust sheet. His legs crossed and his elbows on the armrests, he looks totally relaxed. Harmless. Innocent.

'Mr Eyre,' I say calmly, 'we're currently investigating a murder. I'm sure you've heard about it. It has been on local television and in the newspapers.'

His eyebrows rise. 'Don't read papers anymore. Besides, I've been away. Out of the county.'

Most people want to know more about the victim when a murder is mentioned. The circumstances, the details. He doesn't.

'Mr Eyre, do you know Alicia Poole? Alicia Marshall, before she was married to Trevor?'

He shrugs. 'Trevor? She told me that she was married to Ken.' He narrows his eyes. 'Why? What's with Alicia?'

'I'm afraid she's dead.'

'Dead? Alicia? That's impossible.' He pauses, eyes wide open. 'That's probably a stupid thing to say, Mr Tregunna. I don't suppose you're here to tell me fairy tales, but ... I can't believe it. I was with her on Saturday night.'

'Her death has been in the press, Mr Eyre. Why didn't you come forward when we asked for people who spoke to her, or saw her last weekend?'

His face expresses genuine surprise. 'I didn't know.' He turns, his face blushing. 'Honestly, I didn't. I just told you that my wife has gone back to her parents. They live in West Yorkshire. I went up there for a few days to be with her. The fact that she can't live in this mess anymore, doesn't mean we are splitting up.' A moment silence. 'I hope.'

'And you don't read the papers.'

'Yeah, well, no, to be honest. I don't.'

'When did you go to see your wife in West Yorkshire?'

'On Sunday. I sort of got there just before tea time.'

'When did you come back?'

'Last night. It was a long drive and I went straight to bed when I got home.' He looks sheepish. 'Are you sure it is Alicia? I mean ... I can't believe it. I mean, last time I saw her, she was sort of ... full of life!'

'And when was that exactly?'

'As I told you. Last Saturday night.'

'In Newquay?'

'No, yes, we drove up the coast road.' He gestures vaguely in what he assumes is the direction of the Atlantic Ocean. 'I saw her in a bar in Newquay. Barrie's Bar. I was with a friend. He had helped me with some heavy stuff here and he suggested we go to the pub to relax. I didn't really want to go out, because I was going to see my wife and I wanted a clear head for the long drive. But he had helped me and he wanted to see a film, so I thought I could doze off a bit, maybe. But when we arrived at the cinema, he found out that he'd read the dates wrong. The film he wanted to see wasn't on anymore. We weren't interested in the other films, so we went to have a burger somewhere and we ended up in a few pubs. We were just about to go home when I spotted Alicia. My friend said he'd got to go home anyway, so we sort of split up there and then.'

'You'd met Alicia before?'

'Oh, yeah, we go a long way back. We went to school together. I suppose we had a sort of something going when we were teenagers, but we lost sight of one another.'

'Did you see her before Saturday? Did you have a date with her? Did she tell you where she would be this Saturday?'

'Oh no. I just happened to see her at Barrie's.' He scratches his chin. 'We just met by chance and I bought her a drink and we got talking, that's all.'

'Was she alone?'

'No, she was with a friend. Can't remember her name, though. Dark hair. She seemed a bit pissed. Wasn't very happy when Alicia told her that we were going off … ehm … for a drive.'

'Denise.'

'Huh? Yeah, that's it. Denise.'

'She wasn't invited?'

'Uhm, no.'

As far as she was able to follow his car on the CCTV cameras, Penrose had drawn his assumed route on a map she printed off the internet, with question marks added at some junctions. I try to remember the exact route. 'Where did you go?'

He shrugs, finding a chip on the tree trunk that needs his immediate attention. 'We sort of drove along the coast road to Padstow.'

'Do you own a white Toyota?'

'I do.' He doesn't seem surprised that I know that already. It occurs to me that he still hasn't asked how Alicia died. Or why.

'We were able to follow your tracks as far as the fishing pond a few miles from Padstow,' I say. It is not entirely true, because the last appearance of his car was when he passed the petrol station in St Merryn. There was no sign of his car on the next camera on that road, and he could have taken several country roads before that.

'I see.' He looks up slowly. 'I guess I'd better tell you the truth then, hadn't I? Since you seem to know a lot more than I anticipated.'

'That would be helpful,' I say dryly. 'Best to start at the beginning then, like when you saw Alicia at Barrie's.'

'Okay, but … ehm, what happened?'

'In a minute, Mr Eyre. Please tell me about Saturday night.'

His suspicion is now growing as he realises for the first time that I am not here for a cosy chat, but for a far more serious matter.

'Yeah, well, my mate pointed her out, to be honest. Said what a beautiful woman she was and I realised it was her. Alicia.'

'So you didn't have a date with her last Saturday?'

'Oh no, I told you, it wasn't like that!' He looks down onto his hands uncomfortably. 'With my wife being away … well … ell, it can be lonely, you know. When I come home after work, there is always something to do in this house, so I haven't had much of a social life, lately. I hadn't been out for a while until my mate suggested going to the cinema and … but I told you that already, didn't I? Anyway, Alicia and I met out of the blue at Barrie's. At first, she seemed a bit distracted. She had been at Angelo's with her friend, but something happened. Something to do with a man, I think. Someone harassing her. Anyway, that's how they ended up in Barrie's Bar. I'd never been in there before, you know, it isn't my kind of scene exactly, but Alicia and her friend seemed to go there whenever they went out together. Anyway, I must have said something like I didn't really like it in there, so she suggested going outside. We sat together for a while and then suddenly, she was talking about something else.'

'Something else?'

'Yeah, well, I must admit, it was a bit of a shock to me as well. I mean, I reckoned that Alicia was happily married and she didn't … need anything else outside her marriage. But she told me that she'd heard about this group and … she'd wanted to try it out, but she didn't want to go on her own. And she didn't think her friend - Denise, was it? – would be interested.'

'What group?'

'Uhm.' He hesitates, clearly embarrassed. 'They call it … dogging, I think.'

'Dogging?'

'Yeah. I'd heard about it, but I didn't really know … well, basically, it's people coming together, ideally in the open air, to have sex. They get fully undressed and they … do it, with anyone else from the group. And, apparently, you can also go and watch.'

'I have heard about it.'

'She sort of knew someone who knew how to find out where those guys meet, I mean, men and women obviously, and she knew that one of those meetings was planned for that night.'

'Saturday night?' I try to hide my interest. This is a new, completely different development from anything I'd expected. 'At the fishing lake?'

'Yeah. In the car park. Nobody lives near there and although there are cars driving by, the road is narrow at the bridge and there are some shrubs and bushes, so I suppose you don't see much when you drive past and don't know about it.'

'Did you two go there?'

'Uhm … yes.'

'And did you and Alicia …?'

'Uhm, yes, we did, but we didn't, if you know what I mean. I wasn't keen on it to begin with, because I was going to see my wife the next day and I didn't want to, so … but when I saw the others … it was sort of erotic, you know. Most couples stayed in their cars but a few climbed on top of them,' he chuckles, 'I suppose it was because it was very cold and the engines were still a bit warm. ' He chuckles again. 'To be very honest, inspector, it was rather exciting, like we all shared a secret. I know there were some people hiding in the dark, I mean, people who weren't taking part of it but only watching, but that only added to the excitement.'

'Alicia got undressed?'

'Oh yes, we all did. That seemed to be the 'dress-code' if you like.' He grins sheepishly.

'What did she do with her clothes?'

'I put mine in the car, on the back seat, but Alicia was a bit careless. I remember seeing that she dropped her clothes on the grass. I know that for certain because I said that the grass was wet and she wouldn't appreciate having cold and wet clothes once we were going back, but she only laughed and said she was hot enough to steam her clothes dry.'

'If I take you there, could you show me where you were at that point, and where exactly she dropped her clothes?'

'I suppose I could. It was dark, but the cars were more or less parked in a circle and we all had our headlights on. Her clothes were between two cars.'

'Go on.'

'When we were … finished, I went to the side to have a pee and I assumed that Alicia would put her clothes back on. Most of the others were, you see. It was freezing out there, to be honest, so I thought that would be the end of the meeting. But when I walked back to my car, I heard that some of the others were not … finished. And Alicia was one of them. She got in someone's car. I didn't see him and I didn't recognize him. Anyway, I got dressed and I sat in my car, more or less waiting until Alicia came back.'

'What time was that?' I ask, but he ignores my question.

'You must believe me, inspector, I am certainly not proud of what I did. At one point, I saw her climbing out of the other car and I was … relieved that she was about to call it a day too. But then there was someone else and he took her by an arm. Now, I'm still not sure what happened then. I mean, I couldn't hear what they said and some of the cars had already left, so, there wasn't much light anymore. I couldn't see if she went with the other man or not. I was about to get out and ask her how long she wanted to stay there. I was getting tired and cold and I wanted to go home. As I said, I was going to see my wife the next day and I knew it would be a long and exhausting drive. But when I walked in the direction where I'd last seen Alicia, I couldn't find her.'

'You didn't … hear her?'

'Having sex? No, she was always … quiet. Some women … make sounds, I suppose, but she didn't. But no, I didn't hear them talking either, so I assumed that they were … you know, busy. I got back in my car and waited.'

'Until?'

'I didn't check the time, if that's what you mean. But finally, there was only me. There was one van parked at the side, next to some bushes, but there didn't seem to be anyone in it. Eventually, I got out and walked to the van, thinking that they might be inside maybe. I mean, the van was from some company, fish, I believe, but I suppose there was enough room in the back to lie down.'

'Go on.'

'Well, that was it, really. There was no one in the van. I knocked on the doors and windows and I called her name, but I got no answer. In the end, I started to think that Alicia had gone off in one of the other cars. I didn't have her mobile number, so I couldn't call her. So I thought there was no point in waiting and I went home.'

'Were her clothes still on the grass?'

'No, I checked that, because then she would have still been around somewhere, wouldn't she? But I thought she must have got dressed again as her clothes were gone. Perhaps she was cross with me because I told her I wanted to go home.'

'What about her handbag?'

'What about it?'

'Did she have it with her when you drove out of Newquay?'

'Oh yes, definitely. She checked her makeup on the way. She tried her mobile, but it didn't work and she asked if I had a charger in the car.'

'She didn't leave her handbag in your car?'

He frowns. 'Actually, that seems rather odd, doesn't it? I mean, women keep all their stuff in their bags and I suppose they keep them always within reach. Sort of. Anyway, I didn't see her handbag when she took off her clothes, but you would have thought that she would have left it in my car.'

'She may have come back for it.'

'Possibly, when I was having a pee. But I didn't see her. Or her handbag.'

'Did you contact her later?'

'Of course I wanted to! I felt rather … ashamed that I'd sort of left her on her own there. I wanted to be sure that she had got home alright but I didn't know her mobile number and I gave up when I was with my wife.' He grins sheepishly again and I can guess that his sexual encounter at the lake will remain a secret from his wife.

'Now inspector, what is this all about? I hope you weren't serious when you said that Alicia is dead?'

23

Burke's report on her findings regarding a connection between Torrington and Alicia Poole is in my mailbox. I print it out and attach a copy to the big whiteboard which has Alicia Poole's glamorous photo on it in the middle at the top. Arrows and lines connect her photo to other information, photos and street maps.

My mobile rings as I return with coffee to settle behind my desk. It's the desk officer, forwarding a call. 'Yes Rob?'

'It's Anita.'

'Sorry.'

'You passed me less than fifteen minutes ago,' she says in her abrupt way. 'And you know that Rob is still on holiday.'

I sigh. 'I said I'm sorry.'

'Thank you.' She chuckles as if she's just won a bet. 'I have someone here who says she has information about Torrington. Maloney said you are handling the case.'

'Oh.' I sigh. 'Can you ask her to wait until ...?'

'She's a clairvoyant,' she interrupts, as if this information has suddenly more significance.

'So?'

'She said she knew already that she would have to wait, but she says it is urgent.' She chuckles again. 'Not bad for a clairvoyant, huh?'

'Right. I'd better see her then. Or does she know that already too?'

'I haven't mentioned your name,' she replies curtly and I'm not sure if she appreciates my sense of humour.

Linda Hampton introduces herself as a clairvoyant and a tarot card reader. She's in her early forties, wearing a black velvet dress with multiple strings of coloured glass beads round her neck and several bracelets round both wrists. Her hair is dyed black with a tuft of white on one side of her forehead and her eyes have a thick line of charcoal eyeliner and blue mascara. There is a silver stud in her nose and when she rises to her feet and smiles to greet me, I see another one in her tongue.

'Mrs Hampton, how can I help you?' I say, shaking her hand and making the bracelets jangle.

'I'm here to help you with the investigation of the death of Wilbur Torrington,' she replies grandly, then, almost immediately, her confidence slips off as she sniffs loudly and wipes her nose with the side of her hand.

'Shall we find somewhere quiet and more private?' I suggest, pointing at the open door of interview room 1.

'I'd prefer that.' She nods quietly, fiddling with a handbag made of pieces of coloured leather which are sewn together with large stitches.

'I'm sorry,' she says with a rather husky voice. 'I'm still shocked about Wilbur. I just can't believe it.'

We enter the interview room and she sits down as if she has walked for miles and the exercise has exhausted her.

'Can I offer you a cup of tea or coffee, Mrs Hampton? It's not the best in the world but it will do for the moment.'

'Thank you. Black tea please. No sugar.'

I look at the desk officer who is staring at me as if I am some kind of creature of some endangered species. If it was SpongeRob, I would ask him politely to fetch me a coffee and a tea, both black, but since he is on holiday and the only person currently behind the desk is the woman whose name I keep forgetting. She looks at me across the hall and, reading my thoughts, lifts her chin provocatively as if she is challenging me to the final round in a competition. Our eyes meet and we fight a silent battle of wills until the phone rings on the desk and she has to answer it.

Behind me, Linda Hampton is sniffing and blowing her nose repeatedly, and I don't want to leave her alone in the depressing little interview room Patiently, I wait at the desk for the officer to end the call.

'Would you be so kind to get us a black coffee and a black tea?' I ask, using my friendliest tone and carefully avoiding her name to prevent myself from getting caught in embarrassment.

She smiles sarcastically. 'Of course, no problem, Detective Inspector.'

I nod and smile, not sure if she is taking the Mickey or offering me an olive branch. I leave the door ajar and sit down opposite Linda Hampton who is now sobbing quietly.

'How did you know Wilbur Torrington, Mrs Hampton?'

'We met years ago when we both worked in a supermarket. We never really lost contact.' Her bottom lip trembles and her eyes are like dark puddles.

'What is the nature of your relationship, if you don't mind me asking?'

She straightens and touches the white tuft on her forehead. 'Uhm ... we weren't in a relationship as such, if that is what you mean, but ... I'd like to think that he and I are ... were good friends,' she replies quietly. 'I am a clairvoyant, inspector. Every so often, he used to come to see me and I'd read the cards for him.'

'Cards?'

'Tarot cards. Contrary to what people sometimes think, Tarot cards can't change future events, but they can help people to anticipate them. Wilbur believed in them and found comfort when he was in a dark place.'

'Was he often in a dark place?' I ask, thinking about his life and responsibility for his father.

'Not often, but ... sometimes. He came more often than most of my clients,' she explains, holding up her head with pride and a touch of arrogance. 'Most times he came to have the cards read for ... reassurance, if you like.' Her cheeks are regaining their pink colour. She seems to be recovering her normal control by talking about her obvious passion. 'Some people let their lives be ruled by the cards, but that is not what the Tarot was intended for.'

'Would you say that Wilbur Torrington was someone who relied on those cards for choices he had to make?'

'No, certainly not, but he always felt more confident after our sessions.'

'When did you last see him?'

She swallows, the memory flooding back. Tears are running down her cheeks. She is in the real world now, where the cards have no place.

'That was Saturday night.' She sniffs and blows her nose in a paper napkin that smells of patchouli and ginger. 'Just after midnight.'

Against all odds, I feel myself tense. After Chris Eyre's revelation about Alicia Poole and what was going on in the car park by the lake that night, this looks like there could be another bombshell in the investigation into Wilbur Torrington's death.

The desk officer appears in the doorway, pushing the door open with a foot, her serious face. With a polite, 'sir' she comes in with coffee and tea. Both liquids are so dark that I can hardly tell which one is which.

'Thank you,' I say, making a mental note to get her name right next time.

'I am sorry I didn't come sooner,' Linda Hampton says softly. 'But I promised Wilbur that I would not tell anyone, and I wouldn't, but now that he is dead … it doesn't matter anymore.'

'I hope we can find out what happened to him,' I say gently. 'Hopefully with your help we can achieve that.'

She blows her nose again. 'How did he die?'

'We are not sure yet,' I reply carefully. 'We're still waiting for the post-mortem report.' Inwardly, I curse Guthrie, who seems to be convinced that Wilbur Torrington's death was an accident and consequently, the post-mortem has not been brought forward on the pathologist's list.

'I read that he fell from the cliffs at Bedruthan Steps,' the clairvoyant continues. 'Was he murdered?'

I frown. 'Why do you ask?'

'Because he was afraid of heights. He would never get close to the edge of cliffs.' She looks down at her hands, her fingers playing with a string of silver and red beads as if she is praying. 'From what he told me that night, I thought he could have been murdered. Just like that poor woman.'

I shift slightly in my chair, hoping that my expression hasn't changed. But she senses a flicker of interest and a tiny smile lifts the corners of her mouth.

'How do you mean? Which woman?'

She lifts one shoulder. 'She was mentioned in the papers earlier this week. The woman who was found in the lake.' She sips her tea, seemingly unaware that it is too hot.

'What makes you think that there is a connection between the two, Mrs Hampton?'

She shakes her head as if she can't believe how ignorant I am. 'Because of Saturday night, of course.'

I lean backwards, feeling like I have fallen asleep with the television on and wake up having missed the most important part of a thriller. 'Perhaps you can tell me what happened on Saturday night.'

She clears her throat. Her tears have dried and she doesn't need to blow her nose so ferociously any more. 'I was just about to go to sleep when I heard someone at the door. It was late and I didn't want to get up, but he kept knocking and ringing and calling me. I recognized his voice and let him in. Wilbur. He was in a terrible state. His clothes were dirty and wet and he had a wild look in his eyes. I'd never seen him so upset before. He stumbled in, almost tripping over the threshold, and he started to cry as soon as I closed the door behind him. I made him a cup of camomile tea to calm him down a bit. As I said, I was just about to go to sleep. I had been reading in bed and I didn't ... I wasn't properly dressed. I left him in the kitchen to put something else on ... in case he got some ideas, you know, but he wanted me to read the tarot cards for him. I thought it was rather an odd time of day to do that, but he said it would help him because he didn't know what to do. He might be in serious trouble, he said. I asked him what was wrong but he was only interested in the cards and we went into the room that I use for my regular customers.' She smiles thoughtfully. 'I have decorated the room to satisfy the expectations of my clients, subdued and calming, and I always have some incense sticks on the go to create a bit of an atmosphere. I knew that Wilbur always liked being in that room. It helped him to relax when he was upset about something and ...'

I hold up my hands to interrupt her. 'What do you mean? Was he normally upset when he came to you?'

'Most times, yes. Or just frustrated. He was not very happy with his life. He was lonely and depressed. He couldn't wait to leave his parental home because he couldn't deal with the situation with his father.' She blinks. 'I believe his father has Alzheimer's.'

I nod. I can understand the frustration. 'Did he have a girlfriend that you knew of?'

'No, I don't think he did, although he was trying to find one all the time. He told me that he was on several dating sites and he was chatting to a lot of women but he never seemed to find the right one. Sometimes he asked me for advice. Some of those women were using him, ripping him off for his money or taking the Mickey. It was really sad sometimes, but he wouldn't listen to me when I tried to help him and warn him to leave certain types of women alone. They only added to his disappointments.'

'Did you get the impression that he had a date that night?'

'I'm not sure,' she replies, hesitating. 'It could be, but he didn't tell me.'

'Okay. So, going back to that night, you read him the cards and then what?'

She looks anxious. 'To be frank, I wasn't honest with him. He picked cards and I knew that the first one was not right for him. If I told him the truth, he would only get more upset. I could see that he was worried about something and I sensed that he wanted my reassurance more than anything else. He needed help and I kind of bent the truth about the cards to help him relax. But he saw the last card and he knew it was a bad one as soon as he saw it. He knew what it meant. Bad news, he said. He then started to cry again and told me what happened before he came to me. It was an extraordinary story and at first I didn't believe him. I thought he was upset and confused and that he was mixing things up. I thought, he might have had a few drinks, but he said no when I asked him and, in fairness, I didn't smell any alcohol on him. He said he had been working that evening until eleven and he would never drink during his shift, or when he knew he'd have to drive home.'

She pauses, deep in thought, reliving the last moments she saw Torrington alive, perhaps regretting something she had said or done, or not doing something which could have prevented his death.

'Go on, please, Mrs Hampton,' I say encouragingly.

She drinks her tea. 'He was working at the petrol station when he had a customer he knew who told him that something was going to happen at the car park at Swan Lake. Wilbur knew that it was the rule of the fishing society that they would not allow fishing in the dark. But the other guy laughed and he asked Wilbur if he had ever heard of dogging. Wilbur had never heard about it and the guy explained it to him. It was towards closing time for the petrol station and Wilbur was about to go home. But then he decided to drive past the lake and see what was going on. Clearly, although he didn't say so, I suspect that he thought there might be a chance for him to have sex with one of the women. When he drove past the car park, he said, there were several cars parked in a circle with their headlights on. Wilbur realised that he wouldn't be able to join in because he was not a member of the group, so he decided to park his car further up the road and he walked back through the fields. He approached the car park from the other side to the coast road and he saw that there were several couples having sex in the cars or on the bonnets of cars. He hid in the dark and watched and I suppose he got excited and ... you know ... but then he heard something in the bushes behind him and he was scared that he would be seen as a peeping Tom. He ran away. By that time, several of the cars were already leaving the car park. He thought it would be quicker to go back across the fields to where he'd parked his own car, but he found it easier to follow the headlights out of the car park. Although there was some moonlight, he couldn't really see where he was going. Then suddenly he fell over and he landed on something he described as soft and white.'

Mrs Hampton pauses, an expression of concern on her face. 'I don't think he realized immediately what it was exactly. He heard something behind him and he was terrified. He staggered to his feet and he saw a man dressed in dark clothes. He then realized that he had fallen on top of a naked woman and he thought that the woman was about to have sex with the man, who seemed to be furious by the disruption. Wilbur panicked and as he stumbled to his feet, he lost his balance and he fell against the side of a van. He staggered off as fast as he could and when he arrived at his own car, he noticed that his hands and his shirt were covered in blood. It occurred to him then that the woman was hurt so he drove back to see if she needed help, but the car park was deserted and he couldn't find the woman where he thought she had been lying. He thought of going to the police, but he was certain that they wouldn't believe him. He was in such a state and he didn't know what to do, so he decided to come to me for help.'

'He was covered in blood?'

'Well, it looked worse than it was. His hands were dirty and there was a stain on the front of his shirt, but that was all.'

'What happened to his shirt?'

'He took it off and I gave him an old one of my ex-husband's. I put the shirt in a bucket of cold water to soak, but I couldn't get rid of the stain, so I chucked it in the bin.'

'And the bin men have already collected it?'

'I'm afraid so, inspector. They come on Thursdays.'

'Did he come back to see you after that Saturday night?'

'Oh yes. He came almost every day, especially when he heard about the woman found dead at the lake. He hadn't got much of a look at her and he hadn't recognized her from the pictures in the newspapers but he knew it must've been her. He thought that there would be evidence left on her and the van implicating him and he was scared that he could be in trouble and nobody would believe him.'

This, undoubtedly, would have been the case, I think, not saying so out loud. She wipes a single tear from the corner of her eye. 'That's why he didn't want to go to the police, inspector. I wish now that he had, because then, maybe, he would still be alive. The man he saw that night must have been the woman's murderer and he was scared that his life was in danger. Sadly, that turned out to be true.'

'This is what he told you?'

'Once I'd read his cards, yes. As I said, that Saturday night, I lied to him a bit about the cards and he seemed calmer when he'd told me everything. But once we knew about the dead woman I wish that I had done more to convince him that he should go to the police. I could have saved his life.' She is quiet for a long time. 'I came to you today to tell you what he told me and what I know because I truly believe that his death wasn't an accident like they say in the papers. I want the police to find out what happened to him rather than putting it down as an accident.'

'You have been very helpful,' I say gently. 'Can you remember how he described the man? What he looked like, what his impression of him was? Anything that can help us find this man?'

'He didn't say anything that could be helpful to you,' she says slowly. 'All he said was that he had seen the man before and guessed it must have been a customer at the petrol station. That would explain his fear, I thought, in case the man saw him working at the petrol station and recognised him. He'd be signing his own death certificate.'

I shake my head. 'That sounds rather dramatic, Mrs Hampton. Let's not assume anything at this stage. We'd better concentrate on the facts.' I smile as reassuringly as I can, knowing that she may well be right that Torrington's death could have been prevented.

24

'What is this?' Guthrie is standing in the middle of the reception area, holding up a paper, his face the colour of a ripe tomato. Wisely, the desk officer ducks behind a computer screen, making herself invisible from the DCI's rage. Unfortunately, I enter behind Maloney and, once I am in, there is no escape. Guthrie's eyes skim over Maloney, who is a master of evasion and, consequently, they rest on me.

'Tregunna! I demand an explanation!'

I stare at the newspaper, but it is partly folded in his shaking hand and I can't read the headlines, or anything that has caused his fury. In fairness to Maloney, he pauses to ask the only relevant question. 'What's wrong?'

Guthrie is so angry that he says each word very loud and slowly. 'What's wrong? This. Is. What's. Wrong!' He holds up the newspaper and we can see the headline: 'Clairvoyant to help police solve murder case.'

I swallow. Linda Hampton. She didn't strike me as someone who would inform the press, but it hadn't occurred to me to ask her to keep quiet about it either.

'Who authorized this?' He looks from me to Maloney and back again. I feel like a schoolboy caught stealing a pencil.

'We didn't authorize anything, sir,' Maloney says, at the same time gazing at me. Which he shouldn't have done as, immediately, Guthrie is suspicious and he senses that we are in this deceit together.

'Tregunna? Did you speak to that woman?'

'Yes sir, I did, because she is an important ...'

'I don't need you to tell me how important she is, Tregunna. I just need to know how this article appeared in the paper.'

The statement of clairvoyant "Lyndha", real name Linda Hampton, was initially received with mock and sniggering laughter, but then the significance dawned on every officer involved. Linda Hampton's story confirms that Wilbur Torrington had indeed been in contact with the white van, which explains how his fingerprints in blood got there in the first place.

The continued silence in the room becomes uncomfortable.

'She came forward as a witness,' I explain. 'Wilbur Torrington went to see her on Saturday night because he stumbled over Alicia Poole not knowing then that she was dead but, when he drove home, he realised he had blood on his hands and clothes. He panicked and went to see Linda Hampton, who happens to call herself a clairvoyant, but she was also friends with Wilbur. She promised him not to tell anyone about what happened, but, when she heard that he was dead, she came to see us.' I turn towards the desk officer. 'Annie … can confirm that.'

'Anita.' She looks up from behind her computer screen and smiles coldly. 'Yes sir, that is right. I knew DI Maloney was very busy but Tregunna was available.'

How easy it is to play with words and give out a completely different impression. I catch the look in her eyes and sigh inwardly. The war between us is still going on, albeit under the surface.

'So this wasn't you who leaked this to the press, Tregunna?'

I stare at him, almost wishing I had. 'No sir.'

Guthrie is only half convinced, but as the wind has been taken out of his sails, he doesn't know how to go on.

'We'll have a briefing in half an hour,' Maloney says helpfully, though I'm not sure if he is supporting me or the DCI.

'Okay.' Guthrie's face is already returning to its normal colour. 'I will deal with the press personally.' He makes it sound as if he sees it as a chore, but in reality, I suspect that he relishes it. 'Perhaps we can turn this to our advantage.'

One can always hope, I think, saying nothing.

In the incident room, the rapid tapping of fingers on keyboards of a couple of well-trained admin officers is louder than the voice of DS Ollie Reed speaking on the phone. He waves as he spots me, trying not to involve Maloney, and pointing at his desk. I see a scattered pile of newspapers. The pages are all open at the same story. 'Police need help of clairvoyant to solve murder of wife of Cornish businessman.'

Had Guthrie seen this particular headline, he would have been even angrier. I slump into a chair and, as I wait for Ollie to finish his conversation, I read quickly through the stories. One newspaper has used a photo showing the vague outline of a woman, her hands folded around a crystal ball. A second photo shows me getting out of my car, the bulge under my shirt clearly visible and recognisable even to those who don't know what a stoma bag looks like. I can't find the name of the photographer under the photo, which may be just as well.

Finishing his call, Ollie picks up several printed sheets, stapled together in one corner.

'This has just come in,' he says in a low voice, as if he's apologising for the fact that he is supplying me with information. 'These are the results of what was found on Alicia Poole's iPad. I thought you might like to see it, before ...' He doesn't finish his sentence, letting it hang in the air.

'Didn't she have a computer or laptop?'

'There wasn't a computer in her home and we've only found the daughter's laptop. According to Mr Poole, Alicia stopped using a computer when she got an iPad. If necessary, he would bring his laptop home, but usually she would email documents to his office if she wanted something printed.'

'Modern times, Ollie.'

'I suppose,' he replies, wondering if I'm half joking or serious.

'Let's go though this, then, Ollie,' I say, staring at the first sheet. Someone has scribbled undecipherable comments in the margins and put asterisks and arrows connecting sections of text, and highlighted some of the names and dates with yellow marker pen.

There are printouts of Alicia's emails from the week before her death, filtered out from all the spam, newsletters, advertisements and notifications from social media sites. She exchanged several emails each day with her friend Denise, and occasionally commenting on posts they had shared. From what I can see, the exchanges seem innocent enough, rather boring in fact, with comments on fashion or people they both knew, and some short videos, most of which involve animals doing the most extraordinary exercises, and a lot of emoticons to express their feelings.

The get-together on Saturday seems to have been arranged a while ago, as there is no other reference other than the occasional 'see you on Sat' and unanswered questions like: 'Where shall we go?' Even in her last message on Friday evening, Alicia was casual about what time they would meet as she was unsure about the time she would be ready, depending on when Trevor picked up Briony and Ken left to play. Everything seemed to be normal up at that point.

It starts to get more interesting on Sunday, when Denise sent her friend several emails. The first was just one question: 'How did it go?'

Then, as there was no reply, which must have been unusual and made Denise curious at first and then probably annoyed. From what we can read between the lines, the girls did go their separate ways on Saturday evening, which confirms what Denise already told me, that Alicia left with a man who she introduced to Denise as Chris.

On Sunday, before it was known that Alicia Poole was dead, Denise's messages prove that she didn't know what had happened to her friend. Unless she planned and staged the murder to perfection. Which, to me, is almost impossible. Even the best laid plans can go wrong. A tiny incident, a split second, can change everything. Like the hit-and-run case of last week. The father stopped briefly to tie his shoe laces, missing being hit by the speeding car by a few inches, whereas his daughter, who had walked only one single step forward, got the full blow. In the unlikely event that the driver had intended to drive into them both, he couldn't have predicted that the father would bend down at the very last moment, or that the girl would move one more step before she realised that her father had stopped.

Amongst all the emails, there are some to and from Alicia that suddenly catch my attention. There is no name, only the fact that the other person called himself 'godfather'. There are four emails from this godfather, but Alicia only responded to the second one. Unfortunately, those emails have not been printed out.

'Isn't it odd to call yourself godfather?' I say thoughtfully.

Ollie shrugs. 'Why? My mother used to have a godfather and she was quite close to him, especially after her own father died.'

'Did he call himself 'godfather'?'

'She always called him that.'

'I want to see the emails, Ollie.'

'Forensics hasn't printed them, but I guess we can ask …'

I pick up the phone and dial a mobile phone number scribbled on top of the first page.

'Roger?' Ollie asks, lifting his eyebrows disapprovingly.

'Hmm.'

The number is engaged. I've dealt with Roger Bamfield before and on those occasions, he always had his mobile switched off. Or at least, so it seemed as I never saw it on his desk or heard it ring. Bit it's hard to believe that a guy like Roger would be comfortable without it.

'I'd better go and see him later.' I rise, glancing at Ollie who doesn't look as though he intends to come with me. I guess Roger's relaxed attitude towards the legal guidelines makes some colleagues a bit nervous, especially when we are gathering evidence for the prosecution.

Roger's way of working, and getting results, when his colleagues who follow the rules more strictly don't, is exactly why I like him.

25

I see Josh Warren climbing out of his car opposite the Lobster Hatchery on Padstow's South Quay. The old railway line, which ended at the Quay, closed in 1967 and was redeveloped into a 17-mile leisure trail. Originally built to transport sand for fertiliser, the railway later transported slate and china clay to ships moored in Padstow, as well as taking fresh fish upcountry. From an important commercial route, it is now a popular cycle and walk way.

A young man with a black hooded sweater is placing bikes outside one of many bike hire shops, his jeans barely held up by his skinny hips. His eyes are locked on the area in front of his feet, oblivious to anything going on around him. The sky is pale blue, the sun breaking through a little, but it is still rather chilly with a northerly wind.

Eddie Rowse emerges from the passenger seat of Josh's car and makes his way to the quay where an empty lorry has just arrived to collect sand that has been dredged from the estuary. The lorry driver jumps out and greets Eddie with a pat on his shoulder, exchanging jokes with two other men who have been waiting for his arrival. Eddie beams at them, like one of the lads. They all laugh and grin, relaxed. I envy their companionship. I envy Eddie for his innocence.

All of a sudden he looks up and, even from this distance, our eyes meet. For a second, he freezes, then, by way of greeting, he lifts a hand that doesn't reach higher than his shoulder. The other three men follow his gaze and they stare at me with a hint of hostility. I turn away quickly to avoid any confrontation.

Josh Warren has collected a rucksack from the backseat of his car and is fumbling for his keys in the pockets of his jeans.

'Mr Warren, can we have another word?'

'What?' He looks over his shoulder, not wanting to be seen in my presence. 'You mean, right now?'

'Yes.'

'I'm going to work.' He gestures with his thumb over his shoulder, where a middle-aged woman is struggling to attach an A-frame with pictures of lobsters to a lamp post to prevent it from falling over by the wind. 'I'll have to start in ten minutes.'

'It won't take long.'

He cocks his head to one side and sighs, accepting he can't escape from me. His best option is to take me inside, where we won't be seen by too many of his mates. He walks swiftly towards the Lobster Hatchery as if he's trying to shake me off.

'I doubt if there will be visitors this early,' I say casually. 'What exactly do you do at the hatchery?'

'I look after the little ones. Lobsters. We breed them ourselves, you see.' He casts me a sideways glance. 'We work closely with the local fishermen. If they catch an egg-bearing lobster, they bring it over to us and we collect the eggs. We keep the little ones for about two years and then they'll go back to where they belong.' He pauses. Uncertain. The silence grows. He's staring directly at me, his face stubborn. 'Okay. I work. You talk.'

'No. I ask the questions and you answer them.'

He shrugs. He wants to have the last word. 'I'm not sure if I can tell you anything new, inspector.' He greets the woman who is now picking up some scattered chocolate wrappers, purple and gold, from the doorway, gleaming in the early sun, telling her that I am not a paying customer.

I follow him in and he disappears into a small room, leaving the door ajar. He hangs his rucksack on a hook, takes off his shoes and puts on a pair of green boots, tying the laces of his shoes together and hanging them over the rucksack.

'Were you aware that the car park at the lake is being used by some other people?' I ask.

He bends down to push his trousers into his boots. Shrugs with studied indifference. 'It's private property. There are signs, but obviously, we can't stop people from parking there … unauthorized. We can't be that vigilant, inspector. We are aware that people also come for a walk along the lake. It is a very peaceful area … well; it was peaceful until someone was murdered there.'

'I mean at night, Mr Warren.'

'At night?' he asks, surprised. He looks at the floor and then a broomstick seems to need serious attention. 'Uhm … what do you mean?'

'You know perfectly well what I mean, Mr Warren but, for the time being, your little secret is safe with me.'

'Secret?'

'Mr Warren, we are investigating the murder of two people. The woman you found in the lake and a man we found on Bedruthan Steps beach earlier this week.' I retrieve a photo from my breast pocket. 'I believe you know this man, Mr Warren?'

He stares at the photo, his face ashen. 'Yes. He works at the petrol station in the village.'

'Right. You …'

'But I had nothing to do with his death! Or with that woman! It was …'

'You went to the petrol station on Saturday evening. You filled your car with petrol and you bought two bottles of coke, a bag of crisps and a bar of chocolate.'

His lower jaw drops. 'How do you know?'

'We've seen the images on the security cameras,' I say as friendly as I can. 'Why didn't you tell us that you were there?'

'You didn't ask. You wanted to know about the woman. I didn't think it was important that I got some petrol for my car.'

'No, you are right, but I am interested in what you said to Wilbur Torrington.'

His face turns from white to pink. 'I … I can't remember.'

'Then let me help you, Mr Warren. I think you told Wilbur Torrington what would be going on at the lake later that night.'

'What was going on?'

'You are not stupid, Mr Warren. And neither am I. You knew about the meeting in the car park. You knew exactly what was going on.'

'I … no. Well, yes. I knew about them … having sex.'

'Is that why you went back there on Saturday night?'

'I wasn't … I was …'

'As you were the one collecting the fishing fees, you were in charge of the money. I am aware that you aren't the treasurer, but you told me yourself that you collect the money, you bank it, and you send copies of the transactions to the treasurer.'

'What's this got to do with the death of that woman? I'd never seen her in my life.'

'I'm not talking about her at the moment, Mr Warren. I am asking you why you went to the car park at two o'clock on Sunday morning. You went there with Eddie Rowse on Monday morning to collect the fishing fees, so I would like to know what you were doing there early Sunday morning, and why you didn't collect the fishing money then.'

'I ... I can't tell you ... I ... was drunk.'

'The way you were driving doesn't suggest that you had been drinking, Mr Warren. We have images of you driving in the direction of the lake and back again half an hour later.'

'I can't ... I don't remember. Possibly ... I went for a pee.'

'Let me refresh your memory then. I think you went there because you killed Alicia Poole and you had to go back there to get rid of the body.'

I wasn't at all sure about this but, when I see his eyes darken with undisguised fear, I know that my intuitive shot in the dark has to be close to the mark.

'No! I had nothing to do with that!' His voice trembles and he stares down; his expression suggesting a guilty conscience.

'Then why were you there, Mr Warren?' I ask gently.

He stares at me. It is dawning on him that I have cornered him. If he doesn't admit his true reasons for going to the Swan Lake that night, he'll be charged with murder.

'Uhm ... I had forgotten something,' he tries lamely.

'What had you forgotten?'

There is no easy way out for him and he knows it. But he still isn't prepared to admit anything to me.

'Shall I refresh your memory again, Mr Warren? I think you had an agreement with the organizer of the night time meeting and that you allowed him to use the car park with your permission, as it was private property. In case someone found out about it and went to the police, the people attending the meeting couldn't be accused of trespassing.'

'It's not illegal,' he says defiantly. 'It has been done before and it's not ...'

'I presume you intended to pay the money into the fishing society's bank account and send the paying-in slip to the treasurer?'

He shrugs by way of reply and stares at the plastic trays at his side. They are filled with running water and little round discs that each holds a tiny lobster of less than an inch long.

'This one has just shred its skin,' he says, as if he's totally oblivious to what I said. Then he shrugs again. 'Yes, of course I will pay it to our society,' he says lamely. 'I hope you are not here to accuse me of stealing.'

'No Mr Warren, I'm just making sure that you are telling me the truth. Why did you leave the money from the fishing competition behind? Why didn't you take that as well?'

'I knew there would be more people coming on Sunday. It would have seemed suspicious if I'd gone twice. Even Eddie would have found it weird. And he never bothers about anything really.'

A dead body in water starts to sink as the air in the lungs is replaced by water. After a while, bacteria in the tissue, gut and chest captivity form gasses and the body floats to the surface. Depending on several circumstances this can take a few days to several weeks. In this case, it took one day and one of the forensic examiners explained that Alicia's body came towards the surface so quickly because of an upward current in the water.

'Mr Warren, I am not here to accuse you of stealing from your society. All I'm interested in is what you saw in the car park that night.'

'Uhm ... I found the keys that I gave you earlier.'

Whether it's relevant what time he found Alicia Poole's keys, I can't fathom, so for the time being, I let it go.

'Mr Warren, was there a white van parked there when you collected the money at two o'clock on Sunday morning?'

'There was.' He nods hesitantly.

'Did you know whose van it was?'

'It was Art's. He is a member. All our members get a discount when we buy our gear and stuff from him.'

'Arthur Bristow?'

'Yes.' Nothing seems to surprise him any more.

'Did you speak to him?'

'No, I didn't see him. The van was dark and I ... assumed that he was asleep.'

'So you were aware that he uses the car park?'

'Uhm ... yes. 'He stares at me incredulously. 'How do you know all this?'

I shrug, suppressing a small smile. 'That's all, Mr Warren. Thank you for your help.'

'Okay. I admit that the people at that meeting were charged a small donation to our society for the use of the car park. But Art certainly doesn't have to pay, inspector.' He stares at me, licking his lips several times. If he thought by begging me I would keep quiet about his little business on the side, he would.

He stares at his feet. Lamely. Defeated. 'It's just that our treasurer doesn't want all the hassle. Otherwise the money would go straight to him, obviously.'

'Obviously.'

'Mr Tregunna, inspector … I am not a thief, inspector. Honestly.'

'Mr Warren. I was just interested to know if you saw anything suspicious that night.'

He doesn't appear to hear me. 'Am I a suspect now? Because I was there?'

'We certainly won't rule you out, Mr Warren.'

26

Roger Bamfield has half a dozen mobiles on the desk in front of him. He chooses one. Punches in a number, frowning in concentration as he stares at the screen.

In his mid-twenties, he is the stereotypical IT nerd. Dressed in baggy faded black jeans and worn out trainers with odd laces. I have never seen him wearing anything other than black T-shirts with a Goth prints on the front. He once told me that the company he ordered a T-shirt from, had sent a box of 48 instead of the single one he had paid for and before he was able to return them, the company appeared to have stopped trading. To me, the story makes sense, more or less, as any company doing that is doomed to go down.

His dark blond hair is long and unruly; according to Penrose, someone said jokingly that he won't have a haircut until he finds a hairdresser who can do it online. Tall and skeletally thin, it always amazes me that he never puts on weight, as he seems to spend all his time slumped in a chair behind his desk, eating constantly while working on one keyboard with three large computer screens lined up on his desk. Claims that he spends a lot of time playing games are apparently ignored as it is also suggested that he can manipulate the rules to the benefit of himself and his colleagues. Penrose has no doubt that he would have been arrested years ago if he wasn't under Guthrie's wing. I find it hard to believe that a high-ranked policeman like DCI Guthrie would allow Roger to stay if there was the slightest possibility that he would jeopardise the reputation of the police force. Which hasn't happened to date.

As one of the admin staff recently brought into the force to relieve police officers from administrative tasks, Roger works part-time for us and I suppose Guthrie is smart enough to claim that anything dubious Roger may be doing, he is doing so in his own time.

Pushing the mobile phones to one side, he acknowledges my appearance with a crooked grin. Meanwhile, he is clicking on a mouse - which is actually shaped as a mouse, with two tiny pink ears and blinking red lights as eyes. A yellow paper daffodil, courtesy of the Marie Curie charity, is clipped on its tail.

'I have emailed you the stuff from Alicia.' He sounds as if she was a good friend of his. I guess you get that feeling when you rummage through someone's computer and got to know a lot about them.

'Yes, thanks for that, but I need ...'

He shrugs by way of apology. 'Maloney only wanted the emails from her closest friends and relatives.'

I nod. Maloney is following a line of enquiry that is based on the fact that most murders are committed by family members or close friends. Money and greed, lust and jealousy are the main motives.

Without taking his eyes from his three screens, Rogers's right hand travels to a half-open drawer and finds an open packet of sugar coated chocolate peanuts. Crunching his way through a handful of them, he stretches his legs and pulls up another office chair for me.

'Sit down, Andy. What can I do for you?'

'I would like to know who "The Godfather" is.'

This takes his eyes off the screens, attracting a second of his attention. Then he is quiet for a moment, and goes straight back to his keyboard to google the word.

'Marlon Brando.'

'Marlon ...' I stop, annoyed with myself. 'I have seen the film, thanks, but I mean the person who sent several emails to Alicia Poole and called himself Godfather.'

He grins, casting me a quick, sideways glance. 'Yep. I've seen those. Nothing important.'

'Still I would like to see them.'

We have an awkward relationship. He always makes me feel uncomfortable as if he finds my requests and questions clear proof of my stupidity. The result is that I don't really know how to approach him to get what I want.

He shrugs. 'Of course. No worries.'

He moves his mouse, red eyes flickering, so fast that it's amazing that the daffodil is still in place on the mouse's tail. Then he sighs and I watch him moving windows, text and images from one screen to another. I have seen him doing that before and was silly enough to ask him how he did it. There was pity in his eyes when he looked at me. And he said nothing.

Roger may be working for the police, but there is one big problem; he is not a forensic computer analyst interested in the investigations. He doesn't think about any possible links between cases, comparing modi operandi, motives of people involved. He doesn't look for any idiosyncrasies or missing links. His interest and expertise focus on the technology, accessing and retrieving deleted, damaged or encrypted data. He once warned me not to take any computer device to a top without first completely destroying the hard drive. I didn't really believe him until I read a paperback by a crime writer in which someone was blackmailed shortly after he'd put his discarded desktop computer in a dustbin. I gave Roger the book and asked him afterwards what he thought about it. He shrugged and replied that there was an element of truth to the plot, although he thought the actions of the victim were credible, someone being blackmailed would have gone have gone to the police straight away,' he said.

'Then there wouldn't have been much of a story.'

He grinned. 'Good point, Tregunna, good point. But be warned; don't be careless with your electronic devices.'

'I promise to bring them to you when I want to get rid of them.'

At which point he grinned, shook his head at my stupidity and said I'd better not do that either, as I shouldn't trust anyone. Subsequently, my admiration for him increased, but it had probably the opposite effect on his opinion of me.

'I only printed the emails from the people on the list Maloney gave me,' he says, rather apologetically, yet shrugging with indifference.

'Maybe it's nothing,' I offer gently.

He doesn't answer, grabbing a handful of M&Ms and is only faintly distracted when a red one slips between his fingers and lands on the floor. He doesn't bother to pick it up. He taps on the ergonomically shaped keyboard so fast, moving things from the screens on either side to the one in the middle and, before I can work out what they are, let alone read them, a printer behind me whirrs and produces a disappointingly small amount of A4 sheets. He crumples the top sheet, with only a disclaimer on it, in his hands and throws it in the direction of a paper waste bin that is already surrounded by similar crumpled sheets. This one lands in the bin like the winning goal of the world's best basketball player. Grunting, he shoves the remaining two pages in my direction.

'I think it's nothing but have a look yourself.'

I open my mouth to thank him but he is already engrossed in whatever he is doing on his three connected screens.

He is right. The emails are short and contain no useful information at all. In one email the Godfather says he had seen Alicia somewhere in town and was sorry that she was in a hurry and couldn't speak to him. In another email he suggested having a coffee and a chat sometime somewhere, to which she replied that she was too busy and would contact him if she had more time. Both emails are dated five months ago. Her refusal, at that point, to meet him, can hardly be seen as a motive for her murder.

I am inclined to believe that this is a dead-end line of inquiry, until I see the fourth message, dated ten days before her death. 'We have to meet, Ali. Urgently.'

I shake Roger out of his concentration. 'Can you find out who this godfather is?'

'Could be anyone's godfather.'

I suppress a frustrated sigh. 'But I'd like to know who Alicia's godfather was.'

I know Penrose and Ollie Reed are not really fans of Roger; I begin to understand why, as I'm now finding him infuriatingly annoying.

'Ask her family,' he adds, even more unhelpfully.

I rise to my feet. 'No worries, Roger,' I say curtly, resorting to the only thing I know that in the right circumstances will have an effect: 'I'll ask Hazel.'

'Okay.' There is a slightly uncomfortable pause until, for the first time, he looks at me with his head actually turned towards me. I see the faintest twitch of unease crossing his face and his eyes contract to little black dots. I've hit a nerve mentioning Hazel's name.

She is his direct manager, and the proverbial nail in his coffin. She's in her late forties, prim and, rumour has it, frustrated with her single status. Although she's his superior, in Roger's eyes, she's a digital dinosaur. In short: Hazel and Roger don't understand each other, dislike for each other the only thing they have in common.

'Sorry,' he says, chucking another handful of M&Ms in his mouth, then remembering what his parents must have tried to teach him – manners - and he scoops up the half-empty packet, holding it out to me by way of a peace offering.

'Sorry. Bad day.' His grin is sheepish, expressing more emotion than I've ever seen. 'Late night, to be honest. My own fault.'

'Couldn't get away from your computer?'

'I wish.' He shakes his head. 'I have a mutual understanding with my Tits.'

Tits, I know, is his girlfriend. Her real name is Margaret. I have met her only once. She bears no resemblance whatsoever to her nickname. She is small and boyish, unshapely, and has probably never worn a dress or skirt since she was old enough to defy her mother's taste for girly clothes.

'We've agreed to switch off our phones, tablets, laptops at nine o'clock, and then watch a film on Netflix or Amazon,' Roger explains sombrely.

'And she cheated?'

'Oh no, man!' His face opens in the widest grin possible and his eyes have come to life. 'But she's kept me awake almost all night with some … stuff she'd ordered online. You know.'

'What stuff?' Roger is in the habit of calling everything stuff.

'Sexy stuff.' He becomes more human than ever by blushing like a young teenager. 'You know.'

'Oh.' I accept two M&Ms and start crunching, merely to allow him some time to recover. For a young, switched on man, he seems oddly prudish.

More key tapping and activity on his screen, only one this time, and eventually, he says,

' Okay,' leaning backwards and folding his hands behind his head, tapping rapidly with the heels of his trainers on the floor. A habit that reveals his impatience.

He points to the printer as it starts whirring again. 'Those messages were sent from a mobile phone. A pay-as-you-go card,' he explains, choosing his words slowly and with care, as though he is trying to make me understand that one and one equals two. 'The number has been withheld.'

'So you can't find out who this godfather is,' I say, almost feeling triumphant because I have caught him out.

He looks at me witheringly. 'I have the number for you and I know the name of the phone company which sold the SIM. But it hasn't been used since a few days ago. The only way to find out the godfather's identity is if he paid for the SIM card by credit card. Which he didn't.'

I swallow my disappointment. 'How do you know all this?'

'Don't ask.'

'I don't need to know?'

'You don't want to know.' He shakes his head. 'Criminals tend to use those SIM cards more often than we would like, Tregunna. You can buy these SIM cards so cheaply and all you have to do is destroy it afterwards and buy a new one.'

'I heard they … can be … destroyed … damaged by water.'

'Not a chance. You can disable a SIM card by entering the PIN number three times incorrectly. This will lock it until you unlock it with your PUK code. But if you want to make it impossible to recover any data from it, you have to physically destroy the card.' Ignoring the urge to turn back to his screens, he is on a roll. 'It's more difficult than you think. Put it in a microwave or oven and heat it, cut it in pieces and burn or dissolve the metal pieces in some kind of acid. Then dispose each fragment in a different location.' He grins again, seeing the expression on my face. 'But most criminals don't do that. Like everyone else, they don't tend to chuck away something that is still useful. They may keep the SIM card and use it again for their next job. Anyway … back to our godfather.'

'You just said that the phone hasn't been used since … Saturday?' I say slowly. 'That is the day that Alicia Poole disappeared and died. I need to find this godfather.'

'Of course.' He makes it sound like he's reminding me of the fact that it's my job to find out who he is. He nods seriously but as he turns back to his keyboard and stares at his screens, he's already forgotten me.

'I'm thinking of buying some smelly stuff for Tits.'

I see perfume bottles popping up and disappearing again. I still find it odd to hear him use her nickname in a way that is inexplicable to me.

'Chanel No 5?'

He smirks. 'My mother uses that.'

I suppose I'm the last person to know anything about perfume but for some reason, I seem to have the right answer. 'Try that pop singer. The one with the blue wig and gold glasses. I think I've read somewhere that she has launched a range of cosmetics.'

He jumps enthusiastically. 'Hey man! That's great!' He clicks a couple of times and finds what he's looking for.

'Now where were we, Andy?' He looks at me expectantly. 'Your godfather. If he is involved in the murder, he'd be totally daft to use that phone, that SIM card, ever again. But, as I said, people don't like to waste money, so I will keep an eye on it and let you know if he uses it again. And before you ask, I will email you the location point so that you will know his whereabouts when he sent those messages to Alicia Poole.'

I thank him and I see him return to the online perfume site, click on a blue bottle with a gold top before he half jumps from his chair to retrieve a bank card from his wallet.

'"Blue's-on", I hope it smells as good as it sounds,' he says over his shoulder. 'Thanks man. Appreciate it. Happy Tits!'

27

The most obvious explanation for someone to call themselves godfather is that they were appointed godfather to Alicia by her parents. Another explanation is that they use the term at a self-appointed guru. None of this makes any sense in relation to Alicia and the person calling himself godfather in his emails to her. Kenneth isn't aware that Alicia had godparents, neither is Denise. Maloney's opinion isn't very helpful either. He grinned when he read my notes and asked why on earth I could possibly believe that a godfather is able to kill his own godchild. He makes it sound as if I have lost my mind. Even Penrose looks at me dubiously and comes up with a vague excuse when I announce to her that I'm going to see Trevor Bennett about it; she isn't coming with me.

He works in a warehouse belonging to a Cornwall-based chain of shops that deal with anything to do with water sport. It may have originated as a single surf shop years ago, but it has now grown to a well-known chain for with shops all over the south west.

Trevor Bennett is in charge of the stock, which includes the handling of deliveries as well as despatching orders from the shops. I find him in the doorway of a small office beside the doors that are wide enough for a van to enter and load and unload. He is dressed in his work clothes – dark grey trousers and an ocean blue shirt, the word "Surfing" is sewn on the breast pocket. Again I'm surprised at how tall he is.

In his hands, he is holding a long sheet of a computer print that almost reaches the tips of his shoes and he is instructing someone where to store the boxes that are stacked on a fork-lift truck. Although the driver nods repeatedly, his face has a blank expression and I can understand why Bennett finds it necessary to explain everything again. The driver hesitates, still uncertain about what is expected of him and I can see Bennett clenching his fists.

'Now go and don't bloody waste my time!' He has to raise his voice over the radio, turned on to keep everyone, except him, in a good mood.

I clear my throat, stopping just close enough to catch his attention.

'Inspector.' He frowns, clearly annoyed by the appearance of yet another person to waste his time. 'Don't tell me that you have come all the way from Newquay to talk to me.'

'I was in the area,' I reply matter-of-factly, deciding that white lies sometimes serve a purpose. And I need his cooperation. 'I thought I'd drop in.'

'Do you have any news? Did you find Ali's murderer?'

'I'm afraid not.'

He scratches his ear before he pushes his pen behind it, debating what the best option is. 'Oh. Well, I'm busy.'

'I have a few more questions.'

He stares at yet another driver who has just emerged from a van in the same colour as Bennett's shirt. He scratches his backside and grins to nobody in particular, making his way around his van with frustratingly low speed. The expression on Bennett's face is easily readable; clearly, he considers that the van driver is up against fork-lift truck driver for who is on top of the list for redundancy.

'My time is too bloody precious to waste my energy going over that stuff again,' Bennett snaps at me. 'What more can I say that I haven't told you lot already?'

'A murder is a serious matter, Mr Bennett,' I say gravely. 'In fact, as you know, we're dealing with a double murder and I'm sure that you'll understand that we want to catch the man who did it.'

'Alright.' His expression tells me that I won't get any closer to an apology. Gesturing me into his office and waving towards a rather wobbly looking seat opposite his desk, he closes the door behind me. The radio is now only in the distant background.

'I'm just pissed off,' he offers by way of explanation. 'I'm short staffed and the men I've got today seem to have left their brains at home. If any.' He nods to his left side. 'That twat you just saw started working on the fork-lift for us yesterday. He came in full of himself, boasting that he knew it all, but now that it comes to it, he's as stupid as the rest of them.'

For the sake of his future relationship with the people he works with, I am glad that he has closed the door.

'Right.' He sits behind his desk and opens one drawer to put one foot on the edge. 'What do you want to know now, inspector?'

'Just some background information, Mr Bennett. It might not seem important, but we need to know everything about the past that might lead us to the murderer.'

'So,' his brows arch, 'you aren't anywhere near catching him?'

'We have a couple of suspects.'

'I'm sure you have.' He chuckles without humour. 'I'm also sure that my name is on that list too.'

'Yes,' I admit. Clearly, he expected me to deny it. Or at least he thought I'd give a neutral reply that can mean anything or nothing.

'Oh, well, yes of course. What sort of background are you after?'

'What was the reason for your divorce from Alicia, Mr Bennett?'

He seems genuinely surprised. It isn't the question he expected. 'That was years ago. Five years. What has that got to do with your investigation?'

'Perhaps it's nothing, but I'm just trying to get an overall picture of the situation as it was before she was killed.'

He shrugs. 'Well, it isn't a secret. Neither is it something out of the ordinary, inspector. I suppose we split up for the same reason as so many other couples do nowadays. To put it very simply, there was a third person involved.'

'Did Alicia have a lover?' I ask, although I know the answer already.

He grins sheepishly. 'No, it wasn't her. It was me. I had met someone else.' His eyes are fixed on me now, not swirling round his office to avoid looking at me. It is commonly known that people who are lying tend to avoid eye contact, but people who fear that what they say may come across as untruthful also, do that. In his case, I can't make up my mind whether he is lying, withholding something, or simply scared that he's unintentionally misleading me.

'Maureen?' I ask, though I can't image his new wife being the reason for a fling, let alone a divorce. If Penrose could read my thoughts now, she would probably accuse me of being prejudiced. Discriminating even, maybe.

'No,' Bennett replies, oblivious to my instant, probably unfair judgement. 'No, it was someone at work. Typical. She worked here part-time, odd hours, only when we needed her.'

If he needed her, more likely.

'She was also married. We met at work, we did some overtime and … one evening, it got out of hand … and it just happened. It was mad, inspector. We were both blinded. Secretive meetings, sneaking out of the office to have a quick … shag in the toilet or in our car.' He shrugs almost apologetically. 'You know.'

I don't. I have never been brave or adventurous enough to get myself into situations where you can get caught easily. Even with Lucie, my ex-wife. After our divorce, she accused me of not being romantic. To me, it had nothing to do with love and romance. I wasn't interested in a quick shag somewhere. Lucie laughed out loud with pity in her eyes when I said so.

Trevor is staring into the distance, seeing nothing, by the looks of it, recalling his illicit assignations. Maureen isn't the romantic type either. I knew instinctively when I met her, but Trevor has learned from his mistakes and he has settled down.

'We got caught in the act eventually, by my boss,' he continues, with an embarrassed smile. 'Very embarrassing at the time, but we laughed about it afterwards.' He pauses again and shrugs. 'Our laughing didn't last long, though. By then, the whole company knew about it and the situation became awkward. We decided that one of us had to leave.'

'She left?'

He sees my expression. 'Her choice, inspector. I wasn't keen on staying here either, to be honest, with all the gossip and all that, but she didn't want to ruin my career. She wasn't too keen on the job anyway and she quit three weeks later.'

'And then?'

'She was gone and so were our feelings. It could all have ended just like that, but it didn't. Somehow Alicia heard about it. Obviously, she was furious. Sad also. We … tried, but it never worked after that.'

'When did you meet Maureen?'

'That was about six months later. Her husband had died three years before that. We met on one of those online dating sites and … we got on well and … her children liked me.'

It seems an odd thing to say about someone he married, but I decide to let it rest. Perhaps he doesn't mean it like that.

'When Alicia and you parted, how was the relationship between you? Were you on speaking terms?'

'Oh no. She was angry and hurt. I could understand that, so I left at her request.'

'What about your daughter?'

'Briony?' A dark cloud crosses over his face. 'She ... I didn't see her for months. Which was difficult, inspector. She ... Alicia refused to let me see her. The girl had nothing to do with it, mind you, but still she was punished for my mistakes.'

'But it changed. When was that?'

'That was when Alicia met Kenneth. I'm not sure but I think he softened her a bit and, eventually, she agreed to let me see our daughter every other weekend. Like we do ... like we did until the present day. We also made arrangements about holidays and, to be honest, everything worked out fine in the end, but ... I'm not sure what will happen now.'

'How do you mean?'

'Briony ... I hope she will come to live with us, but if Kenneth ... She gets on with Kenneth very well and he might think that it would be better for her to stay where she is.'

'You would agree to that?'

He shrugs. 'Yes and no. I mean there have been issues with her in the past but ... I hope that's all been resolved now. But for the moment, if it is what Briony wants, I won't push her. It will be hard enough for her to lose her mother, it wouldn't be fair to take her away from the home she's had for the last few years.'

Briony must have been four at the time. They say that people can barely remember anything from before the age of three. Perhaps Briony won't even remember very much of what it was like when her parents were married and they lived as a family.

'What did you mean when you mentioned there were issues in the past?'

'Hmm.' He stares at me reluctantly, already regretting that he'd let that slip. He has decided to answer my questions, but not to give me any further, unasked information.

'At some point, Alicia accused me that I hadn't been a real father to Briony. But that wasn't true, inspector. I love that girl to bits. Always have, always will. But it was at the same time that I had that relationship with the woman at work. Well, I can't say any more than that I must have neglected Briony a bit. And Alicia too. Ken is aware of that and … Maureen believes that he might use that against me if it comes to court.'

'Maybe the three of you ought to have a proper talk about your daughter. You can go to court, but, in my opinion, that's not always the best option.' I have seen too many painful outcomes determined in court to advise him otherwise.

'I think we should wait until this is all behind us,' he says pensively. 'I mean … when can the funeral be arranged?'

'I hope soon.' Changing the subject completely, I move in the seat, feeling it shift to the left. 'Mr Bennett, were you aware of what happened, when your ex-wife and your daughter were on holiday in Portugal last summer?'

He nods, annoyance crossing his face. 'I suspect you're referring to her being taken into police custody for one night.' It isn't a question.

'I was.'

He shakes his head, clearly reliving his anger and frustration. 'Unbelievable. You would expect that a woman of her age had more sense than getting arrested for being drunk and falling over her own feet at night, wouldn't you?'

'How did you know about it?'

He stretches his neck like an alert meerkat, gazing over the top of the bushes, sniffing for danger lurking somewhere in the vicinity. He is uncomfortable and I'm getting the feeling that my vague hunch appears to be right: there is something he hasn't told me. Something that might change our idea that Alicia's death had to do with the dogging meeting in that car park at the fishing lake that night.

'Why? Has what happened on that holiday got anything to do with her murder?'

'We are following several lines of enquiry, Mr Bennett, as we have not been able to determine the killer's identity or his motive.'

'I doubt that incident in Portugal was the reason.' His mood changes rapidly. Anger crosses his face. Defiance. And suddenly, he is less cooperative. 'Look inspector, have you got nothing else to do? Like finding the man who killed the mother of my daughter?'

'We're doing our best to …'

'Not with this nonsense I hope, inspector. This happened … how long ago? Months ago. If what happened in Portugal last summer was the motive, then the killer waited a damn long time.'

'You are right, Mr Bennett, but you know … or maybe you don't know, that we go through everything thoroughly before we dismiss anything.' I smile at him and I see his shoulders relax a bit. 'One more question on this subject, though, Mr Bennett. Do you know why they released her without charging her? I under-stand that the Portuguese police have a rather strong policy on drunken behaviour. They don't let tourists off lightly just with a warning.'

'I wasn't there, inspector.'

'No, but the Portuguese police called you, and not her hus-band. And you spoke to her yourself.'

He shrugs. 'You seem to know everything already, inspec-tor. Yes, I did speak to Alicia at the time. The Portuguese police called me. I suppose it was because of Briony. Her last name is Bennett and perhaps they didn't realise that we were divorced.'

'Did you ask them not to press charges?'

He scowls. 'Believe you me, Mr Tregunna, I would happily have travelled to Portugal to pick up Briony while her mother was spending some time in a Portuguese prison. That would teach her.'

I lean back and stare at him, realising what he just said. 'So you do have a motive, Mr Bennett? With her death, it may be easier for you to get custody of your daughter. Is that why you killed her?'

'Me?' He rises, pressing a hand into his lower back and he grimaces as if relieving himself of lower back pain. 'I think it is time to go, inspector. I don't like to be accused of murdering someone.'

His glares at me with a mixture of pain and annoyance. Then a long fart escapes from my stoma bag. I try to press my hand on it, but it has no effect. Blushing with embarrassment, I open my mouth to apologise, but the look on his face stops me. Somehow, the almost triumphant look in his eyes makes me want to hurt him. I can't find the words and instead I turn back to my mental questionnaire.

'Mr Bennett, can you tell me who Alicia's godfather is?'

His face turns from pink to a shade of yellowish grey. 'Mr Tregunna, I would like you to leave. Now. I find your questions ridiculous and irrelevant. If you have something to say to me, or to ask me, please do so as soon as I have arranged for a lawyer because, clearly, you seem convinced that I killed my ex-former wife.'

'This godfather has …'

He shakes his head disgustedly. 'As far as I know, inspector, Alicia never had godparents, so I can't help you there. Now, would you be so kind as to leave these premises? Contrary to you, I have a job to do, you see.'

28

I don't possess the social skills that help me to make friends in an easy, casual way. Whenever someone comes close enough to become a friend, whether subconsciously or not I seem to manage to scare them off, mostly by refusing to confide in them. Friends are there to help each other and therefore they need to know things about each other. I am generally considered as a very good listener, but I rarely tell my inner thoughts to anyone else. I've always thought nobody would be interested in my thoughts and opinions, a habit that is still a big part of my life.

I would never have chosen my neighbour, Harradine Curtis, as a friend, but things have developed between us. Perhaps it is because he is nosy and therefore knows things about me without me telling him. As he is also quite opinionated, he often lets me know what he would do in certain circumstances, and what he thinks about news items or people we both know, albeit sometimes vaguely, or even not at all, like celebrities on television.

On many occasions he has told me how he feels about the development of my relationship with Lauren. Or rather, the non-existent relationship with her.

I know he is right. I know I have to talk to Lauren, and perhaps explain a bit, not everything, not the real reason, about why I left her house so abruptly the last time we met. Eventually, Curtis managed to persuade me to pick up the phone and dial her number. He just wouldn't leave my apartment, before he'd made sure I'd spoken to her. And I have. Her reaction was cautious and hesitant, understandable in the circumstances. Prompted by Curtis, I told her that I was sorry and could I come and see her, some time, to apologise. Eventually she said yes, albeit too reluctantly for comfort. I know now that I can't afford to wait before I pick up the courage to appear on her doorstep. With a bunch of flowers, if I follow my neighbour's instructions to the letter.

Emerging from the rather dark entrance hall of the police station, I squint my eyes in the bright sunshine. There is a feeling of Spring in the air. Mothers are appearing from the narrow street that leads towards the school with children happy that the school day is over, school uniforms dishevelled and smudged with bits of school lunch and coloured crayons. Staring at a group of three young mothers and half a dozen children, all laughing and looking happy, I feel myself slipping into a dark depression. I think about Lauren and her twin sons who might possibly offer me the closeness of my own family. If it ever gets that far. I think about Alicia and her daughter Briony who will miss her mother dearly, and about Denise whose son Jake is showing the signs of becoming a rebellious teenager.

'Inspector?'

I become gradually aware that someone has called my name but I was miles away. The voice is hesitant. I turn to see a young woman approaching, carrying a young child in a purple and green baby sling in front of her, the top of a small head with wispy blond hair just peeping out. She is out of breath, as if she has been in training for a charity run.

'Excuse me. Are you the inspector investigating the death of Alicia Poole?'

'I am.'

'I saw you come out of the police station and I followed you,' she confesses without a touch of guilt, breathing heavily in and out to regain control.

She has stopped a few meters away from me, which seems a rather odd distance. Not far enough to have to speak loudly, not close enough for a confidential chat either. It's like she's attached to an invisible elastic cord and she's afraid that she'll be pulled back when it stretches beyond its limit.

'You could have come in and asked for me,' I say warmly.

'No.' She adjusts the sling in which she and the young child are wrapped together.

'I might know something.' She lowers her voice, but doesn't come closer. Perhaps she has this weird idea that I will grab her and take her into custody at the police station, where she can't escape.

'About the murder investigation?' I ask, trying not to sound too hopeful.

'It may be nothing.' She shrugs, mentally pulling back.

'Or it may be something.'

Sometimes you come across people like this. Innocent witnesses who feel under pressure to do the right thing but are hesitant because they don't know what the implications of their actions might be, especially to themselves. You don't have to look far for them though because regardless of appeals you make for information, they just pop up, in their own good time. Often,, they don't even realise how valuable their information turns out to be.

'Can I get you a drink? Tea? Coffee?' I look round, finding a little café with tables in the windows, empty ones against the back walls. 'There?'

It isn't exactly her style, or mine, but it is perfect for now. There won't be much risk that someone she knows will see her in there. If that's what she is worried about.

She checks the display on the mobile phone in her hand. 'Uhm … I haven't got much time.'

'I don't know, perhaps it won't take long for you to tell me what you know,' I suggest gently, hoping I am winning her trust.

'Yes. No, I guess you're right.' Her head jerks from side to side, looking around, checking that there isn't anyone she knows. 'I haven't got much time,' she repeats with a hint of distress.

'We'll have tea or coffee.'

She shrugs, her eyes almost tearful, so I add for some reassurance: 'Perhaps they do nice cakes.'

'Alright then.'

She walks two steps behind me. To a bystander, it may not be obvious whether we are together or not. I guess not; she's not my type and she is too young for me anyway. But then why would I be with a young woman and a baby?

She sits down, her back to the entrance, adjusting the child automatically and she pushes loose strands of dark hair from her face. She has bright and intelligent, blue-green eyes and a smile that was at first warm and charming, but now only shows her anxiety.

'Your first child?' I ask, mainly to relieve the tension, choosing my words with care because I am not able to determine what may be obvious to others but not to me: whether the child is a boy or a girl. I don't want to hurt her feelings.

'Yeah,' she says, automatically checking to see if the baby is alright. Then her face lights up with a smile. 'He ruins my nights, though.'

He. A boy. 'Can I take your name?'

Immediately she is taken aback. 'My name? Do you need to know?'

'That depends how important your information is.'

She looks around again. Checking. Nervous. As if she is scared. Something catches her eye and she changes her mind. 'I really have no time for tea or coffee.'

'We can walk,' I suggest. 'Up that street, around the corner there? Nobody will pay us any attention.'

'Uhm … maybe, yes, but I need to go, so is it okay if we walk that way?'

Shrugging apologetically at the café owner, I follow her outside. She gestures towards a small alley between two shops. There is a bin bag shoved in the corner, torn open by seagulls perhaps or some small rodent. Dark stains on the walls, murky puddles underfoot, the alley smells as if it's been used by people who can't be bothered to find a loo or pay to use a public toilet since local councils started charging due to budget cuts and choices had to be made as to where to make savings.

The young mother sees my distaste, shrugs. 'It's the shortest way to my home.'

'Alright.' It's not an area I would choose for a conversation. The alley is barely wide enough for two people to walk beside each other,. She walks in front of me, expecting me to follow her, yet not looking over her shoulder to see if I do.

'I am Andy,' I say, by way of encouragement.'

'Oh … uhm … Rosie.'

It's a lie and we both know it. Yet I make a mental note of the name. If someone has to come up with a name, and has no time to think about it, the first name they come up with is of someone they know or are related to. Not necessarily someone close, but … friends, distant relatives, someone they've recently seen or met. A name swirling in the head subconsciously.

'Is it about Alicia Poole's murderer?' I start encouragingly.

'Uhm … not really.'

'Wilbur Torrington?'

'No, no, not him. It is about the woman. Alicia.'

'Did you know Alicia Poole?' I ask.

'Uhm … only through a mutual friend, really. We weren't friends, if that's what you mean.'

I feel like I've hit a brick wall.

'Did you know her at all? Alicia?'

'We … no, but I knew of her.'

She is tentative, nervous, now constantly looking over her shoulders, but not at me. She stops at the end of the alley, looking round the corner as if she's playing hide and seek. Her baby is waking up, making tiny sounds at first then crying hungrily.

'What's his name?'

'What …? Oh, sorry.' Her lips curl in a proud motherly smile. 'It's Harry.' As much as she was cautious about not telling me her own name, she tells me the baby's name with no hesitation, only realising she's let down her guard when the little one increases his volume.

'How old?' I ask, appearing not to have noticed.

'Uhm … six months.' Even I could have guessed about that, by the size of him.

She turns left into a street of small bungalows on one side and a row of garages and sheds on the other. The road is tarmacked but covered in potholes. Four old battered cars are lined up alongside the garages. One is missing all four doors, the other three are placed on piles of bricks where the tyres have been removed. It is one way to avoid your car being stolen.

The bungalows have small front gardens, mostly paved over or littered with rubble. The odd one has some sad looking shrubs alongside the knee-high concrete walls bordering each of the spaces. A very depressing environment to live in. I hope, for the little boy's sake, that this is not where she lives.

A car engine comes to life and Rosie almost jumps as though she has a guilty conscience. Diesel fumes cloud the car's rear end for a moment and I see her wince, shielding the baby from the poisonous air with a hand over his face.

Catching up with her, I start walking beside her, trying to peep at the little boy's face, and she smiles with the warmth of a proud young mother.

'How well did you know Alicia Poole?' I ask again.

'I didn't know her.'

The car engine is almost too loud to hear what she says. I follow her annoyed gaze. The driver has climbed out and is now almost bent double to fetch something from the back seats.

'Then what …?'

'Over here.' She stops at a small gate made of wood that was once painted green and now has a weathered grey colour. The hinges are rusty. She pushes it open and it gets stuck on the uneven path that leads to a porch, with a few shrubs on either side. The bungalow has whitewashed walls and white window frames covered in a layer of dirt, but the windows themselves have been washed recently and the net curtains behind look clean.

A few terracotta pots with the remains of last year's geraniums are lined up to one side of the porch. The plants have so far survived the mild winter, but only just.

Rosie, or whatever her real name is, unlocks the porch and takes off her shoes. She's wearing bright red socks and slips her feet into a pair of black-and-white slippers with panda bear faces on her toes.

'Adam?' she shouts, but the house seems empty.

'I'll make us some tea,' she says, 'then I'll have to breast-feed the baby. I hope you don't mind.'

'Of course not,' I say, uneasy.

I enter a living room with a threadbare beige carpet, a faded green fabric settee and two non-matching armchairs, and a chipped and painted coffee table. There is a TV set on a white MDF cabinet, its bottom shelf full of DVD boxes. On the floor are some old shoe boxes. There are bright floral curtains, not quite long enough to cover the window, giving the overall impression that the room was furnished on a budget or from a charity shop.

She is unwinding the sling, carefully holding Harry against her body.

'Shall I put the kettle on?' I offer, wondering if she is embarrassed by my presence or to cope with my own embarrassment at the thought of her breast-feeding.

'The kitchen is a mess,' she says, shrugging, but she seems to accept my offer, as she sits down on one of the very uncomfortable looking armchairs and removes the baby sling and pulls up her shirt. The little boy opens his eyes, looks round for something familiar and when he sees his mother's face opens his mouth to let her know that he is hungry.

She was right about the kitchen. It looks like she only does the washing up when all the crockery, pots and pans are dirty. I fill the kettle and push the switch down, but it isn't working. I try again, with no result. I wash two mugs under the tap. The water is tepid. A small round Quality Street tin holds a dozen tea bags, and an open packet of biscuits, half eaten, is tied up in a clear plastic bag.

'Milk is in the fridge!'

I open the fridge. It is almost empty and the light doesn't come on.

'Do you have a pay-as-you-go meter for the electricity?' I ask, standing in the doorway and looking down at her. The baby lies in the crook of her arm, pressed against a small white breast, sucking contentedly. Her other arm is on the armrest, holding a mobile phone. She's tapping away on the screen with remarkable speed.

'Oh, I forgot. The top-up stick is in my bag.' She nods towards her shoulder bag, which she dropped onto the floor as she came in. 'Do you mind? The meter is in the porch.'

'No problem.'

Her bag is full of things that a young mother would need. A large red purse, a plastic make-up bag, tampons, wet-wipes and nappies for the baby, a multi-coloured spectacle case, a cheap pen with the logo of some builders company, a hairbrush and empty wrappers of chocolate bars. I am disappointed that there is no ID card.

'The electricity stick is in the glasses case,' she says helpfully.

She tops the stick up with ten pounds, but as the meter was already on emergency. I wonder how long it will last her.

The fridge hums when I return to the kitchen and I switch on the kettle and dry the mugs with a tea towel that is not surprisingly olean and dry considering the stack of unwashed dishes.

When I return to the room with two mugs of tea and some biscuits, she has moved the boy to her other breast and stares into the distance.

'The electricity won't last very long,' I warn her.

'I know. Adam will come home later and he'll bring some cash.' There doesn't seem to be a need to be secretive about her identity anymore.

'Adam is …?'

'My husband.' She points at the shoe boxes by the TV cabinet. 'Can you open that white box, please?'

I pull the box from under the cabinet. It is old with damaged edges, but there is no speck of dust on the lid. 'What am I looking for?' I ask, putting the lid to one side and staring at a heap of photos.

'A school photo of last year.'

'Perhaps it would be better if you have a look yourself,' I say, pushing a photo of a smiling woman sitting on a sunny beach under another one.

'Maybe.' She rummages in the box and retrieves a white envelope dated June last year on one corner. 'This is the one.'

She takes her mug and blows the steam away. 'Those biscuits are stale,' she grunts distractedly, nevertheless, she takes a bite of one. 'So, inspector, tell me what you see.'

I have opened the envelope and take out a school photo of a girl. She is about seven years old, grinning at the camera, her hair in two plaits that start beside her temples with several coloured hair clips arranged randomly. She is wearing a white blouse that seems to give her face a translucent shine.

'But this is ...' I pause to correct myself. 'No, it isn't.'

'It is a picture of Adam's sister's daughter. Yvonne. It was taken last year at school. She is now seven years old.'

'But how ...?'

She grins. 'That's what struck me too, inspector. I noticed it immediately when I saw that photo in the newspaper.'

I don't have to ask her which photo she means. A special service was held for Alicia in the local church and as Kenneth Poole and Trevor Bennett came out afterwards, they had Briony between them, each holding her hand. The girl had been crying, but there was a glimmer of a smile on her face when reporters ran towards them, shouting their questions.

'This is ... extraordinary.' Apart from an age gap of roughly two years, Briony Bennett and this girl Yvonne could well be twin sisters.

29

A tall and slender woman in her early thirties opens the door. A raven-black fringe almost obscures her green eyes, otherwise her hair is so short it looks like it has been shaven recently. On her neck, she has a tattoo of a black spider with red eyes sitting in a web. She lives on a new estate outside Newquay that was built under a government scheme to help young people get on the housing ladder. In the distance, the iconic shapes of the so-called clay mountains are barely visible in a fog that seems to get thicker by the minute.

'Yes?' She has a toddler on her hip, a little boy who looks sleepy and is quietly sucking a dummy.

'I would like to talk to Susanna Keogh. Is that you?'

'No.' A faint smile. 'She's not home yet. I'm Billie Keogh, Susanna's wife.'

I am barely able to hide my surprise. Perhaps she is used to reactions like mine. Same-sex marriages seem to have become more common these days, but I can't always get my head around it. I do believe that people have the right to make their own decisions and I have nothing against gay marriages, but it can still take me by surprise sometimes.

'What time do you expect Susanna home?'

She glances at a thick, black watch that is too big for her wrist. 'She won't be home before seven.

I look at my watch. It is almost six. 'It is really important that I speak to her, Mrs Keogh.'

'Yeah, well, as I said, she won't be home until seven.' She frowns. 'What is it about?'

'Sorry, I am Detective Inspector Tregunna.' I see her eyes widen in shock and I add quickly. 'Her name has come up in connection with the investigation into the death of a young woman. I'm sure you've heard about it. Alicia Poole. She was found in a fishing lake last Monday.'

'Oh.' Shock is partly overtaken by surprise. She looks at the child as if to shield him from anything unpleasant. 'I heard about it, yes, but what has that to do with Susanna?'

'Probably nothing, but her name has come up in our investigation. And the way we work is that we not only look for evidence to identify and convict the murderer, but it is also important that we eliminate everyone else whose name we come across who may be connected to the murder.'

'You can't possibly think that Susanna ...'

'I didn't say anything of the kind, Mrs Keogh. I am here to find out whether we can remove her name from our list.'

'A list? Oh.'

I smile at her, aware that she is curious. 'Is it possible to wait for her here?' I ask amiably.

She steps back, more or less inviting me in. 'Susanna works until half past five, but today, she's going to collect our daughter from a friend's house and takes her to ballet lessons.' She hesitates. Reluctant, but her curiosity takes over. 'Can I help you?'

'Maybe you can.' I follow her into a hallway. The largest of the white walls is covered with portraits of what could be ancient relatives. Coats and shoes seem are stored behind a door with a black chalkboard nailed to its surface with a short shopping list and some children's drawings pinned onto it. It feels warm and welcoming.

'It would be very helpful, Mrs Keogh.'

'Alright then.' She seems annoyed with herself that she has let me in, albeit as far as the hallway, but she doesn't know how to get out of it. Besides, she did seem keen to learn more about the dead woman in the local media, and no doubt there has been a lot of speculation about the death on Facebook and Twitter.

'Please come through, inspector.'

Opening a door to an open-plan living room and kitchen, she dumps the little boy in a play pen and shoves some toys scattered on the floor to the side with her foot. 'Please take a seat, inspector.'

'Thank you. I have some photos here. I was hoping Susanna would be able to tell me who these people are. But you might also know.'

'I hope I can help you.' Her cheeks redden as she realises that she might be useful to the investigation. Or perhaps she thinks that if she can help me if she can help me, I won't need to wait for Susanna to come home.

I take two photos from my pocket and place them next to each other on the coffee table.

'How did you …?' She stops, staring at the photo on the right. 'That's our Yvonne. I'm certain of it. Where did you get that photo?'

I don't reply. I wait for her to continue. 'The other girl looks older. Like what Yvonne will be like in a couple of years. The … the likeness is amazing.'

'That's what I thought too,' I say gently. 'It may be a coincidence, but I don't believe in coincidences. Do you?'

'No.' She shakes her head.

'Do you know the other girl?'

'No.' Suddenly there is concern clouding her eyes and her mouth has tightened. 'I'm not sure if Susanna can help you, inspector.'

'What makes you say that?'

She pulls the zipper of her navy blue Weird Fish cardigan up to her chin and pulls the collar up to under her lips. I get the impression her face is a few shades paler. 'I'm afraid you can't stay here after all, inspector.'

'I need to wait for Susanna.'

'No. I don't think she'll want to talk to you. She won't be able to tell you anything anyway. I don't know the name of the other girl and I'm sure Susanna doesn't know either.'

Her voice is raised and the little boy in the play pen looks up, frightened, lips trembling and eyes filling with tears, ready to start crying. Protectively, she picks him up and presses his face against the tattoo on her neck. The spider's bright red eyes don't seem to scare him.

'Is he yours?' I ask, merely to distract and relax her. 'Or Susanna's?'

'Yes, he is mine,' she snaps almost violently. 'Mine and Susanna's. You have no right …'

'I'm not here to upset, Mrs Keogh,' I say soothingly. 'I'm just trying to establish who these girls in the photos are.'

'I told you, didn't I? I've never seen that other girl. I can't help you. Yes, the young one is our Yvonne. Full name Yvonne Keogh, Susanna's daughter, but I think you already know that.'

I decide not to react to her accusing words. 'When was Yvonne born?'

'On the fourth of February. She has just turned seven.' She takes a sharp intake of breath. 'But that's all I can tell you, inspector.' She looks at me with despair in her eyes. Then, without warning, she bursts into tears. Seeing his mother in distress, the little boy also starts crying.

'I didn't mean to upset you,' I say lamely. 'Or the boy.'

'Please go, inspector. Leave us alone. I can promise you, we have nothing to do with the death of that woman.'

I shake my head. 'I'm pretty sure you don't but, nevertheless, I do need to know who the other girl is,' I lie. 'To me, it looks as if they are … closely related.'

'But I've never seen her in my life!'

'I was hoping Susanna has. That's why I need to see her, so why don't we wait until she comes home? Then this will soon be over.' I don't want to let this go. Whether it will turn out to be significant or not, I am very intrigued by this situation although I'm not sure if it is in any way related to the murder case at all. It feels like I'm chasing shadows and as soon as one fades, another one pops up. More frustratingly, whichever line of inquiry I follow, the more potential suspects seem to emerge. Further complicating the case.

'But Susanna … I'm sure she has …'

I shake my head, cutting her off almost rudely. Suddenly, I feel tired and I don't want to have to go and come back later. 'Let's make ourselves a cup of tea, shall we? While we wait for … your wife?'

She stares at me, uncertain. In her eyes, I have probably become a monster who is a threat to life and she doesn't understand it. Which is probably all the more frightening. She lowers the little boy onto the floor and he claws to his toys, grabbing a red plastic fire engine and pressing a button on its roof. A blue light starts flashing and a tinny voice says: 'Hello. Where is the fire? Let's go to the fire.' The voice repeats until the light stops flashing, and the boy presses the button again.

'Stop that, Charlie!' Billie snatches the toy from his fingers and without having to look she finds a little switch to turn the battery off.

I see resentment in her muscles when she turns her back to me as she moves to the kitchen area, where she makes tea while she keeps an eye on the boy. He is examining the toy, wondering why the light and the sound aren't working any more. I wonder how long it will take him to find the switch and realise his mother has removed the batteries. Children seem to work these things out at a very young age nowadays and as if on cue, Charlie pulls himself up to the couch and finds a hibernating iPad and pressing his little fingers on the empty screen, it comes to life.

'How old is he?' I ask, shocked to see that he is now tapping away and choose a cartoon film on YouTube.

'Fifteen months.'

'He can do more with that tablet than I can.'

A small smile lights up her face. 'He learns all that from Yvonne.'

'Do you know Yvonne's father?' I ask gently, yet I hope she hears in my voice that I won't take no for an answer.

She shakes her head, concentrating on measuring out tealeaves into a China teapot and pouring hot water over it. 'I don't think …'

'Is it Trevor Bennett?'

'Who?'

'Trevor Bennett.'

'I've never heard of that name.'

'He is the father of the other girl.'

'Oh!' Her voice trembles. 'I thought you said you wanted to know who she is.'

The boy looks up, his eyes wary, ready to start crying, but he finds another cartoon on the tablet and watches it totally absorbed, although probably not understanding a word of it.

His mother puts the old-fashioned teapot under a tea cosy that has rococo stitched on it. Vintage seems to have entered this household. 'I really can't help you, inspector,' she says lamely, shaking her head as if she needs to be convinced herself.

Then she picks up the boy, lowers herself on the couch and, undoing the zipper of her Weird Fish cardigan, lifts her shirt to reveal a swollen breast and a stain on a white vest underneath. As she presses him into the crook of her arm and he starts sucking her nipple, I realise that it is the second time this afternoon that I witness a young woman breast-feeding her child.

'The tea will be ready in a couple of minutes,' she says, suddenly calm.

'I'll find us some cups or mugs,' I say, my voice hoarse.

I look at her, sitting on the couch, her eyes still red, the black fringe on the bridge of her nose, but there is serenity on her face that makes me swallow suddenly.

I think of Lauren and I know I want to see her again. I love her. I need her. Maybe it is not too late. And I definitely need to speak to the doctors in Treliske about this problem of mine. All I can think of now is imagining Lauren, breast-feeding our baby … surely it must be possible to sort this out, make me able to make love …

'I guess it will be easy enough for you to find out about us,' Billie says, as if she needs to fill the silence. 'I met Susanna about five years ago,' she continues, looking down at her child, who seems to have fallen asleep, his bottom lip stuck on her nipple. 'At that time, she was still living with Tony, but their marriage was more or less over. They hadn't slept together for a long time, she told me. I had no reason not to believe her, did I? I never asked about the details of their relationship and she didn't tell me much. Not then. She was going to get a divorce, she promised me, which was all I needed to know.'

'So Yvonne is Tony's daughter?' I ask incredulously.

She shakes her head fervently. 'She got her divorce and we married three years ago. We were happy, until … some time ago, when Yvonne had an accident on her bike. Nothing serious, fortunately, but it looked really bad in the beginning. We were so scared to lose her. But it all went well and Yvonne came home a week later. Susanna and I … our relationship had changed, though. Yvonne's accident had made me realise that I wasn't number one in Susanna's life. That was Yvonne and I knew that would always be the case.' She stops and sighs, offering a watery smile. 'I know it sounds horrible, but I got jealous, really jealous. I even started to dislike Yvonne. I hated myself for it, but I couldn't help it. I was jealous. I tried to hide it, but Susanna knew, she understood.'

She looks up shyly, uncertain whether it would be better to wait for Susanna after all.

'They were too young when they married. Susanna had her doubts, but she didn't realise that she was a lesbian. She hated the physical side of their marriage, but she couldn't understand why and she thought it was normal. She didn't enjoy having sex with Tony and she told him honestly. Then Susanna thought their marriage could be saved by a baby, but Tony refused. Knowing she preferred women, he felt … so humiliated. He left her and Susanna lived with a woman for a while. It didn't work. This particular woman was older, she had three children from two previous marriages and Susanna knew she would always be less important than the children.' She smiles sadly. 'That's how she understood so well why I was struggling with my feelings for Yvonne. But then ... she told me about Yvonne and ... it all made sense, you know. We discussed every angle of it and then the decision was made.' She looks down on her son, a tender smile on her lips. 'We decided that the only way our marriage could survive was if I also had a child. It would make us equals, you understand that?'

'Yes, but ...' I'm not sure where this is going. I am investigating a murder. I feel almost embarrassed listening to the heartache of a lesbian couple.

'We discussed it endlessly and ...' She stops to gesture towards the teapot. 'I think our brew is ready, inspector, would you ...?'

'Of course.' I'm not too pleased by with the interruption, but I daren't put pressure on her to carry on with her story.

'It took only two months before I was pregnant and this is the result. My little man, Charlie.'

'You slept with the father of Susanna's daughter?' I ask incredulously. 'With Tony?'

'Well, not exactly.' She blushes. 'He would ...' She stops abruptly when the door opens and a young girl runs in, dropping a sports bag on the floor in the middle of the room.

'Yvonne!' A voice from the hallway shouts, half annoyed. ''Have you forgotten something?'

I stare at the girl, who has jumped on the couch next to Billie and is cuddling her and the boy at the same time. I recognise her immediately from the photos: she is a younger version of Briony.

'We have a visitor,' Billie exclaims nervously, stroking the girl's hair. 'Say hello to Mr Tregunna, Yvonne.'

The girl turns to see me looking at her and grins. Once more I'm struck by the resemblance.

'Hello Mr Tregunna,' she says politely.

'Mr Tregunna is a detective inspector,' Billie says carefully, omitting to say the word 'police. He's come to see you, Sue.'

'Yes?' She has short cropped hair, though not as short as Billie's, a stud in the side of her nose and dark grey eyes.

'It's about a photo,' Billie says uncomfortably, in her eyes a warning that Yvonne is looking and listening.

'He came to ask about ... who did you say, Mr Tregunna?'

The woman in the doorway hasn't moved. Although she reminded her daughter about her manners, she hasn't made a move to greet me properly herself.

'Trevor Bennett,' I say.

'Who?' There is genuine surprise on her face and consequently, she relaxes a bit.

'I'll get you some tea, Sue.' Slowly not to wake the boy, Billie rises to her feet, grabbing Yvonne's arm with her free hand. 'Will you help me, Yvonne? Charlie is asleep, so I could do with a bit of help.' Diplomatically she moves to the kitchen, pushing the girl in front of her. She doesn't offer to get me more tea, clearly hoping that I will ask Susanna my questions, and then leave.

I explain to Susanna about the investigation and I can see on her face that her confusion is only growing. 'I'm sorry that I have to ask you. Mrs Keogh, but is Trevor Bennett the father of your daughter?'

'I don't know anyone with that name.'

I show her the photo of Briony and she is shocked by the likeness. 'Who is this? Is this a joke?'

'Her name is Briony. She is nine years old and she is the daughter of the woman I have just told you about. Her father is Trevor Bennett and … well, you can see how much the girls are alike. I was just wondering if Briony and Yvonne might have the same father.'

'How did you find us?' In the circumstances, I think that her reaction is rather odd. If she doesn't know Trevor, or Alicia, why not ask me who they are?

'Someone who came forward in our investigation mentioned the resemblance between Briony and your daughter,' I reply vaguely.

'Who?'

'I'm afraid I can't tell you.'

'It wasn't him? The man you just mentioned?'

'Who? Trevor? No, I haven't spoken to him about this but I'm going to do that later.' I'm not really looking forward to another meeting with Bennett. Somehow, I know that he won't be pleased by the latest discoveries at all.

'No, no. I don't mean the man you call Trevor. I mean … Sorry.' She realises that she's nearly said too much. 'I can't.'

'You can't what?'

'Nothing. I don't know anyone called Trevor Bennett.'

'You are saying he is not Yvonne's father?'
'Definitely not. Now, please inspector, leave us alone.'

30

According to his assistant in the warehouse, Trevor has taken the afternoon off. Assuming that he will already have left his work by the time I get to the Liskeard area, I drive to his home. A tatty old Peugeot is parked on the drive and in front of the house is a dark grey Citroen Picasso. I park behind it.

'Is your husband in?' Maureen Bennett's eyes are red and she clasps her neck with one hand. The other hand, holding the edge of the door, has a balled handkerchief in it.

I stare at her, knowing instantly that something is wrong. 'Are you all right, Mrs Bennett?'

'What happened? Is Trevor alright?' Panic makes her voice high and tinny.

I force a smile. 'Are you alright?' I ask.

'Yes, of course … I just got home.' Somehow, she seems to find reassurance on my face. She relaxes and her shoulders drop. 'I had a phone call from Alfie's school. They said that something happened to him in the PE lesson. I thought that he must have had a fall or something like that, so I dropped everything and drove to the school. But when I arrived there … it was weird. Nothing had happened. They seemed surprised that I was there in the first place.' She sniffs and wipes her nose with the handkerchief. 'It then became clear to me that they … I mean the people from the school, hadn't called me.'

'Did you see your son? Was he okay?'

'Oh, I did see Alfie but he was with his friends. He looked perfectly okay and I thought I'd better not bother him with my worries.'

'Worries?'

'About that phone call.' She shakes her head as if she's trying to make sense of it again. 'It must have been someone's idea of a bad joke.'

I nod, not at all convinced. Why would someone scare a mother like that? Why her?

'Did you speak to the PE teacher?'

'Of course I did, but he didn't know what I was talking about.' She bows her head and I see a tear drop onto her chest. 'He said he understood the situation … with Alicia and all that.' She lifts her head again and shows a brave little smile. 'He must have thought I am mad.'

'You were worried.'

'Yes, I was. I thought … well, don't they say that bad things and accidents always come in threes? Alicia was the first, of course, then Trevor, and then Alfie.'

I am still on the doorstep and she hasn't moved either. Alicia. Trevor. Alfie. Something is wrong here. 'Mrs Bennett, can I come in?'

'I suppose so.' She hesitates, as if she has a question on her lips, but is not sure if she wants to hear the answer. 'But you'll have to wait if you want to speak to Trevor. He isn't here.' She steps back and gestures with her hand. All the doors are closed and the long hallway is dark.

'You just said that accidents and bad things come in threes. What did you mean by that? What's happened to Trevor?' I ask, following her into a cold living room. Yesterday's newspaper is spread out on one side of the settee, a pair of slippers, presumably Trevor's, are scattered under the table. Two empty tea cups are on the coffee table, next to a book with a bookmark stuck between the pages. A historic novel. Maureen's.

She turns and scrutinises my face. 'Are you here to tell me that Trevor has had an accident, inspector?'

'No.' I sit down on the nearest seat closest to the book. It feels warm and comfortable and I can easily imagine her sitting there with her book and dozing off while Trevor watches football on TV. Simple family life. I think of my own home. Comfortable and warm, but lonely. Nobody to talk to when I come home, to discuss items what's on TV or in the papers. Or what's happened during the day. Even though, at the moment, her life doesn't seem as rosy as I might think, I envy Maureen Bennett.

'Shall I make a brew?' she asks, flexing and unflexing her fingers, moving the handkerchief from one hand to the other.

'Sit down, Mrs Bennett. Tell me about Trevor. Clearly, you are concerned.'

She sniffs and presses the handkerchief against her nose. 'Just before I got the call from Alfie's school, Trevor had phoned me. He normally gives me a call before he leaves his work and today … he planned to have the afternoon off. He can't get his head round his job at the moment, you see. He is so shocked about what happened to Alicia.'

'They had been together for ... how many years?'

'About twelve years.'

'Oh, go on, please Mrs Bennett.'

'He called me, like he always does. There is a supermarket on his way home and I can always ask him to get me anything I've forgotten to buy. I asked him to buy some milk, as ours had gone off this morning. He said, no problem, and as soon as I put the phone down was when Alfie's school rang. I jumped in my car without even thinking about writing a note for Trevor to tell him where I was. Good job I didn't, I thought afterwards, when I drove back home, because ... well there is some tension between us since ... Alicia's death. I felt rather silly about the whole thing with Alfie. I couldn't ... I didn't intend to tell Trevor where I'd been ... in case he asked. Anyway, I expected him to be home already, but he wasn't.'

'Could he have also had a call about your son and also gone to the school?'

'No. Yes. I don't know.' She shakes her head vigorously. 'But the odd thing is that Trevor has been home, because he left the milk on the counter. Then I thought ... I knew ... he would never do that, inspector. He would always put the milk in the fridge. He wouldn't just leave it there. And he always writes me a note when he goes out. Always.' She finishes with a small sob.

'Have you checked the house? The garden?'

'I've been everywhere. Checked everything twice. Even went in the shed, although the padlock was still in place ... on the outside of the door.'

'What do you think has happened to your husband?' I am thinking about the affair he had with someone at work, when he was still married to Alicia. His deceit and lies eventually caused their divorce. Perhaps he's met his former lover again and they have rekindled the affair. Or he's met someone else.

Maureen Bennett seems to have had the same train of thought. 'I really can't imagine ...' she says slowly, then pausing abruptly

'Have you called his mobile?'

'It was the first thing I did. I got through to his voicemail straight away. I asked him to call me back immediately. Several times.' She sniffs again. 'And then you came. A policeman on the doorstep is never a good sign, I thought. I was afraid that you were here to bring me bad news about him. Like he'd been involved in an accident. Injured. Badly hurt. Dead.'

I stare at her. Something is nagging at me. Something she said, but it didn't register with me. I now sense that it was important, only I can't remember what it was.

'Why did you think the worst?'

'Isn't it obvious? Alicia was murdered. I was afraid that Trevor … he might be in danger too.'

I stare at her, trying to read what's going on in her head. 'What makes you think that?'

She shrugs. 'Well, if Alicia's been in contact with that man, and so has Trevor, he would also be in danger, wouldn't he?'

'Is there something you haven't told us, Mrs Bennett? What man are you talking about?'

'Like what?' she asks, but her mind is elsewhere.

'Mrs Bennett,' I say slowly, 'Do you know something about Alicia's death?'

'No! I don't know anything!' She cries out, then resumes in a calmer tone, 'I don't understand how you can think that.'

'Keeping important information from the police, or giving a false statement, is regarded as a serious crime, Mrs Bennett. I hope you are aware of that.' I hope I haven't frightened her so much that she won't say another word.

'I haven't done anything wrong!' She is in tears now, possibly a mixture of concern about Trevor and my presence.

'Then why don't you tell me who that man is that you're talking about?'

'Because I don't know! I really don't!'

'What do you know?'

'Uhm … it started a while ago.' She glances at the clock on the mantelpiece above a coal-effect electric fire, which has a lead tied together with a piece of brown packing tape.

'Two, three weeks ago, maybe four, Trevor had a phone call. I didn't know who it was, only that it was a woman. Knowing the reason why Alicia divorced him, I was … suspicious that he might do it again.' She shakes her head defensively. 'I could hear her voice, but I couldn't hear what she said. Later, I convinced myself that it must have been Alicia. About Briony. They were generally civil, but sometimes … they argued. I always kept my distance. Trevor was upset about the phone call afterwards, but he wouldn't tell me anything. He said it had nothing to do with me and that he wasn't seeing someone else.' She pauses and shrugs miserably. 'I didn't know what to believe, to be honest. A few days later, a man phoned. He'd called before. I could gather that from the conversation, and he sounded angry. Trevor was angry too. He took the phone into the other room, but I followed him and I listened at the door. I thought, if he had something going with another woman, this might be her husband. But then I heard Trevor telling the man to leave him alone and not call again. I thought that was odd, because if Trevor really was having an affair this man's wife, he would have been telling Trevor to leave them alone.' She hesitates. 'Does that make sense?'

'Yes. I gather that this wasn't the end of it?'

'No, it wasn't. I … I don't want to cause any trouble for Trevor, inspector, but I do believe …that he had contact with Alicia and it wasn't about seeing Briony.'

'When was that?'

'About a week before she was … before she died.'

'Trevor and Alicia had normal contact over Briony, I suppose?'

'Yes, but this was different. The arrangement about Briony was pretty straightforward. He always picked her up on Saturday morning about half past nine, every other weekend. And he took her back on Sunday after tea time. There wasn't any contact between them unless one of them wanted to change the arrangement. Like that day that his car wouldn't start and he was later than usual.'

'But when he spoke to Alicia that day … do you have any idea what that was about?' A woman who suspects her husband of having an affair will go to great lengths to find out about it. I guess Maureen is the exception to the rule.

'They had a row and I know it was about a holiday. I thought it was about this year's holiday, because we've been talking about going to France and we would love to take Briony with us. Although there are two years between them, my Gillian and Briony get on really well. The girls are into horse riding at the moment and we found a campsite near to some stables. And there is a swimming pool and a play ground for Alfie.'

'It wasn't about this summer, then?' I interrupt her. 'Was it about last summer? The holiday in Portugal?'

'How do you know that, inspector?' without waiting for me to answer, sniffs, blows her nose and continues. 'Trevor said something about how badly she had behaved and he wouldn't want a repeat of that if she was taking Briony on holiday again. If she wanted to go on holiday with her friend, he wouldn't want her to take her daughter with her, as we are always happy to have her.'

'So this phone call was about what happened in Portugal last summer?'

'I don't know. He wouldn't tell me anything about it and I … I couldn't ask. I knew they had been to Portugal of course, because Briony told us about it, but I didn't think that they were still arguing about it now, months later.'

'So why do you think this is important, Mrs Bennett?'

'I don't really know. It's just … a feeling I had. Because … I may have got it all wrong, but I believe that Trevor … that he might be in trouble and it has something to do with Alicia.'

'You thought there was an argument between Trevor and Alicia about that holiday in Portugal. But the other phone calls? Were they about the same thing?'

'I don't know. I just had that feeling … because Trevor isn't the type to have arguments with other people. I thought it was odd that he got upset by these phone calls.'

'Do you have any idea who that man might have been? Did Trevor ever mention a name?'

'No.' She smiles and stretches her hands out in front of her, spreading her fingers. 'I checked the phone, but the number was withheld.'

'Have you ever heard the name Torrington? Wilbur? Or Arthur Bristow? Josh Warren? Chris Eyre?'

'No, I haven't heard any of those names. You will have to ask Trevor yourself.'

I look at the clock on the wall. It has been thirty-five minutes since I got here. 'When do you expect Trevor home?'

Her eyes have followed mine to the clock and I can see them widen as she realises what time it is. 'I don't know …' she says softly, almost in tears again. 'I can't think where he's gone. His … his car is still here, you see.' She pauses, hesitating. 'I might be completely wrong, inspector, but I have a feeling that the man who rang him had something to do with Alicia's death. And I am afraid that Trevor may not be safe.'

31

One of the main duties of a police family liaison officer is to communicate with a bereaved or traumatised family and provide practical help and support, but also, as an experienced police investigator, their primary role is to gather evidence and information that may be useful to the investigation. The relationship an FLO has with a bereaved family relies on compassion and trust. Sally Walker was initially assigned as a FLO to the Poole family, but Kenneth Poole didn't approve of having a stranger in his home. He instructed Briony not to talk to Sally, and eventually he told her not to come any more.

I don't know her personally, but I have heard good reports about Sally Walker and I'm pretty sure that any friction was not caused by her. I would have liked to her to have been able to carry on in her role a little longer, but we can't force a family to have an FLO in their home.

Kenneth Poole's son, Christopher and his wife, Marisa, have temporarily moved in with him, mainly to support Briony. When I made the appointment to talk to Briony and ask her some questions about her mother, Kenneth wasn't keen on this idea either, but he had promised his full cooperation with the police investigation so he has little choice but to let me see her.

Marisa Poole is in her late twenties, thin as a willow, with dark hair that is cut too short to be flattering. Her cheeks and jaws are pronounced, and her eyes are set too far apart from her nose. What she lacks in beauty, however, is made up for by charisma and a certain sex-appeal that might attract some men, but not me. She is originally from Poland. Her grandparents lived in England after the war, but one of their three sons, her father, moved to Poland when he finished school. Marisa came to visit her grandparents and eventually stayed in the UK when she met Christopher Poole.

She isn't a warm and motherly figure and I see immediately that she isn't very good with Briony.

'Briony, this policeman would like to talk to you about your mother,' Marisa says insensitively. 'If you don't feel like talking to him, at any stage, please say so and we will stop this meeting immediately.'

The girl nods, looking at me with a mixture of suspicion and caution. It isn't a good start and I wish that I had at least taken Sally Walker with me. Kenneth hasn't emerged from his study yet, but I know he will rush in if Marisa calls him.

'That's right, Briony,' I say gently. 'As soon as you want to stop this interview, or conversation, you only have to raise your right hand. Okay?'

'Yes.' The girl's voice is barely a whisper. 'Yes sir. Inspector.'

'First of all, you can call me Andy,' I say, which makes Marisa frown in disapproval.

'Briony,' I continue. 'I know this is all very difficult for you. I understand that. But I believe that you can help me.'

'Why?'

'I don't know for sure, but I have that feeling.'

'I thought the police relied on facts not feelings,' Marisa blurts out.

'True.' I try to hide my growing annoyance. 'But we can't afford to ignore our instincts either.'

She smiles cynically but, fortunately, she keeps quiet.

'Briony, I would like you to look at a few photos and tell me if you know these people and, if you do, who they are and how you know them.'

Clearly, this isn't what she or Marisa expected. They look at each other with the same question written on their faces: Why? Neither has the answer and I certainly don't give it to them.

I have brought with me a good collection of different photos. Some are copies of the ones that are on the board in the incident room, some are randomly copied photos from adverts in magazines. And some are of colleagues.

The first photo I show her is of Gillian, her step-sister, using the same technique as we use with a lie detector: ask a simple question which won't produce a lie, like 'what's your date of birth' or 'what did you have for breakfast this morning?'. It relaxes people and makes them less wary of the trickier questions and they respond more spontaneously. Any hesitation associated with making up a lie, can be picked up.

'That's Gillian,' Briony says with no hesitation, a fond smile crossing her face. I see Marisa's eyebrows rise, and a look on her face suggesting why I would think that Gillian could possibly be involved, which is too crazy an idea for words and, as the question begins to form on her lips, I shake my head and, surprisingly, she shuts her mouth.

'She's my sister,' Briony says with pride. 'And Alfie is my brother. They live with my Dad and Auntie Maureen.'

'I understand you and Gillian are going horse riding?' It is meant as an innocent question, but it has the wrong effect.

'Mum doesn't want me to go on a horse! She says I will fall off and break an arm or a leg.'

'That doesn't happen very often,' Marisa says sarcastically.

Briony starts sobbing. 'Mum! I want my mum!'

Marisa tries to take the girl in her arms, but she is pushed away almost violently. 'Leave me alone! You never liked my mum!'

'I have never said that, darling.'

'Mum told me herself!' Her grief is replaced by a mixture of anger and spite. At least it stops her tears and Marisa is a bit taken aback by the outburst.

'Perhaps you can ask your father or Ken,' she says diplomatically.

Before she can say any more, I place a photo of Josh Warren on top of Gillian's.

'Have you ever seen this man, Briony?'

She studies the photo as if she is supposed to recognise the man in the picture but can't remember him. 'No. Did he kill my mum?'

'I can't tell you anything about the investigation right now, Briony, but I promise I will do my best to find the person who did kill your mother.'

She looks up, lips trembling and blue eyes filling with tears, but somehow she manages to keep them from rolling down her rather chubby cheeks. 'You promise?'

'I promise.'

I see Marisa looking up sharply, clearly wanting to ask how on earth I can make such a promise, but once more, the words die on her lips.

'How about this man?' This time it's a photo of Ollie Reed, dressed in plain clothes, smiling at the camera. When I asked his permission to take the photo, he warned me that the girl might have seen him when he came to their house. Which is exactly the intention.

'Yes. I have seen him.' Briony's face flushes as she takes the photo in her hand. Then she shakes her head and puts it back on the small pile. 'He had a uniform when I saw him. He's a policeman.'

'That's right. His name is Ollie.'

'Now that you have established that Briony is not stupid, can you get on with the real detective work, please?' Marisa snaps. 'You're wasting your time showing us trick photos.'

Briony is now grinning from ear to ear, and says, 'Next one, Andy?'

But I know Marisa is right. I am not doing the girl any favours by letting this interview last longer than necessary, although, she seems to enjoy looking at the photos and sees it as a game.

'What about this one?'

It is Chris Eyre. I don't think Alicia ever took him home, but you never know.

'Oh yes, that is Chris,' she says promptly, without any hesitation.

I can't hide my surprise. 'You know him?'

'Yes. He came to our house once, when Dad Ken was away for a few days. He had a meal with us and he played a computer game with me.'

'When was that?'

'I don't know. A long time ago.' This isn't very helpful, as children of that age can't really be relied on when they have to establish time. Like when they think someone in their forties is really ancient.

'How long ago?'

'Dunno. He brought a present for me, but it wasn't my birthday. He said he didn't know when my birthday was, so he'd bought something anyway.' She giggles. 'It was a box with beads to make jewellery. Mum ... helped me and we made a bracelet for me and for her.' Her lip starts to tremble again and quickly I place the last photo on the pile.

'Have you ever seen this man?'

It's the photo from the CCTV images in Angelo's bar, where, according to Denise, Alicia was harassed by a man, which caused them to leave the bar and go to Barrie's Bar.

'Yes.' She grins again. 'He was in our street.'

'Do you mean that this man lives in your street?' I ask incredulously.

'No. He was there, at the playground. We were playing football, me and my friends, and he helped us get the ball when Jamie shot it over the wall into Mr Hopkins' garden. Mr Hopkins always keeps the ball, you see, and we wouldn't get it back until the next day. But this man offered to get it and we had it back.'

'Did he speak to you?'

She shakes her head. 'First I thought he knew Jamie, but that wasn't true. Jamie told me.'

'Did he speak to you?'

'Oh yes. He made me laugh. I said, 'thank you, mister,' to him, because he got the ball back, and he said I didn't have to say mister to him. I could call him Daddy.'

I feel the hairs on my neck stand on end and a shiver runs down my spine. I dread to think why he would say that.

'Daddy? Did he want you to call him Daddy?' Marisa cries. 'That is …'

'Briony,' I quickly interrupt, 'what happened then?'

'I laughed and I said that I already have two Daddies, my real Dad and Dad Ken. I didn't want a third Dad.'

'You said that to him?'

'Yes. And he said that I was right. If I didn't want to call him Daddy, I could call him Godfather.'

'Godfather?' Marisa echoes.

Briony starts to look worried, especially as she looks from Marisa to me and back.

'What is a godfather?' she asks, tentatively.

'It's … a bit like a grandfather, but different,' Marisa says vaguely. For once I am grateful that she is here, because it is now my turn to be speechless. Godfather. This can't be a coincidence.

32

Maloney has been away for most of the day to pick up his wife. He told me that she's returned from Weymouth where she left her parents after many failed attempts to get them back together again. She sobbed during the journey home and he confided in me that he was relieved to be working on a time-consuming investigation. Even if Guthrie won't allow him to, and he won't get paid for it, he'd gladly do some extra overtime for nothing.

His brief outburst that she should stop sobbing like a spoiled child and stop interfering in her parent's lives, only caused her more distress and, obviously, didn't help their own relationship.

By the time he arrived at the station, the wheels had already been set in motion. As I quickly fill him in on the latest developments, I see his face redden and his eyes shining with hope and expectation. After the trauma with his wife's family, this must be like some sort of a treat for him.

'Right!' He rubs his hands together as if he has been presented with a five-course meal of all the things he loves. 'What's going on?'

'Ollie is fetching pizzas,' someone says. 'Ten minutes.'

'Okay, we'll wait a few minutes,' Maloney says generously, grabbing his mobile from his pocket to check his messages. At the same time, the door opens and DCI Guthrie emerges, folding his arms across his chest and positioning himself in front of the door, blocking the way in or out to anyone who would like to escape to the washrooms.

'What are you waiting for, Philip?' he asks frostily.

'Uhm … we're just about to start.' Instinctively, Maloney knows that this is not the time to tell his superior that we're waiting for the arrival of DS Ollie Reed with soft drinks and a pile of pizza boxes.

'Good.' Guthrie now sounds sarcastic, his eyes coldly locked on Maloney. His presence is demoralising and I seriously doubt that he can add anything useful to the meeting. Confusion, more likely.

'I've come at the right time then,' he continues, not leaving his position at the door. On the contrary, he spreads his legs and raises his shoulders and he looks like a bull entering an arena. In his hand is a tightly rolled up newspaper. And as if to make sure that we all know what this is about, he taps it on the knuckles of his free hand impatiently.

It was Gerald Hill from West Country News who wrote the disastrous article that suggested that the police wouldn't get anywhere near catching a double murderer without the help of the pretty clairvoyant. Hill has been busy again. He has used whatever little material he had to feed his fertile imagination and has drawn up a sensational headline: 'Murderer makes police dance like marionettes'.

I am pretty certain that this is the real reason why Guthrie has joined the meeting. I'm not the only one who is of the opinion that Hill is the proverbial nail in any policeman's coffin. Hill must once have been an old-fashioned Fleet Street reporter competing for stories on a daily basis. The fact that he has been transferred to the South West, where life is generally much less exciting from a reporter's point of view, has made him into a journalist who is led by so much frustration and anger that he can't see anything wrong with exercising in print his vivid imagination. Clearly, Gerald Hill has rubbed up Guthrie's feathers the wrong way.

'Right.' The DCI begins in an almost friendly manner, which is always dangerous. 'Have we all seen the paper?'

A faint murmur. Nobody wants to attract Guthrie's attention.

'I have only one simple question,' he continues, in the same, soft voice. 'Who has been leaking to the press?'

Silence. I see several heads duck behind computer screens or behind hands. PC Ally Poldeen pulls the elastic band from her hair and bows her head. I notice that Penrose seems to be letting her hair grow a bit longer these days.

'Well?' There's thunder in his voice now. His eyes scrutinise our faces for any sign of what can remotely be seen as guilt.

We all know that someone is telling a lie when they avoid eye contact or go red in the face or get fidgety. But innocent people can also get nervous and sometimes blush or look away, or start clearing their throat when they are confronted with an awkward situation. This means they can easily be mistaken for liars.

Whether Guthrie is aware of this or not, he is searching for the person avoiding his gaze or with the reddest face.

'I know one of you talked to the press. And I have an idea who it may be. But I don't like working with cowards. So if you are guilty, just be a man, or a woman, and stand up before I get really angry about this.'

I remember from similar situations at school that it isn't always the real culprit who raises his hand. Sometimes, it is someone who is fed up with the situation or is willing to take the punishment to protect his mates. I was never that brave but I knew a few schoolmates who were and I always wondered how they could take being punished for something they didn't do.

Guthrie's eyes are still darting across our faces. PC Ally Poldeen's face is the colour of ripe cherries. She shakes her head vigorously and murmurs, 'It wasn't me, sir. Honestly.'

'Who has been leaking to the press?' Guthrie repeats bluntly, but his words don't have the effect he hoped for. At that moment, Ollie Reed arrives with the pizzas and a plastic bag with cans and bottles of soft drinks. Guthrie turns his head incredulously, as if it has never occurred to him that police officers need to eat and drink.

I sigh inwardly, gathering my papers to make room for our improvised meal. Others do the same. Guthrie hasn't finished. He just won't give up. Nobody has come forward to admit any connection with the press and Gerald Hill in particular, and he is looking for a scapegoat.

Squeezing his eyes almost shut, he scrutinizes the incident board and immediately picks out the two names that Maloney has circled with a red marker pen: the 'godfather' and Trevor Bennett.

Ignoring the fact that most of the officers are grabbing pizza slices and soft drinks, Guthrie demands to be updated, his anger about the press forgotten for a moment. Despite his earlier scepticism when I explained to him about the 'godfather', Maloney now shares my optimism that the person using the nickname could open up the investigation in a new direction, if not lead us to the identity of the murderer. Glancing at the pizzas momentarily, he quickly looks away and reads the messages on Alicia Poole's iPad out loud.

'What's the significance of this so-called 'godfather'?' Guthrie demands.

Exchanging a glance with Maloney, I explain that it is too much of a coincidence that Alicia received emails from someone calling themselves 'godfather' and then a man who approached her daughter in a playground told her to call him 'godfather'.

'The bottom line is,' Maloney resumes, 'that we believe that this is the man who spoke briefly to Alicia Poole at Angelo's on Saturday evening, which upset her enough that she mentioned it to her friend Denise Shaw and suggested they use the back door to slip out and go to another bar. We have images of the two women leaving Angelo's by a back alley, and we have two images of the man. Sadly, not as clear and sharp as we would want. He could have followed Alicia to Barrie's Bar, and then followed her and Chris Eyre to the lake. In his statement, Eyre told us that it was Alicia who knew about the dogging meeting, but it's possible she hadn't really planned to go there because she hadn't mentioned it to her friend Mrs Shaw. So someone, and it could be this 'godfather', may have followed her from Barrie's Bar to the lake and killed her there.'

Although initially, Maloney was sceptical about the importance of the godfather, he now seems more optimistic. This could be a breakthrough in the case and in all fairness, it's the only lead we've got.

'We need to find this man,' Guthrie announces as though we haven't already worked that out for ourselves. 'Go over each of the statements from everyone in those bars. Angelo's, Barrie's Bar. All of them. See if he visited other bars in the area. Someone must have seen him. Someone must know who he is.' He gestures at Maloney, who obligingly calls out several officer's names who nod and grab their coats and jackets, half-eaten pizzas forgotten.

'Tregunna?' Maloney looks at me, narrowing his eyes. 'You look like you have something else on your mind.'

I hesitate. I called Maureen Bennett again when I reached the station to get the latest update about her husband. She was in tears and told me that Trevor hadn't returned yet nor called her. All the more concerning is the fact that it has started raining and she realises that her husband must have left the house without a coat. She remembered he wore his navy blue jacket in the morning and now it was hanging on the coat rack.

'Trevor Bennett, Alicia's first husband and the father of her daughter, is missing.'

'Since when?' Maloney looks doubtful, unsure if he needs to do something about it. Perhaps he wishes that he hadn't given me the opportunity to mention this to him

I shrug. 'Not long enough to start searching, but his wife is worried, and, to be honest, I am too. He was last seen today at about 1.20 am, when he got out of his car in front of their house. He'd bought a bottle of milk and he left it on the counter in the kitchen. Since then, we don't know what he did or were he went.' I pause briefly to make sure that I have the attention of everyone who is left in the room. 'We know that Bennett spoke to someone on the phone several times and that he was upset afterwards. We can't rule out the possibility that he was speaking to the man who called himself godfather. Or to the man who killed Alicia Poole and Torrington. If he did, then Bennett's life might also be in danger. We must therefore take his disappearance seriously.'

'Yes, Tregunna, I see your point,' Maloney says thoughtfully, but I can see that he is more focused on finding the godfather rather than spending time trying to find Trevor Bennett.

'I'm sure Bennett will show up sooner rather than later,' he says.

'May I remind you that he is an adult and that we have two murders to investigate?' Guthrie strokes his chin as if he is wondering if he forgot to shave that morning. 'Maybe he got depressed about the death of his ex-wife and he thought ...' He pauses to interrupt himself. 'Does his new wife think he may be suicidal?'

I hesitate. With a missing child, the police respond immediately, but with adults, the police first determine the level of risk as there is usually a reason. In some cases, a serious search is speeded up when the missing person is vulnerable or depressed and, possibly a danger to themselves or to other people. I can't see Trevor Bennett as someone who would take his own life but we do need to find him because I am certain that he knows the identity of the killer, possibly even without being aware of it.

'I haven't asked her that,' I say truthfully. 'But Mrs Bennett thinks that something has happened to him.'

He scoffs. 'Did she check if his passport is still there? Did he take any clothes? Money?'

I shrug. Penrose picks up the phone and, after a brief conversation, putts it down again. 'I've just spoken to Mrs Bennett. She has checked, but her husband's passport is still there. As far as she can tell he hasn't taken any clothes with him. They have a little money box with some extra cash, and he didn't take any of that either.'

Maloney casts me a glance. 'What do you think, Tregunna? Has he done a runner?'

'Not in the sense that he is guilty of a crime, but I do believe that there is something odd about his disappearance. That's why I think that we should at least send an FLO to his home,' I say, careful not to tread on his toes. 'We can send Sally Walker. She's been with the Poole's for a couple of days and she knows everything about the case, which might be useful.'

He nods. 'Okay. Sally Walker. Anyone knows where she is? Get in touch with her and send her up there.'

'Do we declare him a missing person, sir?' Penrose asks, her hand on the phone again.

'Not yet.' His eyes scan our faces. 'Anything else on this subject? No? Alright. Let's move on folks. Tregunna,' he looks at me, still not entirely convinced that this new lead won't send us on a wild goose chase. 'This godfather. You're sure the girl didn't make it up?'

'She told me herself. I didn't ask her anything. She seemed an intelligent girl and I can't see why she would lie about it. She recognised this godfather immediately. Not only him, but she also recognised Chris Eyre. She remembered that he came to their house one day when Kenneth was away for the weekend. And she pointed out Ollie Reed who had been at their home to get Kenneth Poole's statement. She didn't recognise Wilbur Torrington, or Eddie Rowse, Warren or Bristow. We showed her photos of everyone that we know of who was at Swan Lake that night.'

I suppress a snigger. When I showed Briony all the photos, she had picked out Guthrie's face as one of a pair of Jehovah's witnesses who had appeared on the doorstep on a Saturday afternoon, a couple of weeks ago. I'm glad I have withheld this information; Guthrie would go mental if he knew that I used his picture in an unofficial line-up.

But Guthrie isn't impressed with our reasoning, or with the way Maloney proposed to deal with the new information. He is still convinced that the murderer will be found amongst Alicia's closest relatives or friends. As far as Guthrie is concerned, the disappearance of Trevor Bennett fits perfectly well with this theory, proving his guilt.

'Philip, I would like to have a word with you right now, all the others, get out and find our man.' His eyes rest on me. 'Tregunna, you have been assigned as the intelligence officer here. I don't want you to go out. I want you here, collating information that comes in from your colleagues.'

Most times, I know when to grit my teeth and keep quiet, but this time I can't stop myself. 'I'm only working part-time, sir. And I have already worked more hours than I am strictly allowed to this week.'

His eyes are like daggers, but he says nothing and turns on his heels and stamps out of the incident room, duly followed by a worried looking Maloney.

'I'm not sure if that was a very wise move,' Penrose murmurs from behind her hand.

'We're dealing with a serious crime, Jennette. I don't care if I have stepped on someone's precious toes.'

She shrugs but I see her wink also, a tiny smile on her rosebud lips. She looks at the slices of cold pizza left behind in the boxes.

'Why are you more focused on Bennett than the godfather?' she asks.

'Looking for him is like searching for a needle in a haystack but, if I am right, Bennett can help us find the godfather. I think he will be able to tell us his identity, so I think we could kill two birds with one stone.' I grin at her and, stretching my back and shoulders, I add, 'All we need is someone to call us with a sighting of Trevor Bennett.'

She nods and she is about to leave the room, when, as if on cue, the phone rings.

33

The couple are nervous and fidgety. I guess there has been a dispute between them about whether it was right to come to the police station or not. They are sitting in the reception area: the woman is staring at her hands, the man is looking away towards the door as if he is seriously considering leaving before it's too late.

I stand in the doorway. The desk officer stopped me as I came in, asking me to deal with the couple. She is offering them coffee or tea and they stare at her as if they hadn't expected any kindness in a police station.

'Annie,' I say softly, 'I'm supposed to be in the incident room. I'm sure you can find someone else.'

She looks at me clearly annoyed. 'I know,' she says, ' but Maloney isn't here yet and …' She stops with a vague gesture, her body language telling me that she would have called someone else if there had been anyone available.

'By the way, it's Anita.'

'I'm sorry?'

She shrugs as if it isn't important to her any more, as if she has already decided that I am so ignorant that reminding me what her name is, is a complete waste of time. 'I will intercept all incoming calls and make notes for you.'

'Oh.' I stare at her in surprise. 'Thank you, Annie.'

She shakes her head, turns and sticks a yellow post-it note on the back of my hand. 'You're welcome, Billy,' she replies before turning back to the desk where the phone is ringing again.

I open my mouth to remind her that my name is Andy. Then it dawns on me. She seems to have a sense of humour after all.

'Mr and Mrs Jennings?' I read the name from the note on my hand.

'Huh?' Mr Jennings says reluctantly. He is as nervous as you might expect of a guilty person.

'Yes,' his wife says firmly, pressing a black shoulder bag to her chest. 'We are.'

They are both in their mid thirties, with hair that is prematurely greying and lines on their face that suggest a troubled life. On second thoughts, they might be younger than I think.

'How can I help you?'

'It was more hassle to call you than to come here, as we were passing anyway,' she says, grabbing at her husband's arm as if she wants to make sure he doesn't fall asleep. 'We have come forward because we have seen the man you're looking for. The murderer of that poor woman.'

Behind me, the desk officer takes in a sharp breath. Perhaps now she regrets that she didn't insist that Maloney speak to them.

Mr Jennings shakes his head. 'El, we don't know for sure.'

'That is for the police to find out,' his wife says unwaveringly. She rises to her feet, swinging her bag over her shoulders as if she is going into battle. 'I'm Ellen and this is my husband Alan.' She shakes my hand, adding nervously, 'which can be confusing if someone doesn't pronounce our names correctly.'

'Shall we find an interview room?' I say lightly. 'No need for anyone, at this stage, to overhear our conversation.'

Alan Jennings seems to relax a bit at the thought of more privacy than the entrance hall where the phone is ringing almost constantly and the desk officer and an apprentice seem to be sharing jokes between the calls.

'I shall need to take down your details,' I say, grabbing an A4-sheet from the printer and taking a pen from the breast pocket of my shirt as I open the interview room.

'Is that really necessary?'

'Alan, please, we have to help if we know something, don't we?'

'I suppose, but why is it ...'

She interrupts him with a warning glance and they sit on one side of the table.

'Perhaps you can tell me first what you know,' I say gently. 'Then we can decide afterwards how to handle the official side of it.'

Ellen Jennings picks up her shoulder bag from the floor and retrieves a folded newspaper. As she flicks it open, I see a photo of Trevor Bennett. She pushes the paper across the table and I pick it up, reading the headline in horror: 'Murderer on the run: Police get it wrong AGAIN.'

With a sinking feeling, I scan, rather than read, the article. As usual in these cases, there isn't much information, but the reporter has managed to fill the column by padding out what little he has got. In short, it says that Trevor B., former husband of the murdered Alicia Poole, has escaped from the police and is now on the run, probably on his way to Europe. The public are asked to contact an address at the newspaper if anyone knows where Trevor B. is and any information will be treated as strictly confidential.

'That man,' Ellen Jennings says, with a voice that holds no room for doubt. 'We saw him, didn't we, Alan?'

He nods, apprehensively. 'Yesterday.'

I take a deep breath. When someone is missing, the majority of reported sightings are wrong. Although that may be the case here, I have a feeling that this couple is different.

'Are you sure?' I ask, not able to conceal the mixture of doubt and excitement from them.

'Yes, we are sure, inspector.'

'Where did you see him?'

They exchange worried looks, still in disagreement. Alan is not willing to give any more information than necessary. Neither is Ellen but, nevertheless, she sees it as her duty to tell me what she knows.

'I hope you can keep the information to yourself,' Alan says eventually. 'Obviously we don't want people to know who we are.'

'I will do my best, but this is a serious murder investigation and I can't promise you anything.'

Once more they exchange glances. Ellen decides to continue.

'We were … visiting someone who is … an acquaintance of ours. We were nervous, as it was a rather … personal matter. So we sat in the car for a while. We were a bit early. Our appointment was at half past two, but we got there already just after two.'

'What was the nature of your visit?'

'Uhm, we'd rather not say. As I said, it was very … personal. Private.'

'Alright. Go on, please.'

'We sat in the car and we … talked. We were still not sure … well, I was, but Alan wasn't. He wasn't convinced that this … acquaintance would be able to help us and … well, I'd better not say any more. The bottom line is that we were in the car, talking, and deciding if we wanted to go through with this or not. As we sat there, still discussing the matter, a car parked on the other side of the road and … a man got out. It was him.'

The way she manages to avoid the actual reason for the appointment is intriguing and for some reason it makes me feel determined to find out what it was.

'You saw the man you were supposed to meet?'

'Well, we're not sure. We had met him before, but that was close up in a café in Truro and this time he had his back to us most of the time.'

She pauses and looks at her husband to check she should carry on.

'He got out of the car and ... well, at first we thought he was alone and we were about to get out of our car and check it was him, but then he went to the rear door and he helped another man out of the car. It looked like the other man was drunk, or hurt, or drugged. He had difficulty trying to get his balance and ... our acquaintance ... ehm, the man we were meeting, had to keep him steady on his feet.

Ellen Jennings pauses and glances at her husband again. 'We still weren't sure and we didn't ... I said to Alan that the man might need our help, but we didn't want to interfere in anyone else's business, same as we didn't want the other man to know about ours.' She shrugs and gives a small smile. 'We decided to wait until the two men were gone. We watched them go inside a block of flats and then we saw them appear again on the walkway on the first floor, which was where we were also going.'

Shifting on his seat, Alan takes over. 'But we're not here about the man we were meeting, inspector. We're here about the man the police are looking for. We recognised him. The drunken man.'

'Both of us,' Ellen nods quickly as if she's afraid that I am about to call her husband a liar. 'Alan said it at the same time as I did. That's why we are so sure it was him.'

I point at the photo in the newspaper. 'Was this the man you saw? Trevor Bennett?'

'That's him. We saw him in the paper. The man who is suspected of having killed his wife and who seems to be on the run from the police.'

I scribble something in my notebook, hoping they won't notice my excitement. What I don't want to happen now is that my reaction will encourage them to make up a lot more than they actually saw.

'You both saw man on the walkway on the first floor. What happened next?'

Alan nods. 'We waited until we saw both of them disappear into one of the flats. By then, it was time for our meeting. At two minutes before half past two, we got out of the car and went into the building for our meeting.'

'And Bennett?'

'He wasn't there,' Alan says quickly. 'Only the man we were meeting.'

Ellen nods. 'It was a rather small flat, with only one or two bedrooms, I believe. When Alan asked him if his friend was okay, as we thought he had looked rather unstable, he said he didn't know what we were talking about.'

They are speaking freely now, adding information when the other pauses for breath.

'I told him that we had seen them both arriving in his car and walk to the building. He seemed shocked at first, but then he laughed and said it must have been someone else. There was, he said, someone living in the building who looked a bit like him.'

'But you didn't believe him?'

'No. we thought it was all a bit strange, but … we were not there to get involved in any of his personal matters, so we … sort of got on with our business.' She blushes and looks down at her hands that are nervously fiddling in her lap.

'We … I don't really want to explain what we were doing there, inspector, so what we will tell you next, I hope you don't need to ask any further more questions about it.'

'I hope that you understand that this man might be a suspect in a double murder, Mrs Jennings,' I say gently. 'Therefore this information might be important.'

'Oh.' They look at each other, concern in their eyes about what the implications for them may be.

'Go on, El,' Alan says weakly. 'It was you who wanted to tell them this. Not me.'

'Okay.' She spreads her fingers and scrutinises her finger-tips for damaged nails. 'We were in the living room to talk things through with him and … he left us alone for a while so that we could discuss the matter before we made our final decision.'

Again, their secret mission intrigues me, but one look at their faces tells me that they won't say any more about it.

'We were alone for about ten minutes,' Alan continues, not meeting my eyes. 'It didn't take as long as we'd anticipated and ...'

'That was when we heard it.'

'You heard what?'

'We heard voices and swearing and ... we didn't know what to think or what to do.'

'We thought it was best to wait until he came back.'

'He'd made us a cup of tea, but we didn't feel like staying there much longer. It was all a bit ... embarrassing.'

'So you think the man who, according to the newspapers, is hiding for the police, is still in that flat?'

'I'm pretty sure he was there when we left. We heard ... there was a door in the hall. It looked like there was another bedroom; smaller than the other one, but nevertheless, it was a room because we heard someone snoring.'

'So you believe that the man, Trevor Bennett, was there, drunk?'

'Drunk or he might have been drugged,' Ellen Jennings says, rolling her eyes.

I pick up my pen and roll it between my thumb and index finger. 'What is the address?'

Once more, they exchange glances. 'Inspector, if you find something about us ... I mean, our private life ...'

'I will do my best to be discrete, but I can't promise you that.'

They glare at each other, realising that they have said too much to withhold information now.

'8 Penmar Road,' Alan Jennings says grimly. 'First floor, the last flat on the walkway.'

And his wife adds, apparently for no particular reason, 'Next to the fire escape.'

34

I'm not sure if what Alan and Ellen Jennings have told me is of any relevance to the investigation. The Trevor Bennett I have met wouldn't have just gone off without telling his wife and then got drunk. It doesn't make sense to me either that he would be staying with a friend. Why wouldn't he call his wife to tell her where he is? Why doesn't he let her know that she needn't worry? If it is him, he must have seen his own face in the newspapers, on the local news channels and on social media. Even if he hasn't seen anything, surely his friend must have.

I return to the incident room and find Penrose standing in front of the whiteboard, deep in thoughts. She turns on her heels when I approach her. 'I thought you'd had a lie in,' she says disdainfully.

I drop my notebook on one of the desks and point at the few lines I have written in it. 'I've just spoke to a couple who claim that they have seen Bennett. They say that it looked like he was drunk and someone helped him into a flat in St Austell.'

She looks at my face. 'Do you don't believe them?'

'Kind of,' I admit. 'They were certain that it was Bennett., although I can't imagine that he would leave his home and family like that, making his wife sick with worry and then getting drunk and sleeping it off in someone's flat.'

I stare at Bennett's photo on the board. 'What have you been up to?'

'I went to Poole's house.' She frowns with disapproval. 'It's like the poor girl is being imprisoned by her own family. She wants to go to school, but they won't let her. She isn't even allowed to watch TV.' She blows her cheeks and slowly lets the air escape between her teeth. 'I was only able to speak to Briony for two or three minutes, when the damned woman was on the phone.'

'Marisa Poole?'

'Yeah. She wasted my energy and my time. I nearly brought her in for obstructing our police enquiry.' She smiles grimly. 'But I do know that the girl hasn't seen or heard from her father either.'

'Which suggests there's something very odd going on,' I nod. 'I can't believe he would be so cruel as to just go off and leave her for no good reason so soon after her mother's death.'

'You are right. So do you believe he was drunk or was he drugged or sedated when these people saw him?'

'That sounds a bit far-fetched, but yes, that could be the case.' I tap on a keyboard and check the address of the flat which the Jennings gave me. I look at my watch. 'The resident's name is listed as Mrs Marcie Holt.'

'I thought Bennett was seen with a man?' She frowns, already dismissing the possibility that we might have found an important lead.

'Exactly.' I nod firmly, disguising the fact that I am following such a tenuous hunch that I can hardly justify it to myself. 'Are you coming?'

Penmar Road is a three-storey block of flats. The grey concrete walls are stained with so much graffiti you can't decipher the messages. One of the flats on the second floor has scorch marks around the frames and under the walkway of the flat above. Plywood has been nailed over the door and the two windows, and scrawled across the plywood in dripped black paint are the words: 'NO to Migrants'; someone has tried to make a point.

The main entrance door to the building is open. It has no handle, let alone a proper locking system. The square hallway smells of urine and cigarette smoke. In the dark corner under the stairs is an old stained sleeping bag permeated with the sickly sweet smell of soft drugs. On the wall, three rows of metal mailboxes, only half of which have residents' names on them, are all dented and sprayed with graffiti: a mixture of obscene words and body parts, mostly female.

We climb up the concrete stairs where the smell of urine is combined with rotting food. Up on the walkway there are small puddles where the rain has dripped from broken guttering.

Windows are covered with curtains or sometimes with just a sheet pinned to the frame. Some are ajar and a variety of smells drifts our way: spicy food, fish and chips, cat litter trays. The front doors look as if they haven't been painted for at least a decade ago, and are now a faded blue or orange. Some of them have half-opened letterboxes with strings hanging out. Perhaps the residents are careless, or they simply know that there isn't much worth stealing anyway. Only one resident has made an effort and placed a rectangular flower pot next to the door; despite the rain, the primroses need watering. At the end of the walkway is the regulation fire exit: its concrete steps spiralling from the top to the ground floor, enclosed with metal caging. Penrose pushes down on the handle of the metal gate which opens surprisingly smoothly.

'Handy to have an escape route,' she mutters grimly, unaware that she's conveying the exact thoughts of Ellen Jennings.

Only the last flat next to the fire escape has got a name next to the number, 8, on the orange door: Holt. I knock. There is no answer. The curtains are pulled closed and, when I try to peer through the letterbox, I can only see a narrow hallway with all the internal doors closed. I hear the muffled sounds of a television, but the building probably predates proper insulation, I suspect the sounds may well be from one of the neighbours.

'Perhaps we should have called for back-up, sir,' Penrose says, anxiously, staring down onto the car park where a group of teenagers with no apparent goal in life have gathered around a lamp post. One of them is making an attempt to climb it, probably to reach for a rucksack that is dangling from the light.

'Call for back-up? What do you think the response would have been?' I ask rhetorically, shaking my head and grinning at her smugly.

'Perhaps it would have been better if we had talked to Maloney and convinced him about your hunch,' she shrugs disdainfully. The expression on her face tells me that she isn't pleased with my attitude or with the fact that I have brought her here when we are both supposed to be following orders. And she is right. My repeated rebelling against Guthrie is childish and unnecessary. Perhaps I should try harder to work as part of a team, rather than go off on my own accord.

'Annie has offered to collect every snippet of information for me and I'm willing to stay all evening to record it all in the case file,' I say by way of apology.

'Anita,' she corrects me automatically. 'All the same. If you are right and the man we're looking for killed two people … well, we can't even be sure that he hasn't killed more people, can we? And If he's really got his hands on Bennett now too …' She sounds apprehensive.

'Jennette, I'd be happy for us to go back to the station and wait for Maloney if you think that's the best option now.'

She stares at me for a long time, then she shrugs, this time almost reluctantly, but she turns round and knocks on the door.

There are no approaching footsteps.

I peer down at the car park. On the pavement, a young mother is pushing a pram, the baby tucked underneath a blanket. A girl, judging by the tiny pink hat the baby is wearing. Beside the mother is a toddler, unsteady on his short legs but determined to walk without his mother's help. In the street, a car drives by, revving loudly. The little boy, startled, falls over, landing on his hands and knees, crying. The mother shakes her head and I can almost hear her mumble, 'I told you so, sweetie.'

I turn back to Penrose. 'If my information is correct, we should find Bennett here.'

She looks sceptical. 'They saw him here yesterday.'

'Well, perhaps someone can tell us where he is now or ...' I stop abruptly. 'Can you hear something?'

'I can hear some knocking. As if someone is hammering a nail into a wall.' She smiles ruefully. 'These buildings were not built properly. The walls are paper thin. It could be someone in any of these flats.'

I shake my head and knock again. Persistent.

'Hello? Uhm ...can I help you?' The neighbour's door opens just wide enough for a man to stick his head around the door frame. A pair of glasses is askew on his forehead.

'We're looking for your neighbour, sir,' Penrose says politely. 'Mrs Holt doesn't seem to be in. Do you happen to know what time she gets home?'

The blue door opens a bit wider. The man is wearing brown corduroy trousers and a green shirt, the sleeves rolled up to his elbows. His face is pale and he has wide jaws and a flat nose. His small eyes blink as a mole suddenly exposed to the light.

There is something oddly familiar about the way he cocks his head, holding it slightly to one side as he moves. I wonder if I have met him somewhere, but nothing springs to mind.

'Do you have an appointment?' His voice is slightly hesitant before he pronounces the double P, as if he's trying to overcome a stammer and doesn't want us to know he has one.

'No, but ...' I start. I am not sure what or why, but something feels wrong here. The question about an appointment seems totally out of place. Even if I was in urgent need of a dentist, for example, I wouldn't consider coming here.

The neighbour stares at Penrose as though he thinks he should know her but can't remember where from.

The hammering sound from somewhere in the building suddenly starts again and the man looks over his shoulder, a vague uneasiness in his expression. 'I'm sorry about … the n-noise.' P is obviously not the only consonant he seems to have trouble pronouncing.

He shoves his glasses straight on top of his head. 'Holt. Ehm … Is it urgent? '

He stares at Penrose. For some reason, he has decided to ignore me. Or maybe he is just one of those men who think it is much easier to deal with a woman than a man.

'We just have some questions to ask,' Penrose says vaguely.

'Oh, well, actually …' He pauses and smiles, seeming to be enjoy the conversation. I have the feeling that this he is playing a cat and mouse game with us, but I'm not sure who the mouse is.

'Mrs Holt?' The neighbour places one foot on the threshold. He is as tall as Penrose, but more bulky around the waist. Pear shaped with legs that seem too short.

'Or Mr Holt?' Obviously, Penrose has the same feeling as me and I'm aware that annoyance is already creeping into her voice.

'Does he know that you're coming?' he offers a sheepish grin, unaware that his words are only adding to our confusion.

'No,' Penrose replies, without thinking.

'Yes, he does,' I say at the same time.

'Oh. Right.' He frowns, narrowing his eyes. 'Well, I sup-pose I can give you a phone n-number.'

'Thank you.'

His shoulders relax and he takes his glasses of his head, folding back the arms with great care.

He hesitates. 'Ehm … it's cold, isn't it? Would you like … to come in while I get the number for you?'

Taking his glasses in one hand, he motions with them and he goes ahead of us along a narrow hallway. A piece of brown packing tape is stuck on the back of one elbow.

There is the hammering or knocking sound again and he shakes his head disapprovingly. 'I hate to have to admit that living here isn't what it used to be anymore. The whole place is deteriorating rapidly. And you don't know who any of the neighbours are these days.' His stammer has gone with his outburst and his intonation suggests that what he really means is there are too many residents whose native language is not English and, consequently, he is mistrustful of the unfamiliar.

The sound returns more loudly. 'Just a sec,' he says, stopping halfway down the hall and opening one of the doors. As he enters a bedroom, I can see a double bed, neatly made up with a crisp white duvet cover that looks out of place in this dingy flat., two black side tables with a black and white bedside lamp on each of them, a paperback with a pair of reading glasses on one of the tables and a white clock with red digital numerals on the other. He saunters towards the wall behind the bed and lifts a fist and knocks heavily, shouting: 'Stop it, please! I can't even hear my own voice!'

Turning back, he smiles sadly. 'I can report it, obviously, but what will be the point? The police won't do anything about it and it'll be more reason for them to disturb us again.'

'Them?'

'Hm. All these noisy people around us who don't care who they upset.'

He closes the bedroom door and proceeds to the living room where the walls are painted with pale beige emulsion and the floor is covered with a matching beige carpet. Dark oak furniture, the upholstery brown and green. Although every piece in the room looks old-fashioned, they seem new and unused and it feels like we've entered a showroom in a furniture shop.

He scratches his head as if he's unsure about something then, hesitating, his eyes narrowed so that he can hardly see us, he mutters, 'I seem … I'll have to think where the number is.'

'Take your time,' I say, trying not to show any impatience.

He invites us into the living room but the invitation doesn't extend to offering us a seat. We stand in the middle of the room, Penrose a few paces away from me.

He shakes his head. 'There must me a … m-misunderstanding with the ap-pointment.' His frame is blocking the doorway as if he is determined not to let us leave.

He shakes his head again and mutters. 'Normally … people don't make mistakes about their appointments.'

Somehow, it feels like the conversation has taken a strange turn and I haven't a clue in what direction it is going. Oddly enough, I have the feeling that he doesn't know either.

'What makes you say that?' I ask.

He is confused. 'You are a coup-ple, aren't you? Yes of course, you are the same age and there is a certain … understanding b-between you.' He cocks his head. 'You are both determined p-people, I can tell.'

'We are,' Penrose says, rolling her eyes and looking hopefully at the doorway. Clearly, she's of the opinion that the man has lost his marbles.

He clears his throat, swallowing quickly 'What was your name again?'

'We didn't say.' I answer as cautiously as I can muster.

He blinks with a mixture of anger and uncertainty. The remnants of any good humour are dissolving rapidly. 'Oh.' He hesitates, his feet shuffling in the doorway as if he isn't sure whether to come into the room or not.

'Uhm … have we met before?'

'Strangely, I have the same feeling,' I say, unsettling him but staring at him as if I'm trying to imagine him in different clothes and in different circumstances in order to recognise him.

I wait. He does the same. Beside me, Penrose clears her throat. She is used to my silences which are primarily to wait for the other person to speak, but this time the silence goes on for too long and her impatience gets the better of her .

'Actually, we're not a couple, not like you think. We're partners.'

A fleeting sense of relief crosses over his face. 'That doesn't make any difference to me.'

'If we could have your neighbour's phone number?' Penrose reminds him sweetly. 'It would be very helpful for our investigation.'

'Inv-vestigation?'

'Didn't we say?' she grins with an almost mean expression in her eyes. 'We're police. Police partners.' She makes no effort to disguise her dislike of the man.

'P-police? I d-don't understand.' His breathing is shallow and quick. 'Is … something wrong?'

I don't reply and thankfully, neither does Penrose.

'Sorry.' He clears his throat. 'I didn't mean to be n-nosy. It's just that … I suppose I …ehm … may I see your identification?'

'Of course,' I say, retrieving my ID card from my pocket. He studies mine and ignores Penrose's.

'Can we see yours?' Penrose says in a patronising tone, putting her card back in her pocket.

'Uhm … yes, I'm sorry. I'm Sam. Sam … Collins.' The smile disappears from his face. 'If you wait here, I'll find that phone number for you.'

I can see more questions are popping up in his mind but, at the same time, like a lot of people who are suddenly confronted with the police, he realises it is probably wiser to keep quiet. He rummages round until he finds a small black book under a newspaper that looks like it has been folded in haste. As he writes down a number on the edge of one of the pages of the paper and tears it off, I can just see on that page the face of Trevor Bennett.

'I'm not sure if I should give the number to you.' He hesitates, carefully considering the reasons for his confusion. 'I mean … would it be a breach of privacy?'

'We only have a few questions to help us clear up some issues that have arisen in an investigation,' I say. 'But, in fact, you might be able to help us too. Were you at home yesterday?'

'Yesterday? I went out to get some milk and my newspaper.' He scratches his head. One of the corners of his mouth twitches. 'That must have been before nine. The lollypop lady was just going home. Oh, and I went out later, around lunchtime. Why do you ask?'

'We're here because we were hoping that your neighbour would be able to help us with our investigation, but I'm afraid that's all I can tell you.'

Uninvited, I lower myself onto the brown sofa, immediately regretting it. The surface is hard and unforgiving and although most of the surgical wounds on my bottom have healed by now, it is still a sensitive area. I pull the picture of Trevor Bennett out of my pocket, holding it up to Sam Collins. He unfolds his glasses and puts them on his nose, blinking behind them. Then he picks up the photo and studies it carefully.

'Mr Collins, did you happen to see this man? We have information that he was in the flat next door yesterday.'

'Yesterday? Next door?' He smiles as if we have offended him. 'Sorry, but I don't really pay attention to what my neighbours do. But, if it's helpful or not, I can definitely say that I have never seen this man in my life.'

35

The incident room is buzzing. I can feel the sense of hope and expectation. In stark contrast with earlier, when everyone thought we had reached a dead end and Guthrie was threatening to reduce the hours spent on it, the mood is now optimistic. I don't know the details yet, but it feels like the double murder is about to be cracked.

Maloney's face is flushed. He is updating the whiteboard with the latest information. I can see him adding several red arrows, linking Bennett's name to other added information and I feel my heart sink.

'We've got him,' Penrose whispers from the corner of her mouth.

'Who?' I find a seat between Penrose and PC Andrews for a moment staring as the whiteboard where the name of Maureen Bennett is underlined and some exclamation marks after it.

'Bennett.' PC Andrews replies. His jaws are chewing rapidly. Every so often I see a piece of pink gum moving from one side of his mouth to the other.

'Where is he?'

Penrose shakes her head, eyes fixed on Maloney, who seems to be expecting someone to come in with the news we've all been waiting for.

'We haven't found him yet. A warrant has been issued for his arrest.'

I can't believe my ears. 'On what grounds?'

She stares at me. 'Haven't you heard? His wife has changed her statement.'

'Maureen? Why?'

She shrugs, unsatisfied with my reaction. 'Maloney sent Ollie and Watkins to see her again. Eventually, she admitted that Trevor hadn't been with her all the time on Saturday night at the campsite. As we know, Briony was sick and the boy, Alfie, didn't feel great either. Trevor suggested he'd sleep on the couch so Maureen could keep en eye on the children.'

'That doesn't mean that Bennett ...'

She cuts me off. 'Briony and Alfie didn't sleep very well so Maureen got up at about six thirty and made herself a cup of tea.

She didn't check on her husband as she didn't want to wake him. But when she was in the kitchen making tea, he came in. He had been out. He said he'd just driven out to the nearest village to buy a newspaper.'

I shake my head. 'Does that make him guilty of murder?'

'Not as such, of course, but Maureen didn't really believe him. Their car was dirty, the wheels were clogged with mud. Anyway, we checked and he didn't appear on the CCTV at the village where he claimed he'd bought the paper.'

'Perhaps he didn't know the area very well and he went to an other village.'

I can see anger flaring up in her eyes. She's annoyed by my scepticism and thinks I'm sulking because I kept saying that Bennett isn't the murderer and now that it looks as if I'm wrong, I won't admit it.

'Well,' she says defiantly, '… we know for certain that he did buy a paper and a few magazines for the children. One for Alfie about Formula-1 racing and one for each of the girls -horse stuff-because Maureen saw them. Later, she found the receipt stuck between the pages of the newspaper. It was not from some village store but from a petrol station further west, on the A30 in Cornwall.'

She lowers her voice as Maloney taps the whiteboard wiper on the edge on the table. Guthrie is a few steps to one side of him, arms crossed in front of his chest and smirking as though he has personally solved the case. Everyone is quiet as Maloney more or less repeats Penrose's whispered explanation.

'We've asked the petrol station on the A30 to send us the images from their cameras,' Maloney proceeds, not able to hide his excitement. 'It was pretty easy to check because the time was also on the receipt. We've just got the confirmation that Bennett was seen on the images, paying for petrol and magazines and a newspaper.' He pauses briefly for effect. 'It was 6.08 am. The petrol station had just opened and he was the first customer. The woman at the till remembers him, because she has a daughter who reads the same horse magazines. The significance here though is that this petrol station is at least 30 minutes away from where they were staying in Devon. So he was clearly lying. Our next job is to trace his movements for the whole of that night. We're looking at a time frame between one and six in the morning.' He pauses and his eyes wander over our faces. 'Unfortunately, we don't know the exact time of her death. She didn't have a watch on that conveniently stopped at the moment she was killed.'

'But Torrington stumbled upon her just after midnight,' I remind him.

Maloney nods, this time more patiently. 'That's only what the clairvoyant told us. We can't prove it because we have no other sightings of Torrington on that night except when he left work on Saturday night.'

Maloney opens his mouth again, but stops midway, gazing over our heads. 'Yes Ollie?'

'I've spoken to the clairvoyant again, sir,' he starts, blushing when there is a low murmur and sniggering.

'Quiet!' Guthrie thunders. 'This isn't funny.'

'She says that it might be possible that she had the time wrong,' Ollie continues, trying to pull a serious face. 'That night, we had to put the clocks forward for British Summer Time. She says she doesn't remember exactly when she changed the clock in her bedroom.'

'Okay. The bottom line is that Trevor Bennett has no alibi for that night,' Maloney resumes. 'And there is more. We have checked phone records from that night. He received a call from Alicia Poole at 11.31 pm and they spoke for about 6 minutes. About thirty minutes later, at 12.03 am, he received a call from a different number, which we know now was from Denise Shaw's phone. He didn't answer that call but Alicia had left an urgent message for him asking him to call her back on that number immediately because she was panicking and wanted him to come and help her. Which confirms that she was still alive at 12.03 am.'

Casting his eyes over our faces, he stops at me. 'We need to check this with Denise Shaw. Perhaps you can do that, Tregunna. You seemed to be friendly with her.'

I shrug and stare at Penrose, managing not to blush when I hear someone sniggering again behind me. I will have to ask Penrose to talk to Denise because I won't be able to face her. Not after that disastrous night with her. And Penrose won't ask me any awkward questions as to why I don't want to do it myself.

'All we have to do now is find Bennett,' Maloney continues optimistically. 'I'm sure he'll see sense when we confront him with the evidence.'

'Even if he was at the lake that night,' I say slowly, 'can we prove that he killed her?'

'He'll confess when he hears what we have on him.' Confidently, Maloney turns and writes something on the whiteboard. 'So far, we can place him on the A30 between Okehampton and Launceston. Unfortunately, he had no signal there, possibly because he turned off his phone. He knew we would be able to trace him.'

He picks up a sheet and starts issuing orders to the officers. All leave is cancelled. Nobody objects.

I can't see Bennett as the killer, but I suppose I must be wrong. Even if all the evidence is only circumstantial at this stage, there is the fact that he lied about that night.

'What about Torrington? Did Bennett kill him too?'

'We're currently concentrating on two things here,' Maloney replies firmly. A, find more evidence that proves Bennett killed his ex-wife Alicia, and, B, find him and arrest him.'

He pauses and there is a brief applause. Maloney bows his head, then smiles, and says that it was due to good team work. For the record, he adds that we still have a lot of work to do.

'Let's do this, ladies and gentlemen. The sooner we find Bennett and charge him the better.' He pauses, his eyes meeting Guthrie's. 'And of course, not a word to anyone of the press. Do I make myself clear?'

36

Despite our bad start, I have a feeling that an invisible bond has grown between the new desk officer and me. Alert to all the on gossip and everything out of the ordinary that is going on in the police station, she seems to have taken my side against Guthrie. When I pass her on my way home, I can see warmth in her eyes, replacing the mockery that clouded them earlier.

She puts her arms in a bright orange raincoat and fusses with the zipper, wishing the night duty officer a quiet evening and joins me in the hall.

'Finished for today?' she asks good-naturedly.

'I hope so.' When Maloney found out that she had taken the calls for me when Penrose and I went to the address Jennings had given me, he became unusually angry with me and he literally ordered me to stay by the phone until further notice. Seeing his mouth twitch nervously, the tired look in his eyes, I could understand his frustration and I did as I was told. The search for Trevor Bennett hadn't got us anywhere and when, eventually, the calls became less frequent, Maloney released me off my duty and found someone else to spend the night listening to useless calls from time wasters.

'Uhm, thanks for your help earlier, Annie.'

'It's Anita.' She stops and reaches out her hand. 'Anita Barron. And it was no trouble, Andy.'

I feel myself blush. 'Thanks, Anita.'

'No worries.' She smiles. 'I could see how stressed you were.'

'Hm.' I hope she's not going to enquire why I am stressed. That will immediately dilute the first cautious steps to a better understanding between us.

Thankfully, she doesn't. 'No news about Bennett, I presume?'

'No.'

Ollie Reed and his partner have been watching the block of flats on Penmar Road, but even I am now inclined to admit that Alan and Ellen Jennings must have made a mistake when they thought they recognised Bennett.

'Shame.'

With her free hand, Anita Barron forces open the door against the wind, using her body to keep it open. The sky has blackened and jagged clouds are chasing across the sky. The distant hills and clay pits are obscured by a dark blanket of rain. But in the other direction, over the sea, the sky is almost a clear pale blue with a single slice of purple as if someone has glued it there.

'Hm. We'll get him eventually.'

She hears the tiredness in my voice. 'Can I offer you a lift?' she says, pointing at the sky as we feel the first drops of rain on our faces.

'Only if you are going my way.'

'I am,' she says, not offering any further information.

We drive in silence, each in our own thoughts, but it doesn't feel uncomfortable or awkward. There is a smell in her car that reminds me vaguely of Lauren and the thought of it now fills me with a pain I have tried to ignore for too long.

Anita drives along the coast road where we can see huge waves crashing onto the beaches below us, white foam gathering along the harbour walls and against the rocks. Fishing vessels in the harbour pull at the chains and ropes.

All of a sudden, we are in a heavy shower with water streaming across the road. Each time we hit a puddle, water spouts out like a fountain from the tarmac. She hunches forward in her seat, concentrating hard to as the sodden windscreen is sporadically cleared by the wipers. Her lips are pursed and her hands are tight around the steering wheel.

'Not in a good mood?' she asks, keeping her eyes on the road.

Although I hate it being pointed out when I'm in a bad mood, I admire her for her sensitivity.

'If I'm honest, no. We thought we had a serious lead when the Jennings came to the station yesterday,' I say, irritably. 'Penrose and I went to the address where the Jennings said they'd seen Trevor Bennett. I suppose they meant well, but we found it was a dead end. There was no one in the flat. The neighbour was there almost all day, apparently spying on everything that was going on but he insisted he hadn't seen Bennett.'

'His word against that of Mr and Mrs Jennings?' Anita says encouragingly.

'You could say that.'

'They are two pairs of eyes.'

'True.'

'What if the neighbour lied?'

'Why would he?'

'Don't know.'

She flashes her headlights, annoyed as she sees a car with no lights on at all. 'I understand there's been a breakthrough.'

I shrug, wondering if she realises this is exactly the reason why I'm not in a good mood. I don't feel satisfied about my day at work. It is as if I've been wasting my time and everything I achieved has been wiped away.

'Trevor Bennett is now the prime suspect.'

She casts me a quick glance. 'I hear a but in your voice.'

'I'm not convinced he did it.'

'Why not?'

I shrug. 'A hunch, that's all.'

'Hunches don't come from nowhere.'

'True.' But I know Maloney wasn't impressed by my logic. 'It's because of the milk.'

I still can't believe that Bennett would have bought the milk for his wife. Why would he have bothered if he knew he was going to leave his family?

'And your hunch is based on … milk?'

'More or less.'

She stops behind a small white car, tutting when it doesn't move when the traffic light changes to green.

I nod. 'He brought the milk home. Why didn't he take his car? Or his passport? He hasn't been to a cash machine to take out an abnormal sum of money.'

'But is there evidence against him?'

'All circumstantial.'

Not taking her eyes off the road, I can see a smile on her lips. 'When I come home from work and I'm tired, or grumpy, or moaning about everyone and everything, my fifteen-year-old daughter asks me if I want to talk about it. It has become an expression in our house. But really, it helps. I moan and groan and she listens and we laugh about it afterwards.'

'Does she also moan?'

'Of course. School. Teachers. Friends. Disputes.'

'I live alone.'

'Hm.' We drive in silence again. Every so often she taps a rhythm on the steering wheel with a finger. I sense her looking at me and she changes the subject completely.

'It was PC Beth Andrews who is responsible for the leak to the press. She's friends with Hill's wife. They go to the same hairdresser or something like that.' She pauses. When I don't respond, she adds, 'You know, that reporter. Hill.'

'Gerald Hill? I wasn't aware that he has a wife.'

'You are cynical, Andy Tregunna.'

'Realistic.' I hesitate. 'Does Guthrie know?'

'Uhm ... no.' She blushes. 'I was advised to tell you.'

'Why me?'

'You'd know what to do.'

'Says who?'

'Uhm ... Champion.'

She's referring to PC Danielle Champion. One of the young-est recruits on the force. She is as thin as a rake, with hunched shoulders and so short she barely reaches to my chest. In the beginning, I wondered what went on in her head or what she expected when she chose a career with the police. But she's proven me wrong. She'll be a good officer, probably one of the best.

'Are you going to tell the DCI about PC Andrews?' Anita Bar-ron asks, frowning uncertainly, probably already regretting that she's told me.

The increasing wind is making the car rock and she has to hold the wheel firmly in both hands. I look at the torrential rain crashing on the windscreen as we approach the double rounda-bout.

'It will blow over.'

'Maybe, but it isn't right that ...'

'I'll have a word with PC Andrews. Gerald Hill will find an-other way to get his information, or he'll simply make things up.'

'Oh.' She slows down as we drive alongside the park. Leaves are blown across the road and the trees are shaking. 'Where is your flat? Tell me where to stop.'

'It's fine if you stop here. I'll walk the rest of the way.'

'Not in this weather, you don't ...' She shakes her head. 'For what it's worth, I overheard the Jennings talking to one another as they were leaving the police station,' she continues. 'It didn't really make sense to me, but it seemed important to them. That's why I'm telling you.'

I have my hand already on the door handle waiting for her to stop the car. 'What was important?'

'Mr Jennings was angry with his wife after they were interviewed …' She pauses and curses a bicycle rider in front of us dodging puddles and slowing down the traffic on the road. The flashing red light on the back of his bike is barely visible through the rain splashing up off his tyres. When he has moved onto the pavement, Anita seems to have lost her train of thought.

'You were telling me what you overheard the Jennings say.'

'Oh sorry. Well, Mrs Jennings was in tears when her husband announced that he didn't want to go on with the whole process because he wasn't sure about the man's background.'

'What did he mean by that?'

'I don't know.'

'Whose background?'

'I thought you would know that.'

I'm puzzled. The wipers make a sucking sound. I can't concentrate. I have the frustrating feeling that I am missing something here. Something small, but very important. It's at the back of my mind, I can almost grab it, but it disappears when I reach for it. I need to be alone silence, I need quietness, I need to think.

'What else did they say?'

'Not much.' She frowns. 'Only that they'd come so far already. They've paid and it has now gone too far to stop.'

'Can you stop here, please, uhm … Anita?' I say abruptly.

'Is it something I said?' she jokes, not hiding her surprise as she obediently stops beside the kerb, ignoring the hoot of an impatient driver behind us.

'Yes, it is something you said but not in the way you think. Thank you, Anita!' Climbing out, I let go of the car door which almost blows out of my hand.

'Get back in,' she insists. 'Just tell me where you live.'

'No, but thanks anyway.' I lift my head and feel the rain pouring down my hair and face. I almost welcome the wet coldness. An idea is beginning to form in my head. Absurd and totally at odds with everything I know and experienced in my life. I can barely believe what I'm thinking but things are starting to make sense. Slowly.

'I need to think.'

Anita waves goodbye, then she's gone. I pull up the collar of my coat, brace myself against the lashing rain and instead of going home walk back to the police station.

37

My rain-soaked collar clings to my neck and my shoes are making squelching sounds when I arrive at the station. By then the rain has blown over and the sky is clearing to the west, offering a small strip of sunlight just above the horizon.

The entrance hall is deserted. The desk officer is Philpo, short for Phil Philpott, a retired policeman. He 'd been looking forward to his retirement for years, saving money and making plans to travel the world with his wife, but a few weeks before his retirement day, his wife was diagnosed with acute kidney problems and she died within three months. Going mad in his empty house, not wanting to travel on his own, he came back to the police force and is mostly stands in for former colleagues during their holidays.

Clean shaven and sad eyed, he is sitting behind the counter and reading a paper, catching up on the background stories of Alicia Poole and Wilbur Torrington, regardless of whether they have been accurately written by the reporters or not.

'Evening,' Philpo says, gazing over the rim of his reading glasses that are hanging from his neck by a yellow cord. 'Can I help you, sir?' He sounds as if he is wondering if I am a colleague or someone he arrested during his career.

'I'm Tregunna.' I can't blame him for not recognising me. I wouldn't have recognised him either, but for his name on the desk, as we've only met briefly.

He stares at my ID, not seeing any point in apologising. 'Most of them have gone home,' he shrugs, 'They haven't found that guy yet, though. Search is to be continued tomorrow morning.'

I nod. The station would be buzzing if Bennett was being held in one of the cells by now. Everyone would be working very hard to make sure that he wouldn't be released after the designated time he could be legally held in custody without being charged.

'Do you know if Maloney is still here?'

'He left with DCI Guthrie ...' He looks at his watch, '... seven minutes ago. Didn't you see them in the car park?'

I shake my head. 'Penrose?'

'Haven't seen her.'

'DS Reed?' I try my last option.

'Ollie? He's in. He said something about staying here the night.' He frowns. Uncertain. 'His neighbours are having a house-warming party. Or something. He can't stand their choice of music.'

'Thank you.'

I find Ollie staring at the coffee machine as though he needs to read the instructions first. Turning his head to give me a nod, he presses a button and waits for the machine to come to life, coughing and shuddering until it spits out coffee that looks like tar. He stares at it, muttering about having pressed the button for extra milk.

'Try again,' I say. 'I have my coffee black.'

He does. It has the same result. With a shrug of defeat, he sips the coffee and spits it out instantly.

'Sorry. I'm not in a good mood.'

'I know the feeling,' I reply casually. 'Perhaps I should have brought some doughnuts. The sugar rush will help.'

He shakes his head. 'I've just had my tea. Microwave meal, but good. Really good. Chicken Kiev with new potatoes and broccoli. Ever tried it?'

'No. My mother doesn't approve of those meals. Every now and then she checks my fridge and freezer and gives me a bollocking if she finds a frozen meal from a supermarket.' I grin to try to put Ollie at ease. 'She only believes in fresh food. British food. She doesn't even buy sprouts in summer or lettuce in winter. Never used to be available in her childhood, she says.'

'No curry or lasagne?' he asks sympathetically.

No lasagne, but she is of the opinion that curry is part of the British menu.'

The hint of a grin crosses his face. 'Mine is only worried about saturated fats, carbohydrates and sugars.'

As if we've reached a mutual understanding, we walk to a small room that is intended for meetings with superiors or work assessments. The table and four chairs are littered with files and papers spilling out of boxes. Ollie clears one of the chairs and I sit on the edge of the table.

'I'm here because of my new neighbours,' he explains, un-asked. He pinches the bridge of his nose and squeezes his eyes shut. 'They've been knocking down walls and doors, replacing the floors and God knows what else. They've been at it for months, driving me mad with the banging and the noise of electric tools. Not to mention shouting and yelling when they've had a disagreement. And that happened so often that it amazes me that they are still together. Anyway, they finally moved in a couple of days ago and they're still yelling and shouting at each other.'

'Can you still hear them?'

He nods gravely. 'You would have thought that they would have put something some insulation but apparently not.'

'Philpo said something about a house-warming party.'

'I wish. Unless having loud music and lots of friends round all the time is their idea of having multiple house-warming parties. They do it more or less every day.'

'Have you spoken to them about it?'

He raises his eyebrows quizzically. 'Are you serious? They know I'm police. They know the law. They know they turn it off between 11pm and 7am. Besides, they say I'm always welcome to join them.'

'Friendly neighbours.'

'Oh, they are friendly alright, I'm not complaining about that. It's just … the noise they make. Sometimes I can't stand it.'

'Turn up your own TV or radio a bit louder.'

'I don't want things to escalate. They've just moved in. we might have to live next door to each other for ages.' Pulling a face, he looks as though the thought of it makes him consider his options.

We've barely touched our coffees. I contemplate suggesting we find a café near the police station and get some decent coffee.

'Funny thing, insulation,' he continues after a short pause. 'Their house isn't even joined to mine. They share a wall with the other neighbours, but I seem to get the bulk of the annoyance.'

'It's important that you get enough sleep and …'

'You sound like my mother.'

'Perhaps mothers are right.'

'Yeah, well, I don't know. They have a little girl. Three years old, I think. She likes to dance, but it is more like jumping, if you ask me. I can hardly hear the music, but I do hear her jumping up and down all the time.'

'Perhaps this is all about perception. We tend to get upset about noises we don't like and especially music that is not to our taste. It annoys you, like the music in some shops. But if we like it, we like going to that shop.'

'Is that the psychology?'

'I believe so.'

Something clicks in my brain. Something that has been nagging at me for a long while. Sam Collins. Thinking out loud, I tell Ollie all about the hammering sounds. The neighbour, the young mother I met, said it could be anyone in the building. And she's right. Sound travels in the form of vibrating airwaves which, when they bounce off walls, can create echo-like sounds,

Collins was annoyed by the hammering and my guess is that it had been going on for a while. We put up with annoying sounds to start with but if they continue, they can incite our anger. Collins went into a bedroom and banged on the wall. Why would he bang on the wall if he didn't know for sure where the noise was coming from?

I take my phone out. Find Mrs Holt's mobile number in my contacts list. Press buttons.

She answers with caution in her voice as if she's not expecting anyone to call.

Ollie reed is staring at me, wondering what he might have said to distract me from our conversation.

'Mrs Holt, my name is Andy Tregunna.' I glance at my watch. 'Sorry to bother you at this time of the evening, but I have a question. You spoke to my colleagues earlier and ...'

'You are the police inspector?' she interrupts, sounding happier. She sounds like she had a couple of glasses of wine with her evening meal.

'I am. I have just one short question for you, Mrs Holt, if you don't mind?'

'Of course not. We've just finished our tea. So, what's your question?'

I hear the rattle of cutlery on crockery. A tap running briefly. We, she said. Our meal.

'Are you with someone, Mrs Holt?'

'Yes, of course. Sam always does the cooking. He has ...'

'Sam Collins? Your neighbour?'

'Yes, of course, we're ...'

I shake my head with frustration. I omitted to ask Collins anything about his relationship with his neighbour. He called her Mrs Holt and I assumed that they were just that. Neighbours. A nod, a polite greeting, helping each other out in an emergency. Nothing more.

'Mrs Holt, one quick question, although I might know the answer already.' The question I had for her has dissolved. Instead, I ask, 'Does Mr Collins, Sam, have a key to your flat?'

'Does he … yes of course he has. What …?'

'That's all, Mrs Holt, thank you.'

'What was that about?' Ollie asks, intrigued as soon as he heard Collins's name. He's heard about my little escapade to the flat with Penrose. He knows that Maloney wasn't pleased about it.

'Would you bang on your neighbour's wall when you heard a noise, any noise, but you knew they weren't there? Wouldn't you have a quick look if you heard something in your neighbour's house, if you knew there was nobody there, and you had a key?'

I don't wait for his answer. I pour the dregs of my coffee into a sad looking plant in a dark corner and crunch the plastic cup in my fist.

'Sorry, Ollie, I need to check something.'

'Would you like me to come with you?'

'That won't be necessary.'

'I'm not convinced,' I say, smiling briefly. 'But I think I need to do this alone. In case I cock it up again. Go home, Ollie, wear some earplugs and, if you can still hear your neighbour's music, just try to enjoy it.'

38

There are twice as many cars in the car park since I was in Penmar Road with Penrose. And twice as many teenagers are hanging round. Their presence makes me feel a bit uncomfortable. Or perhaps I am prejudiced, which makes me as bad as people who spray paint on boards to let the world know that they don't want migrants in this neighbourhood. Maybe not as bad though as the 23-year-old guy who could have killed someone when he set fire to the flat on the second floor. I have checked it out: an only child of a respectable couple who have always worked hard to be able to afford his education. He has become a selfish young man who fucked up his jobs, stole petty cash from the company he worked for and was too stupid to realise that he would be caught. He's now become a couch potato, flicking through TV-channels his only physical exercise. Bored and lazy and blaming everyone else for his own failures.

Once more, I climb the stairs and walk along the walkway, hearing loud music and laughter, a dog barking, arguing voices. The smell of curry hangs in the air, mixed with burnt onions.

I can see light behind the curtains in Mr Collins's flat. I can visualise him sitting on his sofa watching an episode of David Attenborough's travels around the globe. Sipping milky tea. Dunking cheap biscuits. He's just that type.

I'm relieved to see that the lights in Mrs Holt's flat at the end of the walkway are on.

The kitchen blinds are down, but the slats are half open. I cup my hands against the glass and peer through the gaps between the slats, letting my eyes adjust to the bright fluorescent light inside. The otherwise tidy kitchen is disturbed by something broken on the floor. Glass.

Somehow, it seems as if time is standing still, as though something is about to happen. A sense of unease is growing within me. I imagine Penrose standing still beside me, a question of doubt in her tone when suggesting calling for back-up. I should call, Maloney maybe, but will he listen? I don't even know what I'm doing here myself. Everyone is focused on finding Trevor Bennett as the main suspect in the double murder case. They're checking train and bus stations, questioning cab drivers, talking to his friends, relatives and work colleagues, widening the area as they search the towns and rural areas.

But I know that the extensive search for Bennett isn't the reason why I don't make the call for back-up. It's my stubbornness that I try to conceal which would be regarded as arrogance.

I walk past the front door without knocking on it. The curtains of the room next to the front door are partially open. The bed is covered with a layer of sheets and blankets and a duvet without a cover. On top of it is an open suitcase, partially filled with rolled-up socks and folded shirts. Mrs Holt, packing for a holiday? Or a weekend away to see a mother, a sister, a relative, somewhere up country?

I knock on the door. Nothing happens. Knock again, harder. Nothing. I can hear footsteps, but they could be of someone on the walkway above or below me. I wait. Hesitate. I contemplate calling on Sam Collins again to ask him if he knows where Marcie Holt is. When I spoke to her I'm sure he was with her by the sound of rattling crockery. She might have told him about my call. She might have repeated my question to him.

I put my hand on her door handle, thinking, listening, almost hoping that someone will turn up with a key. Unconsciously, I press the handle. The door opens. I am too surprised to act immediately. I look over my shoulder, checking to see if there isn't anyone behind me playing tricks on. A shiver runs down my spine. I feel uncomfortable, exposed and vulnerable, as if I'm being watched.

The door opens into a narrow hallway.

'Hello? Mrs Holt? Are you there?'

No response. I am only greeted by silence. The flat is cold and musty, as though the heating hasn't been turned on for the last couple of weeks. My footsteps are absorbed by a beige carpet. It reminds me of the carpet in Mr Collins's flat. The only open door leads into the kitchen. Broken glass litters the floor. It looks so out of place in the neat, orderly flat that I stare at it. Did Marcie Holt have an accident, did she drop a glass, two maybe and cut herself on the shards? Did she go to Collins for medical help?

I call again, but there doesn't appear to be anyone in the flat. I know I shouldn't be here. I know I should go. I stand in the doorway to the kitchen, my eyes scanning every item. There is an electric kettle on the spotless counter. It's cold. The fridge is humming softly. I open it. It's empty, except for a bottle of milk. Unopened. One of the cupboards holds a diversity of a few coffee mugs, one with two teaspoons in it, an opened package of sugar, a small jar of coffee granules and a 'get 50% extra' box of teabags behind the mugs.

The lounge has the feeling of faded decadency, with its L-shaped sofa, embroidered pillows and throws printed with pink and red roses. The crystal bowls with potpourri take me back to my childhood, when it was fashionable. At one side is a small desk with a computer on it. It's turned off, but when I check the unit, it is still warm. Clearly, it has recently been used. If it was used by Marcie Holt, then she must have been here since I called her. But where is she now?

She let it slip that she had a meal with Sam Collins and that he always did the cooking, so she must have been in his flat. Not hers. She may still be next door.

Once more, aware that I might frighten her to death, I call her name. Repeat it. Let her know I am here, who I am. Still nothing.

I open the bathroom door and slide the plastic shower curtain to one side. Nothing. Staring in the mirror of the cabinet above the sink, I open it. A new tube of toothpaste and some dental floss. Deodorants. Five different brands. The cupboard under the sink holds a pile of clean folded towels and boxes of tissues and wet wipes. Bleach and toilet cleaner. I can see no painkillers, throat lozenges or other medicines. It seems like nobody lives permanently. It feels like I'm in a hotel.

Calling Marcie's name again with little hope, I cross the hallway, listening keenly, filtering out muffled sounds from elsewhere in the building: the murmur of a television, music, footsteps.

The main bedroom is almost as unlived in as the rest of the flat. The bed is king-size, with a classic looking, metal frame in a chrome and white finish. It has pink satin duvet cover and matching pillows, bedside tables each with the pale pink lampshades and clear glass ashtrays. On one is a remote control for the flat screen TV on the wall opposite the bed. The red standby light is on. A DVD player sits on a white dressing table. Above it, is an oval mirror. Opening the only drawer I find there is no ladies underwear or make up or any of the usual things you would expect to find in a bedroom. Instead, there is a neat row of

DVDs. Scanning the titles, I see a selection of porn films, ranging from soft to hard porn.

The large white wardrobe has three doors, the centre one with a full-length mirror. It rattles when I open is. Once more, I am surprised to see its contents. I have never met Marcie Holt but I was expecting to find more than just a couple of black skirts and blue blouses and a printed scarf.

The only items that seem slightly out of place are a man's black towelling bathrobe and a ladies pink satin dressing gown with white lace and little fake diamonds sewn along the edges. The scent of something flowery mixes with that of dust.

All of a sudden, I become aware of the hammering sound again. It seems closer than when I heard it in Collins's flat, but I smile inwardly, thinking about what I told Ollie Reed about the movement of sound waves.

There is a cold draught around my ankles and I turn on my heels. 'Marcie? Mrs Holt?'

Nothing.

There is one other smaller bedroom which I peered into from outside. Surprisingly, the door is locked but the key is in the lock. The door opens inwards and the hammering sounds stop abruptly. It's a bit dark with its partially closed curtains. My hand finds a light switch and a bright energy saving light bulb slowly comes on. There's nobody here either, but the smell is different. Sweat and stale breath.

The only furniture is a double bed, the same style as the one in the main bedroom, only smaller. The open suitcase I saw when I looked through the window is on the unmade bed. On the floor beside it is a pair of trainers, mud and sand stuck to the sides which is uncharacteristic of the rest of the clean and tidy flat. For no apparent reason, a chain, the size of a dog's leash, is looped around one of the legs of the bed.

I can hear noises from some neighbours again. Running footsteps, laughter, the bang of a door closed by a gust of draught.

Straightening up, I look around, bothered by something that I can't put my finger on. Something is wrong. Something doesn't add up.

Apart from the double bed, the room looks empty. I'm about to leave, when I hear a sound. It seems to come from the space between the bed and the wall that adjoins Mr Collins's flat. I can barely hear it. Soft. The scraping of feet against something hard. Or it could be a voice, a low moan, someone trying not to make a sound.

I turn back to the door and raise my voice. 'Mrs Holt? Marcie? Hello?'

Frantic movements come from behind me and a muffled voice trying to shout.

Crossing the room, I see his legs first. Dark socks and ankles bound together with brown packing tape. It is the same type as I saw earlier stuck on Collins's elbow. No shoes. The dog chain is looped around his feet and a leg of the bed. I bend down and see that his hands are tied with plastic ties to the buckle of his belt in front of him

The man is rocking his head from side to side as if he is stuck in a nightmare, his body jerking in protest. His nose is running and his breathing seems to be a struggle, making his body twitch in panic. From what is visible of his face, his skin is pale, perhaps a bit bluish. The same brown packing tape is wound around his head and neck, holding a piece of cardboard over his eyes, and a piece of cloth is pushed into his mouth. Snot drips from one side of his nose. He can't afford to get his nose blocked; he will die.

His suddenly lies motionless, perhaps sensing that whoever has entered the room, could be his abductor, or maybe not. Clearly he doesn't want to take a risk.

Just as I open my mouth to reassure him that his ordeal is over, he lifts one elbow and kicks it against the wall. The hammering sound returns and I swallow; I should have realised much earlier what it was.

I crawl towards him. My fingers touch his arm. 'Hello, Trevor,' I say, holding his hand. 'You're safe.'

His fingers try to squeeze mine. He rocks his head, urging me to take the blind off his eyes. Gently, I remove the tape that has got stuck in his hair and I can see him flinch as I do so. The sharp pain overrules the anxiety of not being able to see.

His eyes flutter open. Pupils dilating with the sudden light, and then he shuts them again. When he opens them again more carefully, he stares at me until he recognises me. And he relaxes.

'Mr Bennett, Trevor,' I say comfortingly, my voice hoarse. 'How good to see you.'

He squeezes his eyes shut and a tiny marble-like tear rolls down his cheek and disappears in his ear. He cries openly like a man who's been given a second chance, who wants to tell everyone that he nearly died but was saved miraculously.

I try to untie his hands, but I need a knife or a pair of scissors to cut the strong plastic of the ties. He's straightening up and I see his eyes widen. He still can't believe that help has come for him eventually.

'I need to find something to cut you free,' I say, reassuringly, swallowing as I see panic rise in his eyes. 'I'm only going to the kitchen.'

I think of the empty cupboards, and wonder if there might be something useful there. Like a knife or scissors.

He jerks his head, mutters something that sounds like a 'no' and I realise he still has the packing tape over his mouth. Attempting not to expose him to the sharp pain again, I try to tear it off his face carefully. His eyes are rolling in their sockets, he is almost passing out.

'Trevor? Mr Bennett? Stay with me! Everything will be all right.'

He opens his eyes. I see more fear and panic. I don't understand. There is a moment, a heartbeat of silence, when we stare at each other. He is trying to tell me something, I am trying to understand his silent message.

He lifts one finger from his tied-up hand and points at my shoulder.

I want to ask what he is trying to tell me. My mouth opens. No sound emerges. Instead, I hear something else. The rustle of footsteps on the soft carpet. Bennett is pointing again. I realise what he means when I feel something hitting me hard on my head. My legs buckle. Someone steadies me but my body crumples and I feel myself sliding onto the edge of the bed, and then falling onto the floor.

Then there is only darkness.

39

A face is peering down at me: a woman with swollen eyes and a dark red smudge across one ear. The earring is missing, ripped out. The other ear has a large gold loop in it. Strands of dull brown hair are hanging down beside her face. She is sniffing and sobbing; clear shiny fluid is running out of every orifice in her face, dripping onto me.

It's Marcie Holt. I recognise her only by the clothes I saw in the wardrobe. She is dressed in a black skirt, but it is now spattered with dirt and torn at one side. One of the buttons on her blue blouse is missing and I can see the edge of a plain white cotton bra. No lace on the edges. Nothing fancy. There is a dark red stain just above her waist, though she doesn't appear to notice that she might be hurt.

'Hello?' she whispers. 'Are you awake?'

I try to nod, but the movement sends electric shock waves through my body. My head is pounding and there are little dots of light shooting from one end of my peripheral vision to the other. I don't know how or why, but I know instantly that these light dots aren't a good sign.

'You're Marcie,' I half say, half ask. My mouth is dry and my lips are cracking. Every word is painful to speak.

'Yes. Marcie Holt.' Her voice is dull and I realise that she is in shock. Her eyes are vacant. She's staring into the distance, not seeing anything. Her face looks like white and grey marble, like those ancient statues in museums. She's holding a mobile phone in her hand. The screen is cracked but I can see the distorted letters of some notifications of messages.

'You called me?' She gestures with her mobile.

As I lift my head, a sharp pain shoots inside my skull and I nearly fall back into unconsciousness.

'You are Tregunna?'

'Yes,' I say, but she doesn't need an answer.

I move my head slowly. I recognise the wallpaper but it takes a while before I realise where I've seen it before. I'm lying next to a wall and on my other side I can see a cotton sheet printed with lavender and lilies-of the valley. A cold draught comes from underneath me and I realise that I 'm lying on the floor in the narrow gap between a bed and the wall, my head half under a wooden dining chair.

Shards of memory are coming back.

'Where is Collins?' I try to see what's behind her, but she is blocking my view, hanging too closely over me. 'Marcie? Is he still here?'

'He's gone.'

'And Bennett? Trevor Bennett?'

'He's gone. He's left me.'

I try to think. Bennett has left her? It doesn't make sense.

'He left me.' Her eyes are locked in horror.

'Marcie, I need to know where Trevor Bennett is!'

'I'm so sorry. I could have … I should have stopped him.'

I'm not sure if she's talking about Collins or Bennett.

All the same, I become aware of the silence, which seems more frightening somehow. A shiver runs down my spine, a foreboding of danger. I need to get out of this place before Collins comes back. I'm not sure what he is capable of, whether he is responsible for the deaths of Alicia Poole and Wilbur Torrington, but I do know that he brought Trevor Bennett, voluntarily or not, to this flat and tied him up, and that he lied when Penrose and I spoke to him. And he knocked me unconscious.

'I'm so sorry,' she says, her voice hoarse with crying. 'I'm so sorry.'

She's constantly repeating herself, shaking her head as if she still can't believe why her life is in such a mess. I want to tell her that this isn't her fault at all, but somehow I know I'd be talking to deaf ears.

'Where is Trevor Bennett? And where is Collins?'

She stares at me, a flash of emotion in her eyes. There is something unfathomable in them. She's stuck in a single moment, the moment her personal world collapsed. Possibly mine too. I feel a small tremor vibrating inside me, expanding from between my shoulders, filling my chest and throat. I try to move, but I can't.

'Marcie, you need to help me. Please!'

'Don't shout at me.' She looks over her shoulder with raw fear in her eyes, ready to jump up and run away. Something tells me that, once she's gone, she won't come back.

'Sorry. I'm sorry. I won't shout at you, but you need to help me get up.'

Her eyes are blank. It's pointless. Something horrifying is blocking her brain. I close my eyes and concentrate on trying to get up myself. Ignoring the pain and flashing lights in my eyes, I lift my head slowly until my forehead touches the leg of the chair above me. I move my shoulders. It's painful, but I can do it. My arms. My legs. I can feel them, but they won't move. I move my fingers. I wiggle my toes. I feel a prickling sensation and I can almost cry with relief. But then I fear that this could mean that the nerves to my limbs have been cut off, sending the wrong information to my brain. I move my fingers and toes again. Sharp pain, pins and needles. I can't remember from the compulsory first-aid courses I attended whether this means that there is some permanent damage to my head or spine. And I still can't move.

I panic. I try to focus and then gradually I realise that my wrists have been tied tightly behind me. I'm lying on my arms which have gone numb, making my shoulders ache by my uncomfortable position. I can move my fingers, but not my wrists and arms. My legs have been crossed over and my ankles are tied-up.

Whereas people, especially in films or books can escape miraculously from situations like this, I can't. I shall need help.

I close my eyes and feel some energy beginning to return as though it has been drained out of me. I'm sure I'm not fatally wounded. I can move a bit but I need help to untie my arms and legs.

'Marcie? Look at me! Is Collins still here?'

She blows her nose using a crumpled handkerchief she pulls from in the sleeve of her blouse. 'He's left me.'

'Marcie, you have to help me. You have to untie my hands and feet.' I remember the plastic ties around Bennett's hands and feet. They were the type that are meant to be so strong that they can lift really heavy weights without breaking, which is one of the reasons we police use them more often than the traditional handcuffs when we make an arrest.

'I'm sorry.'

I shake my head. 'I can sort this out, but you have to help me get up first.' My voice sounds convincing and I see a flash of understanding on her face, then her shoulders slump.

A fart escapes from my belly. At the same time I become aware of a terrible smell. Her nose still buried in her handkerchief, Marcie isn't aware of it. Another fart. She stares at me. A gasp escapes from her mouth but I'm not sure why until I notice that my stoma bag is protruding and has grown to abnormal proportions. It is more or less the size of a cricket ball. There is a dirty mark on my shirt beneath it. I don't want to think about what it is, but the smell is almost unbearable.

'How long have I been here? What time is it?'

'It's past nine.' It's her first sensible reply. It's light outside, so it must be morning.

I gaze at the dark red stain on her shirt. I'm not sure if it's bigger than a few moments ago. 'Are you hurt?'

'He left me.' Her eyes vacant again, she touches her side with her fingertips. As she lifts her shirt, I can see pieces of brown packing tape crisscrossed over her skin. There is blood around the edges, but I can see it's dried blood, not fresh blood.

'Are you alright?'

She shrugs. Indifferent. She's still in shock and doesn't seem to understand we need to get help. And she isn't aware of the sense of urgency which puts us both in more danger.

I remember the kitchen, almost bare. Mugs in one cupboard, no proper cutlery in the drawers. No knives, let alone scissors.

'Marcie, can you go to the flat next door and get a knife or a pair of scissors?' I try to sound casual. If she senses my fear and panic, she may become frantic and not be able to do anything useful.

'What do you need them for?' Her eyebrows rise and her eyes are like saucers.

I need all my patience to remain calm. 'To cut the ties around my hands and feet.'

'Oh.'

'Did you hear me, Marcie?' I need your help. Go next door and get something to cut the ties for me. Please?'

She doesn't move, she doesn't speak. The moment of clarity, when she asked why I wanted a knife or scissors, seems to have worn off. Yet, somehow, I have to get through to her to make her aware of the situation, of the imminent danger to both of us.

'Marcie, pull my legs. I can't sit up. My head is under the chair. Pull my legs.'

She moves from the bed, staring down at my feet. 'Pull, Marcie, please.'

'Yes.' She rises to her feet, stumbling as though she's been drinking too much. I don't know how long it takes but she repeats my words until they start making sense to her and she follows my orders to the letter.

Eventually, I am sitting on the end of the bed and she is standing beside me, panting, on her face an expression that suggests that, now that she's fulfilled this task, she's gone back into her shell.

'Thank you for this, Marcie, you've been a great help. Now, I need you to find something sharp to cut the ties around my wrists and ankles. I can't walk like this, can I?' I end with a forced wink, as if this is all a game, but she doesn't respond.

'Go to Collins's flat, Marcie, and get the sharpest knife you can find. Please.'

She nods, but my words haven't registered. Or perhaps her brain stopped working when I mentioned Collins's name.

By now I am pretty certain that Collins has gone but at the same time, I am aware that he might have been watching us all the time, listening. Waiting.

'Marcie, be careful ...' I say, but she withdraws, walking backwards to the doorway, arms outstretched defensively and her eyes fixed as though she's in a trance.

The flat is empty and silent, but I'm uncomfortably aware that she must have left the front door open. I can feel the cold air coming in, the mizzle dampening the atmosphere

Gradually, I come to the conclusion that I can't expect any further help from Marcie. She hasn't come back. She has either decided that it's not in her best interest to help me escape or she's slumped in a seat, wondering how the world around her has changed so much and so quickly. Either way, I have to hurry. I have to find out where Sam Collins is and where he has taken Trevor Bennett. I don't allow myself to speculate about what might have become of Trevor. If I hadn't been so stubborn and foolish coming here on my own, he would have been back home safely by now. I failed him, I failed Maureen, and I failed Marcie.

Sunlight filters through the drawn curtains. A black leather handbag is sitting by the mirror of the white dressing table.

Marcie's handbag.

Most women carry a wealth of necessary and needless items with them. My mother had a leaflet with the bus timetables in her handbag for months; she never uses the bus as my father drives her everywhere. She also carried a small purse for foreign currency, empty since their last holiday abroad, four years ago. I hope Marcie's handbag will be a similar treasure-trove for me.

With a mixture of determination and desperation, I rise to my feet, slightly out of balance with my hands and feet still tied up and my crossed legs.

A movement catches my eye. I don't recognise the man in the mirror. He is staring at me with tired eyes, his clothes dirty, something the size of a cricket ball at the side of his belly, dirty stains on his shirt.

It seems to take forever to totter over to the dressing table. I lean and turn, grab one of the handles of the handbag before I fall over. Out of breath, I go back to the bed. My heart is pounding and my head is spinning when I lie on the bed again. It feels like something or someone is hammering so hard on the inside of my skull that I fear I'll faint. I lie on my side waiting for my headache to go, catching my breath, trying to calm down and think.

I don't know where Marcie is or what she is doing. More importantly, I don't know where Collins is. Marcie claims that he's left her, but she was so confused that he could just have gone to the corner shop to get milk. And now he could be holding her hostage and waiting for me to appear.

I struggle for ages with my hands still tied behind my back to open the zipper and empty the contents of the handbag on the bedspread. Unable to see them I take each item in my hands and try to work out what it is as though I'm blindfolded in some sort of television show and I've got to name each item within a limited time to win a TV set, or a holiday to a sunny island.

Then I feel it. Nail clippers. Bless you Marcie.

40

They take me to the hospital. I share the ambulance with Trevor Bennett. People are shouting and shining torches in his eyes. He is strapped to a stretcher, briefly opening his eyes before he falls back into semi-consciousness. I sit next to him, my hope fading that he'll be able to tell me what happened before the police interview him properly. The paramedic is crouched at the other end of the stretcher, checking in the evidence bag the pharmacy boxes which the police found in Collins's flat and scribbling on a clipboard on his knee. He has already confirmed that Bennett had been drugged but they're not certain which drugs Collins gave him, or how many.

Skipping the waiting area at the A&E department, we are steered towards a small cubicle. I feel quite guilty as we pass patients on trolleys or slumped in uncomfortable hospital wheelchairs, waiting to be consulted. Some of them look a lot worse than Trevor and me.

On the basis that we are both victims of attempted murder, I manage to remain at Bennett's side until Maloney has arranged for someone to keep an eye on him. He seems only half convinced that Bennett is a victim rather than a suspect and he's quite happy that I can stay with him in case Bennett disappears again.

A Junior Doctor playing with the stethoscope hanging around his neck and a range of pens in the breast pocket of his white coat comes in. His name tag says he is Callum Wyatt and he asks the same questions the paramedic had already asked us. Within minutes he disappears behind the grey cotton curtain, he issues his instructions to a nurse and he's gone without examining me. The nurse relieves Bennett of enough blood to fill a dozen test tubes for examination to determine how to proceed with his treatment. Then she looks at me quizzically.

'Have you been looked at by the doctor?'

'No, but I'm fine.'

'The paramedics think you might have concussion.'

'I'm fine.'

She nods, scribbling Bennett's name on small labels and sticks them on the tubes. 'I'll get the doctor to have a look at your head. Better make sure most of the damage is on the outside.'

Her voice leaves no room for argument.

'I'm fine,' I repeat, whilst at the same time, like a child, trying to cover the lump on my head with my hand. It makes her smile and she tells me, for my own good, not to move until someone has examined me.

The Junior Doctor returns with a deep frown, looking at me as though I'm not the first obstinate patient who has tried to avoid him. He checks my reflexes, looks into my eyes with a bright penlight, mumbles inaudibly and writes his diagnosis on a blank form. He confirms that it doesn't look as if I have a serious injury, but I need to be aware of certain symptoms and come back immediately if I develop any of them, As soon as I get the chance, I let one of the nurses know that I need a fresh stoma bag. She's very young and very shy. She blushes and looks at me as though I'm taking the Mickey or perhaps I have a serious head injury after all. When I lift my stained shirt, she looks even more embarrassed. Earlier, I punched a small hole in the blown up bag to release the air, but the smell is still disgusting. She admits that she's never seen one before and doesn't know what to do and, I sense her relief when I tell her that I'd rather deal with it myself as long as she can provide me with what I need.

The soles of her shoes squeak on the laminate floor and she's gone.

Our voices have woken up Bennett. For a moment, his eye-lids flutter and stares at me. I can see his nostrils widen, but he is too drowsy to say very much.

'Where is …?' he starts, fear building up in his eyes.

'Everything is alright now,' I say quickly. 'You are in hospital.'

'Where is … Collins?'

I don't yet know where Collins is but I tell Trevor I expect he's in police custody by now.

'Oh.'

Half satisfied, he slips back into semi-consciousness, but this time I won't let him. I think of Marcie Holt, who is also somewhere in this hospital, still in shock from the ordeal. Her condition is stable, but she is under close surveillance. I can't wait for Trevor to wake up properly. There are so many questions I need to ask him to clarify the half-broken chain of events in my mind. His condition is also stable and one of the doctors has reassured me that he'll probably be released from hospital by the end of the day, once the drugs Collins had given him have worn off and they are sure there are no signs of other injuries.

'Trevor! You need to help me.'

I recall the moments after I freed myself with Marcie's nail clippers and went into Collins's flat, not knowing what to expect there. Marcie had been telling the truth. To my relief, Collins was gone. However, I found Marcie sitting with her back pressed against to the headboard of their bed, shivering and shaking under the duvet, eyes wide open with horror and fear. Amazingly, her first words were: 'I don't want him caught.'

'He is a murderer, Marcie.'

'No! I don't believe that!'

I didn't think Collins would come back for her, but I bolted the front door and we sat together and waited until help arrived. Like warriors in a computer game, heavily armed police officers spilled into the house wearing bullet-proof vests and helmets, following orders they received in their earpieces. I don't know what they expected, but, fully armed and fired up, they found in one flat a woman in shock, a tired and dirty colleague emanating an awful smell, and, in the other flat, a half sedated Trevor Bennett snoring in a bedroom.

In the turmoil, Marcie Holt managed to whisper: 'He is a good man. He's a godfather.'

She was then taken care of by the paramedics and, while they put her in an ambulance, I received a bollocking from Maloney about being stubborn, selfish and foolish. I told him humbly that he was right after which he softened a bit and let me go back to the other flat to stay with Trevor.

'Trevor, you must help me.' I put my hand on his shoulder and almost shake him. 'Is Collins the godfather?'

He opens his eyes, possibly checking if we're alone. 'Briony … He is mad.' His eyes widen as something dawns on him. 'He hasn't taken Briony, has he?'

'Why would he do that?' I freeze. Why didn't I think of that possibility? Why didn't I take the necessary precautions?

'Briony is … she is … Collins is mad … dangerous.' A tear escapes from between his eyelashes and his voice drops off to an inaudible mumble.

'Trevor, stay awake please. Do you know Suzanne Keogh?'

He opens his eyes and blinks. His pupils are too big to focus clearly. 'Who?'

'Susanna Keogh. Her daughter looks exactly like Briony.'

'No … I don't know … Oh. Then … he is also …' His eyelids are getting heavy. 'I can't tell you … Sorry.'

Before I can press on with more questions, his wife arrives. She is accompanied by her brother and her two children. They are pale and timid, the horror of the events still etched in their eyes. She shakes my hand, thanking me, but at the same time I see something in her eyes that tells me her real thoughts: that Trevor wouldn't have been kidnapped if the police had done their job in the first place. I leave them hugging and sniffing and crying, mumbling words of encouragement and reassurance that the ordeal is over.

When Penrose emerges from the lift, she avoids my eyes and says curtly, 'Home?'

'No.' I shake my head. 'What's the latest news about Collins?'

She stares at me, debating inwardly whether to tell me that it is none of my business since I made such a mess of the investigation. 'He is currently being escorted to the police station. They picked him up in Plymouth when he tried to board the ferry to Roscoff.'

'Let's go then.'

'Where?'

'To the station. I need to speak to him.'

'Maloney won't let you.' She looks at my face. She doesn't even bother arguing with me any more. 'Wouldn't it be wiser to take you home?'

'No.'

Her face softens. 'You look tired.'

'I'm okay.'

I follow her to her battered little car and fall immediately asleep, waking up when we arrive at the car park behind my home. I wipe a dribble off my chin, running my tongue over my dry lips. Thirsty and hungry.

'You were snoring.' I hear a glimpse of humour in her tone.

'This isn't the police station.'

'I know.' She looks at my shirt and I follow her gaze. I have changed my stoma bag but I'm still wearing my stained and smelly shirt.

She smiles faintly. 'I thought you could do with a quick wash and change and then I'll take you to the station. Promise.'

She follows me up to my flat as if she's been instructed not to let me out of her sight. She inspects my fridge and finds a packet of cherry tomatoes, courtesy of my mother. She pops one tomato in her mouth, her lips pressed together not to spill the juice.

'Guthrie's in limbo,' she says, still chewing. 'He doesn't know if you deserve a medal or the sack.'

I shrug and go to the bathroom. I wash my face and run my hands through my hair. There is a lump on the side of my head, but the nurse at A&E has cleaned it and sprayed some plastic plaster onto it to prevent it from bleeding. I fill a glass of water and swallow some painkillers. I change my stoma bag again, this time replacing the one from the hospital with one that I find more comfortable. With Penrose's last words in mind, I guess I am now delaying going to the station.

I put on a clean shirt and dump the dirty one in a plastic bag in the bin. Although I use a lot more deodorant spray than I normally do, I'm still not convinced that the smell has gone completely.

'Ready?'

Penrose jumps to her feet, sheepishly putting the punnet with the remaining cherry tomatoes on the table.

I nod, but my phone vibrates in my pocket. It's Maureen Bennett, her voice full of resentment. 'Trevor says he wants to speak to you.'

'Now?'

'Yes. They're keeping him in the hospital overnight.'

'Is he alright?'

''He says you asked him about a woman. Susanna?' I hear the uncertainty, the concern in her voice. She is scared that she might find out that her marriage is on shaky ground and her whole life is about to unravel.

'That is right,' I say gently. 'Susanna Keogh. I'm sorry, Mrs Bennett, but I can't talk about the investigation right now.'

We disconnect and I make a mental note to tell Trevor to talk to his wife and tell her the truth.

'Change of plans.' I grin at Penrose, but she looks back at me blankly. 'Trevor Bennett wants to talk to us.'

Her face lights up. 'A confession?'

'I don't think so. The motive for the murder of Alicia Poole, hopefully. Are you coming?'

Trevor Bennett is still drowsy which is probably why he hasn't been released from hospital yet. He has been moved to a room designed for six beds, but a seventh is squeezed between two windows at the end. A bulky woman is snoring in it. Every now and then she groans and pushes the bed sheets aside, revealing a faded red vest and arms covered in tattoos of blue and red roses. Then she starts shivering and pulls the sheets back under her chin.

Trevor has half a dozen pillows piled up under his back, but he has slipped down so that his feet are touching the foot end of the bed. He frowns when he notices Penrose behind me, but he shrugs.

We sit on each side of his bed, Penrose with her little note-book in one hand and a pen in the other, waiting. Bennett looks like he is going to tell me that he won't say a word until she disappears.

'Mr Bennett, you lied to us about the night Alicia died,' she says curtly.

He nods. 'I lied about it because I knew how it must look. I had no alibi or witnesses.'

'Can you tell us about it?' I ask gently.

'There isn't much to it. Alicia called me while she was out that evening with her friend Denise. She was scared because she said Collins had seen her and had been very menacing. She knew that he has been threatening me too. I told her to leave the bar and go home where I thought she would be relatively safe. She called me again later that night but she used a different phone number which I didn't recognise so I didn't answer it. But she left me a message asking me to call her back on that number urgently because she was really panicking. I … I couldn't get hold of her any more and I thought … I don't know what I thought. Collins was … threatening us and we needed to sort this. Anyway, I drove to Cornwall, to her house, but there was nobody there and eventually I went back to Devon.'

'And you didn't see her at all that evening?'

'No. If I'd known she was at that lake … I mean, I almost drove past it! But I didn't know, honestly.'

'What was all this about, Trevor? Is this about Briony?' I ask.

'Uhm, it's complicated …' He pauses, fingers fidgeting with the edge of his blanket. 'You asked me about that woman. And her daughter.'

'Susanna Keogh. So you do know her? Her and her daughter Yvonne?'

Penrose started scribbling but she stops after she's written down Susanna's name. She's angry and confused and can barely control herself.

'I've never heard of them before you mentioned her name, but … you said the daughter looks like Briony.'

'Yes, she does. I've seen her.' I ignore Penrose who is staring at me in disbelief, willing me to explain what's going on before I take this any further. 'The resemblance is astonishing.'

He nods gravely. 'It makes sense. They must be sisters. Half sisters.'

'You had an affair with … Susanna?'

'Oh no. It was Sam. Sam Collins.' His face expresses a mixture of hatred, fear and disgust. 'He calls himself the godfather.'

41

By the time we get back to the police station it's almost dark. There is more activity than on a normal weekday evening, but the earlier buzz of excitement has disappeared. The desk officer nods and grins. Congratulating me. Clearly Philpo thinks I'm the hero who caught Collins single-handed while everyone else was looking the other way. I don't explain to him that it's pure luck that my unprofessional actions have turned out to be so fortunate. I could easily have got it all very wrong. He tells me that Collins refuses to be represented by a lawyer and is currently being interviewed by Maloney and the DCI. He shakes his head disapprovingly, but I'm not really surprised. Collins is arrogant. He may have convinced himself that he is completely innocent and believes it.

I sit down behind the desk next to DS Rowlands who is responsible for the recording equipment, a task he fulfils with a serious face, given the importance that the right procedures are followed to the letter. He only blinks to acknowledge our presence.

'How's it going?' Penrose asks, almost holding her breath. After what Bennett told us, she's as hopeful as I am.

Rowlands points at the three men in the interview room. 'The guy is a clever bastard,' he replies with a mixture of admiration and disappointment.

Sam Collins is dressed as if he is going to a wedding party. He is clean shaven and his gelled hair is combed neatly across his skull. He looks completely different from the man I spoke to earlier when I went to Marcie Holt's flat. He seems to have the ability to change into a different person, which is probably why my thoughts didn't go any further than the idea that he was vaguely familiar. I certainly didn't recognise him from the CCTV photos from the bars in Newquay.

Opposite him are Maloney and the DCI, both looking extremely frustrated.

'Has he confessed?' I ask DS Rowlands.

He looks at me briefly, an expression of 'are you kidding?' on his face. 'Nope.'

'I need to speak to Maloney.'

'He said: "no interruptions",' Rowlands says flatly. 'They want to crack on in case Collins changes his mind and wants to be represented by a lawyer.'

'Has Maloney got his earpiece in?' I ask, aware of Penrose staring at me again. I know exactly what she's thinking: it would be in my best interest not to disturb the interview at this point. The story Trevor Bennett told us is too incredible for anyone to take seriously, especially in a murder case like this, until at least we have checked what he told us before we tell anyone else.

'He has got his earpiece in,' Rowlands replies hesitantly. 'Guthrie hasn't.'

Collins has placed his hands, palms down, flat on the table in front of him, staring at them as if he is considering whether he should cut his nails. His face is emotionless. He looks bored like someone just waiting for a bus.

As if he senses that I am looking at him from behind the one-way mirror, he glances at his reflection and although he can't see me he is looking right at me. I feel a flicker of discomfort, as if he is putting a spell on me.

'I have information for Maloney. It's urgent.'

Rowlands hesitates again, looking over his shoulder in Penrose's direction for moral support. She only offers a shrug.

It has gone quiet in the interview room. Collins's repeated line 'I didn't kill Alicia' still hangs in the air. Maloney stares at a single sheet in front of him on the table and Guthrie makes a show of fiddling with a bundle of files as though the case has so much evidence he can't decide where to start.

Collins barely looks up, seeming unperturbed. He is relaxed and there is a constant little smirk on his lips, as if he is confident that this will all turn out to be a big mistake for the police force.

Every so often, he takes his glasses off his nose, polishes the lenses with a tiny cloth from the glasses case, and puts them back on, oozing arrogance and superiority. He waits patiently when Maloney reminds him of his rights, asking him again if he is sure he doesn't want a lawyer. Everything about the body language of all of them suggests that the interview has come to an end and has produced few results.

Ignoring Rowlands' faint protest, I grab the microphone and lean closer to it. But then Maloney unexpectedly speaks and what he says stuns me to silence. 'Mr Collins, can you explain to us why one of our officers, DI Tregunna, was found in your flat.'

'I told you, it is not my flat. He was in my neighbour's flat. Which reminds me that you haven't answered my question. Where is Marcie? I am concerned about her.'

Maloney looks up. 'There is no need to be like that, Mr Collins.'

'Is she okay?'

Guthrie frowns, looking at Maloney quizzically. I have a suspicion that he doesn't have a clue who Marcie is or how she is connected to Collins and the enquiry. I secretly smile to myself as Collins, with his arrogant defiance, is one of the few people I have ever seen to put Guthrie off balance. He has managed to unsettle the two detectives and take command of the situation. He sits calmly, as if he knows a bomb is about to explode and he is certain that he'll be the only survivor.

I lean toward the microphone, flicking the button to speak in Maloney's earpiece.

'Philip, don't say anything about Marcie.'

Maloney is the last person I would trust in a game of poker. He turns his head and stares at the one-way mirror, as if he can see me, wondering why I'm interfering. His expression has changed in such a way that both Collins and Guthrie instantly look in the same direction.

'He wants to know if we have found her and what she has told us,' I add, hoping that Guthrie keeps quiet for a few more seconds.

'Mr Collins,' starts Maloney with admirable calmness, considering that Guthrie is now fidgeting with a pen, still looking perplexed. 'Where were you between midnight and 3 am, on the night of Saturday 25th and the morning of Sunday 26th March?'

Patiently, Collins shakes his head as if he is tired of the whole situation. 'I need to know if Marcie's all right. She's my friend. I care about her.'

Muttering under my breath, I shake my head. This is going the wrong way. Collins is clever; he has an evasive answer to every question.

'Mr Collins, you have been charged with the murder of Alicia Poole.'

'I didn't kill her.'

'You are denying the charges?'

'Of course. This is ridiculous.' Collins seems to be enjoying exaggerating the role of the victim of mistaken identity.

'Where were you at midnight on Saturday 25th March?'

'At home.'

'Can anyone corroborate that?'

'Yes. My friend Marcie. I'd like to know if she is alright.'

My fists are clenched. Collins seems to be in charge of the conversation. I must admit that his position is strong. Any evidence we have found so far, is only circumstantial. There is little hard evidence to prove that he was at the fishing pond and killed Alicia. He has admitted that he spoke to her in the Central Bar, and that he followed her to Barrie's Bar. From Newquay, he said he drove on the coast road in the direction of Padstow. It was a clear night and he wanted to watch the stars so he headed towards Trevose Lighthouse, but turned back when he found the gate to the toll road closed. He then went to the National Trust's car park at Bedruthan Steps. Conveniently, he can't remember exactly where he walked and any evidence we might have found at the scene of Torrington's death could be from that occasion. He came home just after midnight and he is certain that his friend and neighbour can corroborate that.

I press the button on the microphone. 'Philip, ask him about his role as godfather.'

I see the first syllable being formed on Maloney's lips. Then he nods vaguely and obediently repeats the question.

The result is beyond comprehension. Even I am astounded by Collins's reaction. His eyes widen and he sits up straight, putting his hands around the edge of the table as if he is planning to rise to his feet and give a sermon of doom and gloom to an unrepentant congregation. The police officer standing in the corner has so far been looking stoic and disinterested but is now moving his feet, ready to grab Collins in case he gets up.

'Why do you call yourself godfather, Mr Collins?' Maloney asks.

'This has nothing to do with Alicia's death!' Collins hisses between his teeth. His cheeks are flushed pink and his eyes narrow with sudden weariness: his confidence is visibly deflating like someone sucking air out of a plastic bag.

'It helps us form a complete picture of you, Mr Collins,' Maloney continues unperturbed. 'We'd like to know why you call yourself 'godfather.'

Collins is rapidly losing control. He slaps his hand on the table. Yelling. 'I am proud of what I did!' His whole face is now turning bright red with anger and frustration. Then, for a moment, he is silent. Perhaps he is shocked by his loss of control, wondering what triggered the outburst. His eyes shoot from Maloney to Guthrie and back. A wild animal suddenly in danger not knowing in which direction to flee. Then his arrogance, fuelled by anger, takes over again. He stretches his shoulders as if he expects the detectives to tap on them to congratulate him.

'Nobody understands how important I am!' he yells, his voice full of self-importance. 'They call me the godfather. I am the godfather.'

Although the expression on Guthrie's face tells me that he doesn't have a clue what Maloney is driving at, he seems quite happy for him to carry on.

'A godfather is not as important as a father,' I say in Maloney's ear and he repeats my words in almost exactly the same tone

This time Collins explodes. The officer in the corner steps forward, reaching for the hand cuffs that dangle from his belt. Maloney stretches out an arm to warn and stop him.

'Tell us about Briony. Why you were so angry with her mother.'

'I am the girl's father! Don't you understand? I am her father. I have a right to interfere when Alicia neglects her role as a mother.'

Ignoring everyone except my voice in his earpiece, Maloney proceeds. 'So that was the reason why you killed her?' he asks flatly.

Collins can't stop himself. I see panic in his eyes as he realises that he is digging his own grave, but he can't control himself to calm down and think before talking.

'The bitch! I just wanted to scare her off. But she laughed at me. She laughed in my face, calling me a pathetic little nothing. A useless sodding bastard. She said I was the scum of the earth. Worthless. Not even worthy to say her daughter's name, let alone get to know the kid.''

Red blotches form on his now pale face. As he becomes aware of Maloney casting a sideways glance at the one-way mirror, I see hatred appear in Collins's eyes.

'He's here? Tregunna? That bastard? Watching me? I should have killed him when I had the chance!'

'Mr Collins,' Maloney interrupts calmly. 'I must warn you again about your rights. If you change your mind and you want to take the opportunity to have a lawyer with you, we can stop ...'

Collins doesn't listen. Instead, he continues, almost triumphantly, 'That guy Torrington was just a ... nuisance, a mistake ... but she ... she deserved to die. She lied to me. She never intended to let me see the girl. My own daughter! And when I confronted her with the fact that she wasn't even a good mother, that she was nearly arrested by the police in Portugal, she laughed in my face. She laughed and threatened to tell everyone about me. She said it was illegal to sell my semen to desperate couples and she would expose me. Stop me. She didn't realise how important I am.'

He folds his arms again across his chest and looks at us with a weird smile on his face. It is the smile of a mad man.

42

Although I had a vague idea about it, the details of the combined stories of Trevor Bennett and Marcie Holt have astounded us all.

In their late teens and early twenties, Trevor Bennett and Sam Collins belonged to the same group of friends. They became rivals when they both fell in love with Alicia, nee Marshall. She married Trevor. Despite the fact that she was never interested in Collins, he didn't stop loving her and he remained hopeful that she would turn to him eventually. He saw his chance when he learned that Trevor Bennett, after a string of disappointments and treatment in fertility clinics for nearly six years, was almost infertile. He offered to become a sperm donor and father a child with Alicia. His reason was pure selfishness, not generosity; Sam Collins hoped that a child would bind him to Alicia, and that, eventually, she would leave Trevor.

The couple couldn't foresee what would happen in the future. They were delighted with their daughter Briony and when Sam said that he wanted to have a special relationship with the girl, they understood his feelings and granted his request by naming him their daughter's godfather. A situation that seemed to work in Briony's first year.

Collins had had a lonely, loveless childhood and he'd vowed that he would never have children of his own. He had never met his own father and grew up with a mother who could never set her bitterness aside. He found it quite liberating that he could have offspring without the responsibility of having to raise them. He formed, in his own words, 'a master plan' to set up a private little business. He placed small advertisements in local papers and came in contact with couples like Alicia and Trevor, who were desperate to have a child but had been unsuccessful with fertility treatment. Alicia and Trevor weren't pleased at all when Collins boasted that Briony would soon have a half-sister or half-brother, the first of many, he hoped. A boy, Sammie, was born and the situation changed when the mother of this second child was left by her husband and in desperation she turned to Collins for help. He was pleased that he was able to see his son and his contact with the boy, seeing him growing up, made him determined to get more involved in Bryony's life. However, his efforts had the opposite result: Alicia and Trevor started avoiding him and, eventually, they moved without telling him their new address. At first Collins was angry and frustrated and finally he became obsessed with finding them.

When he discovered that Alicia and her little family had moved to Cornwall, he followed them.

Marcie Holt was a troubled young woman whose husband left her after the death of their premature baby. She refused to accept the divorce and, when Collins met her, she let him believe that her husband had gone away for a short period of time.

For Collins, she was perfect, providing him with a plausible cover story. He managed to rent a flat next door to her and persuaded her to move in with him so that he could use her flat to run his 'business'. To secure his relatively anonymous existence as a sperm donor, the flat still remained in Marcie's name. He spent a lot of time in his 'office' to keep in contact with the mothers of his children through email, telephone and video-calls. In this way, he knew all about their home life, their progress at school, even about illnesses and minor injuries. He also arranged initial meetings with couples who were potential new customers in various coffee shops and as soon as they reached an agreement, he invited them to Marcie's flat where he explained the procedure. The women would let him know when they were ovulating and they would then return to Marcie's flat with their partners. Collins had made it clear that he wouldn't be emotionally involved in the procedure, but he was willing either to inseminate the women by having sex with them or he would provide his semen so that they could use it in more relaxed privacy in the specially furbished bedroom. He even set up a TV and DVD player to create the right atmosphere for the nervous couples and make the conception feel as natural as possible.

Collins kept denying that killing Alicia that night was premeditated. He knew she and Trevor were divorced. He'd found Trevor's new address and he admitted that he had contacted him to try to force them to let him be in contact with Briony. Trevor refused. He claimed that he accidentally saw Alicia having a drink in a bar in Newquay with a friend. He offered her a drink, but she refused and, he stated, he accepted her wish to leave her alone. After a few drinks, he decided to try again, but he couldn't find her and he assumed she'd gone home, after which he also went home to Marcie, who, he was sure, would be able to confirm this. When I called Marcie and he overheard the conversation, he panicked. He realised that by kidnapping Trevor Bennett he had made a big mistake. Trevor had no idea about Collins's involvement in Alicia's murder, but thought that when Collins kidnapped him it was in order to force him to sign over the parenting of Briony to Collins. But with Trevor missing, the police were closing in on him and he knew then that Bennett had to die too. The situation was becoming precarious as he realised that I was on my way and that Marcie knew too much as well. He saw me arriving, he knocked me unconscious and knew he had no other option than to run.

43

It's after midnight when I arrive at the house that is now my home. Mine and Lauren's, Stuart's and Joe's. There is talk about a dog, but it hasn't been decided whether it will be a puppy or a rescue dog. The front door key is in my pocket, on a new key ring: a small metal oval with the word 'home' on it. Letting myself in, I use the glow of the street lights to find my way along the hallway, dodging trainers and boots and school rucksacks. Trying not to make a sound, I go into the living room and slump on the couch, closing my eyes and pressing my thumbs against my temples. I'm too tired to get up the stairs, too wired to sleep.

'Hello.'

Lauren is standing in the doorway. Her red hair catches the light from behind her. It's like she is surrounded by a halo of light and sunshine. She's wearing a long satin nightdress the colour of champagne, which I bought for her to celebrate ... I can't remember the exact occasion. She looks gorgeous and I feel my heart swell with love and pride. And with lust.

'I saw the news,' she says. 'What a horrible man. The idea ...'

'Yes.'

'Has he confessed?'

'Eventually.'

I look into her eyes and see love and compassion in them. I feel tears coming. I try to hold them back, but she sits beside me and presses her face to mine. She wraps her arms around me, hugging me like I am one of her boys.

But I'm only dreaming.

Dreams can come true, but nothing happens by itself. My hands are trembling and my heartbeat has gone up. Just thinking of Lauren has that effect on me. I'm in my own flat. It's cold and empty. The kettle is boiling and I make my coffee, spooning ground coffee beans into a paper filter and waiting for the water to drip through, then I sit at the window with the view of the hills beyond the Gannel spread before me. The moon is only a crescent, but it is spreading a silvery light on the landscape making it look like I'm living in a fairy tale. I close my eyes as I let the warmth of the coffee slip back over my throat, and try to focus on what it is I need to do now. The case is about to be closed and technically I'm not needed any more. It's up to other people now to make sure that Sam Collins gets what he deserves. A life-long sentence, if I have a say in it, thinking not only about the people he'd murdered and the impact on their families but also about the couples like the Jennings desperate to have a child and the children he fathered whose lives would never be the same once they know the truth about him.

DCI Guthrie has counted up my hours and, in his usual, un-sympathetic way, gave me the devastating news: I have worked so many hours that I have to go off duty for five weeks. The thought of being in my own company for a whole day is terrifying enough. I can't bear the idea that it will be more than a month. It almost makes me want a new murder to be committed …

With mixed feelings, I turn my head and stare into the kitch-en. I struggle to face what I know I'll have to do now. There are no excuses to postpone it any longer. I have waited too long already.

The bouquet of mixed white and pink flowers has been in the sink since yesterday. I can't leave them there and let them wither away. I pick up the flowers, let the stems drip for a while and dry them with a tea towel.

I haven't called Lauren. She told Curtis, my neighbour who was playing Cupid on our behalf that she was waiting to hear from me. I'm not someone who can't say sorry. I am sorry about the whole thing. I should not have left her like I did on that evening. There are no excuses for that sort of behaviour. It was stupid and unnecessary. On several occasions, she came with me when I had an appointment with my doctors in Treliske Hospital in Truro and she has been very supportive and under-standing. I should have told her about my struggle with impo-tence. She would have understood. She will, hopefully.

Tonight, if she lets me in, I will tell her about it. I will explain how insecure I felt, and still do, and how I was afraid I wasn't worthy of her. I will explain everything, even perhaps tell her about my true feelings, and then, as instructed by Curtis, let her decide if she wants to have a relationship with me or not.

I will explain, without telling her the details, without telling her about the embarrassing, humiliating episode with Denise Shaw, that I know that even the Viagra pills aren't working for me.

For that reason, I feel I haven't got much to offer. Other than my love and support. I can only hope that she will say that the physical side of the relationship isn't so important. True, but how long for? Are there any alternatives? Yes, maybe, but still, none of the options will make me feel a hundred per cent a man. I'll be a failure to her. The bottom line is that it is very possible that she will send me away.

Today, I have much more stamina and optimism as I walk along the path on the steep hill near the boating lake. I feel pleased that I have finally made a decision. I can't do any more than that. It's up to Lauren to decide what she wants. Whatever that might be, I will have to accept it.

The street I know so well is deserted. I can see her house as I get closer. My hands are clammy. A woman opens a door nearby and stands on the doorstep, looking at me, smiling, lighting a cigarette. I feel ridiculously vulnerable, holding the flowers against my chest for support and confidence.

To get to Lauren's front door, I have to walk past the window of her living room first. I wasn't going to look, but I can't stop myself, hoping to see her sitting on the couch, watching TV or reading a magazine or a book. She isn't. She has just entered the room. Dressed in a simple black dress, her hair held on top of her head, long, golden earrings dangling in her neck. She looks gorgeous and I feel my heart warming. I can't believe that I waited so long to see her again, how many weeks it has taken me to swallow my pride and make up my mind.

Then I freeze. Something is wrong. She has two mugs in her hands. One is yellow, the other purple. I see the smile on her face widen as she kicks the door closed behind her with the heel of her shoe. Then she laughs and I can see her saying something to a man who is sitting on the couch. I don't know him. I don't need to know. He is handsome and relaxed. I have no doubt that he is a good lover.

He says something and she throws her head back in laughter. She looks happy and carefree, confident.

I turn on my heels, walk away as fast as I can, passing the woman who is still on the doorstep of her house, smoking.

'For you if you want them,' I say brusquely, and I lay the flowers on the low wall in front of her house.

ACKNOWLEDGEMENTS

Although the idea for this book is remotely based on a true story, it is a work of fiction. Names, characters, places and incidents are either products of my imagination, or are used fictitiously or accidentally, however, with the exception of the real Trevor and Maureen Bennett – they bear no resemblance whatsoever to the couple in this book.

The process of writing is a lonely one, but I could not have achieved this without the help of my editor Mollie Goodman and proof-reader Anna Turpin – hopefully they have spotted most of the mistakes and typos. Also thanks to The Lobster Hatchery in Padstow, Magdalena Pieta and Hannah Vaughan of TJ International and Erik de Bruin of Varwig Design. And as always, a big thank you to my children who are always there for me; especially Astrid, who helped me through the last winter, when I nearly gave up on Tregunna.

A big thank you also to the group of Cornish authors, for the wonderful lunches and tips and do's or don't's and last but not least Mike, for listening to my crazy ideas and supplying me with enough coffee to encourage me and keep me going.